Born before the internet was even a twinkle, Alder Markson was raised in Newcastle, finally leaving in 1983. The last twenty-five years he has worked in the IT and Telephony industries, mainly in Service and Project Management. He still works in that industry today. A recent graduate of Teesside University with a BA in Creative Writing, which he completed with the aim of improving his storytelling. He lives in North Yorkshire.

To all those voices in my head – you can have a day off now.

Alder Markson

IN THE COMPANY OF DEMONS

AUSTIN MACAULEY PUBLISHERS

LONDON · CAMBRIDGE · NEW YORK · SHARJAH

Copyright © Alder Markson 2025

The right of Alder Markson to be identified as author of this work has been asserted by the author in accordance with sections 77 and 78 of the Copyright, Designs and Patents Act 1988.

All rights reserved. No part of this publication may be reproduced, stored in a retrieval system, or transmitted in any form or by any means, electronic, mechanical, photocopying, recording, or otherwise, without the prior permission of the publishers.

Any person who commits any unauthorised act in relation to this publication may be liable to criminal prosecution and civil claims for damages.

This is a work of fiction. Names, characters, businesses, places, events, locales, and incidents are either the products of the author's imagination or used in a fictitious manner. Any resemblance to actual persons, living or dead, or actual events is purely coincidental.

A CIP catalogue record for this title is available from the British Library.

ISBN 9781035897179 (Paperback)
ISBN 9781035897186 (ePub e-book)

www.austinmacauley.com

First Published 2025
Austin Macauley Publishers Ltd®
1 Canada Square
Canary Wharf
London
E14 5AA

This novel mainly owes its birth to the voices in my head. On occasion I have needed that spark of something new. Pauline Ludgate kindly gave me the bones of four characters, without her input Tiff, Andrea, Tommy, and Stanley would not have made it to the fore. So, thanks as ever Pol. She also became my reader in chief, and as those that know me will be surprised, I took most of her suggestions and edits. Thanks goes to all those who have given me feedback as this project took shape, as ever it is appreciated, especially those at my workplace who have been battered into reading this. My mother kept telling me I should either go on a quiz show or write a book. Well one out of two isn't bad.

5:29 pm

In the normally simple, uncluttered and unhindered world of Tina Rawson, the current situation she found herself in was now ranking as one of the biggest wastes of her time yet. Here she was, a senior executive officer for the much-heralded National Crime Agency, and what was she doing? She was tailing someone, which in itself was something she was more than used to being engaged with, but what made this so frustrating was that at the moment her target was in a car about two metres in front of her own company Volvo. Her skills at following and observing were hardly needed here. Tina was so close she could have exited her car, walked a few feet and had a chat with the object of her surveillance.

All because the traffic was doing nothing, only a stop-start dance of the frustrated. Instead, she would have to satisfy herself with sitting here glaring daggers at the man in the Audi who was clearly completely oblivious to her presence. If he had looked in his mirror even once, he would have seen her, perhaps he would have recognised her for what she was, but then again, there was considerable doubt about that.

The clouds of smoke he emitted regularly from his window, complete with the background knowledge they had on the subject, would tend to indicate his known weed habit may be in play here. He, therefore, might only have noticed if she was painted purple and was a unicorn, and even some doubt could be cast on that hypothesis.

The traffic had been brought to an abrupt halt a little while ago, which had prompted Tina to quickly take the opportunity of moving her car to be directly behind her target, just in case. Just in case of what, was impossible to know, but she did know through experience of many operations just like this one that being ready never hurt, although the downside was that she was now in plain sight. Her partner Ray Pickard was in the other vehicle, as they had been engaged in a game of surveillance tag with the Audi all the way from Stranraer, which was where they had been ordered to pick it up.

It was standard operating practice that they would swap places at intervals, ensuring that Matt Connors, the target, did not notice them. Now they were stuck with the problem that they couldn't swap places without completing a complicated do-si-do manoeuvre, which would involve the hard shoulder, an invisibility cloak, and some unlikely-to-be-offered goodwill from the public, all without drawing attention to themselves.

Tina could see Ray every time she looked in her mirrors, and each time he had been chatting away to someone; knowing him it was more than probable that it was work-related, as it was highly unlikely that Ray would be doing anything as frivolous as shooting the breeze to alleviate the tedium.

This was exactly what it was, a tedious traffic jam, a thing that was the bane of the modern traveller, and even more so when you were an officer of the law and were tailing a courier with a large quantity of cocaine in the boot of his sparkly Audi. Tina was obliquely listening in to the radio chatter coming through her earpiece, all the chicken squawks that were going on, and she deduced from this that it was an accident further ahead that was causing this current delay.

While normal people may exude sympathy for anyone hurt or injured, it would not be something for Tina as it was impacting her day and therefore was seriously irritating her. Tina understood the concepts and ideas behind sympathy and empathy, she just lacked the tools or the will to put that understanding into action.

If Ray had been in the car with her, then they could have chatted and at least passed some of the time, but all she was left with was to watch the Audi and look at all the others that were trapped like her in this mechanical melange of shite. She could see a white, or mostly white, van that was wallowing in the middle lane—an obvious pile of crap and shouldn't be on the road.

In a past life when she had been, albeit briefly, in her scratchy uniform, straight out of training school, then she would have possibly done something about it; now all she would do was puff out a breath and resume watching the Audi.

*****

The gentle downward pressure from my right foot brought the dirty, dented, nearly white, three-and-a-half tonne box van to a halt, not quite as quickly as it should because the brakes felt shot. From the outside, I was just another run-of-the-mill vehicle joining the long line of red lights stretching into the distance, giving the bright impression of a gaudy and particularly unimaginative Christmas tree. The odd flash of orange occasionally breaking up the dull, uninspiring palette.

"Fuck" slipped out of my mouth, an address to no one and everyone, it was more of a question as to what was this latest delay in the journey. It seemed to be more serious than anything earlier, a fact emphasised by the lack of headlights coming in the opposite direction. A complete lack of illumination except for the emerging sodium glow of the gantry lights. An artificial radiance just commencing in its latest attempt to hold back the encroaching darkness, a counterpoint to the sun as it slipped away on the early autumn evening.

The instructions had been clear and drummed in repeatedly. If I was even a minute delayed, then I would have a catastrophe on my hands, that's if I still had hands. There was a feeling that I know is my blood pressure slowly rising and that soon a clammy and unwelcome perspiration would make a fresh appearance on my brow.

In hindsight, which is a luxury I appear to be able to indulge in with abundance as I sit in this traffic, then I should have tried to run, to try and get my sorry arse out of this. Had this been a normal job, then it might have been possible, but the incentive that had been put in front of me was something that could not be ignored. If I am honest, which is another thing I seem to have plenty and yet no time for, then the people offering the incentive had me by the balls.

Focus, man, get a grip, I will be no good to anyone if I lose control of myself now, something I had been repeating as a mantra for most of the journey. A refrain that I had trotted out every time there was even a minimal delay, and now it would look like the fates that clearly weren't listening had thrown up a far more consequential one. If there was no oncoming traffic then the motorway was shut, either for the air ambulance or because the problem was in both carriageways, and this was more than significant, this could be devastating.

The orders I had been given were simple, all I had to do was follow the satnav, get there by six and not look in the back as that does not concern you. The little screen of the satnav was now mocking me, as it showed the flashing arrow on the display in the middle of the motorway. The unemotional voice telling me, 'Caution, possible stationary traffic', was not even ironic in tone, no, it was practising being bloody annoying.

I don't want to risk fiddling with the bloody thing to get rid of the voice, because I had a fear that I might lose the address detail and that would be another nail in my metaphorical coffin. The consequences are not even worth thinking about, although looking outside it may be that I would indeed have time for that now, along with hindsight and honesty.

Not that thinking was my strong suit, as Lizzie would attest, and it was that lack of thinking, going back over the years that has led me to be sitting in a van, with a load of fuck knows what, and a far from idle threat underpinning the whole shebang. It would appear that I have nothing more time-consuming to do for a while than to apply what I try to pass off as intelligence to it all.

The vehicles on either side of me were moving occasionally, but only in little bursts, this was not a case of the normal brightly coloured flash in the outside lane or the grumbling trundle of the wagons on the inside ones. This was more a metallic sludge, rolling alongside like a galvanised painted slug, or the drivers trying to establish some sort of slow-moving pecking order.

The only differentiator was the number of pairs of eyes that I caught sight of as they passed me or as I rolled past them. Every vehicle was now compelled to join the nearest strand of red jewels, like a mocking demonic necklace, laid out across the motorway ahead in front of us all. Every one of the occupants was intent on their own cocooned lives apart from when it was broken only briefly by that slight flicker when they saw me.

If they did see me, that is, and if it was so, then what did they see? An ordinary-looking bloke of an indeterminate age. Could he be a family man? Or did they glimpse into the man and see somebody trapped in something that was not of his making? Would they even be able to recall him later if they were asked or would those memories be confined to that dark place in their mind, only to be triggered and released by something much darker?

This heap of crap I was driving didn't even have a working radio, so I had no way of knowing what was causing the delay, other than my less-than-informed guesses. If only my erstwhile employer, and that was a very loose term, had not insisted on me leaving my phone behind as well, as I could really have used it right now. The cargo in the back was sensitive to radio waves, they said, ha! more than likely, it was dodgy, and they didn't want it to be tracked.

However, how anyone would know my number and therefore track me was beyond my limited comprehension of technology. I became almost entranced as I gazed at the monochromatic fairy lights, of which I could still only guess the cause, but I could see a long line into the distance, possibly miles, so it must be really bad. Bad in this instance, however, had the potential to become a much better-defined nightmare for me.

The traffic was still groaning very slowly past on either side and must be producing enough pollutants to kill the last few polar bears or certainly melt the ice they were perching on. A look of profound regret on their gaunt and starved faces, or certainly one that might be read as, *'We told you so'*. I tried to imagine someone breaking out the party hats and streamers if the traffic managed to get above ten miles per hour. Not that I would have much reason to join in the party or even think about the big ones that would be happening in a few months.

My mind was constantly being focussed by the ticking of the clock. Which was not so much ticking, but the flip of one digital blue number to the next in the recognised sequence. Glancing at the satnav I watched my estimated arrival time slip further and farther into the future, as the machine calculated my speed and the distance left to travel, a weird sort of backwards time travel, without the need for a mad scientist or a taxpayer-funded sports car.

I almost felt a small surge of relief with the realisation that if the traffic started moving soon, I could still make the destination, just about on time. But as I looked out of the window for what must be the umpteenth time, my relief deflated like a week-old balloon, as I saw the miles of red lights appearing to laugh back at me, and that hope was what it was—forlorn.

As the traffic again moved slightly around me, an almost precoordinated shuffle, it gave me a different set of strangers to look down on from my slightly and subtly elevated position, not in the HGV class of superiority, but enough to give an imagined level of dominance or at least a marginally different perspective to those wrapped in their saloons. There were three of them in a row on the inside row, which was unusual in itself, an Audi and what looked like matching Volvos.

I certainly did not feel superior to any of my fellow road users, a feeling they would not reciprocate if they knew me, and what I was. I could spend a few of my precious minutes trying to imagine the lives that were going on behind those other partitions of safety glass. Using this as a distraction from the slow flip of the digital clock and the static and passive-aggressive blinking of the little arrow on the satnav.

As I shifted the van forward a few more yards, losing sight of the strange saloon convoy, my left-hand view was now blocked by one of those eighteen-wheel mechanical brontosauri that grazed on the UK's motorway network. Herding together with its brethren, protecting themselves from the imagined jackals and hyenas circling around them as if they were trying to detect any sign of weakness in the herd.

This one was liveried in the familiar logo of one of those fast-food companies that have been insinuated into our twenty-first-century lives, a similarly marked pack mate was idling about ten inches off its back bumper.

All Fenced In

The traffic all around can only be described as stationary, with an accident up ahead according to the radio bulletin. The same announcement only confirmed what I already knew—being at a complete standstill usually pointed to that scenario. There was no point in me being worried and in truth, there was nothing about the situation for me to be in anyway concerned. The wagon was refrigerated, fully fuelled, and fortunately, I had loaded up with personal supplies at the last stop.

I was, therefore, basically and smugly good to go, though, ironically, unable to go anywhere. There was no point in thinking that my destinations further down the line would be over the moon about the delay, as there is not a lot, they or I could do about it.

I can see Ed, poor old Ed, in his own company wagon in my mirrors. He was off to Doncaster and beyond, and we will split up our convoy a few junctions further on, when I head to Derby. Our vehicles are loaded with all the portable workings that were needed to operate the franchises that proliferate the land like a rash—or an STI that smelt of chips anyway.

Sitting as high up as I was, I had an unobstructed view of most of the other drivers. My reflection in the glass appeared smug, and no wonder—I could almost see them panicking because they were down to their last smoke. Others would be getting flustered as their bladders start to put a real or imagined strain on them, all underlined by the wishful thinking and hindsight that will cloud their thoughts as they envision the previous service station.

How they had ignored it or even the toilet that they passed on the way out of wherever they had come from. A few may even be wishing they had stocked up with overpriced e-numbers at the last garage, that thought making their mouth inordinately dry and causing their bellies to rumble.

Thankfully, my smugness is elevated by my wagon, one that has the enviable space behind its cab—a mini man cave, if you like, or a woman cave, as the industry is inclusive. When the traffic had ground to what looked like a long-term stop, I had taken the opportunity to make a brew and pee in a bottle I had for that purpose. Now, I was now supping tea and munching through a packet of guilt-free chocolate digestives. I hope the other drivers weren't too jealous, it would just add to the list of things that drivers disliked about those who drove HGVs—not quite as bad as van drivers, but that was setting the bar quite low.

We loved ourselves after all—who else would? But we know that the other road users have no love for us. To be perfectly honest, I don't care. I am warm, had a brew in my hand, biscuits and importantly an empty bladder. My only worry was being late, and getting a slight headache from all the flaring red lights.

The van driver in the next carriageway had a pained look when I caught his eye, suggesting a full bladder perhaps. "It's your own fault, mate" is my less than charitable voiced comment. The glance stopped as the other driver looked towards a minibus slightly in front and to the right of his ropey old van. Wonder what his story is really. A cargo of crap, just like me? Too many hours at the wheel or just pissed off to be stuck in a van in a jam?

A large SUV passed slowly and carefully in the gap between the van and a BMW behind it. The driver was a middle-aged woman. There was no need for a car that size if only to show off wealth—one of the points my daughter raised this morning. What did they call them? Chelsea Tractors?

That conversation at home had really floored me, bringing home a whole series of, while not home truths, certainly things to think about. I think my daughter, Caroline, Caz or Caro depending on the phase of the moon, has now finally outgrown me. Intellectually, yes, ethically, yes, spiritually, most definitely, morally, even that was a possibility. The only thing I still have left, it would seem, is that she won't outgrow me physically, although she would no doubt fancy her chances if we had a scrap.

This process had been happening for a while, and in an act of strategic cowardice, I had deliberately avoided discussing it with her mother. That had been my policy, therefore hoping to avoid the accusations of jealousy, insecurity or paranoia that would have no doubt been levelled at me. After all, as we reach maturity, aren't we supposed to be the fount of all knowledge to our kids, all-seeing, all-wise, omnipotent and all that? Breakfast this morning made me re-evaluate most of those grand and probably frivolous ideals, shattering my preconceptions of what I was to not only my kids but to the planet.

This is what was predominantly playing on my mind as I cast my gaze over the red lights ahead of me, wondering whether I should call Ed and chat it through. After all, he had kids and still had a wife he lived with, so he might offer some sort of perspective. However, the company had a very strict policy on mobile use in the cab, and this was the thing preventing me, though it didn't appear to apply when they wanted to speak to you.

The morning started simply enough. We were having a conversation over toast. Well, I was having toast, and Caz was force-feeding herself something green that managed to give off a vague air of sinister. Not for me that goop, no thank you. No matter what the alleged health benefits, starvation would be an option before that. That means I'd stick with my thick sliced white with butter—olive oil spread really—and marmalade that contained enough sugar to feed a colony of wasps. Proper food, as they would say, where I come from or probably did twenty-five years ago.

That, however, wasn't the subject up for discussion. We were amiably talking about how blue the sky was on certain days, and yet on others, would look paler. Neither of us could fashion a sensible and convincing explanation for it, and as I had banned phones from the table, we couldn't do the internet lookup, that would have solved it. Ben, her brother, my other younger progeny, was also present, but as the only thing he ever uttered is "Can I have," followed by whatever it is he needs, I usually don't expect any valid input from that third of the family as a rule.

What we did do was we agreed that we would look it up later, and that was that or so I thought. I really should have known better, but for some reason, I had left my wisdom and common sense with my phone in my jacket. As soon as the words came out of my mouth, making a casual throwaway remark about global warming, I knew the error I had made, this was the equivalent of me killing a chicken on the kitchen table.

Yes, I may have jokingly said that with the ice caps melting, the animal life would just have to move, the same as the people who got burnt out by wildfire or flooded out. Apparently, my dry witticism was lost on Caz, as she went into full-on ecowarrior mode. I would not have been surprised if she had spontaneously sprouted dreads, piercings and a pervading smell of body odour.

I am sure they don't smell but certain preconceptions are hard to shake. You can blame, what was he called—oh yes, Swampy, that was it—for that.

Trying to swallow a mouthful of what suddenly was very dry toast while being confronted by an angry metaphorical cross between a womble and Stig of the dump is not the way I envisioned my morning going. To be fair, I am sure Caz was having similar feelings too, but she was difficult to read beneath the red hue she was now wearing, like some weird form of camouflage.

Putting it all back together, I tried to summarise her rather impassioned tirade. It wasn't just the animals that lived at the extremities of the planet that would suffer, it was the whole ecosystem that relied on it, in other words, everything. The change in the oceans would affect all coastal settlements—permanently erasing some. The quality of the air would change so much that we would all have to wear masks to avoid getting all sorts of unwelcome infections.

The COVID thing is a case in point, she said. The food chain would not cope unless we all moved, like she had, to a plant-based diet. It was all my fault, she had said. At this point, I took one for the team there, as I think she meant my generation rather than me personally, although I thought it best not to point this out. What I did do then was interject, to say that we could all blame generations going way back and that it was my generation who had allowed theirs the freedom to do anything about it.

At this point, she went from red to what can only be described as a deeper shade of puce. A colour that, if I had achieved it, I would have been calling for an immediate medical intervention. There was no froth yet, but spittle wasn't far away, as she raised her position of defending Maia. The passion rose another notch, the rich were only interested in getting richer and this was on the back of the poor of all nations, whether they be developed, developing or one of the ones not on any holiday wish list, this last being my words, as I think she used underdeveloped.

Pointing out that all the online marketplaces made their fortunes by selling stuff nobody really wanted, stuff made by people who could never afford to buy it. Then the really hurtful nail, the job I did for the company, the wagon I sat in and the waste I created, was doing as much harm to the planet as if I had personally set fire to all the remaining peat bogs. I was about to rejoin with the old parental adage of food, roof, clothes, yada, yada, yada. There was not a chance of getting a word in edgeways now, as she was in full flow, and didn't seem to care that she was haranguing her dad.

The amount spent on warmongering was obscene. The amount spent on sending stuff into space was obscene. Her final point was that if I ever wanted to see any wildlife, I had better do it soon, as the only things that was left would be in zoos. Silently, I finished my cup of tea, reflecting on what Caz had said and the fact that the kitchen door survived Caz's exit.

Ben was looking at me with wide eyes and said, "Wow, Dad. Can I have some money for lunch?"

At this point, I realised that my little girl had grown up. In fact, it was more than grown-up, it was a new maturity, and in doing so, Caz had completely bypassed me and my set of beliefs. This had given me an awful lot to think about, and the day so far had not been the ideal vessel for doing that, however, this traffic has created the time to contemplate what I could do.

Not only to take some responsibility but to try and gain a smidgen of respect back from Caz. Taking a look at the brew sitting in the cupholder and the packet of chocolate digestives, and those two things, for some reason, concentrated my thoughts. Firstly, there was the tea, which was imported from somewhere overseas, Sri Lanka, India or anywhere, but definitely not Wakefield.

The sugar and milk were also laced with different sets of issues. Sugar possibly had a get-out, in that its origin could be from beet and therefore not dragged across from another former colony, so I could park that one for now. Milk from cows that were efficiently generating methane, which according to Caz was the natural chemical equivalent of a WMD. The simple answer to that one was I could solve it by not taking the milk, and that could be score one for me.

There were more issues close at hand—the biscuits—I didn't know the provenance of all the ingredients, but the chocolate was definitely not grown in our local hedgerows. I would hazard an uninformed guess that at least half of the other stuff would be imported. Not even counting the plastic wrapper and all the evil connotations around the production of that stuff for a minute.

Then there is my wider environment, I was sitting in a traffic jam in a large wagon with an engine that runs on diesel. It is idling away underneath me as I sip my allegedly unethical and definitely not green tea. The engine belched out all sorts of nasty elements into the atmosphere, that's the engine, not me, fairly similar to a cow, but I wouldn't know the composition of this lot.

The fact that I am surrounded by thousands of other vehicles all doing exactly the same, just in my immediate vicinity, was quite eye-opening, and I will freely admit that I have paid lip service to this over the years. I could discount the smug ones in their hybrids and electric vehicles, as apart from not questioning where the power was produced from, they would be not pumping out very much. Caz and her rant had rammed home that we need to do something about it.

The manufacturers tell us technology has improved with start/stop. However, I read somewhere that this technology uses more fuel in this manner than it would in a normal state. You can get the internet to offer blame or excuses for anything these days, it appears. Also raising the question of safety but that's another argument for a different day.

The fuel companies postulate that the fuel is cleaner than it was twenty years ago. That may be the case, but as Caz had pointed out, you still wouldn't want to sit in a room full of its fumes for long, and I would agree. If I told you that is all I thought about, that would be a downright lie, but these revelations were to the fore, and I was starting to look at things completely differently.

The trailer attached to my tractor unit is packed full of allegedly everything that was the environmental end of the world—my new illuminated perspective on it. Half of it masquerades as food, the type that people don't need but, because of the ingredients, want—possibly to the point of addiction. The whole lot sits in refrigerated and frozen sections, maintained by a unit that runs off the engine, which is also chucking out all of its muck.

So, more muck, just to keep the chilled and frozen products at an ambient temperature. The irony is not lost on me that some of the meat, in its natural form, has already emitted another substance of mass destruction. So, in effect, a double whammy. Then I thought about the other part of the trailer—it was not chilled or frozen, making it environmentally slightly superior to its neighbour.

But this stuff would, no doubt, within seven days, be decorating a high street near you—and not in a good way. All the ironic paper cups, which can't be broken down without a huge investment, the plastic lids, the printed cardboard and the plastic fruit containers—it goes on. At least the straws were paper now. Goodo, that was all that sorted then.

Caz was right, and she would love that. But not just her—we are surrounded by stuff that is, at worst, destroying the world we live in and, at best, cluttering it up with crap. All the voices I had studiously ignored, who kept telling me this, were now parading in front of me, against the backdrop of several thousand vehicles idly filling the air with shite. The first thing I decided to do was to fall on my sword—made of recycled metal, of course. I would do this when I returned to the depot: hand in my notice, then find a green job.

One that would make Caz proud of me. If it caused hardship, then so be it—the kids would just have to understand. Morally, they couldn't argue. If I could make a stand, then so could everyone else. Time to act, as enough lip service had been paid to it. This whole revelation felt good, though with nothing but the casual bystanders in the vehicles around me to appreciate it.

Coming to a momentous, life-changing decision, all I had was some red lights and reflections. Who said achieving the moral high ground was easy—let alone sainthood?

*****

5:30 pm

With what may be a slow, karmically driven shuffle, the vehicles had moved around, and Tina now had a slightly different view. Her vision was still inexorably glued to the back end of the Audi, but the outside world had shifted around her. She glanced further ahead and noticed the logo on the back of an articulated wagon, which only raised her mood to a new level of pissed off as she realised she was hungry.

The fast-food delivery now in her view seemed to be taunting her, closing in as if deliberately mocking her. In some sort of Pavlovian response, she felt saliva build. As if she needed reminding that she had not eaten for at least six hours and had nothing in the car that would ease that situation anytime soon. This was all she needed.

Ray was still chattering away, and Tina wondered if he was doing something not related to their work. She knew his wife, Cheryl, had buggered off and left him—according to the office gossip, she had even done the packing up by email.

Tina had a callous streak—her string of exes would attest to that—but this struck her as particularly nasty. Hardly a blow for the sisterhood. *So perhaps,* she thought, *'He was trying to patch things up. But why would he want someone back who had consigned him to history in that way? It was beyond her understanding.'*

However, as she refocussed on the Audi, still where she had left it; who was she to talk. Her last ex, Chris, had upped and offed without a by-your-leave—or an email. Apparently, Tina was just too Tina to live with. Chris had been sick of her me, me, me woes and decided that posting a key back through the door was an appropriate course of self-preservation.

On that self-pitying thought, she looked to her right and caught sight of what looked like a party happening inside a very jolly-looking red minibus. This didn't help her mood one jot.

*****

Catching the glance from the driver of the artic had unnerved me. To avoid seeing that smug look again, I glanced to the right and saw that the minibus had drawn level again. Its occupants were enjoying themselves big style, engaged in vigorous discussion and drinking beer from cans—probably illegal nowadays. But considering the crap that I had in the back of my van, a few tins on a bus ranked quite low on the illegal scale.

The blokes in the minibus—and one woman, for some reason. I mean what was that all about? Well, they certainly were displaying a middle-aged vigour and the latent confidence of those comfortable with one another. I wonder what they were discussing. More than likely, it would be sports—if I had to bet, that's what I'd go with. Though there was one older gadge who appeared to be asleep, his head against the window. He looked a bit of another token to me.

Still, at least someone was enjoying themselves. I knew what that feeling was—I just hadn't felt it in a while.

I wondered if I could pass the time by creating a story for them all. It didn't matter if it was real or not; it might take my mind off everything.

After all, I could do fuck all about it. Stuck in the proverbial gap between a rock and a very hard place. Maybe it would serve as a distraction from what was probably going to happen to me in half an hour or so.

But perhaps. Just perhaps.

Who am I kidding? Of course, it won't. My mind will wander, no doubt, but at the back of it will always be the reason that I am sitting here. There's no escaping that.

Definitely A Different Language

The bright red minibus was not moving far and was doing so at a very sedentary rate, its driver having adopted the customary practice of fitting in with the other vehicles around it. The gold lettering and logo of a stylised bird, denoting the bus's owners, flared in the artificial light like a badly imagined or child-drawn phoenix.

An even more amateur depiction of what could be a Viking, alongside the words *Kings Head*, was created on what looked like a self-laminated sign, perched in a slightly foggy window—giving the casual observer a possible clue as to the identity of its occupants. They were either role players from a pub or both.

The correlation between a Viking and a king was more akin to Eric Bloodaxe than to any dynasty that had plundered this sceptred isle in the last thousand years. The passengers were sons of the Dales, hardened by lead mining, farming, wind and snow, and about as likely to kowtow to royalty as they were to call an egg and bacon pie a quiche.

The pub in question resided in a remote part of North Yorkshire, and its occupants were off on a road trip to see the Peacocks—the mighty white—or, to those more prosaic, Leeds United Football Club. Their team were playing in a cup fixture in Leicester. None of the assembled travellers had any idea who had originally suggested the trip, but they had all signed up readily enough and were now moving steadily, albeit slowly, away from their beloved valley.

The pub they hailed from is, as are most, a listed building and typical of the style found in the Dales National Park: stone-built, draughty, thick-walled and stacked with what visitors would call *character*, but what those who were still able to be called *residents* would say was *home*. An addition attached to those people would probably be *reet*, as they were *characters*—particularly some of the more voluble ones.

On this evening, despite the absence of so many of the regulars, a log fire would still be burning at both ends of the main bar. There would still be several groups of people, of various ages and in various styles of dress, gathered around the bar. This is the case year-round, as the pub was popular with day visitors and those few remaining locals. The *commerinners*, as they are known, also used the pub on their infrequent visits, which was always a point of contention after a few pints had been sunk by the hardcore villagers.

Any visitor opening the door could not help but have their attention immediately drawn to a notice board right in front of them. A sign proclaimed: *Happy Hour—every Friday 5–7 pm*. Somebody, with the dry sense of humour associated with Yorkshiremen and women, has added a stick-on note reading *not so grumpy* next to the word *happy*.

This sign had been duplicated—if adulterated—onto a beautifully unprofessional laminated piece of card, which was also stuck in the front window of the minibus. *The Grumpy Bastards' Day Out*, it proclaimed.

It was strange indeed to see these men of the Dales outside their home territory—other than market days. As many of them would attest, *Why would I gan anywhere? I live 'in't' Dales.* Parochial it most certainly was, but it had a certain allure—a flashback to simpler, less well-travelled times.

There are sixteen of them on this trip, filling up just over two-thirds of the minibus—not a bad turnout. There was a seventeenth, but as he was the driver and from a different dale entirely, nobody paid him the blindest bit of notice. Apart from the slight nod each had given him as they boarded back at the pub—considering that many aboard might be related to him, this could be considered rude. But, as no doubt one of them would say, *if you have webbed feet, you do not draw attention to it.*

Greg, Mike, Kieron, Ian and Steve sit towards the back of the bus, dressed for rural life, with no concession to travel or city living. Multiple styles of fleece jackets, heavy denim jeans—with no fashionable rips, only accidental ones—and all were shod in good-quality, if slightly battered, footwear.

Two of the men wore the distinctive, green-checked cloth cap associated with the gamekeepers in the land of their birth—not a fashion statement but a statement of vocation, as genuine as the strands of DNA that ran through their wearers.

There were only a couple of additions to their normal pub huddle, one being Sandra, who was acting as unofficial guardian to the other: three slabs of Yorkshire Bitter.

Her role as chaperone and peacemaker may have been explained by the motif on her pale yellow and blue t-shirt: *You can take a man out of Yorkshire* on the front, countered by *You can't take a Dalesman out of me* on the back.

Some of the younger van assemblages had passed ribald comments as Sandra loaded herself—and the beer—aboard the charabanc, mainly directed at her chest. The t-shirt, a couple of sizes too small, was a clear, unambiguous and usually ignored mating signal for Greg, the de facto leader of the group. This was always unlikely to bear fruit, as Greg was immune to all advances of that nature—possibly explaining why he had never married or indeed knowingly had a female companion.

However, a few stern words from him to the youths—or, more accurately, the younger ones—had put them in their place and earned a delicious and slightly predatory look from Sandra. An observer might have described it as *rapacious*—a hungry lioness on the hunt.

On the periphery of this little group sits Eric, the elder statesman. Not officially part of the *Back Seat Boys*, he was more of a mascot, and nobody had the heart to shift him. Matt had given him a beer, and he appeared to have dozed off, his flat cap askew—like a particularly jaunty or flamboyant version of a shepherd.

These men looked and were comfortable—even away from their normal surroundings—and especially with each other. They all had cans in their hands, and the bin bag, already half full of empties, was testament to their enthusiasm for the task at hand. Nobody had mentioned—yet—that it was no doubt illegal under now redundant EU regulations to be doing what they were doing.

Spacing themselves easily around the rear seats, they could in no way be described as resembling naughty schoolboys.

They did, however, emanate a certain frisson—an exclusive membership vibe—that came from being comfortable in their own skins and with each other. None of them were under fifty years of age.

The air circulating around the bus was filled with the odour of beer and wet dog. The latter seemed to have followed one of the gang. The King Power stadium didn't allow dogs other than assistance ones. They knew this because they had checked—otherwise, they would have had a pack of hounds with them, had it been acceptable.

As to who was the odour bearer, it could have been any of them—they all owned dogs. Even Sandra, who owned a Saint Bernard the size of a small horse, which was called Douglas for some unfathomable reason.

Occasionally, the smells were interspersed with a waft of food that would reach the men as one of their fellow passengers unpacked a bait box. The prevalent scents were cheese, onion and pickle, occasionally accompanied by the rather distinct odour of cooped-up hardboiled egg. Nobody at the back was concerned with solid consumption at this stage; they had all had a pie within twenty minutes of setting off, mainly so they could concentrate on the serious business of ale and putting the world to rights.

Greg had also pointed out that he was fairly sure the southerners of Leicester should have discovered snacks for sale by now, so they should all be fine. After all, they invented crisps, did they not? He also added that those down south had invented everything, hadn't they, and would have it all on sale to prove their superiority and affluence.

The conversation rolling around at the back could have been one taking place in their normal stomping ground. It never ceased; it covered all topics. It was like the tide—never diminished, not by numbers or situation. It was just, as one of the younger ones at the front might have said, how they rolled. To the outsider, they may appear simple men, but they were up to date, though sometimes their views were not academic or cutting edge—more archaic.

It was sweet in a way. It could be offensive sometimes, generally tempered or formulated by the lives they lived. They tried, when in the pub, not to discuss either visitors or commerinners, as this usually upset Keith, the pub owner. His livelihood now depended on this new way of life, a change that all on this bus had faced reluctantly and with a grief they would never display.

The village could be like a cowboy ghost town once October had rolled out. Lights in windows or chimneys belching smoke were in the minority once the wasps had buggered off. The current topic on this slow-moving but adequately beer-fuelled evening was around the World Wide Web and the world of unsocial media.

"Read t'other day that one out of four people has a mental illness or summat like that," said Mike, raising a can of ale to his lips after making this statement.

"Read where? Wasn't even sure that you could!" said Ian, his words laced with humour, typical of the pattern within this close-knit group.

"I saw it on Facebook as well," chipped in Greg, glancing quickly at his mobile screen.

"Must be true then!" responded Ian with a laugh.

"It's where I get it all. If it in't on Facebook, then it in't true," responded Greg, without a trace of embarrassment or irony.

Several incredulous looks passed among the group. Even though they had heard this before from Greg, they were still amazed when he repeated it. Gobsmacked was the best word for it. Kieron and Ian laughed out loud, unable to suppress the humour of the latest iteration of Greg's gullibility.

"You aren't serious? I thought we'd covered this before." Mike paused mid-sip.

"Yep. And just 'cos you mentioned it, don't mean I listened." Greg showed no awkwardness about this, something else that was not included in the group's DNA.

"Jesus…" Kieron said, shaking his head, still failing to understand the mentality of a man he had known all his life and who was, in Dales' terms, a close relation.

"Ignoring Greg and his theory of evolution—if it's one in four, then as there are five of us, one of us is mental," he said, looking pointedly around the group.

"Yeah, Mike, think Greg just proved that."

And they all looked at Greg.

"Bit harsh. Also, it reminds me of that Tommy Cooper line about one in five people being Chinese. What's tha point, Mike?"

This made them all smile. The seventies comic was one of their favourites, particularly as he had died on stage, doing what he loved. All of them here would be happy to die in a field with their wellies on and a dog at their feet—or in the pub with a pint in the hand. It was a toss-up which option would win that vote.

"Well, I'm sure it weren't always like that. So what happened?"

As a conversation saver, this was actually a genuine question—quite unusual in the playbook of their sessions. However, if the past was anything to judge your horse flesh or lamb size by, someone would bring it back to reality with a comment.

"Probably the water. Speaking of which, another can, please, Sand," said Ian, waving his empty at the guardian of the ale.

"No, can't be t'water. Apart from Greg, none of us is affected—only the young'uns apparently." He cast a glance towards the front of the bus.

This prompted much shaking of heads and raising of cans to mouths as they contemplated the implications of Mike's announcement.

Kieron raised himself off his seat and shouted towards the younger ones, "Oi! You lot of scrotes at the front, why are you all mental now?"

The responses, while many and varied, were largely of the type telling him what he could do with his non-scientific enquiry.

"Fook's sake, K, make an arse of yourself, why don't you," said Greg with a smile at his cousin.

"Greg! No need for that!" Sandra looked up from her phone to admonish the object of her desires—an action not missed by the others, who, to a man, smirked like naughty little boys.

"Something must have 'caused 'n', and before you say anything about conspiracy theories, Greg, t'int Roswell, Princess Di or t'Moon Landings. But summat has changed," Mike went on.

"When do you think it changed? Greg will reckon it was due to the millennium."

This was a popular theory for Greg. It bettered Stephen Hawking for simplicity and would probably be an easier read once you got past all the other conspiracy bull. Steve loved poking that particular nest.

"Dunno," said Ian. "When was t'internet invented?"

"Seventies, I think…" Steve ventured.

"Aye," Mike threw out, then seemed to ponder a while, his face a picture of concentration—or something anyway. "But I didn't see'm till, don't know, what—nineteen-ninety?"

"Nah, Mike, was earlier than that. Think I had it when I left college in eighty-six?" This still had not produced another word of conspiracy from Greg.

"That sounds about right. So you blaming t'interweb, Ian?" Steve seemed genuine as he reached round and grabbed another can of ale.

"Well, Greg will want a conspiracy, so that would fit, wouldn't it?"

All eyes looked at Greg, who remained stoically silent.

"Oh, don't set him off on that'un as well," poked Steve.

"Aye, well, I was reading on't Facebook t'other day. Think about it—we are all relatively okay…" Greg could not stay quiet for long and amusingly had completely missed the irony of referring to an app for confirmation of a web-based conspiracy.

"Four of us anyway…"

All four shook their heads, knowing a theory was about to be aired, no matter what they said.

"But look at the kids today, they are always on tharn phones." Greg had assumed the posture of a man about to preach—only sitting down.

"Not just the kids! Look at Sand," said Kieron, trying in vain, and probably fruitlessly, to head Greg off at the pass.

They all pointedly look in her direction. Sandra, in true screen-lock mode, completely ignored them—entirely impervious to the monumental discussion around her, though she would pick up any swear words chucked out. That was what she called women's intuition.

"And all these ism's, they mess with me head. Our lass reckons she is a modernising feminist liberal environmentalist now," Ian said with a shake of his head.

"That will mean you are as well then, Ian mate, knowing your lass." They all laughed, knowing who was in charge in that marriage.

"Bloody ha-ha. I just don't like change. Wherever I lay me hat, I expect it to be there when I get back." Ian tried to act offended without risking anything that might be reported back.

"We should call the BBC."

All four turned to look at Steve. Even Sandra had caught this one, raising her head to glance in his direction.

"What the fu…sorry, Sand, fudge for?" queried Mike.

"Make a fillum about Ian, his missus, his fear of isms and living in the dark ages," Steve threw out with a slight grin at the under-fire Ian.

"I'm not that bad; I know how to iron and washup," he said with implied pride.

"Please don't sound so proud, Ian. We aren't just here to serve you." A look of slight revulsion mixed with a soupcon of acceptance crossed Sandra's face.

"Well, you are—ow, there was no need for that, Sand." He rubbed his thigh where Sandra had punched him, slightly harder than she meant but slightly less than he deserved.

"So, this rise in mental illness and wellness, and diversity, and then bullying, and what about all this hate stuff?" Greg steered the debate back on track.

"True enough, lad. Weren't they on BGT?"

All nodded at this, even Eric, though he was asleep, so probably not in agreement, more likely just rocking in time with the brakes being applied.

"Who?" Greg appeared genuinely confused.

"Diversity," Steve said with a straight face.

General laughter followed, but Greg felt the need to clarify. "No, what I were reading about was neurodiversity. I mean, what in the name of all that is sacred is that?"

Nobody could answer Greg, as they were all ignorant of this new phase of mental categorisation, and it was easier to stay silent.

"The bullying though, not sure about that," Ian said, breaking the silence.

A lull followed as they all refreshed their ales and took a moment to look out of the window. It was a subject none of them had answers to, so they let it drop.

"Back in the day, if you didn't like someone and wanted to take it further, you got in their face. None of this cardboard soldier stuff. You couldn't hide." Steve tried to sound aggressive, but dressed mainly in tweed, the effect was comical.

"Cardboard what?" said Keiron.

"Cardboard soldier. He means keyboard warrior." Greg shook his head.

"Thanks, Greg. Mebbes. Aye, that'll be right." He gave a knowing look and a slight nod.

"Aye, cowardly bastards."

All of them grumbled in agreement. They had all seen someone in the dale being picked on this way.

"Language, Kieron. You know the rules. There you go, Ian." Sandra handed him another tin of ale. "Also, I wouldn't be without my Facebook and Insta. Even TikTok."

"What in the name of all that is sacred is bleedin' TikTok?" Bewilderment was apparent on his face. You could only mix a Dalesman and technology so far before it became heretical. And Greg was the one who actually used his phone other than as a way of keeping an eye on lamb prices.

"I'll show you, given half a chance." The innuendo and double meaning in Sandra's voice were barely concealed.

"But, Sand, your so-called friends or followers wouldn't help you if you really needed it, would they? In t'old days, it would be your neighbour, and I bet you can't even name yours nowadays?" Ian threw in, hoping to keep the innuendo at a minimum.

"Erm…" Sandra did something none of them had witnessed before—she blushed.

"See? So, if you fell down your stairs and couldn't reach your phone, who would notice?" He was determined to explore this phenomenon more closely.

"Thanks for that, cheery sod. You lot would notice when your pots didn't get filled." Sandra tried to regain both her composure and the upper hand.

"He has a point, though."

They all smiled; never a truer word had been spoken.

"There must be some good on the net, though." Another genuine question popped up.

"Online banking? Streaming sport."

Several heads nodded at Steve's suggestion.

"Porn?" Kieron volunteered.

Mike burst out laughing. "I knew you would say that. Kieron, you'll get a reputation, you know."

"But don't tell his missus," Steve jabbed Kieron in the ribs playfully.

A few minutes of companionable silence followed as they all either grabbed another beer or drank noisily from the ones they had. A couple looked out the window, but as dusk was falling and they hadn't moved in at least ten minutes, there was little to see.

"Not wanting to stereotype my gender, but what about shopping?" Sandra broke the silence.

Mike pointed outside the bus. "Take a look out the window at all this crap we're sat in. Look at them all; it's not just cars. Take that van over there. No markings, but I'd lay a pound to a pinch of snuff it's full of crap nobody really wants."

He waved casually at a worried-looking van driver, sharing a glance that seemed to convey both of their frustrations. The driver raised his hand briefly and looked away. The bus occupants stared hard at the scruffy van, each with different thoughts about its possible contents.

"Seriously, though, some of this environmental stuff is all right," Steve said, bringing them back to the bus and away from the battered old van stuck in the same traffic.

"Yeah, we'll all be dead or have grown webbed feet within fifty years." Mike laughed at his own joke.

"Think that might be an exaggeration, mate. The research published on Facebook reckons more like one hundred and fifty." Greg, the self-declared SME on conspiracy theories, weighed in.

"Whoa, what have you done with the real paranoid Greg?" Mike did a comical left-right glance, then lifted his cap off the seat next to him, pretending to check underneath.

"I know you all take the piss about my conspiracies, but I've read a lot on this one. Think about it—when was the last time we had real snow? Ten years ago, we'd be snowed in at least twice every winter. Haven't even had to get the chains out for two years."

This earned several pursed-lipped nods.

"Aye, true. And look at the rain and t'floods two years ago."

Mike had been more affected by the days of flooding than anyone else—most of his land bordered the river.

"Oh God, it's depressive corner now. Can we have the grumpy one back, please, or I'm going back to my online friend?" Sandra said with an air of resignation, like someone who enjoyed herding cats.

"You may laugh, but it's your kids I feel sorry for—and mine, for that matter. We'll all be long gone by then. They'll have to live with it all." Mike was on firmer ground now with this, unlike most of his pastureland.

"Never thought about it like that," Sandra said, looking genuinely surprised.

"That's what I mean. We can only cheer on those who are trying and do a little bit to help," Mike continued.

"Not joining any of that stuff Sand was talking about!" chipped in Steve.

"Why, Steve?" Sandra asked with a glint of mischief, knowing it would set him off.

"Haven't we just talked about that? It's fucking evil. Sorry, Sand, but you can do good without it. Or if we must use it, then you can't hide who you are. All this anonymity and crying foul when someone shows the world who you are—civil liberties have a lot to answer for. Goes back to what Greg said about fronting up. I'd listen and take notice of Greg Sunter, but I wouldn't if it was ballscratcher47." Steve raised his can in acknowledgment of his friend.

"How did you guess that?" Greg said, making a rare sortie into comedy.

The laughter took some of the mounting anger out of the conversation, bringing it back to the comfort of their usual piss-taking and counter-piss-taking, interspersed with real-world insight into what a bunch of middle-aged men really thought of the world.

The conversation turned to the match, the price of beer—a fairly common theme—Greg's love life, or lack of tit, as Keiron was fond of saying, and other mundane aspects of rural life. The bus hadn't moved more than five yards when Ian suddenly burst into the chat.

"And what the hell is a snowflake? Or woke, for that matter?"

"Woke is for the kids—*awareness* is too hard for them to spell," Steve said, opening his next beer, the smile still in place.

This comfortable camaraderie was the product of a lifetime together, and he was determined it wouldn't be spoiled.

Shaking his head and laughing, Keiron answered Ian, "Snowflake is an insult, mate—if they think you care too much or are too liberal. Did somebody hurt your feelings?"

"Hardly. I voted to leave," grumbled Ian.

"No, *snowflake* isn't what I'd call you—unless it was to wind you up." Keiron smiled.

"I'm sort of touched that the bloke who delivers logs and coal called me out for caring," Ian said, looking thoughtful.

"So, the bloke who encourages people to pollute t'planet calls you a snowflake? That in't all that bad, really," said Mike, joining in this new strand of chat.

"True enough."

This from the last of them—Greg had stopped thinking about Sandra and rejoined his real-world mates.

Steve raised his tin as if about to propose a toast. "We all agree, then. The world really started going to shite with the internet—we just don't know when it happened. Social media in't social at all. The world is going to die soon, which is a good thing—not that it's dying, but that we know about it. We are snowflakes because we care, and woke because we are all aware—and can spell it. I don't know about you buggers, but I'm confused as to who and what we are now. God, I need a drink. Break out some more cans, Sand."

A new voice joined them. Eric had roused from his slumber.

"Wheear 'as ta bin sin ah saw thee…"

Laughing, Greg said, "Oh Christ, who set him off…"

"On Ilkla Moor baht 'at?"

"No more beer for Eric, Sand—it's a long way yet," Steve said, as he noticed they'd drawn level with the shabby old van again. He caught the driver watching them and raised his can in salute.

"Wheear 'as ta bin sin ah saw thee?"

Despite it all, they couldn't resist the urge to join in, and the entire bus rendered: "Ah saw theeeeeeee… On Ilkla Moor baht 'at? On Ilkla Moor baht 'at?"

*****

They had been steadily trailing the Audi for over two hundred and fifty miles when news broke of a major hold-up ahead. Their target had not reacted to any of the signs; he had simply remained in the inside lane until the traffic came to its inevitable halt. Fortunately, they had access to more information than most of their fellow travellers caught in the blockage.

They knew the crash was a major one, with multiple minor injuries and several ambulances en route for the worst cases. Three police forces were involved, as the site was one of those UK oddities where three boundaries met at a single point. Ambulances had been called from seven major hospitals across the cities surrounding the motorway and its environs. The same applied to the fire service.

Tina and Ray had discussed the situation when they first heard about it, debating whether they should switch on their concealed blues and twos and join the response effort. If they broke cover, their boss would have torn them apart, despite the moral argument that they would be saving lives.

The counterargument was that their current operation would have a far greater impact, as the gang's activities were destroying far more lives than they could save by playing white knights. The guilt of inaction still sat with them, and Ray, in particular, felt uncomfortable with it. Orders were orders, though, he reminded himself as he readjusted his holstered Glock, which was digging into his side.

They had been a team, a partnership, for three years. Ray had been paired with Tina after his former partner retired—more dramatically, after Tina's partner, Steve, had suffered life-changing injuries in a shootout with the very gang they were still pursuing. Steve was now confined to a wheelchair and had been invalided out. Tina had returned after two months of enforced leave and counselling. At one point, she had even considered leaving the desk role she had been assigned, probably prompting that thought.

Tina had repeatedly requested a more active role and was growing desperate until the day arrived when she was partnered with Ray. It suited them both—they were both a little bit individual, loners, even, but they lived for the job. They clicked immediately, recognising themselves in each other. While neither would admit it, they both used the other to get through the days that were getting harder and harder as crimes seemed to rise at an alarming rate.

Ray only had two years left before he could put in for what he considered a hard-won and more-than-deserved retirement. He hadn't talked to Tina about it—he knew it wouldn't end well. While he was not a coward, a certain level of self-preservation had kept him pretty much unscathed throughout his career. She did carry a gun, after all!

That would be a conversation for another day. Thinking of the day you could hang up your spurs and tin star when you were staking out a gang that was known to shoot first, bomb second. And only talk when all other acts of violence had been exhausted, would all go to hell if you thought even about the weekend when an op like this was in play, you just listened to your radio, your partner and reacted as quickly as you could.

The minibus with the party—would that be him soon? Was this a glimpse of normality that had been missing for so long? Looking at the Volvo in front of him, he could see the back of Tina's head. He thought he would recognise that auburn ponytail anywhere. The calls he had confirmed they were right to stay on their target. That was all he needed for now. If the traffic didn't shift soon, he would call Tina and get her thoughts.

*****

5:31 pm

That bloke—the one who had waved at me, twice in fact, the last time saluting me with a beer—it was almost as if he was trying to tell me something. My mind kept returning to it, unsettling me more than I wanted to admit. This was not something you expected when stuck in a motorway jam, except for little kids who hadn't yet understood the rules of normal human engagement. I looked away briefly, hoping for a distraction—anything to avoid the thoughts that little hand gesture and the metal salutation invoked.

The fucking clock has passed another minute, changing just one number at the end. This was interminable. The satnav was still taking the piss, and the lights were showed no sign of doing anything but snaking off into the distance. Without a phone or radio, I had no clue or idea what was going on ahead—the only thing to do was assume the worst.

Not that I gave a fucking hoot about whoever was involved up the road. No more than they would give a flying fuck about me. Not that I needed anyone worrying about me—I was making a fine fist of worrying about myself, thank you very much. All these people were within spitting distance, almost surrounding me, and not one of them knew what I was going through. No surprise as I had nothing to go on either. I was in a situation of my own making yet I had no idea what it was.

Glancing to my right, I spotted the scourge of the motorway. Look at it—that one, big brash Beemer. Could only be a sales rep or someone of a similarly pointless ilk. Probably pumped up with their own self-importance and moaning about being late for the next meeting to sell something nobody really wanted.

But as I thought about that, another popped into my head. My van was probably full of something that nobody would admit to wanting. It's possible? No, make that probable. Illegality was like a cloak of invisibility. No—scratch that. I knew it definitely wouldn't be legal, and as a guess, that a select demographic would be very needy for it.

Blood as Thick as The Mud

This bloody traffic—it's the last thing I need. The connotations of it being present are something I could really do without. Its meaning was clear, and it necessitated my having to call James. All down to his inability to do anything without me, even though he tries to think he can, despite what he tells everybody who is silly enough to listen and believe him.

To be honest, this whole relationship thing has caught me completely by surprise—admittedly, a pleasant one. After all, here I am, thirty-eight years old, having spent most of the last half of my life enjoying—no, that is not the right word—enduring the life of a dedicated singleton.

Like Bridget Jones without the fags, booze and the distinctly sexy Colin Firth. It was essentially passable, in no way controversial, and it caused no ripples or waves in society. It was what it was, it was passable. When my dad, bless his soul, went and died suddenly—as in very suddenly, as in setting off for work one day and not coming back at teatime—I had forced myself to step up.

It was not something I had intended for my life, but fate has a habit of kicking you when you least expect it. So, I took on the family business and made it my own—not necessarily in my image, but definitely with me as its pilot. I surrounded myself with a close circle of friends and a slightly larger one of acquaintances, and even I would admit that most of my social interaction came through work.

Then—boom—James entered the playing field, smashing into my virtually insular orbit like a defunct satellite returning to the mother planet's reluctant atmosphere. My whole world was shaken to its previously very steady—some would say stolid—core. I had not expected to find love like this, nor—even wilder—to be married after only twelve months. Now, I know why the word *stellar* applies in stories like this, and how I would dismiss them out of hand previously, because I am now living out of this world.

Some may say that I am now living in a real world, where people have relationships, marriages, kids and stuff. I am not complaining—not at all—just still in shock, and I think that will last for a long time. Married, for crying out loud. My parents had been delighted, if a little amazed, but, as I said to them when breaking the news, getting married was not the most outrageous thing in my history. They turned up at our little affair and seemed genuinely happy for both of us, accepting James with a warmth and tolerance I had not known they possessed.

The call to J will have to wait a minute—there were more pressing matters than whether he had lost his keys, the kids or some other potential husband-induced drama. I needed to think through my impressions and the figures from that meeting. Using this downtime to ponder that, rather than the great imponderable that is love and all that entails, was a sound strategy.

It had certainly been an interesting day—one that could mean the potential survival and flourishment of my company. My team, which consisted of Annie and me to be precise, had spent most of the day tidied away in one of those nondescript office buildings located in a barren and soulless Lego business park.

The type of damned place that looks all corporate and grand but, if you remove the well-known logos printed on anything static for more than ten minutes, could have been anywhere. The meeting had not been that dull though—by any stretch. The new customer we had been schmoozing had been very laid back, positive and surprisingly entertaining.

There had been the inevitable, death-like, water torture drip of PowerPoint, but the coffee and Danish had been good quality, alleviating some of that pain. We had both worked on this for the last two months and were well prepared. We had practised a run-through only last night and thought we were slick. More importantly, we were confident we could handle any questions thrown at us.

The key was not to show any hint of fear or weaknesses, because if they knew we needed them more than they needed us—trying to keep the company afloat—then all the figures would mean nothing. If we had they would then have screwed us over with more applied discounts and punishing penalty clauses. I did not want the seventy-five-year history of our business name to be wiped off the face of the market. Pouring everything and anything into this meeting and contract was the only way forward.

If the figures were right—not some smoke blown out of a PowerPoint-designed hole—then we would be more than in clover. It all looked nice and shiny on the screen, but, as the old saying goes, *if it looks too good...*

There was no escaping it—my mind flip-flopped back to my personal life. After all, they were inextricably entwined. I really hoped he had remembered to pick up his kids from school—one of the reasons I knew I had to call him. I mean, he really is useless. How he managed in his previous marriage was beyond me—his wife must have been a saint.

Though, to hear him tell it, that was not quite the case. She had upped and left him eight years ago—completely vanished—and James had been left with a mortgage and two kids under three. Then I came along. Or, to be more accurate, J crash-landed into me and my little world. He had been working part-time for an agency we used, fixing IT—or, as he put it, telling people to turn it off and back on again—when he had turned up at my office.

Not quite the ignoble start, as he had barged into a meeting with some sort of flashing gadget, announcing he was doing a trace. I assumed it was an IT term, not some sort of misogyny. That was that. I went out on a limb—something out of character—and got his number from him before he left. Only in case there were any problems, of course.

I did leave it a few weeks, so that he could ring me first, naturally—I'm not that forward. And anyone who knew me knows I did not do that sort of thing. I suppose I may have been shy. When I finally rang him, we just hit it off. Coffee at first, then dinner, then inevitable overnighters. Next thing, he proposed—the day after his divorce came through—and here we are.

With another flip, I was back to the deal we had put together—something again from my work life. This had only come about because it involved him supposedly being a house husband while I did all the career stuff. I assumed he was happy with this, but, as anyone will tell you, assumption will make an ass out of you and me.

But now, it seems I am doing his job by proxy, as I must remember everything for him as well. I have tried writing lists and Post-It notes but all that happens is J forgets to read them. If he were not only thirty-six, I would think he was going senile. I mean, early-onset dementia would have to be reclassified if that were the case, wouldn't it?

Here I am, sitting, wondering and worrying about the kids and James, when I should really be thinking about work. I will give Annie a call and see if she thinks it is kosher and not just a polished turd. That refers to work, not home and the kids.

One joy of being in the fast-moving corporate world—the one I occasionally appreciated—was the quality of the equipment. With one push of a button on the steering column of my BMW 7 series, I called Annie, the ringing coming through the expensive B&O speaker system.

There is some danger in this—I sometimes wondered about the integrity of using this, as on several occasions I have overheard what should be confidential calls, including once, someone getting told they were being made redundant. And that was through two layers of safety glass and eight feet of car park. Being a Luddite, I wasn't quite sure how to turn it down, so I would just ask Annie to keep it basic, non-specific, and as clean as she could, in case she chose to use some celebratory industrial language.

"Hi, Kelly," she answered as if she had been sitting on it.

"Hiya, thanks for today. Just thought I would have a quick debrief while I'm stuck in traffic. May not have time later with the kids going feral at home—that is, as long as he has picked them up."

"You love it, they adore you, which isn't bad considering."

Our relationship was based on my laissez-faire attitude towards the ivory tower and the longevity of her service to me and my family before me. She was only slightly older than me but knew the business and the company as well as, if not better, than I did. She was more than an asset. Of my small circle of trusted friends, she was among the best—on a par with the man I had married.

"Yeah, OK. Anyhow, how do you reckon we got on? Just keep it general, as I am on speaker." Realising I sounded like my mother and her aversion to the phone, I said, "I felt it went better than well."

"OK, seemed good to me—not having to change the figures or take any penalty clauses was a result. I think they definitely understood where we were coming from and, more importantly, what we can give to them," came the immediate, business-like reply.

"Thanks, Annie. That's what I thought."

Why I was doubting myself was strange—perhaps it was an insecurity, and I needed affirmation from someone else.

"No problem. As I said, it did look OK, and when I got back, I had another look, and it stacks. We should live to fight another day. Your dad would be proud—the name lives on."

"You're back already? I am stuck on the motorway and have been for ages." I tried to ignore the less-than-positive *should* in her statement. We needed it firmer than that.

"I am staying up here as I'm using the local office tomorrow for some reviews and appraisals."

"Oh, yes, you told me—lucky you. I'd best ring J now, as he will have forgotten to breathe or something." That lack of enthusiasm was picking at my head, but this was neither the time nor the place, and you never knew who might be listening outside in the jam.

Laughing, she said, "You love him, so you best hope he hasn't."

"Speak tomorrow," I added with a smile, trying to keep it positive.

"Say hi to him from me." And she was genuine about this, as she had accepted my new relationship and all that brought to the company with ease—something I wished I could exhibit.

"Course. Bye."

She was gone, and I was left with my flippy-floppy thoughts.

So, the company looks like it will survive, despite a lack of surety from Annie. And as I believe and trust Annie—which I do implicitly—I will put the reticence to evoke some gusto and enthusiasm around it down to it being something she was waiting to get back into the office with. She was basically backing up my own gut feeling, but it is nice to have even a timid affirmation.

Now to see if my husband has survived—and if he has forgotten the kids again, he had better find a very deep hole to hide in, as this traffic is really pissing me off. The whole mess of it must have moved two hundred metres in thirty minutes. I mean, I ask you, what must these other road users be thinking?

As I studied the traffic, which still showed no sign of moving at any pace, if at all, I wondered what all the other people were doing, trapped in their metal shells. A dark grey Volvo—or rather, a pair of them—slightly to the front and left of me caught my attention, as they both had a funny little aerial on the bumper. Slightly odd. Must be some new sort of tech that I was not aware of—and, to be honest, had no interest in.

The occupants appeared normal enough: a young middle-aged man and a younger woman with a magnificent mane of red hair. They looked, to be truthful, too staid to be taken up with all that stuff, but each to their own. There was the inevitable infestation of white vans—and many other colours—and they were everywhere. Unless they were labelled, I could not even begin to guess what they carried. One to my left was sitting quite low in the water, so was obviously bordering on being overloaded.

In my mirror, I could see the flashing blue lights of an ambulance as it tried to get through the traffic behind me. But where was everything supposed to go? It had stopped about two hundred yards behind me, lights flashing forlornly in hope more than expectation.

If it was occupied, I felt sorry for the poor soul who was the unwitting passenger. There was also an irrational anger at the idiots who had blocked the lanes and would not get over, even though there was little wiggle room. It may have been harsh, but it was probably justified. The red lights just stretched into the gloom, the weird effect heightened by a light rain that sprinkled sporadically, making the lights even more gem-like—an impression of a very big necklace.

Time to call J.

The kids are home—hallelujah—he had actually remembered. Perhaps I do him down too much. I just get so frustrated that he seems to think he can just muddle around while I am out busting my butt to support us. It could have been the other way around, of course. J could have insisted I stay at home and look after them. But I had the company to save and run, so that was a non-starter.

Our relationship has flourished even with the kids inserted into our lives. Our marriage had been a normal registry affair—no bells and whistles. The kids were just accepted as part of the equation. I had told J he could contact his ex and get her permission for me to adopt, but she has literally disappeared off the face of the earth.

I made a joke once about it being funny that she went because she did not like the new decking, but J said that was not funny. He would only say she was a troubled woman and was best left wherever she was.

J's childhood may have influenced his intentions when he suggested I officially adopt them; he had been fostered and adopted, so it was a move made from understanding the need—and it made sense to both of us. I think he wanted to create that stability, and if his ex-wife really was gone, then it made just that.

The process, however, was an absolute nightmare. Getting married was a complete doddle, as it should be. The horror stories out there—the tales of red tape and bureaucracy—all of them came painfully true. The councils that promote a diverse and tolerant attitude try their best, but the combined effect of all the bureaucracy and leaflet-driven eye-rolling had the effect of making them appear as homophobic as a group of nineties football fans.

A same-sex couple wanting to formally adopt one of the couple's own kids, could not have raised more eyebrows or created more paperwork. Perhaps it was just this one council, but I had the distinct impression it would have been easier if I had breasts and a vagina. But we got through it all, and I ended up adopting those two wonderful kids. In truth, I seemed to have adopted three if you include my husband, J—but I do love him.

*****

Ray could still see the blue Audi saloon up ahead, about fifteen metres or so, with only Tina's Volvo between him and it. Their target had again drawn parallel with a knackered-looking white van that was riding quite low on its axles—the type of van that, like cockroaches on any motorway, was always there, doing who knew what, and seemingly would do so until the end of time. He laughed to himself, thinking they would probably survive a nuclear holocaust as well. A smile remained on his face even as he caught sight of the driver.

The bloke in the van had glanced across, looking directly at Ray, and Ray swore he looked nervous and fidgety. But he knew it wasn't their presence on the motorway that was causing it, as they were both in unmarked National Crime Agency Volvos. The only clue to their being anything outside of the norm was a smaller aerial on the back bumper, which fed their secure radio comms.

The radio was alive with chatter, despite the request from on high for minimal use. Ray knew, though, that the size of this operation would be pumping adrenalin through the team like an air conditioning unit cranked to the max. Tina was a case in point—she had been positively oozing the stuff since the briefing this morning. She always got like this when there was action in the offing, and today was no different.

Ray knew something else—something he would never voice, even to Tina—that mistakes could be made with all this excitement. Or something would be missed, something crucial that would allow the gang to slip through their fingers, leaving only the detritus of the disposable foot soldiers to carry the can. Ray's long years of service in the army, then the GMP, and finally the NCA, had given him the experiences that produced this thought. If he was honest, it had first come to him when this was being planned three months ago and had reappeared as a genuine worry this morning when he had been strapping on his Kevlar vest.

5:32 pm

The Beemer had slipped from view, it's driver almost exclusively concentrated on his phone call. Now, a little red Mini was just visible. I had been watching the driver for a very short while—she was grinning manically, as in seriously manically. Something was making her happy, it seemed. What was with all these loons on the motorway? What with the minibus, and now this woman? She should go and join them—she could take her smile and join their little party.

I wish I had a reason to do that. I'm sure I was once happy too—when I was first married and then when the kids came along. We were happy then, or so my ex-wife would tell me—our little family. Even though my life meant I could be, and on a few occasions was, rudely removed from it. What has happened to bring me to this? To culminate in doing something off-the-scale dodgy for some very nasty people?

Admittedly, I had known them from school, but they weren't friends. They had basically manipulated, threatened and pushed me into this before I knew what was happening. Now, I was so tied into whatever this was, and I had no way of getting out without causing further harm. That harm would include people I cared about a lot.

The woman was on the phone now, still grinning. Well, good luck to her. She looked like she wanted to dance, or maybe she was on something. But I won't judge her. I only hope she would judge me favourably if she knew me—even though the likelihood of that was slim.

I am Blessed

This insane grin—I must get it off my face. I know it's there; I caught a glimpse in the mirror a few minutes ago. I can sense the blooming thing—it feels like it must be almost reaching my ears. Who needs Botox? You just need to grin inanely and permanently, which will tighten everything up—well, facially anyway.

The rest, no doubt, will just keep moving nearer my feet. It doesn't look that bad when I am lying down—a position I have done a lot of over the last few days and nights. More than I could reasonably expect at fifty-seven and probably far more than when I was twenty-seven if truth be told. Who would've thought that I had it in me, metaphorically and physically? Hee-hee. I mean—fifty-seven and being shagged rotten by a man I was madly and deeply in love with.

The thought of what we had got up to on our midweek break was starting to make me tingle again, in places that should be saying, *No more, Julie, we have done our part and need a rest.*

I know right? When did sex become so bloody good and fantastically great fun? Certainly not in the last fifteen years of my marriage, and to be honest, probably not in the first ten either. I may be being a little harsh there, as there had been the occasional episode of feeling vaguely satisfied with David.

The kids were clearly a testament to that—although, as everyone knows, but probably not men, an orgasm is only necessary for one of you in order to conceive. We had managed to achieve something through it, but that doesn't ascribe any satisfaction level, and that pretty much sums up my whole marriage. David may have provided an alternative narrative, though—not that he would ever go public and tell anyone, let alone me.

Sorry, kids. Love you to bits, and I know you would be doing that pretend vomiting thing or sticking your fingers in your ears if we ever had this conversation about me and your dad. On the other hand, I think you would need prolonged therapy if I told you what I have been up to over the last three days. Seriously, the kids would divorce me for acting like a porn star—albeit a slightly saggy one, and not quite as energetic as I once was. But what the hey—who cares?

Someone once told me, when I was a little drunk at a dinner party, that I should start acting my age. What a crock. I wish I could go back and tell them of my antics—that I was making up for lost time, or lost orgasms, anyway. Not that I could, of course, as they all had pretty much blanked me as soon as I announced that I was divorcing David.

The thing is—I feel like I am glowing, like a ten-foot-high pink and blue neon sign pointing at *the extremely dirty girl in the red Mini.* The other thing is—and this was making me sit up and pay attention—I was missing Mac like crazy, and I had only left him two hours ago.

The sex was not the only reason for this euphoria—he had asked me to move in with him. And it wasn't even a post-coital episode—one which could be laughed away once the sun came up. This had been over the more prosaic setting of a hotel breakfast this morning.

For one panicked moment, I thought he was going to ask me to marry him, but luckily it was nothing that seismic. After all, we have both done that before and what do we really need to do that again for? Especially at our age. What does it prove? Let's just live together and have great sex whenever we want.

Not that I had said yes to living with him. Not yet, anyway, as I was supposedly *thinking about it*. Yeah, right—of course, I was.

The sad part of all of this is that the last three years could have been my entire adult life. I had met Mac when I was seventeen, and we went out for eighteen months or so. He may well have been my first love—he was certainly my latest one, and hopefully my last one. Schoolgirl crush it most certainly wasn't.

Our parents had even met back then. They were thinking long term here, and for two naïve youngsters, we had accepted their proffered wisdom. The sex has still been great, if a little new—it all just seemed to fit despite our inexperience.

All that time wasted from then to now—just a forlorn wish and all that. Hindsight can be a real sod. But what could I have done? We didn't drift apart; it was more a case of explosively separating.

My parents had been torn—they genuinely liked Mac, but they wanted the best education for me, and with that came the inevitable sacrifice. Being packed off to a far-flung university—Manchester, actually—both of us making promises that, at nineteen, we were going to find almost impossible to keep. They lasted a little while, but realistically, we both sort of moved on.

Going home that second Christmas had been hard, especially as Mac had found someone else. After that, time passed at uni—I met David, married him, had satisfactory sex with him, had two great kids and was comfortable. Very bloody bored but comfortable.

It had been so easy to find Mac—I can't get over how simple it was, and that in itself reinforces my grin.

We had both been on our own again—Mac only recently—but hey-ho. It was like fate, or the god of the internet had intervened. Hermes, apparently, according to the internet. The god of the internet, that is. I looked it up on Google, whether you believe that or not. Sure, that is a case of something self-proclaiming a god—there will be a name for that, I am sure.

But here we were—two lost souls, keen to reignite. Or so it seemed, even at that first contact. Well, I was, and bits of me had enjoyed the reignition significantly more vigorously than others. Hee-hee.

For three years we had been doing this, and he had touched me in more ways than I could imagine. Hee-hee.

I had found a new happy place that wasn't a visit to the hairdresser's every month—it was taking my place in Mac's orbit whenever we could manage it.

Mac wanted more—assuming that was the reason for the question. And I wanted more, as I was also sick of driving up and down this motorway. One way in anticipation and the other in a state of despond—because I wanted to turn around and go back.

Thank you, internet. Thank you, social media. And thank you, the gods of everything.

I had found happiness in my mid-fifties. I had achieved multiple orgasms in my mid-fifties. I had found my true love and soul mate again. All of these were intrinsically linked and ultimately created a winning formula—all through the electronic catalyst of the World Wide Web.

Even the stumbling block that was our collection of kids had not been as big as we thought it would be.

Six months in, we had taken mine out for dinner—a little awkward, but they now message Mac for stuff as much as they do me. And I'm not jealous at all. Or perhaps a bit.

It was a little harder with Mac's, as they were slightly younger—only by a couple of years—but it did take a little more invention. We used the home ground of Mac's house as a sort of casual meet, and this broke the ice.

I want them to be like mine are with Mac, and I think they will be. It might just take a little longer. The university experience they are both on now will probably sort it out. Realising there is a bigger world than your home one will smooth out any misconceptions. We wouldn't tell them about the physical side—this is by mutual silent consent—as nobody's kids need to know what happens in the bedroom, bathroom, kitchen, lounge or garden shed. Hee-hee. As they say, what happens in Vegas?

God, that tingle is back. It isn't just the sex—it's the whole package. The excitement, the safety and a very different level of comfortable. Not having to be on my best behaviour all the time, allowed to just be me—this is a revelation, and one Mac has made come true. As well as making me come.

Why was I flapping about? Making the decision was really easy. Of course, it was. I knew where I wanted to be—my whole body knew where it wanted to be. My mind knew it was right. So why had I gone through the pretence of saying I was thinking about it? Mac must think I am a fool.

Let's be practical—ooh, yes, let's. This from the tingle, which was doing its best to distract me.

I could rent my house out. Then, if it doesn't work—and why wouldn't it?—I will still be fine. Sexless, but not homeless. There you see, you can shut your yap, tingle. Practical works now and again.

Before I change my mind—let's do this. First of all, where's my handbag? Got it. Every woman knows you need to add some lippy and a dab of Chanel No. 5—other perfumes are available—to get your confidence up to the right notch.

I was making my biggest decision for years—the biggest one since I decided single life was better than looking at wallpaper books or debating with David what to do on our middle-class holiday in the south of France. Yep, there we go—ready. Give me that bullet to bite on. Press number two and hope he picks up before my courage fails me.

"Hello, sexy gorgeous girl. You home already?" Answered on the third ring.

"No, lovely, stuck on the motorway in a horrendous jam." And missing you like mad, I almost added. But we would leave his ego alone until I had done this.

"Oh, Jools, sorry—you should have stayed here and gone in the morning. We should have checked." I mean, considerate as well—what is a woman supposed to do?

"It is what is. Anyway, the reason I rang…" I started to say.

"You missed me?" *Duh, yes.*

"Of course, from the moment I left. No, the reason I was calling is I…" I tried again.

"Want to shag me rotten." Double duh, yes, and my tingle flared so much I was sure the Hubble telescope would see it, and it would be on the late news.

"Mac, yes, I do. Will you just listen?"

As much as the casual flirting and banter were great, this was me making a life-changing decision. To be fair, he did.

"OK," he sounded like a little boy.

"I've decided that I'm going to rent my house out and move in with you if you still want me to?" Keep it blunt, make it sound like a business arrangement and avoid pumping his ego.

"You are saying yes? Wow, just wow. I thought you were having second thoughts or that I was pushing too hard." I could hear the excitement in his voice and was fairly sure any self-doubt he might have had was also flapping off into the sunset.

"Should've said yes straight away." Pump it a little, baby. Hee-hee.

"Oh, you have just made a middle-aged man very happy. Wish you could see my grin." And the thing is—I could imagine it.

"I will soon enough. It's time to stop dithering." I grinned at myself in the mirror.

"It's just…wow…" Mac seemed lost for words.

"It is. And now I've told you, I am going to ring the kids. They will be chuffed, I hope." Not that I was bothered by that—they would be fine.

"They will. And yep, give me a ring when you get back. I am going to ring everyone I know. Drive safe love." And he probably would do just that. Not that I could criticise—I would be doing the same.

"I will be. Goodbye." Regrets—I've had a few, but this wasn't one of them.

"Always. Bye." And the man I loved had gone, but only for a short while.

As I looked around the traffic surrounding my car, I hoped the other road users were ignoring me—or at least couldn't see me. Although, I had caught that van driver watching me in his mirror. I wondered what he thought was going on. I shudder to think.

Bloody hell—I had actually done it. The grin spread even wider, if that was possible. I wanted to get out of the car.

I wanted to dance to the flashing red lights like I didn't care, like nobody was watching, and all the other cliches. I wanted to go and hug the intense-looking man in the yellow Fiat. I grinned inanely at the man in the white van. He just looked straight through me.

I don't care. I really don't.

Everyone should be happy for this fifty-seven-year-old sex kitten. Mac's words, not mine. I deserved this. Yes, I did, and I was going to enjoy the rest of my days with Mac.

Calm yourself a little, Julie—it's time for the kids.

*****

The phone in the car cradle in Ray's Volvo suddenly flashed up with Tina's name. When he answered it, she chirped up from her Volvo, about five metres away, "We could do without this pissing traffic, Ray. All the timings could go to pot unless we move soon."

"We will just need to keep him in view, T. Not that we can do much else," Ray replied, which sounded to him—even as he said it—very much like he was stating the obvious. "It will clear soon. Remember, we can lose the driver but not the car—he's a no-mark."

This brought the response that he had expected—a muttered "Fuck"—and then she hung up.

Clearly, Ray thought, *Tina was back in her world, where the need for civility was limited.*

*****

5:33 pm

Looking away from the mad loon in the Mini, I could now see the minibus again and the old fella on it, the one who had been asleep against the window.

However, he was no longer like that, and, yes, it was true—they appeared to be having a sing-song, led by the same bloke in the wonky cap near the back. He was the oldest by some way. Bless the old fool, he was giving it some real welly, yet the others were joining in, only to a slightly lesser degree, and they showed no sign of relenting.

Smiling—something that I had not done much in the last few days—I hoped I would have as much gusto when that age caught up with me. But living life to the full would never come easily to me, as my life choices dictated that I am always on the edge.

That old chap probably had some medals from some sort of war, which he would wear with the passing and dying pride every November. He certainly looked old enough. It wouldn't be one of the big wars, but Korea or somewhere.

The old guy had looked completely at home belting out whatever it was, with a beer in his hand, and he was part of the group again. Even if the others in the bus were still only half-heartedly joining in, their singing was in marked contrast to the old 'un's enthusiasm.

This latest respite from my woes, over the last few minutes, meant a distraction—and it had made me happy. It was good to be distracted in such a way. But as the smile faded from my lips, my thoughts almost instantly and sharply returned to the darkness engulfing me, inside and out.

A darkness punctuated by the steady red pulse threading out in front of me.

I Miss the Gifts You Gave

It was common yet unspoken knowledge that they had invited me because they felt sorry for me. I knew this; they would acknowledge it too, yet they would also show no shame. I could never hold them to account for it, as this simple act can be counted as the kindness that it was—and in essence, in all its embodiments, that was exactly what it was.

Looking out of the bus window wasn't exactly great entertainment, and the temperature inside was warm—too warm for me. It was almost like being under one of my old mum's handmade comforters. Although they always smelt of dog—funnily enough, like this bus. Maybe that's what had brought the memory back.

All the times when one of them slipped into the bedroom unobserved—although they would never smell of beer, which was the other smell surrounding me. What my Methodist mum and dad would have made of their son sitting in a bus, on a pub trip, with a beer in his hand, I will luckily never find out. They were long gone to the abstemious afterlife, so I'm not sure why I was even wondering about them. Best just to turn my attention back to the stationary traffic.

Most of the models out there I would struggle to identify nowadays. There was a tatty old Land Rover, and I only knew that one because I used to have one of them back in the day. The rest were just a mash of modern shapes and colours—similar yet unfamiliar. What would have been the chances of seeing one of them back then? In fact, I can never recall having seen a yellow car—not like that tiny little bright one. Squinting at it, I could just about make out it was a Fiat something or other.

You wouldn't have stood for that, would you, Nellie? All that colour, making you stand out instead of blending in with the crowd. There were white ones, grey ones, big ones, little ones, some wagons, and a couple of vans. All of them changed places slowly as the traffic edged forward and back. It was sort of mesmerising, really, and the warmth inside was making me feel sleepy. The view changed every few minutes, and I got a different set of faces to look at each time. I could try to imagine their stories, but it would be too taxing—though I was sure they were out there. Families, singles, couples, drivers and even what looked like a chauffeur or two.

Ian—or was it Greg? I could never remember any of their names these days. I was okay with faces, but names usually eluded me. One of them had given me a can of beer. Another small kindness, I suppose. It was quietly warming in my hand, and I didn't want to seem rude by refusing it. You know me, Nellie—a small whisky on a Sunday or a half in the Kings, that's my limit.

But still, it was a kindness. I can sip it occasionally, and if I close my eyes now and again, they won't insist I have another. Hopefully, at the rate they were throwing them down, they'd soon forget about me—which would suit me for now, as it let me think about you.

Oh, Nellie, I miss you so much, even now. It's been ten years, or thereabouts, and yet you still sit in my thoughts as if you had just nipped out for the messages and were due back soon. Remember that blue silk scarf of yours? I carry it with me everywhere now, but no doubt, if you are watching, you already know that. It's here now, tucked in-between my shirt and vest. I still spray it with your perfume every now and then—4711 by Maurer and Wirtz. I remember the first time I met you—that smell took me, and I was yours.

I am still yours-, and that perfume just holds me in a world I want to stay with. The soft feel of your scarf is a comfort, and if I move slightly, I catch a draft of your perfume. I don't think anyone has the heart to ask why I smell like that. Perhaps they can only smell Fly, my constant sidekick—or maybe just their own dogs.

Fly's face was a picture tonight when I went out without him. You would have laughed to see him—head down between his paws as if I had just flicked his nose for misbehaving. I will buy him a treat when we get there. I am sure a nice pie or a bag of crisps will stop his sulk.

The traffic is still lazily rolling about, Nell. It will send me off soon. Had you been here, you would have taken the beer off me and nudged me when I started snoring or drooling—your hankie always at the ready. I miss those little things. The girls that come in and do the stuff you did are nice enough, but there are three of them, and I can never remember who's who. I get the feeling sometimes that they would rather be doing something else. Did I mention that it takes three of them to replace you? I could have told that nice man from the council that—you were irreplaceable.

But at least you know that I am fed and have clean clothes. Apart from your scarf—nobody would touch that. They even do all the cleaning and tidying up. I feel like I am a kid again. Sometimes, the way they talk to me makes me think I am six years old. I know I haven't long left till I can join you on your cloud of 4711, ready to put me straight again.

Fifty years together, and I have had to wait another ten to see you again—it in't right. The guys in the pub, the ones who brought me along tonight, are friendly enough. I think they just see me as a relic of days past—and I should be treasured or a lucky mascot or summat. Still, it was a kindness, wasn't it, Nell?

I can feel myself slipping off—my eyes are getting heavy. I should put the can down or hand it to the guys.

I must have dropped off, as my cap in't straight. Must have pressed it up against the glass. You would have sorted that, girl. No scruffiness on your watch. Remember that bus trip we went on to Castle Howard and Whitby? When I dripped ice-cream down my mac? You were livid. It wouldn't come out. You insisted the driver point you to a supermarket so you could get some cleaner. I loved you for that. How we laughed later.

I wish I had the same pride when you had first gone. It took a while for me to be picked back up, and I think you would be happy, my love, that I managed it.

The last year has been hellish. You would have hated it, Nellie. The talking at people through windows, the masks. I was banished to my bedroom while the girls came in and did what they could. Food parcels on the doorstep. It was worse than what they used to tell us about the war, love. If I hadn't had Fly, I don't know what I would have done. At least I was allowed out to walk him, so it wasn't as bad for me as for others.

Everything was shut, and I had to get Lorraine next door to get my shopping. Even had to trust her with my card. It was madness, and people were dying. I got my jabs early on, as would you if you had been here. It didn't hurt—you will be pleased to know. We lost a couple of friends, and we weren't even allowed to the funeral.

We could only say a prayer at home. No church, nothing. Nell, it was horrible, and I missed you even more than before. It's over now—well, the worst of it, according to the news—and we are sort of back to normal.

I am getting too maudlin. You have never been to a football match, have you? Well, you are going today, so I hope you enjoy it.

Listening in to the chaps and their chat—most of which I didn't understand—I felt a strong urge to sing. It would help everyone forget and would cheer me up. It would remind them all that we were the sons of Yorkshire. We may be old and slightly dated, but we were proud.

"Wheear 'as ta bin sin ah saw thee?"

Greg or Ian or one of them said.
"Oh Christ, who set him off…"
"On Ilkla Moor baht 'at?"
And you know what, Nellie, lass? They all joined in.

*****

5:34 pm

Tina had cut Ray off, as he had done that bloody annoying thing of his where he thought stating the obvious was needed. She knew she should apologise and was on the point of phoning him back to have a more in-depth conversation about the scenario when her attention was caught—and not by the yellow bin on wheels or the giant pink monstrosity she had glimpsed.

It was the radio, and she had picked her callsign out of all the noise—not only miraculous but also fortuitous, because it meant she could avoid humble pie for a little while.

"Lima 46, Lima 47, this is Lima 1. Can you go to secure channel 4? Over," focussed Tina. The fact that Ray was sitting up straighter when she looked showed that the shout clearly had both of their attention, as these were their call signs. How they both picked it out was something that would always remain a mystery.

"Received, Lima 1. Switching now, over," Tina said into her throat mike, adjusting the dial on the belt-worn radio to the required channel.

"OK, are you there, boss?" Tina heard as she linked to the channel—Ray quicker on the button than her. Lima One was the main man, sometimes called Gold—and Colin Philpott in his normal life.

"Ray, are you and Tina still snarled up on the motorway?" A note of concern was apparent.

"We've only moved around fifty yards in the last half hour or so, boss." Ray was old-school and would no more use metres than he would ask for a half litre of beer. Tina loved him for it.

"OK, we are reviewing how we handle this, as the pond is getting a bit choppy down here." Considering that Tina and Ray only knew limited information, the rest of it was of little use in keeping them abreast of anything.

"Is the other ARV still behind us?" Tina had to ask, as she had not seen them for a while.

"They are Lima 32. But I may pull them out, as the intel tells us your target isn't armed and has no form for violence." Something they had already learnt this morning at the briefing, but Lima One was known as being a bit of a pedant.

"Though that might be the case, Ray and I should be OK, boss, as we have enough firepower between us to counter one guy." Which was very true—or so she hoped.

"OK, I will call off 32 and put them on intercept nearer the job here. We may have to change plans at short notice, as we can't lose Golf 1 and 2 this time. If they look like moving, we will act and take them out. You can then just move against your target when you need to."

Golf One and Two were the principal targets—the whole reason for this shebang. They were the kingpins, the functioning heads of the organised crime gang the NCA was targeting.

"Ok, boss. Received and confirmed. Out," Tina said, and they were back to radio silence. Or rather, they were back to the chicken-shed twitter of the general channel.

*****

Why had I not asked more questions about the contents of this bloody van? This thought had now popped into my head. The very nature of the incentive offered, in all fairness, precluded asking too many questions, and the very characters who had asked did not tell me what was expected, underlining the point. I knew my cargo would definitely be illicit, if not completely and ten-to-life illegal.

The very nature of the people who forced me to do the job—and the incentive they had offered—easily pointed to the provenance of whatever was locked in the back. It certainly wouldn't be fluffy unicorns or penguins, biscuits or otherwise. It could be drugs, booze, guns or fags. I was fairly sure it wasn't people, as there was no air in the back, although that was not a cast-iron guarantee, as recent news stories had highlighted. I knew that the mobile phone's absence was some sort of basic security, and they had tried fobbing me off with the *sensitivity* thing. That was hogwash—that was clear. It must have been so illegal they didn't want anybody tracking it or even having the ability to follow the van.

I must admit, as I drove, I wondered if that was why the radio was disabled, but I didn't know enough about it to know if you could track a radio. But then again, I had a satnav. Could you track that? Surely you could, as the damn thing, apart from being bloody annoying, was sending out a signal. Not knowing the answer was frustrating—but not really something to worry about. The no-phone thing also gave them peace of mind that I couldn't call for help or dob them in. Not that I would, as the incentive was too big and would ensure my silence.

The woman in the Mini was now chattering away on the phone, the rictus grin still in place. Was it with pleasure or pain? If she wasn't careful, she would be wiping her grin off her face and all over the back of the bright yellow Fiat 500 that had now caught my eye. The drivers of these things must have balls of steel I shook my head at the thought—something the size of a small outdoor hot tub, with wheels the size of dinner plates.

The thought of what it would feel like to have one of the HGVs thunder past it must make it feel like the end of the world. Balls of steel were the only answer—unless it was a death wish.

There Will Be No Pudding

There was a familiar creeping tension building inside me, and if I could, I would scream—I really would—but there were too many, far too many people around. Probably none of them were actually looking at me but knowing the way my life was then there was a very strong doubt that they could even see me.

Shedding a tear or two was an option, as there was even less chance of anybody noticing that, surely. But if I did, I would not be able to stop, and in the end, it would probably get all snotty—and I had no hankie. Wiping snot on my sleeve would only draw attention. There was nothing else for it—I would just have to hold in the incipient tears for a more personal time later. The screams were also building; they could sit with the tears until I was somewhere away from the bullies, somewhere nice and safe.

The fact that nobody would notice me even if they could see me was the story of my life—the sort of bloke you only vaguely become aware of if you knock into him. These drivers around me thought they were insulated from observation in their metal cocoons, but they would get a shock if they looked over and saw some random bloke in a car screaming his head off. They would no doubt hope that he didn't get out of the car.

I could imagine that, just as a precaution, they will make sure all the doors are locked up tight. *It would be best if we don't open the window, Mary, just in case—you will just have to wait for a smoke.* My entire sad little life had been spent having people look at me and wonder whether I was up to *it*—and if I was, what that *it* could possibly be. Or even what the hell I was doing there in the first place. The thought that I was invisible again didn't cheer me enough to batten down the urge to scream, but it faded just a little.

My family, when I told them my plans all those years ago, thought I was completely mental. God, even I thought I was mental—so what hope did the underachievers in my family have? You know the story: first in a long line of no-marks to go to the big house. And I don't mean Armley Gaol, as quite a few of my clan had already indulged in that accommodation. But this particular big house was the stately realm of further education—in other words, university. In some less enlightened cultures, I would no doubt have been burnt over a fire or eviscerated with a blunt spoon.

My home? Not so much. There was more of a slight shrug of the shoulders, a furrowed brow, and a comment from my dad—jokingly, I believe—asking where he could get a DNA test. I had been made to feel completely worthless before I even reached this epistolary moment, but this was the icing on that particularly ill-tasting and prejudiced cake. I was going to be one of *them*, joining a genre or club they continually and vehemently derided. It was as if I had picked up the shotgun and made sure it was fully loaded for them.

The fact that I did not want to go into the family business of casual labour, criminality, recidivism, and idleness was a crime. Not a heinous one, perhaps, but still worthy of comment every time there was a bloody family do. Rather naively, I thought they would grow out of it—probably with the same level of innocence with which they thought I would. If only they knew. The abasement didn't even stop after I left the nest; they still jibed and jabbed at me as if I were some sort of sport to be partaken in on public holidays. I was as sick of it now as I was then. I had no escape from the persecutors in all their forms.

I had thought at the time that my decision was based on it being the easy option. Despite a life of being harassed, demeaned, and assaulted during my education, I knew that if I was on the other side, I could also have that aura. I could join their gang. Then I would become one of the tormentors, with the undervalued protection of being in charge—the one given a government-approved mandate to harass, demean, and assault during the hours of nine to four.

All safe in the knowledge that if the little bastards went home and complained to their parents, they would get further humiliation at *their* hands. People say that experience during your formative years is a wonderful and joyous thing, don't they? Well, news to those who spout that—it's a pile of crap. My family still treated me as if I were something alien to them at best, something noxious they had stepped in at worst. *The illusion of seizing power. Ha!*

That illusion of a new power dynamic lasted about three days from when I came out of the training classroom. The government and its liberal-leaning advisors had removed the shield of protectionism that had been exercised during my formative years, taking away the whole reason I had taken this route. It was replaced with a big, fat, red target—one that appeared on your back if you turned it, or on your forehead if you faced up to it. We were now the proverbial sitting ducks, like the plastic ones at the fairground you had to hook to win a prize—only now we were caught on mobile phone footage or CCTV.

If you glanced at the kids wrong, asked them to do something, criticised them—or, heaven forbid, told them to turn their damn phones off—the abuse you received was off the scale. The ultimate? Being reported to a counsellor or branded a paedo.

So, aiming for the ancient wisdom of being a teacher had sadly eluded me, and I was left in a purgatory inhabited by kids I could only have dreamt of when I was one. The type of kids who would grow up into adults with such a crap education that they would spray-paint *paedo* on a well-respected paediatrician's house walls. Life was so unfair. How could this have twisted into something even more painful than my childhood? It was enough to make me weep—for myself, and for all those yet to come.

Reflecting now, looking down at myself, I tried to reconcile the blue suit trousers—slightly rumpled—and the white shirt. I mean, for God's sake, I was wearing slip-on shoes and a frigging tie. A *frigging tie*. Gone were the tatty jeans, the Motörhead t-shirt, the long hair. The earrings—yes, they had gone as well. Only three little holes remained; you could just about see them if you were really close. And only my wife got that close, which was a rare thing indeed.

This old look had been another rebellion against the Ben Sherman shirts and Harrington jackets of my loving home environment. This one had been just as successful. I don't even know why I had bothered. The abuse multiplied and even spilt out to complete strangers in the street. *Fucking hippy Greebo* was a common refrain from the denizens of my homeland.

I had even thought I could use my previous rebellions to achieve some sort of rapport with my classes, but as you can guess, it didn't end well. Even though some of the memes they produced were positively brilliant, I couldn't validate this behaviour, which meant chastising them. Which resulted in—yep—more revolting memes. And, ultimately, in my complete rejection and deletion of all my social media.

Although I knew stuff was still out there—by the sympathetic, sometimes smug, looks I received from my companions in the trenches. More a case of *there but for the grace of God*. Some support from the system would have been nice, though. Even a tacit nod to my pain would have helped.

The thing is I know I expected too much. Going into a career, that some even called a vocation or a calling, I certainly wouldn't go that far, that had such a negative effect on me, was a strange choice. The thought process was along the lines of – how bad can it be? I mean some of the teachers I had encountered could hardly be called threatening or even vaguely intimidating. What they did have was the power of the word, they could make you feel small, stupid, cruel, guilty, and worst of all they would do this in front of your mates, your peers, and the girls you wanted to impress.

If all that failed, then the casual flick of a board rubber at you or accidentally spilling water on your work would work just as well. Then there was the ultimate sanction of being held back in detention, where the bullying and intimidation could be more overt and archly insidious.

Don't get me wrong—there were a couple of these despots who actually behaved like members of the same species. There was even one who inspired me so much that I did my degree in that subject.

It's possible that it was also the reason for my career choice, or it could be that I was a bully or a coward at heart and could see myself recreating my experiences for today's bunch of bastards. Whingeing about it didn't seem to help either. You have made your bed, Phil, so just grow a pair. I told myself this regularly, but I can tell you—it only helped when I was on my own. My cowardice, my put-upon-ness, my abjection at being stuck in this circle of bullying and familial intimidation—my own as well as the kids'—had brought me to a long motorway drive to escape it all.

My future was mapped out in front of me like these lights stretching off into the distance—only a little more colourful. Red had never been my favourite, as it screamed warning. Distracted, I saw a bloke who looked like he had a joint on the go—lucky bastard—even though, technically, those days were behind me. A future consisting of diazepam and Gaviscon was a much more likely one. I wondered what was going on ahead.

The traffic news, updated every fifteen minutes, indicated a full closure and possible delays—trying, obviously, to put a spin on what could only have been a calamitous occurrence. Some poor soul being cut out of a car they hadn't even finished paying for yet. Although, just as likely, it could be an escaped llama on the carriageway or a swarm of killer bees—our society having as much regard for any of those scenarios.

Suppose I should call Maire and let her know I'll be late, which will lead to the question of why I'm on the motorway and not slogging through the normal city rush hour.

Hmmm. Not sure how to answer that. Maire, my wife of many years—she tells me I'm happy. She tells me I'm doing a good job. She tells me that everything will be fine and that my wobbles and victimhood are normal. She doesn't believe that fourteen-year-old children could really bully a fully grown man. She would know, right?

Of course, she would. She told me so. I can't skip over the fact that she was educated by a nun-run Catholic school in Ireland—because bullying there is impossible, due to the wrath of God or the Mother Superior, or whoever was on the rota that day. However, the stories that appear tell of a far more sinister method of control in those establishments.

I'm sure I can't be a nun or even a Catholic priest, as much as I'm sure I can't be the second coming of Maire's blessed messiah. In a way, I understand how she can't see beyond her own experience—that's how she was brought up. A bit like those who think something can't be true unless it's on Facebook—and, ergo, everything on Facebook is common knowledge and therefore true.

I should also say that Maire isn't really that blinkered—unless she wants to be. More like a dog with selective hearing. It does make for some interesting conversations, I suppose; at least she doesn't deny dinosaurs, as some of the uber-religious fundamentalists do. That would have been the final camel-breaker. If that had come up, I wouldn't have gone on repeat dates, let alone married her.

Yes, I knew she was religious, but she only hits me with the Great Sky Lord every Sunday and assorted random days off, known as religious holidays. It got so bad at one point that I drew the line—a rare phenomenon indeed—when she put a picture of Jesus in the downstairs loo. No one needs that in their normal activities. I refused to be judged by a stylised depiction of a preacher, or, as one friend put it, peeing on a hippy watch.

The repercussion of that line-drawing was that the picture reappeared—above our marital bed. I learnt an important lesson from that: be careful what you wish for. And I think Jesus would echo that.

My eyes were drawn again to the never-ending lights. Perhaps I chuckled rather darkly—this could be the twenty-first-century equivalent of Jacob's Ladder, particularly as there might be someone—or several somebodies—who had passed to the afterlife at the top end of the red creation. Perhaps this was a conversation to have with Maire over dinner. Or then again, perhaps not.

Still, the thought amused me, which was a different end to the day than usual. There was nothing normally to chuckle at unless some other poor sap on the teaching staff was getting a doing from the feckless little shits—which I would accompany with the refrain: at least it wasn't me today.

Maire is off the call list for now. She'll call me either when she's eaten dinner or when *Pointless* is over—whichever of these life-changing events comes last. I'll just have to enjoy the glaring, the rumble of the traffic, and the inane drivel being spouted from the radio. If pressed, I think I'd say it was something about Brexit, even though that was done and dusted—although it could have been about breakfast. Which just reaffirmed that I wasn't listening.

My reason was that I had tuned in for the traffic and the sport—the rest of it was just background noise. There were times when I'd listen to a music station, but only when I could sing along—and I needed to be happy to do that. Not doing my impression of a restructured seventh of the Dwarves. Considering Dopey was in the car next to me, and there was an ambulance—probably with a doc—blue lights still flashing like a manic disco behind, trying to get into the emergency lane, was pretty funny.

I wondered how many more of the entrapped I could attribute to the Disney classic. There was a bloke with big ears one car over, but that was a different film entirely. So, I'd listen to music when happy—when I could sing when I could laugh. That only ever occurred on the last three days of any school holiday, when I'd recovered something of myself, before being dragged back into the maelstrom of a refreshed batch of Year Tens. Happiness was a very brief and cruel construct.

It had always been there—the hassle, the trouble, the abuse—ever since I first walked into that room without my chaperone, aka my mentor. The truth was, I was armour less—I was exposed for all to see. A virgin at a feast of roast unicorns.

This wasn't written in any manual—no textbook explained this phenomenon. A fecundity had taken place, spreading its vileness like a particularly pungent disease. A silent chorus of *He's ours now—He's on his own. Let the games begin.*

It was subtle at first—little pranks, minor yet mostly harmless irritants to a nervous soul. Not full-on warfare or uncivil disobedience—that would come later. The first six months were a tentative prod, testing the elasticity of the newbie's boundaries. My response was counterattacking with what I hoped were engaging lessons, tolerating lively discussion if needed—and therefore, I made the fatal mistake of trying to be down with them.

Thank God—or the goat—I was delivering English, and not something that involved sharp implements or other dangerous materials.

I am not sure how my colleagues at war in those particular fields or trenches could survive without some of the protagonists being hospitalised. The only defences I had were severely limited. Words—yep, I could use these. Boy, did I try, hoping they would realise that English could be a useful tool.

I thought my sense of humour would act as a shield. I was only ten years older than them, for God's sake, so I got the references used in their coded exchanges. Sadly, as I grew older, the faces staring back at me year after year didn't, and my culturally appropriated shield waned in power—failing completely when I had to ask which app they were referring to when TikTok arrived. Oh, how I wish I could have joined in that particularly raucous bout of mirth.

The last weapon was the power over their futures and what level of achievement they could attain in my subjects. This sounds like the most powerful weapon of them all, doesn't it? I wish. If the little, bullying, nasty shits put in the reading and submitted work as required, there was nothing—and I mean literally nothing—I could do. I was stuck inside my personal hell, frustrated, frequently worried, occasionally frightened, and more or less constantly wondering how this was a vocation.

Grow a pair, Phil. Yeah, right. Growing them would make an even bigger target.

To sum it up, one of the tormenting legions issued the proclamation, "What are you here for? All I need is in this book or on the net, and I can read and type, so literally, what do you do?"

In its essence, I should have had a great answer to this, shouldn't I? If I was doubting what I was doing there, then how was I to answer? Back in the days of my learning, there was a mythic atmosphere around a teacher. Yes, they could be cruel, nasty bastards, but at least they would impart wisdom. The internet wasn't there—no clicks and hyperlinks, no detectable plagiarism, and no ready-made answers. We had to listen; we had to put in the hard yards.

Even reading books was encouraged—failure to do so was akin to future job suicide. So, twenty years had passed, and indeed, what was I, indeed we, there for? Keep order? Possibly, but not noticeably. Instil discipline? Letters home to incalcitrant parents and detention—if you could get away with it—though Amnesty would probably stop that soon.

Exclusion was the last resort and, while sounding draconian, only resulted in the offender being let loose on an unsuspecting general public, who assumed they were safe on the streets as it wasn't the school holidays. Normally, the miscreant would reappear, like Harry Potter from under his Cloak of Invisibility, after a week or so. Great deterrent then?

My old man used to bang on about naughty boy schools. I think he meant Borstal, but while they had long since gone, the idea did hold a whiff of appeal. In my days of learning, I had only seen a fellow student expelled once, for fighting. He went on to be home-schooled, got a good degree, and now runs a large multinational business. Perhaps it didn't work then either. So, indeed, what was I here for? Chalk that one up to the inquisitive one who posed the question.

For fuck's sake, I had been at the same school since I finished my training—over twenty bloody years—ground down by a system that doesn't work and by the swarm that appears every year, like particularly malicious wasps, only with worse stings. It wasn't a bad school, but it wasn't the best either. Straddling numerous demographics, we had sink estate kids and still-just-about-afloat estate kids.

Every new year brought new staff, and after my tenth intake, I started to notice the new ones. Full of enthusiasm and vigour, counterpointed by the old stagers—of which I now belonged—who would only venture out of the staffroom if they had to or to escape at the end of the day. Bunker mentality hit all of us eventually. It just appeared to be taking less and less time, as the newbies seemed not to be quite as resilient these days.

The last year had been a sort of blessing—ignoring the pandemic stuff. As a teacher, I could sit in an empty classroom, presenting via the internet to the darlings. I could mute them; I could kick them off, and there was sweet FA they could do about it.

When the powers that be announced that exams were to be scrapped, and we—the arbiters of education—would be given sanction and could extract revenge if we felt that way… It was so tempting to screw them over completely, but it was as if they were watching me, slyly over my shoulder and in my sleep. I will say it was professionalism, but not really. They would be back eventually, and why invite the repercussions? The ammunition was freely available. I left that particular wasp's nest unpoked, as did most of my colleagues, I believe.

Now they were back, and the games commenced, with a few new rules—most of which would be consigned to the file marked *ignore* in a few weeks. There was an insidiousness that drove the herd—the direct challenge to any discipline or even to a simple request. The online stuff was foul. Yes, I know we can turn it off and ignore it, but why should a bunch of kids dictate my life or anyone else's?

What was really hurtful was the fact that your non-school friends and relatives saw the vile abuse and pornographic memes. It became another way—bullied by inclusion. Discussing it at drinks do did not lessen the effect; it just rammed it right back at you, but politely and accompanied by a glass of merlot and some cheese.

The no-phone-in-school rule didn't work—the little shits just got creative at hiding them, ensuring a constant supply of video and photo material for their missions. Uniform was a joke, although a zero-tolerance strategy a few years ago had reduced hostilities slightly, but one complaint from a parent about discrimination resulted in an online petition, and that policy was shot down in flames. I shed a tear then, I believe—born of frustration and despair at my plight.

We were powerless, and yet, during my school years, it had been so different. It is difficult to see where the blame lies for the change, but I am sure someone can answer it. That person will be safe in their bunker somewhere and unlikely to share or to push a reversal policy. It was too far gone now.

I can honestly see the day when metal detectors will be in place at the gates and razor wire around the outside—but to protect the teachers. The kids didn't need protecting from us anymore. Things could get that bad.

There was one blessing—Maire and I didn't have kids. God, in his worldly wisdom, had decreed Maire's womb a desert—an insult to her Catholicism, if I understand right. Secretly, I was relieved and had the benefit of practising conception on a risk-free basis. Immaculate? Probably not, but it wasn't bad.

At least I could escape kids completely this way. The thought of going home to a house full of my own would have filled me with horror.

There had been no pressure either from our parents, as Maire's were both partying with Jesus et al now, and mine had won some money on the lottery and buggered off to Spain, where they lived in a world of sangria, endless games of bowls and day-old *Daily Mails*. I hadn't seen them for over eight years and only spoke to them at each year's end—that was the limit of my familial loyalty.

At least they couldn't pick on me, although my sister had tried to pick up that nasty baton. She was easier to ignore, though. So, no clamour for us to produce, and our friends had now stopped mentioning it—mainly because they realised how lucky we were, really. Well, that was my take, as they all had kids in or approaching teenagedom. I even had the pleasure of teaching some of them.

Is there anyone else wondering, as I do, why I was still doing this? It paid okay, had okay hours, and, apart from six hours of mental and sometimes physical assault, the working conditions were just peachy. There may be, in my thoughts, something that denoted a hint of irony bordering on outright sarcasm. What else, for the love of all that is sacred, would I do? When people who have never had to stand in front of thirty foul-mouthed pieces of work in a parody of a uniform trot out the phrase, *If you can't do it, then teach it.*

I could literally smack them with a shovel before digging their shallow grave with it. We should all get medals, not smart-arsed comments like that. They should all think before they trot that one out, as I would defy anyone who has *done* it to try and *teach* it—I would quite happily watch them from the back of the class, casually walking to the front to hand them a new shovel once they realised, they were not quite as clever as they thought they were.

The collective might of thirty pubescent minds would overpower their learned skills. Sure, there was a *Doctor Who* episode along those lines, but who knows? I would like to see them walk away with their tales between their legs— a kicked puppy in a designer suit and Loakes. Ha-fucking-ha.

Sadly, the adage has an element of truth, as my predicament and predilection to yearly torture appertains. I have taught English in its various guises for over twenty years, and what could I do in the big, wide and shiny corporate world? Write pamphlets or web pages? Librarian? Forty plus and, really, I have taught it but have no idea what else I could do with it. Perhaps my self-righteousness is a little misplaced.

The level we had reached was best summed up by an incident earlier this week. One of the supply cupboards had been vandalised—not seriously. Some creative hand had written *fuck this school* on one of the walls in magic marker. Not the most erudite statement, nor likely to be the last piece of graffiti to adorn the school's unhallowed walls.

Initially, this had caused behind-the-hand amusement in the staffroom and condemnation when front and centre with the little darlings. The new deputy head, in her wisdom, called us all together and, in an *Agatha Christie* plot denouement, proudly announced that she had a list of all the classes that had been in that room's vicinity on that day. We, the ones who had overseen any of that horde, were tasked with obtaining handwritten evidence from every student in that cohort.

Asked to coerce every student to submit a piece of paper with *fuck this school* on it for handwriting comparison. Whoever had written it had used a lowercase *f*. Nobody had the heart to point out that the perpetrator knew this and could, therefore, avoid CSI High School by, oh, I don't know—using a capital *F*. Putting aside the comedy value for the kids, and the legendary status this act would attain and the complaints from parents that would ensue once darling Charmian/Tyler went home and regaled them…

No, she was missing a fundamental piece of information—it was just as, no, it was far more likely a teacher had committed the crime. That was the place we had arrived at in our glorious education system.

Glancing around me, I tried squeezing my eyes nearly shut. The effect while interesting, didn't make the lights go away, but the tears were coming and, as with screaming, this was not a place to cry. This just made the world a long red tunnel rather than the *Jacob's Ladder* effect. A slight spatter of rain on the windshield encouraged the lights to become slightly prettier until the automatic wipers erased that prettiness.

At least if it started to rain, I would have something to watch in the encroaching dark other than taillights. The patterns it would cause in my headlights would be interesting, and I could use my wordiness to ascribe characters to anything that tickled my imagination. God, I sounded like I had been sitting in the car with Dopey up ahead.

The minibus to my left caught my attention briefly. The passengers looked like they were laughing. They even had beer—lucky sods. They were singing, for goodness' sake.

A pang of envy wormed its way into my consciousness. They were obviously not teachers, as they were having way too much jollity. Beer aside. Knowing how I felt, they were probably laughing at this bloody car. I mean, Maire, for fuck's sake, what were you thinking? A bright yellow microcar—it was as if you were just trying to underline my personality, as few men would have gone along with this.

Of course, the kids understood green issues and all that. Did they fuck. They just asked me if I had come to school in the *pus wagon*. One extraordinarily talented individual—staff or pupil is open to discussion—had placed a red hat with a bell at its end, on my desk. Such wits.

Deflecting back to those faces in the bus, the fact that they were older would also mean that their fellow motorway travellers were not likely to have bare arses shown to them if the minibus passengers' beer ran out. However, that would cheer me and stop me from depressing myself further. I almost willed it to happen.

The report on the radio cut off—one about public sector policy, I think, but may have been pubic lice—as my phone rang. Maire.

"Hi, love." I tried to keep my emotions out of my opening repartee.

"Where are you, Phil? I have had to put your dinner in the oven to keep." She made no effort to keep the aggression and self-implied sufferance out of hers.

"You had yours then?" *Keep it light, Phil, she doesn't mean it.*

"I have eaten mine already. You know the routine. So where are you?"

Rat-a-tat. Back to it. You can see why the Catholics invented the Inquisition. There are only two things you need to know about the Inquisition: it was brutal, and Maire would have fully endorsed it.

"Stuck on the motorway. There's been a big smash." Smiling despite the grilling—I mean, *Monty Python*, come on, should make any manic-depressive smile.

"Why are you on the motorway?" The personal affront level raised, along with the pitch.

"Just went for a drive, Maire. Really shite day at school." *Manic-depressive, am I?* That was new. It would be good to hang a label on something rather than just being a useless twat.

"You don't normally do that. Why today?" *Oh, give it a rest, Maire, does it matter?*

"Just because. Wouldn't have done it if I had known this crap was here." My distraction by the shininess of a mental disorder had made me vague, which I also knew I would pay for later. A possibly psychopathic god-botherer for a wife would not let that lie. Or this. Or anything at all, in fact.

"It's just been on the news. I will turn your dinner right down." She skipped right over my lack of informative discussion, which definitely would not bode well.

"OK, or you could microwave it for me when I get in." An olive branch.

"I am going out."

My dove spat out the olive branch and responded with one of those statements along the lines of saying nothing when asked what you are doing.

"Out where?" A duty kicked in—feign some interest and get back in the good book.

"Phil, I told you this morning. Typical of you, self-centred as always."

This came as a surprise, as I normally paid full attention to Maire—it would be a fool or someone with a death wish who did otherwise.

"Maire, I had a lot on my mind, so I'm sorry. You will have told me, I know, but it has slipped my mind. So can you just remind me, please, love?"

Appealing to her sometimes worked, depending on the level of perceived transgression.

"You know what day it is. I am going to light a candle for Ma and Da—you know it's their anniversary…" And she was gone, leaving me to contemplate my inability to grow a pair, and the revelation that I was capable of being a real fucking arsehole. A realisation that everyone who had told me so was probably not that far off the mark.

Why did I do this—not only to myself but to Maire? Even the fact that it was the anniversary of her parents' death in a car crash was being weaponised. I am such a shit. She doesn't deserve it, and I sure as hell don't. She will tell me it's okay when I get back, but I know it isn't and won't be.

All this with the knowledge that I will have to step through the gates of hell again tomorrow, and tomorrow, and tomorrow. The woman in the huge SUV and the guy who was watching me from the van—I wonder what they would make of it all. Would they judge me favourably, or would they, as I suspected, lock their doors? Suddenly, *Jacob's Ladder* became very bloody appealing.

*****

5:35 pm

Tina's phone did its thing. It was Ray, clearly in the mood to talk despite Tina's previous implication.

"You get all that, T?" Ray said as soon as she answered.

Tina gave a quick glance in the mirror at her colleague, who was looking at her.

"What do you think?" she replied with a hint of *duh* in her voice.

"OK, my take is that the boss man may be acting against the OCG earlier—and without us—as they're getting twitchy about something and may not wait around." Which, if Ray was honest, was about all he knew.

"Surely, they aren't twitchy about our guy up front? He's only a little fish."

Although in saying this, Tina was glossing over the large quantity of what was believed to be cocaine in the boot of the Audi. Little fish he may be, but the product was certainly important.

"No, there's something far bigger going on. You've seen the scale of the op—our guy is just another small part of the bigger one."

Ray had his suspicions, but he wasn't going to voice them yet—not until he knew more. The clock on the dashboard read 17:35, so they had time on their hands before any takedown.

"OK, so what's the craic?"

Ray knew Tina would get frustrated soon and would want to go full *Action Mandy*, preferably with her Glock out. That would no doubt involve a lot of violent shouting, which he always assumed was more about officers winding themselves up than the shock-and-awe tactic it was purported to be.

"32 is going off as soon as it can to go on intercept somewhere else, and we may have to take our target out sooner rather than later."

Ray hoped that lessening the number of coppers running around would appease Tina's need for action.

"We can do that," Tina said by way of confirmation.

*****

The way I got into this predicament was simple. The *why* of it—that was equally blatant. The truth was, I love my wife and kids. No, I am being untruthful there, and the thought was more than a little inaccurate. I love my kids, and I *had* loved my wife. I would do anything for the kids, but the wife—well, she wasn't that anymore, so my obligation there was purely a moral one.

My kids mean everything to me, and I was doing this to settle an implied debt, to avoid any of the hinted-at repercussions. Although the debt was real, it was the other incentive that kept me pinned to this situation—stuck in a web spun by a gimpy spider. The fact that this shit heap of a van had moved very little, and the satnav was still in the mood for taking the piss—while proving that time travel was apparently possible and indeed necessary—only highlighted the possibility that the repercussions hanging over me might be closer than I thought.

A bright flash caught my eye, distracting me momentarily from this set of worries.

The intense-looking man in the yellow Fiat looked like he had just received some bad news—or needed a piss. The expression on his face was one of extreme discomfort, or he was about to burst into tears.

Seriously, mate, thought the van driver, *if it's that bad, just get out and piss at the side of the road. It's not like we're going anywhere quick, and all the other drivers would probably praise your courage. Or go and talk to the blokes in the bus, or the grinning loop in the Mini—they should put a smile on your twisty face.*

That would be hoping that those around me didn't have the same level of not caring as me. Although looking across at the woman sitting in the white, top-end SUV beyond you in your Belisha beacon of a car—she's got the wrinkled face of middle-aged disapproval squeezed across it like badly applied prosthetics.

Perhaps I'm being a bit harsh—she looks genuinely unhappy, yet not on the pained-yellow-bloke level. There can't be *that* many things making her that unhappy apart from being stuck in a traffic jam.

Gin prices up? Offer on two-for-one pants in M&S finished?

I wished my discomfort was something as simple as that. The ironic satnav, the worry about the contents of the van behind me, and the dilemma I was stuck in seemed far more real.

Perhaps I should stop and tell Mrs Middle-Aged SUV my problems?

The answer I got from her might not be as simple as I imagined—and would probably not be the one I wanted to hear.

The Fools and The Sages

Being thankful was not something that I had experienced much recently, but for once, I did. John had bought this car before he became ill; if we had still had the old one, the journey would be even more of a nightmare. At least I am comfortable and warm, and having the foresight to use the loo before I left was heaven-sent. Stop thinking about heaven—John's not there yet. He is in a personal hell, though.

The home is definitely a good one, but why did I bow down to Janet, his sister? It really grated on me, as I know I should have stood up to her. She had said she wanted him close, which meant more strain on me. Ostensibly, she claimed she could ease that pressure. The visits I'm making are starting to take a toll on my health—I feel like I have aged twenty years in the past eight months.

Janet visits the same number of times that I do in a week, and I do this journey three times a week, sometimes four—not that I am counting or keeping score. So that reasoning did not really work out all that well, did it, Janet? I think she secretly hopes I will leave her to tend to John and that if pushed, I will just disappear into the background. She wishes.

When we married, it was with the traditional sickness and health bit, neither of us quite anticipating early-onset dementia taking John at forty-nine. The clue was in the name, I suppose, but in John's case, it was so rapid. One day, he was there, doing his crossword and talking about the garden changes for the summer he was planning, and the next, he did not know me from a begonia. He knows bloody Janet, though. Sorry, John, for swearing, but that makes me so angry. He even remembers Terry—bloody Terry—Janet's husband. Sorry, John.

There should be no doubt that he is comfortable and looked after, should there? Not that I had much time from the dagger-like diagnosis to the point where I could no longer cope. When John started nocturnal wanderings and trying to set a fire in the false fireplace, then we—or should I say I—knew a point had been reached. Even the day-care that we were given could not stop the worry at night. No wonder I feel old, but the guilt is crippling me as well. It's just as debilitating as the worry. Guilty because I could not help John, guilty because the feelings I had were raw, guilty because I feel guilty.

The kids had thankfully left home a few years ago. Or was I thankful? If they were at home, I would have help. Now I feel guilty for thinking that. I just feel guilty for everything. Guilty when I enjoy a cup of tea, guilty when I smile at something on the telly. How can I live with all the guilt and still paste a smile on my face when I visit John, who does not know me from his own front door, which he does not know either?

That year of visits during the pandemic had been another version of hell—one of Dante's circles, no doubt. This one was reserved for those who felt perpetually tired and guilty. It started with waving at John through a window—essentially a zoo—watching this creature die from behind the safety glass. Don't worry, it will be extinct soon. The fact that John did not know me made it even more zoo-like.

The plastic screen had been the next development in our unholy distancing, but at least I was in the same room. John had no idea what was going on. The staff tried, but all the residents in the home were pretty much in the same very rocky and leaky boat. Once the last lockdown was over, I could hold his hand again, even though I was suited up like an alien—or so it felt.

Not that it mattered. I may as well have stripped naked and painted myself blue for all the recognition I got. It's not all about me, though, is it? I had some sort of envy going on for John—it must be nice to be blissfully unaware of all the stuff going on around him, and he looked happy enough.

I had talked to one of the sisters during one visit, and she told me they were all living in to avoid any contamination. Bloody heroes, the lot of them. I knew that John was in the best place—they were all trying to keep it the safest place. Although the news did its best to paint horror stories, which I can tell you did not help my frame of mind at all.

Never mind clapping on a Thursday, I would be taking the whole lot of them out for a meal when we were allowed. For that year, I had lived with this, and now we were just about back to normal. As John did not recognise me anyway, the addition of a face mask was not earth-shattering. It was just nice to hold his hand.

Guilt crept up on me when I let out the fact that Janet had been in the same boat for the last twelve months. That will have really curdled her milk.

I know I am not unique in this situation, and yes, I feel guilty for thinking, *woe is me*. I can look around me now and see other occupants in their cars, vans, and lorries and know that I must be unique—for this particular time and place, that is. Who else would have these worries?

The guy in that ridiculous little yellow Fiat looks a little younger than me. He just looks angry at something, a little worn around the edges. The guy in the white van only appears to be worried about the time, probably late for his delivery, as he keeps looking at the satnav on his dash.

That small bus that passed a few minutes ago—everyone in it was older than me and having a rare old time, by the looks of things. Who am I to be passing judgment on these people? I don't know them; they could all have terminal illnesses and are just processing it better than I am. Which is not fair, because I am not ill. The only thing dragging me down is the guilt—and the bloody, sorry John, traffic.

So now I feel guilty for assigning stories to the other people around me. I do not feel guilty about my viewpoint, though—John did me the favour of buying this 4x4 before he got ill. So, I can sit here and look down on most, which is quite refreshing, assuaging the feeling of being looked down on by John's family a little bit.

I know—sorry—we are comfortably off. We have no mortgage, inheriting my parents' house when they died. My conscience wants me to feel guilty about that too, as I see so many of our friends—mainly ex-friends now—struggling with money. But I will not go down that route, as it was not my fault, and I have been doing my bit for charity and fundraising, so my conscience can file that one away.

We have always had nice things and never wanted for anything, and neither did our two kids. There will not be many who have kids coming out of university with only an overdraft as a debt. I should feel proud of that, and I am inordinately proud of the kids overall—as was John, as is John.

They are both working abroad now. John used to say it was the best place for them, and I agree. It does cause an issue now, though—they cannot visit very often, and as John does not know them when they do come, I do not think their incentive is very high.

The COVID year scuppered any visits at all, which they may have looked on as some sort of relief. I feel guilty for that thought, as they love their dad, and I should not have to ask them to down tools and fly back to the nest, even if they could. They do have their own lives and loves to lead. Not facing that dilemma with my parents, due to John and me living down the road from them, ensured no great hardship in helping. Watching them die was not so great, and at least the kids are spared that, I suppose.

I still get uptight about the memory thing. John remembers Janet and Terry. Yes, his parents named them Janet and John, and I can on no occasion forget that. I never did have the courage to ask his parents why they would do that, although it made our early relationship present-buying very easy. I am sure the joke wore thin with John.

He never let it show, which is one of the things I loved—love—about him: an easy-going and accepting demeanour. He never had to try to get people on his side or to be friends; it just happened as easily as putting on your favourite slippers. Not that he was—is—a pushover. He had an edge, but he saved that for when it really mattered—the emotional equivalent of a nuclear deterrent. You knew his temper was there; you just acknowledged that you had gone too far if you saw it in all its released glory.

I know the experts say that EOD means that it is the short-term memory that goes first, and the sufferer will relate more to the distant past. Hence the memory boxes, a concept that I get and have created with bloody Janet—sorry, John. What hurts is that we were married for twenty-seven years and together for thirty. I mean, we are married, and we are together. Guilt, guilt, guilt for that thought. He is not dead.

So, Janet, Terry and some bloke called Dunc, whom he recalls from school—that is it. Everyone else is a complete stranger. I do feel sorry for him, as the inherent gregariousness of his being has gone, replaced with a nervousness—or trepidation if you are lucky. Bewilderment if you are not. I should feel sorry for Janet; it cannot be nice for her either, I suppose, being the only one he asks for all the time. So now I feel guilty about that as well.

Looking in my rear-view, I see the lines around my eyes and mouth that I am sure were not there six months ago. I know I am getting older—it just seems to be happening so much faster than I had anticipated. Why am I even thinking about myself? I am healthy, I still lead a fairly active life, and I still have some friends. The only blip is travelling a sixty-mile round trip to see John three or four times a week. I feel guilty about the visits getting shorter too.

The interaction is declining. There is no tenderness between us, and I miss that. I am being selfish, thinking only of my wants and needs and what I can get out of this situation. Guilt. The white light in my rear-view temporarily startles me. I wish it was the type of white light that I could just step into. John would still have Janet.

I started to have an overdue conversation with the bank yesterday. I know I said we were financially okay, but the home is costing eighteen hundred pounds a week. The care is great, and John is probably as happy there as he is ever going to be again. Our resources are getting to be critical—not yet terminal, though—hence the call to the bank. Releasing equity from my—sorry, our—house is the only way.

There should be enough to keep John there for a few years, although his doctor does not think he will be around that long. The decline, being so sharp, confirms the diagnosis he had explained. Can I ignore the risk that John will live up to character and stubbornly hang on? Of course, I cannot. I will need to cash in and see what happens. I know this because my conscience has chipped in again.

I am not sure what Chris makes of this. Oh, Chris—yes, well, another reason for guilt, I suppose. Hang it, no, I will not feel guilty for looking to my future happiness. John would not want that. Chris was—is—a friend first. He supported both of us, never more so than when John got the initial devastating diagnosis. He would take John on outings to give me a break, usually involving a pub that John would remember. I was just thankful for the break. I could depressurise, even if only for an hour or two.

When John went into the home, I was even more grateful for Chris. Most of our so-called friends dissolved into the background, like John had a contagious disease. Apparently, this was common, according to the gurus on the web. Still did not stop the hurt. I was left virtually alone in a house that was too big and too full of memories. The callous so-and-so's ran away and left me to my own devices; the human psyche never ceases to confound me.

Yet Chris stayed. He gave me space at first but was always there if I needed him or wanted to talk. It may be—in fact, it probably was—due to him losing his wife to cancer seven years ago that he had that empathy. He understood what I needed and what I did not. Do not get me wrong—I had not been particularly close to him before the bomb went off, not as close as we had been to some. Those who had been closer did the suburban equivalent of circling the wagons, only they left me on the outside. Bastards. Sorry, John.

Anyway, Chris got in touch and stayed in touch, and then it became more frequent. Nothing untoward has gone on, but it could have, and maybe should have, and maybe it will soon. Once I have parked this truckload of guilt, then perhaps I can move ahead—presuming Chris wants the same.

It was Chris who told me to write things down, helping with the memory book for John, and bizarrely told me singing helped—music as well. The singing I was not so sure about; I always considered myself tonally challenged, if that is such a thing. Chris was persistent, telling me of the time when his wife, Grace, was getting to the end—she only wanted to hear a certain song or a certain piece of music.

Chris had learnt all the words to *Wonderwall* and, for some reason known only to Grace, the entire *Wall* album. The things you do for love, I suppose. Chris was adamant that it would help, so I prepped some playlists, learnt the lyrics to *Waterlow* and *Hello*, and I was set. I am not sure if John knows what I am doing, but his reaction was never negative.

Those who share my fate with their partner know that negative reactions are usually born of frustration, so the fact that John did not react, I took as a good sign. Still tonally challenged, though, as Janet keeps pointing out. But does it really bloody matter? Sorry, John.

The memory book—I thought it would be challenging. I mean, how do I know what John would regard as worth remembering, as opposed to what I thought would be? It stumped me originally. Janet was being her usual superior self, but it was easier for her. The memories of growing up and family holidays were already present in John's mind, so it was a simple matter to trigger them. A picture of a donkey in Ireland, an ice-cream wrapper or the order of service from some cousin's wedding—all did the trick.

I was against the brick wall that was John not knowing who I was, and not sure how I could get around it, let alone batter it away. It was Chris who came up with the solution. I used pictures that included Janet or Terry or both. That way, I could pretend he was remembering me when, deep down, I knew it was those two who kept him with me. It was not nice, but to see John smile or laugh at something I had produced was worth that little bit of pain.

A sly chuckle at a Christmas snap or one from a birthday was worth it. It was. I did not feel guilty for the subtle subterfuge—guilty for where the idea came from, but not for the delivery. The book is with John now, mainly because I could find nothing else to add that he would remember, and certainly nothing that was solely me or the kids.

The last eight months have been tough, yes. Although the routine is now set, and with Chris's support, it has become easier. I tried a support group at the behest of my daughter. When I say tried, I went twice a week for about two months. The other people were nice for the hour or so I was there, although I cannot confirm what they were like away from the meeting room. Some of them went for a drink afterwards, but that really was not me.

The stories they recalled at the meetings were, at first, hilarious—or so I thought. It only later became clear, once I examined my own situation, that it was all really quite sad. There are only so many times you can hear about accidents with cookers, door locks, pets, etc., until you realise that, as an outsider, it might appear amusing. As an insider, as I now firmly was, it was debilitating. Some of the group still had their partners at home, so I was spared that, and yet that just brought on more guilt.

That's why I did not want to go for a drink. I would want more information from these strangers, and then my guilt would have made me want to bear their burdens as well. That could not happen. I did share the singing tip, though, and that went down quite well.

The main support, other than Chris and the kids, was the web—and that is in that order because the kids did not really offer much. Well, they could not, could they? Being so far away, and time differences and all that, meant it was difficult to keep in touch. The internet, with all its pitfalls, foibles, and downright lies, did offer something. There were some great blogs that I took inspiration from, mainly because I was not in front of them hearing first-hand how their husband or wife had put the cat in the fridge. It was impersonal territory but, in a way, personally touching.

Today's visit had been particularly draining, possibly explaining the exaggerated bags under my eyes. John had not been responsive to me at all, just sat staring out of the window and folding and refolding a Leeds United scarf—the relevance of which escaped me, as he had never professed a fondness, in all the years I had known him, for Leeds United. It was a rather tatty one, so perhaps it was from his early years. I will ask Janet when I see her again.

Even my atonal rendition of *Waterlow* had failed to ignite a response, apart from some other resident telling me to shut the hell up. There has been a regression, even between visits. The care staff were showing a brave face to me, saying everything was much the same and that John was eating well and had laughed when Janet visited yesterday. Of course, he bloody would. I get nothing, not even a facial tic to acknowledge my presence. And that really hurt. The staff telling me about it just added to the cruelty. I know they were probably not doing it deliberately, but it felt like they were just making sure I knew I was not up to the job.

That I was not even up to being a wife. John would have had something to say about my thoughts, except he has very little to say about anything now, and there is the ultimate irony. The one person who could put the world to rights and let them know that I was the best wife, his best friend, and that he loved the bones of me, could not.

The source of my guilt was becoming apparent. As much as I loved him and missed him, he was not really there anymore. It would be better if he just left—sad, but for the best. He was not going to get better, and I know he would not want to prolong the agony or even refinance the house. Pragmatic would sum John up, but I cannot let these thoughts out. I cannot voice this, as the accusations of callousness, uncaring, and gold-digger would follow the selfish one.

So even though logic would tell me to hope for a swift end, realism and guilt kept me all buttoned up. I mean, for fuck's sake, John—and no, I am not sorry. There is no real light at the end of any tunnel. John was already absent—to me, anyway—and nearly to Janet.

The dark was creeping in, the day drawing to a close—a metaphor, if there ever was one, for the end of my relationship with my husband, his dusk more painful than the one happening outside. Looking around me, considering the other vehicles, did anyone else have the guilt or the weight of wishing someone dead hanging over them? I sincerely hope not, because I am a nice person really—just so tired. So, so tired.

*****

The truth was they could. Ray and Tina were both carrying sidearms, and there was also further artillery in their lockbox in the boot of their Volvos. They acknowledged they shouldn't need that if the intel was right, and both had been involved in takedowns as part of small and large teams in the past. Both had also been shot at—Tina carrying the scar of a nick on her upper arm—and crucially, neither had any qualms about drawing and using their weaponry.

Ray had even had the dubious privilege of being part of a fatal shooting inquiry when he was in an assault team that permanently removed the top of a people-smuggling ring in a raid. Three officers had been taken off duty for months, all down to the fact that a bloke who needed removing had been gunned down with a Sig in his hand.

All three had fired and hit their target, but the bleeding hearts screamed breach of human rights and excessive force. Three months of enforced inactivity had followed for Ray, sweetened only slightly by the freedom of the sixteen young girls they had rescued from the dead Albanian trafficker.

Most officers, whatever their rank or role, voiced—either privately or publicly—the sentiment that was hampering the safe policing of the UK. Anti-police feelings were very high, the public thought there were too many armed officers, and that they were all racist thugs.

The Senior Officers' Association, ACPO, and the Home Office produced statements and statistics they thought proved that the percentage of armed officers was only up five per cent in ten years, blatantly ignoring the seventy per cent rise in Taser-carrying officers. They produced more graphs and tables proving that the service was as diverse as any other organisation or group of organisations.

Sadly, in Ray's experience, you were far more likely to get nicked or shot if you were coloured or foreign-looking. Ray didn't need a graph or a table to prove this—it just was.

They both felt they were fighting not only crime and its doers but also the general public. This was something they had discussed at length when they were inevitably on a stakeout. Had they been in the same car, they would no doubt have been discussing it further. The current state of affairs could quite easily be proved if Tina flipped on the hidden lights and sirens at this moment—it would be fifty-fifty whether the vehicles in front moved out of their way.

It was also one hundred per cent guaranteed they would receive a wide variety of mouthed obscenities and a collection of offensive gestures involving imaginary genitals on their foreheads. This was the environment they now worked in. When they had both started as rookies, it was a good bet that if they were in trouble, some well-meaning member of the public would pitch in and try to help.

Now they would more than likely stand there and film the action to post on social media later. In some cases, even bringing cases of brutality against the officer. Ray knew that was why he would be going after his thirty—no hanging around to shuffle papers or do cold cases. He was off. Even if he keeled over the next day while planting potatoes in his garden, the current world was not one he wanted to police. Criminals were now heroes to some, entrepreneurial businessmen to others—not the scum-sucking pond life they should have been labelled as.

All of this played through Tina's mind as she stared at the Audi in front of her, and her doubts surfaced as to whether it was all worth it. A movement caught her eye, and she saw the confirmation that it was—a bizarrely coloured Renault with a family that had snuck up on her. Tina could see the small family unit, the movement of the mother checking on the kids in the back was what had caught her eye.

Then a new depression hit her. Due to her sexual preferences and her complete inability to hold onto a partner for any length of time, this was likely to be a scene that would never play out in the life of Tina Rawson.

*****

5:36 pm

I can't lose sight of what's important here. I need to keep a clear focus on that, never mind the others surrounding me. The kids are what matter. A thought I was becoming an expert at while the traffic seemed to multiply outside the world I was occupying. My girlfriend Lizzie—well, she would more than understand my thought processes. She was more attuned to me than anyone I had ever known, probably including myself in that.

The years I had spent aimlessly drifting after splitting up with the kids' mum—I had told myself it was because I didn't fit in, that I could never be happy as I was not part of any community. My wife had been too busy buying flat-screen tellies and redecorating rooms in shades like dead duck sage or other such hipster bollocks. I could be nothing other than an outsider to all that.

That's why I had left—because, deep down, I knew she didn't need me. Once that hurtful conclusion was reached, it would only ever be confirmed as an unmitigated truth. Yes, she needed the money and the childcare, but not me. Well, now she had both of those without having to accommodate me. In the meantime, I had bounced around between partners with no visible second or first thoughts.

No thought at all. I was just trying to find a place, somewhere I could be still, could be invisible in a community—but only because that community was visible. Then I met Lizzie, and something changed. And for the good, which was a change in itself.

It was surprising, then, that Chaz hadn't known that little fact when the fucker offered up his too-good-to-ignore incentive.

It was just so tiresome. Not only being tired of all this around me, but tired of the way my life had panned out. Yes, I had done some dodgy—some would say downright nasty—things, and my life's trajectory was not a nice one. But that had changed recently. I wanted nothing more than to settle down with Lizzie properly and put all this shite behind me. Even be a proper dad, if I was allowed.

For once, the darkness that had been crowding me and surrounding my every waking move had been speared in a spotlight and was being forced back.

And then fucking Chaz and his fucking threats. He may as well have ripped the cable from the spotlight out of the wall and let the blackness take me. Reminding me that I was one of their own when it came down to it, and who was I to think I could escape into normality?

He was right, wasn't he?

A nondescript, weirdly coloured Renault with indescribable metallic paint pulled into the lane, and I was happy to see a family, kids and all. Contentment in a snapshot.

Oh, the kids.

Chaz and his bunch of bastards had my kids.

I hoped nothing like what I was experiencing would disrupt the lives of that little family unit in the Renault.

The darkness started to fall as if carried down on the light drizzle that was now descending.

Welcome back, it was saying.

Perhaps I should apologise for trying to escape into the light.

Whisper of Love Loudly

There was an atmosphere of contentment and considerable achievement inside the car; it felt like something had finally changed for the better. They were all tired, that was true enough, as evidenced by the two kids who were soundly asleep, strapped into their booster seats in the back. It had been a great idea, and like every great idea in recent months, it had come from the woman sitting in the passenger seat.

It was not as if the man did not have ideas, and indeed, some of them might be great—it was just a struggle for him to voice them, as if unsure how they would be received or what he should do with them in the first place. Confidence had not been a problem before, but ever since that day, he had to put so much effort into purely existing and ensuring the kids were okay that he had no room for anything else.

Today, though, had been worth making room for, he thought, as he watched the taillights blinking into the distance. Even the inconvenience of a delay going home was not going to dampen it. Whether this feeling would remain with him when he woke up tomorrow was not even worth thinking about—he was letting himself feel the moment.

"That was a cracking day out, Dina," he said, watching two wagons that belonged to the monsters in the back seat's favourite fast-food place, hoping they didn't wake and see them. It would be a while before they could do anything about eating any of it, by the looks of the traffic.

"Shame we are stuck in all this now. Hopefully, the kids will stay sparked out till we get out of it." She was looking at him—seeing him and nothing else.

"Tempting fate, that." He gave a little laugh.

"Ha, true, Kal."

She glanced again at Kal and saw that he was looking slightly strained, the red light from all the brake lights highlighting the lines around his eyes that hadn't been there before. Or had they? He looked tired, but there was also something else. Was it possible that hope could be seen in someone's face? Not the opening-Christmas-presents type of hope, but the starting-a-journey type.

After all, Christmas was usually a disappointment in her mind, and she preferred the possibility of a new adventure. Perhaps she was so blinded by this relationship that it was only now, in this unusual circumstance, that she had the time—or even the inclination—to notice. Over her right shoulder, she could see the kids, amazingly fast asleep.

Considering they were strapped in by seat belts on booster seats was a miracle in itself. I am not even sure how they do that, she thought. Pretty damn sure I couldn't fall that deeply asleep in a position like that.

Their day had started with the task of getting two very grumpy—and, she would have said, distrustful—under-eights out of their beds on a non-school day. The two little darlings, Kem and Kai, were not best impressed until it was explained that a day out somewhere that was probably every little boy's dream was on the cards. A day spent in the presence of all the medieval weaponry they could fit on the end of a stick—or shake a stick at, whatever the stupid phrase was.

A reward for their continued good behaviour and a chance for Kal and Dina to be the parents they wanted to be—Kal back as one and Dina exploring her new role. The day was an attempt to raise everyone's spirits, to bring some joy back into their lives. A joy sadly sparse ever since—well, just ever since. Dina, with a skill she used often at work, had used foresight to book tickets, which, when they arrived, proved to be a stroke of genius, as the queue to pay at the door was snaking around like—well, a snake.

Outside in Yorkshire, on a grey October day, is not a great place to stand with your offspring—not if you want a peaceful start to your day, that is. Dina had felt rather smug about the whole thing, and the kids had thought they were VIPs or something as they waltzed up to the prepaid collection point.

The kids, Dina thought, had contained their excitement until they arrived. It was as if they thought it was a trick—that they were really going to end up at the dentist or, worse, Nana Poppie's. A cruel hoax to lure them out from their quilts. At seven and six years old, they hadn't developed a real sense of spatial or directional awareness, so the element of doubt that lurked had quelled their initial boyish exuberance.

Kal could feel Dina's gaze but didn't look. He was tired; the stress of the last two years had taken its toll. Days like today had really started to help and begin the process of taking some of it away. I love Dina for that. She just seemed to know what was needed, he mused. Not only for me, but for the kids, who also seemed to love her to bits. She wasn't hard to love—that sunny disposition topped off with a smile that could show ships the way in the fog. That smile was what I had been drawn in by. I suppose I was like a ship floundering in a fog, and suddenly, there was a clear path back.

Even my mother, God bless her, had accepted Dina, and that was worthy of one of the miracles, as she had not been that accepting in the past. I am not sure what I have done to deserve Dina and two fantastic kids, but there must be hope for me still. I have been given this chance, and I am damn well going to grasp it. I know there will be bumps—there have to be—and the baggage will not allow a completely smooth passage, but with Dina, I am sure we can sail through it.

The whole day out had been Dina's idea. Not that I was incapable of coming up with anything—it would just appear that my head was so far up my own arse, according to my brother Melvin, that I couldn't do anything but function. Ever since that day, since the day that—well, ever since. He was right. I hadn't so much dropped the ball—I couldn't find the damn thing in the first place. I made sure the kids were okay—that was it.

I was paying scant attention to Dina, and I do wonder why she didn't say anything. She just smiled, lit up our lives, and whatever thoughts she had about my behaviour, she kept to herself. Even in the early days, when she held me as I cried myself to sleep, I could still feel that smile—just there, waiting to make it all okay. After a while, I do believe that this had worked. I focussed more on the real stuff, and not just my misery. Thank you, Dina, for bringing me safely home.

The kids, I am glad, don't really know what happened. I will tell them one day, although I am sure they must know something. For now, they can just be the fantastic and annoying brothers that they are—even now looking after each other.

I feel guilty for that—as if I had been less self-absorbed, then they might have had me as a crutch as well. It's too late for me to do anything about that, but I will rebuild that bridge, so we can be a proper family again. Today could have been the start—*no,* he thought, '*it was the beginning.*'

The kids had run around like loons most of the day—hence the kip, Dina surmised—seriously engaged in what the Royal Armouries had to offer. Not that it should have been a surprise. They were bright kids, always asking stuff. She had to smile at the day's most gory question, which had come from Kem: "If I stick that spiky thing up Kai's bumhole, will he stop being annoying?"

Dina had smothered a laugh while Kal had tried to explain that giving them ideas on how to harm their brother wasn't the point of the day. To curtail Kai's search for more extravagant methods of revenge, they went for lunch in what proved to be the most expensive part of the day. Dina had been shocked by the amount the two trays of refreshments had come to, especially as Kai had then removed all the green stuff from his sandwich and smothered his tomato sandwich in sauce.

Could they get a refund on lettuce? The chips were good, though. They had spent nearly an hour sitting and looking at the guidebooks, with the kids drawing more and more imaginative uses for some of the weapons of war—most of which ended up with either a Pokémon stuck on the end of one or a member of Paw Patrol gutted. It was a genuinely enjoyable, if rather gruesome, hour, and the laughter had been good for all of them. Perhaps they were turning a corner.

The final part of the day had been the best for the kids, Dina thought. The mock battles and jousting had kept them rapt for the best part of another hour. They were greatly dischuffed when it was over and wanted to see the whole thing again. There could have been tears if not for the bribery of a drive-through meal of their choice when they got home.

So, armed with a few snacks from the shop at the garage, here they were—stuck in a jam thirty miles from home, the kids thankfully asleep. All around them lay the detritus of a good day out—crisp packets, pop bottles, sweet wrappers, and random items of clothing. Dina thought if she drew a deep enough breath, she could take in some e-numbers with a dash of child sweat.

Dina looked through her reflection in the side window, and her gaze was drawn to a woman in a white SUV that had just been piloted into the lane inside theirs. *God, she looks as knackered as Kal. Dina thought Wonder what her problem is? Doubt it could be as bad as Kal's, but you never know, do you? I hope she gets to turn her corner soon,* she pushed a positive wish towards her.

As Dina glanced away from the window, she turned back slightly towards Kal and caught him looking at her, his tired eyes showing the love she hoped he felt. She turned on a smile—not the full-wattage one she used to lighten up someone's day, but the smile that Kal would know was just for him. One imparting the knowledge that she understood the pain he had gone through with Kass's death two years ago. A smile that told him it was okay to still grieve. A smile that told him she loved him.

A smile that she hoped would help him turn around the final part of the corner. She knew he would never forget Kass or the stupid accident that had robbed him of his wife, his life, and his kids' mum. Dina had told him when they first got together at that church event that she hoped he wouldn't forget her—just as she wouldn't, since Kass had been part of the church too.

Dina, while not friends with Kass, had known and liked her. She hoped Kass would be smiling—not a Dina smile, but one that said, It's okay, Kal. Let me go a little and let Dina help you and the kids. Dina knew they were getting there. The crying in the night had stopped, and the silent staring into space was becoming less frequent. Now the court case was done, and the driver was locked up. That was another slight bend negotiated. The smile Kal gave her back made her believe she was right.

"This traffic is really crap, D." A note of tiredness in his voice.

The sudden break in the comfortable silence caught Dina by surprise, causing a frown to momentarily slip across her brow. "Yep, sorry, was miles away."

"What were you thinking about?" He was trying to push the fatigue away with interest.

"Oh, you know, the usual—you, the kids and all that." She gleamed at him.

"Good thoughts, then?" Kal laughed, which was definitely a good sign. "We might have to wake the monsters, though, or payback will be off the scale when we get back."

"I know. Excitement, fresh air and e-numbers are like the perfect storm. Add in a kip, and we will be up till four with them." Not a hint of concern or criticism—just a statement of fact, underwritten by the element that she would quite happily stay up with them.

"Why aren't we home yet?" Right on cue, Kai had woken up and didn't sound too grumpy.

"Hello, sleepyhead. We are stuck in some traffic—won't be long now. Do you want a drink?" Dina said, turning to the first of the monsters.

"Yes, please. Can we still have a drive-through?" First thoughts and all that.

"Typical, only thinking of feeding itself." Kal laughed. This was going to be okay. Definitely okay.

"Yes, you can wake your brother if you want, as we will be home soon." Dina knew they weren't old enough to see the distortion for what it was.

"Then you can decide where we are going." Kal was concentrating on the vehicle in front of them, where a party seemed to be going on in the minibus—albeit one involving middle-aged men.

"Well, will you look at that?" he said, nodding at the minibus.

"Takes all sorts, Kal. They would say the same if they had seen these two tearing round the Armouries." Dina had briefly looked at the van and shrugged. Everyone had their own story, and she wasn't really interested in the one from the minibus. Her new one with these kids was far more important to her right now.

"True, what was your favourite bit, Kai?" Kal asked, looking in the mirror.

"When they were tw…smacking each other with the swords."

Kem had joined in now, agreeing by slurping some juice through the drinking straw of the carton his brother had given him.

"Yep, that was good. Glad you had a nice day out, boys." Dina smiled at them both.

"Thanks, Mum," Kem said around a crisp.

The silence that followed Kem's statement was incredible—if not a little uncomfortable—and left Dina, for once, bereft of a smile, staring at the monsters in the booster seats. If she could have had a Groundhog Day moment, then this would be it.

"Well, that's you stuffed, D. You are stuck with us." Kal was smiling, but Dina knew the end of the corner was closer today than it had ever been.

*****

Tina had turned away from the family, finding the sight more upsetting than a woman of her age, sense and occupation should. She wanted to shout "What the fuck" at herself, tell her stupid emotions to get back where they normally lived in her system—a place that, by necessity, was normally dark and isolated. She had no time for this, and, more fundamentally, why—on a damp, arse-end of an October day while she was stuck in a traffic jam—had her thoughts turned to family?

Chris, her ex—who was still recent enough to cause a momentary hurt at the abandonment—had always claimed that Tina should never be allowed to look after anything more sentient than a houseplant. While it was quite hurtful, it was also true. She broke most things she handled in her personal life, and as much as she hated the fact, she was better off on her own. As this seemed to be her most common state of relationship, it seemed to prove the point.

The blue Audi, which was being driven by a bloke who, if anyone met, they'd think was just a normal one with a regular job in IT—and not a drug mule, which was what he was—had Tina's attention again. She wondered what made him do it. She knew there was a story there. But he wasn't your atypical drug runner—good family, good job and everything else. Yet something had pushed him into driving around the country with upwards of one hundred kilos of pure coke in his boot. '*It was even his dad's car, for fuck's sake,*' she thought, as she focussed herself away from families and her hormones.

*****

5:37 pm

The moment that Chaz had shown me the picture—*that* picture—one of my wife and kids, it had been indelibly inked on my brain, like an internal prison tattoo. The photo, with that lump of steroid-pumped meat in the background, hinted at a gun and carried more than an overture to threat in the posture.

That picture had shattered my world and had led me to be right here, right now, in a hole that hadn't existed until the other morning. What had been a simple, if dubious, job a few days ago—pick up van, drive it, job done—had turned to shit and a very deep hole as I stepped into the cab.

It was more a fucking chasm than a sinkhole.

Yes, the fucking bastard sons of bitches had my kids. And their mother. But they had my kids, and that was what had caused this predicament. Yes, I knew I owed Chaz a favour from years ago, from the before Chaz, who is now called something else, but I thought the debt was settled, especially as I had done some jobs for him. I had gone to school with not-now-Chaz, and we had been mates of a sort.

Not quite the same gang, but the same football team, with a mutual acceptance based on similar backgrounds and acquaintances. Chaz had solidified back in my life a few months back, having previously only been seen in passing like a ghost. One you could talk to, anyway. He had said he might have some work for me. I knew it would be slightly iffy, but I needed cash to pay for the kids and all that. So, I had done a couple of little jobs—a bit of driving, a bit of collecting, nothing overly heavy and only stuff with a threat of violence. Nobody really got hurt.

The traffic was doing one of those weird reshuffles, where there was a promise of movement, yet nothing really ever happened, except you got a different view. The sound of an overblown exhaust reached me and appeared to be coming from a Ford Fiesta of all things. I bet the bloke in the Golf behind it is loving that.

The two in the Fiesta were having an animated discussion, and, bizarrely, I felt like I was watching myself twenty years ago. With all those bags in the back, they have probably been on the rob—no doubt a right pair of chancers then.

Not One of Grimms

The whole day would have been funny, Patrice thought, if they had not been stuck in this traffic, and as they had nothing better to do, he would ensure that Ty was made to feel as uncomfortable as possible. There would be no comeback, as they had been friends since meeting at primary school—this was just the latest in a long list of scrapes and situations that one or both of them had ended up in over the years. The fact that all of Ty's worldly stuff was in the back of his car only elevated the scale of this latest fuck-up.

"You really are a dick!" Patrice had been reminding Ty of this for over an hour now.

"I know, I know, I know," Ty said with a smile. As far as he was concerned, it was just one of those things, but he needed to keep it light for very personal reasons.

"I mean a Class-A one." Patrice banged the steering wheel to emphasise the level of Ty's dickness.

"Repeating it doesn't make it any better." He tried to keep his grin but nearly failed.

"So, did she really kick you out after listening to a song?" A note of incredulity was in the question because, as Patrice could guess, there would be more to it than that.

"That was one of the reasons. She isn't that shallow—there was other stuff. She just threw the song at me towards the end. I thought I knew what was going on in Rosie's head and could sort it out. She must have been storing it all up, and then—wham. The rest of what she said was quite brutal too."

Which was more than he had said since Patrice had picked him up. There had been hints, but if he was going to get the full story, he would need to keep digging in the dirt of Ty's life.

"Go on then." Slide the spade in. See if he could get the whole story.

"That I obviously didn't care for her, thought she was easy, a control freak and, to top it all, fat," Ty delivered, completely deadpan.

"Wow! You ticked some of the no-go areas there. You could have gone the whole hog, denied God and said you were a Tory, and I would have been planning your funeral." Patrice laughed.

"You don't need to take the piss. How was I to know that she would have all this shit in her head?" Ty did not laugh. He had a serious expression, which in itself was unusual, and as a development, clearly highlighted something else.

"Well, talking to her about it would be a good start—and not taking a lend." After all, Patrice always talked everything through with his girl; they had no secrets.

"That song—you know the one—I kept singing the first lines. She loved it. She kept asking where it came from, and I sort of deflected. Turns out her mate told her to listen to it on Spotify. Had it all set up when I went in, and she did. Then it all came out. Next thing I knew, I was sitting in your car with a TV remote-shaped bruise on my forehead. Bloody Spotify and the internet have a lot to answer for."

There was indeed a slight bruise on his forehead. This story was coming out better than he expected. He would be able to live off these scraps from Ty for months.

"She pinged it when you got in?" Patrice continued digging.

"Hit me with a whole load of stuff—chucked it at me, she did. A whole load of verbal." Ty had the grace to try and look like he was bothered and had some sort of conscience, even though Patrice knew that would be a lie too.

"Then a TV remote?" Patrice was trying to keep his mirth from bubbling out fully.

"Yep. And threw the thing like a bloody gunslinger—hit me right above my eyes. If it wasn't me that was hit, I would have found it funny." Ty was attempting to look sulky.

Patrice did not have the heart to tell him that it was indeed very funny—not yet, anyway. "Not so funny now, is it? You'd better tell me the whole story." Trying to be a mate and hoping that he would get more than he had already.

Ty started his story. "OK, as we ain't going anywhere quickly, I suppose it would fill the time. So, I was a bit late getting back…"

A few weeks earlier

The relationship was rocky already. Rosie knew this. It wasn't that Ty didn't love her—she thought he did—but it was just that he was an arsehole sometimes, or, to be honest, more often than not. He didn't seem to care about anyone but himself, although he did care how much money she had or earned, as if it was his own to play with. She knew that couples shared income, but that was in an equal partnership, where there were shared bills and all that normal cosy stuff. She had caught him going through all her online accounts, without a care in the world or any hint of shame.

Where he had got the password from was a mystery. It would be best if she saved it all up for a day when she could confront him properly. To avoid losing any respect or causing one of their little arguments, she had used a diversionary tactic—a question about a brew—diffusing the potential emotional landmine. Not only did she ignore this transgression without confrontation, she even managed to ignore the nights away with his mates.

The rumour that Sal had repeated—that he was seen in the Akhtar with Janie and appeared to be having a great time—had been harder to ignore, forcing it into a mental box for the time being, one which would be opened when the time was right. The simple fact was, she had loved him more than anything or anyone, and the emphasis was very much on the *had* bit, though he always came home.

Even the time Ty went to Majorca with his mates, and strangely, for a holiday, there were no photos—which was exceedingly odd in these Insta days. That this was untrue only came to light later when some pictures appeared on Lee's—one of the Majorca Six—Facebook account. It was plain as day that Ty was sporting a rather large love bite on his neck. Rosie had asked Ty about it, and the implausible response had been that the lads had done it. Yeah, right. Did he really think that little of her? Another thing for the box.

A few hours ago

Now sitting in the kitchen, waiting for him to make an appearance, Rosie was not sure she had ever really loved him. She certainly had been under that misconception and was sure at one point she had thought she loved him a little, but now she wasn't exactly sure any more about the real depth it had gone to. The intensity of any feelings may have faded; the mental tick list she kept in her head of the good and bad seemed to be pushing the line of not love, bordering on detest.

This confrontation was inevitable, but the history of the last five years had stayed her hand a little. That was down to the fact that no matter what, he kept coming back to her, and she did not want to be alone. It was like an incredibly bad detective novel—the clues were all there, and the reader could see the end coming, but the author still ploughed on, not even trying to chuck in a red herring or two.

More like a giant foam finger being pointed at the culprit. Not a case of whodunnit, more like why she hadn't stopped this nonsense eight chapters ago. So, why hadn't she stopped this earlier? Because she thought she had loved him, she pondered. Even a little was better than nothing, right?

As Rosie was picking over the takeaway, her mobile rang. It was Sal, her best friend and rumourmonger-in-chief, the caller ID informed her.

"Hi, Sal," she said around a mouthful of chicken and rice.

"Have you got a sec?" There was no greeting or preamble, which had Rosie on point.

"No, I can't really talk. Ty is just on his way back, and we haven't caught up yet." And I have used this as an excuse more times than I can count, she thought.

"Okay, well, I will just say this—you know that song he sings at you? Ask him about it. Don't think you'll be happy." Rosie was sure she could hear a trace of malice in the statement, but at what?

"Really?" Rosie was now curious and had forgotten her tea.

"Yep. Do it before he has had a drink, as you need the truth, not the normal Ty drunken rubbish."

Which was almost a mantra where Sal's opinion of Ty was concerned.

"Will do, talk later. Might message you when I get a chance." Which she would.

"Love you." Sal's indication that she was going.

"You too."

The call ended. As conversations go, not only was it brief, but it was more cloak and dagger than anything they had ever really had before. Sal was her best friend, and she also hated Ty—for reasons that had seemed harsh when she first voiced them but were now coming home to roost. Leech, parasite, dog with two dicks, and arsehole of the grandest order had been a few of the many.

She, however, had never really pursued the song, as she had been tickled by it, and even though Ty swerved her when she asked, she wasn't that fussed. Sal had piqued her brain; she cued it up on Spotify and picked her fork up to resume her tea.

The takeaway had been just about passable—disappointingly so, as the Palace normally was so reliable for a Chinese takeaway run by a couple from Laos. A Laotian takeaway doesn't have the same ring to it, although Londoners would probably lap it up. Now the remains of the meal sat like a Gaudiesque mess on the table as the song faded out from her mobile. She was literally stunned. How could the bastard do this to her?

Her anger, which had been simmering, was now crowing to be released at something. She had not been quite ready to let it free yet, but this may be the time to have that chat with the bastard. This was the fuel she needed for her flame.

Calmly, Rosie put Ty's dinner in the oven to keep warm, but she needn't have bothered too much, as the door made its peculiar crunching noise, like a packet of crisps being trodden upon.

The door that he was always going to fix—and had been for at least the last eighteen months now. Which was alongside the dripping shower, painting the garden fence, and the promise to take his mother out for lunch. Just one more thing on Ty's list of things not to be arsed to do. She was now going to add being honest with her, actually treating her with some modicum of respect, and not being a twat of the highest degree to that list, as she could guarantee that he would do none of those things either.

He had gone straight to the fridge, hardly even acknowledging her presence. He had briefly debated water over beer, largely done for effect, as the decision had been made as he came up the path. His thinking was that if he showed a little bit of dithering, then there would be no pointed comments or barbs about his alcohol intake.

Ty looked up from his Kung Po chicken, which she had retrieved from the oven, showing only a minor interest in Rosie, as usual.

"You okay, babe?" said with all the enthusiasm of a fish thinking bus travel would be for it, and secretly hoping a reply wasn't forthcoming.

"Yep."

That limited the conversational repartee on that subject. Rosie reached for her phone and Spotify, finding the required track. Rosie poised her thumb over the play key.

"Can I ask you something?" With no hint of what was about to literally play out.

"Course you can, love," Ty said around a mouthful of chicken and rice and with as much relish as if she had asked him to wipe her arse.

"That song you always sing at me…"

Pressing play, Rosie sat back and watched Ty's face as realisation worked its way past the pleasure of warmed takeaway.

He was on a hook that had not only caught him but had hauled him into the sunlight, into an atmosphere that he was struggling to breathe in. His mind worked quickly to think of a way he could swerve this and clear the decks.

"It was a sort of joke, babe. I don't think those things at all—you know that—and you aren't fat."

"You have been doing that in front of my friends, my family, and total strangers. So now I know the rest. How do you think I feel? Not that I expect you to answer that, as you wouldn't know how I felt unless I tattooed it on your dick." Her voice rose as her ire took over, years of Ty forcing her hand.

"Babe, it was a joke…" His brain could find nothing else to help him.

"Aren't jokes supposed to be funny? What about the other stuff—are they all supposed to be jokes as well? Things like the nights away, the checking my emails and bank accounts…" Rosie started to count things off on her fingers.

"I didn't…" His face told a different story, and in the face of accusations, he was floundering.

"Where did you get the password from?" Ignoring the denial—the lie that it was.

"Off your phone, in case, like, anything happened to you and I would be stuck without access. You know, like a contingency or whatever." His brain and survival instinct were really kicking in, and he thought this sounded plausible.

"You have been in on my phone as well? I mean, what the fuck?" This was a new one for Rosie.

Ty, at this point, realised his error. Normally, he could head off Rosie's arguments as she was usually so predictable. A little banter and occasionally a counter-offensive would burst her bubble, but he had not seen the signs and walked straight into it. Now he had begun digging a deeper hole by mentioning her bloody phone.

A retreat policy would be needed without dragging himself further over what looked like a very steep cliff.

"It was like I said, doll, a contingency. You wouldn't want me to struggle if you were knocked down or something. Seemed like a good idea. You know, like a strategy." He was trying to maintain the idea that he cared.

"Spying on me, more like. You wouldn't know a strategy if you fell over one. Do I mean that little to you? Obviously, I do if you have a special song for me that really sings my praises. You're a wannabe control freak, Ty—or trying to be. That ambition will just have to wait, as you are a complete twat." The look on Ty's face was a picture, and Rosie would have loved to capture it.

"Babe…" he said in a plaintive little-boy voice that sometimes worked on Rosie.

"Don't, Ty, just don't. I don't want any more of your shite." But not this time.

"Honestly, babe, it wasn't meant like that." Ty was trying to retreat from the onslaught. He was unprepared and needed to think about how to wriggle out of it. The strategy excuse obviously wasn't a starter, and the little-boy-lost act was a no-go, apparently. "I didn't look at anything else, just got your passwords, as…" He was repeating himself, as well as admitting guilt—a new feeling for him. Not that he would even consider acknowledging it.

"I know, a strategy in case I was no longer around to hold your hand. I've changed them, by the way, including my phone—just as a fuck you, Ty." Her voice had receded from aggression; she was now far more in control, as she knew what she was going to do.

"OK, your stuff is your stuff, but I thought we were in a relationship, like, you know, a partnership." He could ask her to marry him or something—would that work?

"Oh, that's good, Tyrone. Tell you what, give me your phone and passwords, if that's the case."

Rosie held her hand out in a request. This was getting out of hand.

"OK, I would, but I left it at work, with me being so busy and all."

He tried not to let his hand stray to his pocket and give the game away.

"Uh-huh, course you did. I'll save you the bother of having to delete all your messages and pictures—particularly the Majorca ones." She twisted her ice-cold knife another notch.

"Oh, those again." Fucking Lee and his Facebook.

"So, what else would you be hiding?" Twist, twist—get him to lie again.

"I promise, nothing." Ty tried to keep his face devoid of any telling tics.

"I'll have to take your word for that—unless it was just another strategy." It sounded like a question, but there was no rise, so he wondered if that was it, if he was now off the hook.

Ty could feel the heat in Rosie's argument starting to fall—not quickly, like the sun on a spring day, but slowly. Perhaps he could get out of this relatively intact, regroup, and do some serious Rosie work to smooth it all over. He liked the roof over his head, the comfort—and, to be honest, he liked Rosie. Just not as much as some. Or the ones he chased on days out. As the saying goes, the chase is better than the catch. Well, sometimes.

"OK, baby doll," he said with a smile.

"No, Ty. Not OK. Very much not OK. I was letting most of it ride, just for the peace and quiet, and because I loved you," she said, without a smile.

"I love you too, Rosie." Almost as if he had come into the light, and he could return to his dinner and his beer. The L-word was out.

"I said loved. Or I thought I did. And I've now come to the point of no return."

The tone of Rosie's voice was calm, Ty noticed. Gone was the vim and venom. At this point, even he realised he might be in deep bother.

"I was letting it ride, as I said, until you were spotted with that woman, having a cosy Indian. That was, I now know, the final nail in your rotten coffin."

"Oh, shit…" A dawning realisation broke across his face.

"Get the fuck out of my house. Yes, my house. Not ours—mine. Take what you can carry, then you can collect the rest of your stuff later. I don't want to see you anytime soon."

Rosie folded her arms, indicating the discussion was over.

Ty's only response was to start laughing, grinning like the Cheshire Cat. He had nothing to come back with—literally nothing. However, Rosie must have thought this reaction was not the required one. Casually, with a deliberation born of vindication, she picked up the TV remote with her left hand. With a wicked flick of her wrist, she sent it on a perfect trajectory, shocked and satisfied as it connected with his forehead. The impact clattered it to the floor, its batteries scattering like eggs from a free-range chicken.

"Just. Get. Out."

Her voice rose above and beyond anything he had heard before.

"And that was that…"

As Ty finished, Patrice—his rescuer—just shook his head. Ty was his mate, but he really was an arsehole, and despite their friendship, he might need telling. Properly, this time.

"So that's what happened. And here I am. She just freaked out over that song, the Majorca pics, my having her passwords and looking at her stuff. I could kill Lee, though—why didn't he block her? Tool. I don't understand women sometimes."

Or at any time, thought Patrice.

"Nothing else? I mean, who was the woman?" Because Patrice might have to warn her.

"No, mate, I would tell you if there was. I think it's just run its course, sort of petered out, and she was looking for an excuse to end it. It doesn't matter who she was. You know what I'm like—always on the hunt," Ty said with a pride that made Patrice grimace.

"OK, mate. Think you gave her more than one excuse, but what do I know? Take it you want to stay at mine for a bit?"

He wasn't sure he wanted Ty to, but he was a mate, wasn't he?

"If you don't mind. Get my head straight around this, sort out what I do from here," Ty said, with no hint of subterfuge.

"No bother. I'll just give Janie a call to OK it." After all, Janie always said she liked Ty, so it might not be that bad.

Ty looked out of the window and caught some chancer looking away—old gadge driving a knackered old van. What's your problem, pal? he aimed at the van driver.

Patrice started the call to get Janie to let Ty into their house. Which should be fun, he thought. And at least I might get the odd shag.

*****

5:38 pm

I am still curious about the grey Fiesta and Golf that were nose to tail. Both were loaded to the brim with stuff in the back. Perhaps I am doing them wrong, thinking that the two in the Fiesta are chancers—judging them by my own low standards. I wonder whether the two cars were actually together. They looked about the same age, not that I am a good judge of age these days.

Anyone under thirty just sort of blurred into an amorphous mass. You couldn't even really define them by fashion anymore. The contents of the two vehicles suggested that it might be house moves. It was too late for university, wasn't it? But then again, I am not really sure when all that starts nowadays. Reversing that, I wonder if people would be thinking about the contents of this van, especially with all this time on their hands.

I bet, they just think it's another van of useless crap that nobody really wants but still has to have. I wish I could answer that question myself, popped into my head as a thought, but I am sure that most of the other motorway occupants would be horrified if, as I suspect, the contents were not as legal as they might assume.

That was the price you paid for getting into the life I led—the one I was trying to get away from. But someone always had something over you unless you were God Almighty. I was sure somebody would have something on Chaz, 'cos he was hardly God Almighty—just a lowlife twat who thought holding my kids as collateral was perfectly normal fucking behaviour.

Gone Are Those Clouds

I think I can even put up with all this traffic now that I have finally left. Yes, I packed up my bags, stuffed them all into my car, and headed out on the promise of something else. This is a massive step—new job, new place to live, new people to meet—a brand-spanking-new adventure, and yet I still can't believe that I finally did it. The grin plastered on my face when I entered the motorway system must have had people thinking, *Who is that nut in the Golf?* but I didn't care.

There would be no regrets, no recriminations. I will admit I may miss a few things and a few people, but this was for the best—not only for me but for my mum and dad and everyone who knew me, really. I would be back, I am sure, when I could afford to live there, but then I would be just like all the other people who had now taken over my homeland. So perhaps that was something to avoid.

No, instead, I will be happy. I know I moaned about the damn place so much, and now I have done something about it, so yes, I will be happy. It took me some serious soul-searching, as that place was all I really knew until I was eleven years old. Even the travel then didn't involve much farther than the nearest large town for school. We had been on family holidays, yes, but they were like something from a Dalí painting. You got the gist that you were somewhere hot—well, the later ones were anyway—you just didn't know what it meant or what to do with it once you had worked the first bit out.

It usually felt like as soon as you were unpacked, you were repacking to scuttle back to where we had come from. Well, this boy from the Dales had packed now and wouldn't be packing or scuttling back anywhere for a good while. I had a little smile to myself as I recalled an old boy, Wilf, who once said, "Why would I want to go on holiday? I live in't Dales."

That was the attitude that had kept a way of life going for centuries. Sadly, it was a dying way of life now, and there would be fewer Wilfs and more Tamaras and Xaviers as the current century progressed.

I am twenty-four and free. My old man had put up a sort of token resistance, which I knew was half-baked, as even he could see that the writing was on the wall. My job in a local restaurant was not a career, it was not what I was trained to do, and ultimately, it would never pay me enough to buy anything other than a tent in Wensleydale—or anywhere else around there, for that matter.

I am sure my folks debated my living at home late into the night, as they could see the dilemma. It was a place I loved and always would, for the very fact that my family history was so tied into the valley that I couldn't escape it. Yes, it was beautiful, but that beauty was fading as the years passed and the old traditions fell by the wayside—like a fading actor who no longer got the lead parts but still had the stateliness akin to a dowager duchess. That was the Dales.

Of course, I was just about woke enough to realise that things had to change—well, some things anyway—yet I just knew that the only change I could really make was to leave. So here I am, going to London, going to a shared house, going to a job in digital marketing, going to make something of my time on this earth. God, it's a good day.

If I had time for honesty—and sitting here in all this traffic has given me that time. The alternative to navel-gazing was that I could call people, I suppose, instead of indulging in introspection, but it was too soon to call people I had only left three hours ago, and it was too soon to call the mates I would be sharing a flat with in London, as they would all be at work or on the tube. That will make a fantastic change from a community bus that appears on a timetable that pays more than a passing lip service to the gods of chaos.

So, honesty it is—yes, let's do some good old-fashioned thinking. This whole journey for me really started five years ago, when I rather stupidly asked my mother why I was called Ronald. Yes, I know, right? She thought this would be an opportunity to get me involved in her pet project, the family tree. It wasn't. It was all about me trying to find out why I had been given a name that had died out in the 1940s.

I know my father, and all the male forebears before him, had a version of it somewhere, but some traditions are best left to wither on the vine. Or at least use it for my sister—that works, and she could have carried it off in this day and age. Like that character in *EastEnders*. I mean, even Ron or Ronnie was worthy of ridicule for an eighteen-year-old lad.

The reason I hadn't noticed before was that up until then, school had been populated with a whole battalion of others bearing the same hereditary flaw. I knew three Wilfs, for God's sake—and that's not even counting the older version. These were all within three years of me. University changed that. Once I realised that flatlanders had broken the mould—although sometimes with great alacrity and an overstimulated imagination, to be honest.

Anyway, the family tree and the stimulus that made me realise I had to leave—that I should have the courage to leave. To venture out into the flat pagan lands of Sodom and Gomorrah, as Wilf—the old one—would have had it. It transpired that in late March of 1775, a family loaded their cart with some crates and other meagre belongings. The leader of this innocuous family group of six—two other adults and three children—was a Baptist minister, a rarity in the Methodist stronghold of the Dales.

This relative—this god-botherer—was an eight-times-great uncle, to be precise, and had decided to emigrate with his family and his sister to America.

Bearing in mind that this was still not the USA, as that history was yet to soil the pages of any tome. I thought if he could take that decision and up sticks without really knowing what was at the other end, then working hard at university and getting a good job away from the Dales would never be defined as a hardship.

My illustrious forebear—who had the middle name Ronald, as you may have guessed—had not only left and arrived, which was a miracle in itself, but had also settled in a nice green valley and founded a town. He named it after himself, rather narcissistically—which would also be rather cool if it wasn't so bloody up his own arse. I did not have the ambition to set up my own town, but I would make my mark if I could. I would do the name proud, and I am sure that Great Uncle John had looked at the new lands and thought, '*This is going to be a good day.*'

Satnav was telling me only three hours to London. Admittedly, it hadn't changed much recently, but at least that annoying, ironic voice had stopped telling me about possible congestion. I am sure Uncle John suffered some similar eighteenth-century delays—probably in a lot less comfort as well. Also, I felt quite smug, having stopped earlier for a pee break and some supplies. I could only imagine all the pressurised bladders around me—not to mention the imminent famine about to erupt on the motorway. Perhaps Uncle John could relate more to that last one, I am sure.

One of the other reasons for my departure—other than sanity, money, and the hope of living a little—was the depression that had been wrought in the valleys around me. They were slowly dying, and there was nothing anybody could do. Greed had driven up house prices. Greed had encouraged second-homeowners to buy their getaways at any cost.

The greed was also from those selling, as they knew they could make some serious bang. There was a time when you could be comforted in the winter months by the sight of smoke from the chimneys and the warming glow from all the houses.

As families and locals settled down for a night in God's own country, all of a sudden, these villages became ghostly parodies of what they once were. The carbon footprint would be lower, I suppose—I'd never really thought of that—but, Jesus, it was depressing wandering around a dark village. Shops were shutting, pubs were closing, and even cafés only opened in the summer months. The whole place was dying. The new weekend residents couldn't care less, as long as Waitrose delivered and they had somewhere to escape to from their busy and much more important lives.

The similarities between now and the abandonment of the seventeenth and eighteenth centuries were obvious. This wasn't a mass deportation of labour as had happened then; it was far more insidious—turning a national treasure into a monied theme park. I was doing the right thing, and perhaps one day I would be back to buy my second home in my first one. That's why I had to believe it was a good day.

My new job was in one of these trendy places, where they have air hockey and free smoothies. It was the polar opposite of my dad, who, unless he came home sweaty and covered in some form of manure, would think he had been shirking. No more manure for me, no more 5 a.m. calls during the summer to go and help collect dry grass. No more spending long winter days repairing walls where hikers had damaged them. No more freezing my nuts off in January when I was on early milking.

No more late suppers with hot chocolate, sitting on hay bales as the sun fell below the dale top. No more being the only living being for miles as I raked a field. No more air that tasted like it had never been anywhere other than in Yorkshire. No more drinking water from a spring or milk straight from the dairy. No more watching rain showers chase the rainbows down the dale. No more pints in front of a roaring fire and breathing in the smell of damp dogs.

I would miss it all, but when I went back to visit, most of these things would taste that much sweeter. I was sure of it, and those days would be as good as this one.

I wondered at the assorted motorway dwellers around me. I wondered about their stories. I wondered if they had made the momentous decision I had. I looked at the family with the kids strapped into their chairs in the back and wondered if the kids knew yet how hard life could be. I didn't think they did, as they still had their mum and dad there, and the smile on that woman could stun a tup, as my old man would say.

My mum had smiled at me as I left—I think it was jealousy, really. We had already had the tears and the half-hearted pleading not to go to that there London. The guy in the fast-food artic looked content, even raising his cup to me in a salute, acknowledging his good day and good fortune in that simple gesture.

I wondered if they were all having good days too. Some of the fellows looked a little stressed—bladder, possibly; hungry, possibly; life worries—who knew?

The only certainty was that this jam would clear soon, the light drizzle that had just started would stop, and we would all continue on our merry little journeys. The day would still be as good and as exciting as it had been three hours ago.

The traffic was still moving a little, so that was a positive, and we should all realise that the ones in the accident ahead were definitely not having such a good day. There but for the grace of God, etcetera. Cruel, but nothing was stopping my escape to a bright new future away from the home I loved.

*****

Tina because of this boredom that had settled onto her like a high tog duvet had stopped thinking of more and more creative things to do that involved firstly the balloon in the blue Audi, secondly, anyone who had looked at her in the traffic jam and lastly those responsible for allowing this boredom to be created in the first place. She was now reverting to type and employing a rather less-than-endearing trait of hers, when Tina was bored, then she would deliberately irritate someone else. That someone else in this instance was decided and therefore Ray got the short straw.

Tina pushed redial and was connected to her oppo about twenty feet behind her. Without waiting for a hello, a 'kiss my arse', or anything, she cut straight in.

"So, what do you reckon?"

That would drag Ray back into the here and now and, therefore, into her world of boredom. The clock on the dashboard now read *17:38*.

Ray didn't miss a beat. He was less bored but more frustrated. He also knew Tina well, which meant he could deploy his 'baffle her with facts' tactic—or, if not facts, rumour, supposition, and conspiracy would do at a push.

"This op has been planned for too long for it to be called off now, T. The boss will do anything to keep it all on track. Bear in mind, we are only one part of it. No doubt the planners are all running around trying to sort it, throwing in their what-ifs. After all, if the public found out about all the time and money wasted on this, and it was then lost due to an accident on the motorway—let alone if we walked away and the bastards did whatever this big thing is—then we may as well all go home."

Ray tried to keep it upbeat, but he was from Yorkshire, so optimism was not generally a comfortable bedfellow.

This tallied with what Tina knew—or thought she did.

"I know, I just have this bad feeling. Do they know what the main op is targeting?"

Tina relied a lot on what her gut told her, both personally and professionally—not something she would tell anyone. But at the moment, apart from Ray, it was the only thing that would listen to her.

"Only the top guys. Other than that, I don't. If I were to guess, then it would be another explosion in an unoccupied building."

Ray only had this info from attending exactly the same briefing Tina had been at.

"Shit."

That was a response Ray expected from Tina—she was a woman of one-word answers where she could get away with it.

The whole thing with the OCG was a top priority because of their alleged—or rather yet-to-be-proven—tactic of creating diversions in this way.

"Yep. The intel is that the gang are behind two, possibly three, recently—funding them through their normal business. It's a twat of a tactic. Even if it's just hitting property, it's one hell of a diversion, and they know we would have to respond."

As he said this, Ray realised he was in danger of depressing himself.

Tina chipped into Ray's thoughts.

"The flak would be immense if there was another one. The Joes hate us anyway, and if we don't stop it, then, as you say—taxi for Ray and Tina."

As Tina was frequently heard to pronounce: shit always rolled downhill.

"And everyone else. I don't know that it definitely is—they didn't brief that bit out—but it would be my best shout. I'd put money on it." But he was a son of Yorkshire, so that was highly unlikely.

"In that case, why are they keeping us here, basically babysitting that no-mark, when we could be helping the main op?" Tina's hand dropped from the steering wheel to where her Glock was holstered, a subconscious tic that would have told Ray she wanted some action.

He had noticed her shuffling and could guess what she was doing, as well as thinking. "T, if you'd been listening and not fiddling with your phone at the briefing, you'd know there are eleven others being babysat, as you put it. Assuming all eleven are stopped, it'll be a big spanner in the OCG funds, which should stop any further trouble for a while. If we mess up the main op and they slip away—or, even worse, if they do what I think they're planning—then we'll need more than body armour. We could breathe a little better knowing it'll take a while for them to get back up and running, even if we get a good kicking because of it."

Ray wanted to add that infighting in the criminal world would also escalate, but that had repercussions for the forces of good, and he didn't want to think any more about that. After all, as he kept reminding himself, his thirty were nearly up, and he could leave them to all that.

"Makes sense, I suppose. And you know what my attention span is like at these multi-agency things. Just don't like being a babysitter. But eleven paints a different Muriel," Tina said sulkily.

"Will you ever stop with your outdated *Corrie* references?" Ray shook his head.

"Ha, for you, Ray—never," she said with a smile as she hung up, catching Ray's headshake in her mirror. The smile, though, disappeared as she watched some clown in another Audi suddenly appear like a ninja in a gap in front of the ropey white van—a gap most people would have struggled to get their armchair in.

The inevitable sounding of horns and sharp braking followed, and all Tina could do was marvel at the arrogance of some road users.

*****

5:39 pm

They could keep my ex-wife if it meant I'd get the kids back. But knowing my luck—a small laugh escaping—they'd give them all back as a package, and I'd have to explain to her why she'd been bound and gagged, and who did I think I was, and all that. She'd want to call the filth, and that was a nailed-on death sentence. There may not be honour among thieves, but there certainly were vendettas, and I didn't fancy getting caught up in any fallout from Chaz and his mates.

I just crossed my fingers and hoped she was keeping her gob shut, not mouthing off at them. She could look after the kids, which was a good thing. If I had my phone, I'd have called Chaz and told him to gaffer her gob closed—as I knew, and they would soon—what could come out of it. Better she got a tape burn from taking it off than a bullet in the head because she'd nagged them into it.

Not that I particularly cared. If they'd just snatched her based on out-of-date info, then I wouldn't be sat here. Wouldn't be sat in a jam—physically and philosophically. I wouldn't have the dilemma and the worry. When they first met, I knew that a woman always views the man as a ship that's going to take her somewhere. She had learnt, as many do, that a man is just an anchor who will eventually stop you and drag you down.

I had to stand on the dodgy brakes with some force as some arsehole with a death wish tried to cut in front of my van. A gap big enough to house a washing machine now seemed to want to have an Audi inserted in it.

"Stupid fucker," escaped as I leant on the horn and flashed the van's lights.

Sometimes Confusion Will Rule

What a day! What a fucking day! And now this. The worst fucking day in my fifty-five years, and now this—stuck in bloody traffic. I should have been home hours ago. All of it is my own stupid fucking fault for having a drive to clear my overstimulated brain. Now this. Why did I think it would be a great idea to clear my head by going for a long drive? Not sure I really thought about it, to be fair. I just came out of that room, got in the car, and now here I am.

Four hours ago, I had been sitting in a plastic chair that was neither fit for purpose nor formed for my—or anybody's—comfort. I had taken in my surroundings, which were hardly designed to inspire; they were more designed to strike fear into the occupants of the drab and dismal environment. It most certainly was not God's waiting room, but more than likely, it was the other one. His or her nemesis may have had some input into the design, but as neither existed, then it may just have been a designer with no actual design skills.

The French have a saying that I find to be particularly pertinent: "Plus ça change, plus c'est la même chose," roughly meaning, I believe, that the more things change, the more they stay the same.

Going by the beige décor and the dying plants hanging out on the one windowsill, underneath a window so opaque that it was incapable of performing its one function of letting in light, this was true. The lack of natural light also explained the interminable buzzing from the overhead strip lights, which were contributing to global warming in the middle of the day. It would appear that nothing much had changed here since the early seventies.

But you would think that someone would do something about the light. The décor was a throwback to when the palette was either industrial neutral or garish swirly in-your-face—no middle ground. I would blame the Victorians if they were still about, as their taste was pretty much epitomised in this room. Dismal it was. Throw in the magazines and the posters—designed chiefly to impart horror—advertising diseases you did not think you had until you crossed this threshold, or for procedures you had never undertaken but should have if you wanted to live any longer than the current moment, and it was almost a perfect storm, sans George Clooney, to cause some form of depression.

Throw in the lack of natural light, and it was no wonder so many people felt worse after visiting these places. Surely this must have crossed someone's mind. The irony couldn't have escaped them. Then again, as I looked around at the mess, it clearly had.

My companions in this endeavour could not have been more varied. One of them had looked as if they had only seconds to live, judging by the noise and pallor. So much so that I spent a few precious minutes trying to recall some first-aid training from a past job, just in case it was needed.

The last thing I was going to do was ask them if they were OK, as this would mean either losing my place in the queue while the alleged professionals dealt with them or becoming embroiled in a conversation that could be one-sided and of no interest to me. The only result would be more oxygen being removed from the immediate area, and with the plants already dying, there was no hope of rapid replenishment.

My car was not the place for all this reminiscing. I was already going through the gamut of emotions—grief, anger, disbelief, and denial. I really shouldn't dwell on the appointment four hours ago. It was just hard not to.

The second fellow could not have been more disparate. The nervous energy radiating from him allowed my subconscious to have a mean-spirited and possibly unjustified conversation about mental health or, heaven forbid, drug abuse.

The level of activity from this companion was surely inappropriate for the formal surroundings, so some enhancement must have been supplied for such a causal effect. The alternative was that they were just excited to be there, which, considering why we were there, would be viewed by many—my subconscious included—as wholly inappropriate.

I can rationalise what I was doing there. It was quite simple, really; I had received that phone call—the one asking me to attend this dismal little place. Some would have said, "If it's that bad, why didn't you just say no?" Well, I tried and was told that it was imperative and not really negotiable. So there I had ended up, arse going to sleep on a plastic chair and nothing to do but speculate, worry about why I was there, and speculate some more about my travelling compadres.

I had even tried reading the provided literature and some of the magazines. However, the magazine distraction didn't appeal, mainly because I think I had read most of it back in the nineties when it was published. Also, the musings of the cover personality did not really resonate, as I believe he died fifteen years ago and was therefore no longer deemed current or relevant.

Although a message from the other side may have had a certain ironic quality. The leaflets were no doubt supplied as some sort of backup to the horror-inducing posters, for those who wanted to read more about what was going to kill them if they were in any doubt.

One of the things we have drummed into us constantly these days is that we apparently have a basic human right to health. Amongst other things, food and education, I think, are chucked in there as well. Funny that—I don't recall ever signing anything, so I'm not sure where these rights come from. As far as I could see, ever since we decided that caves were better than trees, we have been trying to destroy each other and everything else we can possibly see. Plus ça change and all that. I would find it amusing and quite worrying if I wasn't so selfishly worried about my reason for being here.

The fact that certain organisations will spend billions trying to discover either how we came to be here—think Big Bang—or looking for other places we can go to kill off should have all the do-gooders frothing at their foam-covered chai lips. It was not the action of sentience at all but the result of a certain blinkering to what is really important, and what appears to me to be a degree of intellectual smugness.

So here we all are. We know the future is bleak, and we know we may not be able to do anything about it. We all know—plus ça change—that we are all going to die, some sooner than others, but it was as certain as sprouts making you fart.

You may feel there was a tad of morbidity here, but needs must. Our ultimate journey is the only real certainty.

Yet there is very little promotion of this. You can live healthily, exercise, and all that hoo-hah, but it doesn't hide the fact that you will die. Both of my neighbours here were at extreme ends of the spectrum but would still die, as would I, as much as I tried to ignore that fact. The NHS could save their budget and drop waiting times if they just put up a sign saying, "None of it matters really, you will still die." It may shock a few, but the ones whose taxes dropped would probably counterbalance that truth.

Now, spiritually and physically, I could see why I had been in that room, even if it was for a lesson I may not have wanted.

If you look at it in a more universal sense, the Earth is basically on life support, waiting around to die, and as for the bringer of light into our very short existences—the Sun—well, there is a death sentence hanging over that as well. Cosmically, we are all in the same rather full lifeboat.

My thought process was going off on a really sharp tangent now, all because of that fucking waiting room, those dead flowers, and what had occurred in the next thirty minutes of my so-far blemish-free life.

The door opposite my tortured position had opened, and my name was uttered by the unglamorous doorkeeper—definitely not one of the angels, unless they had swapped wings for hand-knitted, crumpled cardigans. I was shown into another beige room, with even more of the horrific image series plastered on the walls, and bizarrely, as this was a male clinic, one for ovarian cancer. There had been an apology for keeping me waiting, which was when I pointed out the room was called that and therefore was fulfilling its only raison d'être.

The tight smile was not quite what I expected, and neither were the next five minutes and thirty seconds of dialogue—most of which I can't remember now, as once the first words were out, my synapses started going off like fireworks. Suffice it to say that the tests and invasions I had suffered a few weeks previously pointed to the imminent termination of my fundamental right. Yes, I was going to die. Plus ça change.

I had left that room feeling slightly violated, a victim of some sort of mugging. Something had been taken away from me and replaced with some pamphlets explaining what I could do with my remaining days—pain management and jolly old helplines. I think there was also something about a support group. I mean, I ask you. I had only come to the first appointment because the adverts told me I should get checked out due to my age.

I told them I didn't feel ill, just a bit tired, and I peed a lot—but who doesn't as we get older? Well, apparently, I should have come earlier, as now it was too late, and there was nothing to be done. It had all spread, and I was fucked.

For crying out loud, we had—and by that, I selfishly mean I—just survived the pandemic. Secreting ourselves away from just about everything, we had then been released like a horde of laboratory mice set free by the freedom fighters. So, there should have been a reason to feel some level of joy. Then fate decided, "That's enough of that, Ricky-boy. Have some of this." And here I am, back in a slough—being in Slough would be bad enough. This one was far more invidious.

Now, as I look at that moment, it could be viewed as a point of change—where my life could take on meaning from what may have appeared as an apparently meaningless one. I had meandered and prevaricated through life, railing and raging against everything and everyone, pointing out the flaws and deficiencies of all and sundry.

At that moment, I had just received the ultimate kick in the balls from a seemingly ironic god, who I did not believe in. "I have now pointed out your flaws and declared you deficient," I believe he or she would have said, had he or she actually existed. I can laugh at the fact that all that hanging around in that holistic, all-encompassing waiting room called life had finally been prescribed. Plus ça change.

The others sharing our vehicular prisons—what must they be thinking? I had been given a death sentence, or rather, my death sentence had been promoted for early commutation. Everyone else surrounding me had their lives to continue—until they didn't. Lucky bastards.

Whoever was in the ambulance coming up the hard shoulder, and anyone caught up in the smash ahead, may have been sundered from life early, but I assume they didn't know about it. So, what should I do? It was a case of sucking it up, I suppose. Do what I can until I can't. What's that annoying phrase? "It is what it is." Well, I will amend that to say, "It is what it is until it isn't." That's far more philosophically apt.

I had believed I was different—a revolutionary who could and would change the world. A world I now railed against. I am now just a number, still wanting to change the world, but now constrained in my ability to do so. The world still needs to be changed, and I will continue to rage against the machine.

However, I am now the worst possible agent of change—I have become a statistic. Plus ça change.

Why was that van flashing me and sounding its horn? He had left the gap—a typical white van man, thinks he owns the bloody road. Back off, pal, I'm dying. What's your problem? Are you mad because you're slightly late for your chippy tea? I mean, fuck right off.

*****

5:40 pm

I needed to calm down. Getting wound up was not going to help anyone. There was literally nothing I could do. Surely, they would be tracking me somehow. Therefore, they would know I was stuck here with no way of getting to where I needed to be. As a thought process, this was a logic I couldn't pick holes in. All I knew was that if I were planning this sort of thing, then I would have made damn sure I knew where this bloody van was at all times. It was all perfectly sensible.

You can forget all the stuff about my mobile—that was just so they knew I was clean and wasn't being tailed by the filth. However, they would have one of those little trackers you can buy off the net that allows you to follow your missus or stalk some random. That'll be the answer.

This thought process managed to bring a little relaxation into the mix—something I had not felt since I set off, with the image of my kids burned into my head.

They had left that bit of the plan until the last minute, allowing me to think that I was only collecting a van from Burley Road, until I realised my mistake far too late. If they knew I was stuck and therefore going to be very late, then surely they would factor that in and nothing bad would happen.

Whether or not logic like this could be applied, however, was debatable. What it did do was give me some hope to cling to. In fact, the more I considered this train of thought, the more kudos I tried to give it. Rolling my shoulders to release some of the tension, trying to steady my slightly panicked breathing.

Satnav was still blinking at me, announcing that I had fourteen miles until I reached the rendezvous at the underground car park in the city centre.

I could see in my right-hand mirror a ratty old Land Rover, belching crap out of the back. It had just pulled level with a silver Mini that was directly behind me. The guy in the Rover looked like he needed a chill pill. What is it with these people today? Was it just the jam, or did they all have shit going on and I had only seen it because I was actually looking for once, in an attempt to damp mine down?

What did they think when they looked at me? No doubt some of the same. I could send the Rover guy some of my newfound positive vibes, as nothing was really that bad when you thought about it.

Ignoring the kids and the threat, of course.

Black Roses or Was That Hail Mary's

Perversely, it was my fault that I felt like this. After all, I had told the CO I would do it, even though that was over two years ago and mainly because it was the only fair and right thing to do. Now, to compound the effect, this traffic was messing with my head, giving me unneeded time to think about my man, my Masters.

Stretch had been under my command when it all went down—when it all went to rat-shit. And because I felt like I knew his folks—Stretch had told me enough about them during our tours of Afghanistan—it felt like it had become my duty.

Whenever we were on a tour, I was like a surrogate parent to most of the squad, those that were fresh out, anyway. Stretch was like a son and my chief sidekick; he had been there for me on all our tours. Even though the squad on all the later ones were all veterans and specialists, as there was no use for fodder, he was still always my go-to. His experience was invaluable in maintaining some sort of discipline and helping me keep everyone alive.

That's why they pay me the big bucks. Ha. I fucking wish. My reward for the latest cluster fuck was being in a lockdown for the last twelve months. Not like the civvy job, where you were paid to sit at home and get paid for doing it. No, this one had been confinement to base in Catterick, as if that would help. I mean, what the fuck would I want to go to Catterick for? I had enough of that, all those years ago, when I was in training.

This was the whole squad, though, and someone had realised that we were fucked. All the stuff we had been pumped with had finally failed, and they needed us out of the way—to become deniable. We weren't supposed to feel anything anymore. That was the sell. And yet I could tell them that I fucking felt. I felt a fucking lot. And right fucking now.

I would always know the fuckers that killed Stretch and Matty and the others were still out there somewhere. Not only the fuckers that caused me a visit to

Stretch's parents, but all of the motherfuckers—the whole camel-shagging fucking mess of them. The anger was coming, but this wasn't the place, and it sure as hell wasn't the time. I needed to keep this in check.

Back in the barracks was where I ideally needed to be, but that wouldn't happen again. Now that they have thrown me to the wolves, I could no longer be anywhere where others could help me sort myself out. Now that I'm on a regime of tablets to counter all the shite we were injected with, I have to damp this anger down. The place for this is not in a fucking traffic jam on a motorway.

Fucking lights. They weren't helping. The red lights, firing off into the evening sky—red like blood, bright like the sun in Helmand. But this was the red of the devil. Mocking me. Mocking me like the old Landy I was driving. I should have brought the other car. This one smelt and sounded like the thing it was—a relic from the army. Too many memories. The stupid slits at the front letting in all the fumes from the others around me.

The uncomfortable seats and suspension would kill you if you didn't hang onto something. Where are my shades? They would help. Fuck. They're in my kit. Didn't think I'd need them on an October day. Fuck. Even shutting my eyes briefly will bring back the day. The day the fuckers took away a good man. A man who doubted why we were there but was still a fucking good soldier and did what he could to help.

A man with doubts who would have agreed with the Taliban had they asked—about the legitimacy of our presence, that is. Not the other fucking religious shite. Then they shot him. He was out on patrol, stepping in for one of the other lads who was ill. Bet he feels as shite as I do. Or perhaps he just offers a prayer to Stretch and crosses himself every time he goes out. Probably bought a fucking lottery ticket as well.

Every time I sleep or drift off, I see Stretch bleeding out in the dust, a round from some fucker getting up under his armour. The medic gave him morphine as I called in evac, but we knew he was fucked. All because he was a good soldier—a mate who didn't want to see me short-handed.

When I had got there, I had not been sure what to expect, with it being so long. But his parents had been Sunday-best polite, making tea and all that crap, though they were clearly still devastated. The uncomfortable visit had been, thankfully, short, and I had got out of there as sharp as I could, retreating to the sanctuary of my Landy—only after leaving them with Stretch's personals. I felt like a coward, running away from them, but I couldn't stay any longer because I would see my folks' faces on them and how they would feel.

They asked me to keep in touch and all that, but I won't be doing that. I don't want to be a reminder to them. They don't know the whole story, and I wouldn't tell them. How would it make them feel better to know he shouldn't have been there? For fuck's sake, I know what it was doing to me. So them? Not a chance they will hear it from me.

The pressure is building. I can feel it, like being in a plane, except the only lift-off would be me getting help, not sitting here—anger pressing in from all sides. The visit had done it. The moment I had left his folks, I had pulled over round the corner, and the first wave was there. I knew what would happen. I have been through this so many times since I came back. The inability to get my breath, a sweat coming from every pore, the urge to shout and scream, wanting to hurt something or curl up in a ball.

Tears were new. Tears for Stretch? Or tears for me?

What was that film? The one with the bloke—cleft chin—Spartacus. No, *I'm Spartacus*. Certainly, a fucking slave. You know the one. The guy goes off the rails. Michael Keaton? No, he was a crap Batman. Or Beetlejuice. Or something. Who the fuck was he?

Stuck in a traffic jam in the US. Fucking just loses it. Goes mental. Gets out and wanders off down the road. It could have been set here. All the fuckers in their cars looking at him. Fuckers. Fuckers. Do they know? How can they know?

Falling Down.

Michael Douglas. That's the twat. Goes and shoots up something. Went postal. Feels like I should get out and shoot up something—all those fucking civvies in their fucking nice cars. Or how about a couple of van drivers? Wandering around the country delivering their shite. A couple of those fuckers would make up for it.

Wouldn't it, Stretch?

C'mon, Stretch, help me out here. You would know the answer, Stretch.

Stretch, don't leave me wanting to shoot these fucking civvies. I know they aren't towelhead motherfucking Taliban, but I need to hurt something—to stop the noise in my head. Stop the pain building. Stop the noise.

Please, Stretch. You have never let me down before.

Is this because I broke my promise? I said I would look after you. But you left me there. Holding you while you bled out because of those motherfuckers. That road in Helmand.

You shouldn't have even been there. And then you weren't. Why did you volunteer, boy? That should have been me lying in that hell-blown ditch, with it all ebbing away. I wish it was. I wouldn't be here, with the noise, the pressure in my head, and the lights looking like tracer rounds firing off into the dusky sky. I must be deaf, as I can't hear any rounds going off. You need revenge, Stretch.

When they brought his body back—repatriation, they called it, which to me sounded like they were saying he had lost his patriotism—it had been a full-on army cover-up. No band, no dress uniforms, no rifle salute. All it did was depress me, I think. Sending him off into the burning sun of a foreign land in a wooden box, another number to some Whitehall fucker. Not even a flag draped over the box. But we knew the score—this unit was deniable, and fuck me if they weren't denying us to fuck.

The numbness had crept up through my boots, the sun-dried ground doing its best to add to my misery. The dust from those few present, stomping and moving about, created a pall like gun smoke. The loosely executed salute added more poignancy, and I did well to hold it together even then. The senior officer said a few words, even though he didn't know Stretch from anyone.

His folks seemed to appreciate it, though, when I told them—clutching the folded UJ that I had provided and they would never know—like it was a life preserver. Ironically, in a way, I suppose it was. Stretch would have found some humour somewhere—that was a given. I could almost hear him uttering his little asides as the service of putting him on a flight home progressed, much like when we were stuck in the back of a Mastiff on patrol.

I needed to hear him now, telling me to breathe, you twat, telling me to ignore the lights. Something about stepping into the light, probably. Though I hope he had done that and was whispering words of delinquency and juvenile humour into the ears of the angels. The stationary position was making me nervous. It broke every rule of patrol—keep moving, you cunts! That's where I was. Stretch was on point, and we were moving stealthily through cover.

The goat track we were following had been swept of IEDs, and we were confident we'd be back in barracks in an hour or so. Got to keep moving. Tab, tab—move, you lazy bastards. No, we weren't. I wasn't. I was stuck in a traffic jam, with civvies who don't give a flying fuck about us. Yes, they bleat on about helping the ones who harass them in the street after a night under cardboard. But what about us, you fuckers—the ones that still have to pick up the pieces. Literally.

Then be asked to do it all again, and again, and again. And when you think you have no more luck—you haven't. Ask Stretch. He ran out, and only because he was a good soldier. A fucking mate. One of the boys. Yes, you fuckers—I am looking at you in your nice little lives. You are fucking bastard motherfuckers.

The guy in the Audi was smoking a fucking joint. The fucker. Stretch died because you wanted to get a hit. You bastard—bastard motherfucking piece of junkie shit. You should be bleeding out on the roadside. You should have your mate go and tell your parents that you were a good man and didn't deserve to die. Except you did, you twat.

That's the difference—because of people like you and the appeasers, we would be told to bleed and to die for a cause we weren't sure about. Bleed in the sand, bleed in the jungle—and for fucking what, you cunts? For a flag and a public who couldn't give a shit about us. Yet you sit there with your drugs, and everything is well in your world. I hope you get cancer or have a bad trip and top yourself, you worthless arsehole.

This was no good. The red mist was coming down, and I needed to get out. I needed to take action, or I would—I don't know what. And that's the scary part. Need to respond, need to move. Can't stand still—fucking Taliban will sight you. Watch for the wires. Call for a medic. Evac. The situation is SNAFU. Where's the heli? Where are you, Stretch? I love you, man. I love you, brother.

The day was drawing down into dark now, the lights firing off into the distance, and yet, despite that, I felt my own personal dark lifting a little—because I could see a way out now. They thought I could not feel anymore—that I was a super soldier, immune to empathy and sympathy and that new-age hippy shite. They would be right, but only when I had my eyes open. If I closed them, or even blinked hard, then the fucking pain was there right enough.

No number of pills to suppress the memories would ever work—would ever stop me from feeling the pain of what we had done and what we had suffered. There were victims of what we pulled, but we were also the victims in this. And I knew what I had to do. I pulled my daysack closer, rummaging around inside until my fist closed around the stock of my Glock 17—the one that was filed as missing in combat but had come out with Stretch's stuff. It felt good in my hand—my personal sidearm, my friend, and the means to an end.

Luckily, nobody was paying attention to the scratty Land Rover or its occupant. I could do this. Get out, find one of the fuckers' cousins driving a van, and make them feel the cold hand of death—just like Stretch. That would be justice. Fucking A.

Or, with one shot, I could end my pain and sorrow.

Fucking Stretch, what should I do? I can't do this anymore. I don't want you in my head anymore. I love you, brother—but you've gone, and yet you haven't.

Stretch?

*****

Another minute had ticked over, and Tina estimated that the whole mess of traffic had moved about ten yards or so. She glanced around at the slowly changing traffic outside—apart from to the front, that is—knowing it meant the motorway was being cleared, slowly. But it was still shite.

To amuse herself, she wondered about the stories of the others in their cars. Applying a little fantasy to her day would hardly test her powers of concentration. Then she felt saddened, remembering the little family she had seen earlier, and to distract herself, she wondered about what other secrets were playing out in the traffic.

They were all a metaphor for life, she concluded—all these people who were visible and yet whose lives were cocooned away. All encased in a metal box. Only those they were in contact with would know their real stories. Tina knew she could guess at a potted history of some, but only because they had logos on their van or wagon.

The rest could be anything. What was the story with that pink dildo-stretched thing she had seen earlier? Or the yellow whatever-it-was? Even the ropey old van that came into view now and again? There was an old Land Rover, a taxi, a couple of high-end SUVs—all of them interacting with each other, yet not. The stories they held would stay within.

Then she was hit with—I wonder what they think I am?

Unless, of course, they just think hot babe. That was kind of funny. But then, as she hadn't attracted any of the usual male attention techniques all day, perhaps not. They knew as much about her as she knew about them—not counting Ray and Connors, of course. She was as much a mystery to everyone else as they were to her.

Tina realised she was starting to depress herself—and not wanting to turn out like Ray was a good enough reason to think of something else.

5:41 pm

If I had caught that COVID, would I be in this van now? It was doubtful, as Chaz would not have had the balls to front that out, and that would've fettled this. But no, I had been as clear as a bell. If I had even been in a proper job, I would have been furloughed or whatever it was called. Money for sitting on your arse—like being on the dole or one of those city wankers. My line of work didn't come with that benefit. Everyone being at home had sort of fucked me over. More eyes about, fewer empty properties.

Luckily, Lizzie, who had been working from home, hadn't minded me falling about the place. Though I was technically working from home, I suppose, and that nearly made me smile—although burgling yourself is no fun after a couple of times. So, I had dossed about until that day when they were allowed to mix again legally. I might admit to a few forays, mainly to clear a warehouse and deliver a couple of vans, but all in all, I behaved.

That day of freedom had dawned with bright sun and the shadow of Chaz wandering up the path, limping along, followed by the gimp himself. This day was the start of the end play. *Just a few jobs*, Chaz had said. *Just a few more jobs*, Chaz added. *I know it's been tough, but do you need a loan?* Chaz had offered. Fucking idiot that I was, I had taken it. Now I couldn't repay, and I was stuck in the middle of a right fuck-up. Why the bastard had to threaten my kids still made no sense, though.

There was some sort of commotion at the back of the van—I could swear I caught a glimpse of someone getting out of a car—then it was gone.

*****

Can I Drown My Sorrow

Andrea sat up very straight, as if someone or something had suddenly flipped a switch. She began looking around, taking in her surroundings through a focussed tunnel, which meant all she could see were mainly parts of a car. As soon as she moved her gaze away from the blinkering and looked beyond her hands, she became aware of the outside—an outside that was far, far too busy and unfamiliar. A world filled with traffic that, unfortunately, was not moving much or taking any notice of her, judging by the looks on the few faces she could see.

Although, she thought, *I have got here, wherever here is, so the situation can't be all bad.* She wondered about the problem. Speaking of which, where exactly was she? There was no ready knowledge of how she had ended up in this traffic jam. Please, God, it's not starting all over again ran through her head. She hadn't had a blackout for some time—or at least she was fairly sure that was the case. And as there was nobody to ask, she might have been creating a falsehood in her own mind.

The road signs were blocked by wagons and vans shunting along the left-hand side of her. If she craned her neck, she could just about see the sign on the other side. Bloody hell. Almost in a panic, she wondered what she was doing here. This wasn't her normal route to anywhere, which left her with the reasoned conclusion that, for now, she was stuck in this line of traffic, crawling at a snail's pace, with no idea where she was precisely—just a general sense.

The lyrics to a song spilt out of the radio, a well-known song by Tears for Fears, and they slowly seeped into her consciousness. She could nearly laugh at the aptness. Yes, it most certainly is. The clock read after five-thirty. Where had the day gone? It was getting dark, and those bloody brake lights were stabbing into her overtaxed brain. She could feel the pressure building again. No, she can't. Stop it, Andi, you silly old fool, she admonished herself. Get a grip. Her story and this predicament would take some unfolding.

Come on, Andrea, think straight. Shake off this grogginess. Have I been drugged? To the right of her, a sleek stretch limo with blacked-out windows filled the lane like a giant pink oil slick. When did pink become a colour for a car? Must be someone important. To her left, a silver Mini sat in the next lane. The girl driving looked about ten years old. She was staring straight at Andrea with a sneer on her face—and then gave her the finger.

What's that about?! Must have upset her somehow, although Andrea couldn't see how. After all, if asked, she would struggle to say what she was doing here, let alone what she had done. Ahead, the red rear lights of a white van taunted her, pulsing a beat as if telling her she wasn't going anywhere very soon. Oh, God, I wish I knew what was happening and why there was a hold-up. I need to get out of this traffic. My stomach is in knots, and bile is rising in my throat, making me want to throw up. When did I last eat or drink?

Glancing into the rear-view mirror, her stomach did a giant somersault, nearly releasing the bile that was trying to escape. There was somebody sprawled on the back seat, partially covered by a tartan blanket—like someone who had been in a hit-and-run at a ceilidh.

Shit! Shit! Shit!

Who is that? Twisting her body round to get a closer look, she could see it was a dark-haired, stockily built woman wearing a tweed skirt, tan tights, and sensible brass-buckled court shoes. Definitely not ceilidh-bound then. She looked vaguely familiar—though most people looked only vaguely familiar on a good day. On a bad day, though, Andrea could safely say that even she looked only vaguely familiar to herself.

The radio played on. The tune was so, so apt, it felt like it was describing her exact situation. 'Mad World' indeed. Her heart was beating fast, a pounding in her ears. A pain crept across her brow, and she fought the urge to close her eyes. Stay focussed, woman! Try and figure out what the hell is going on. Who is that person splayed on my back seat?

Who the hell is it? I don't recognise her face. More to the point, how did she get in my car? I can't figure it out. Then again, I can't even figure out how I got in this car, so perhaps she has a similar story? She looks way too heavy for me to have put her there. Not that I'm being unkind, but she is quite a bit chunkier than I am.

A gentle snore emitted from her mouth. As she turned her head, Andrea could see her face more clearly.

Do I know you? Do I bloody know you? A feeling of déjà vu washed over her as she scrutinised the woman's face—a round face verging on puffiness, with a double chin. A drool mark stained the collar of her fawn blouse; she'd be embarrassed when she saw that. Her eyes were closed, so Andrea couldn't see their colour. Her eyebrows were plucked within an inch of their life and pencilled in with dark brown—a job that looked more like a child had done it with crayon.

Her hair was obviously dyed dark brown, and the lines on her face indicated a woman who had resorted to the magic of a bottle.

Glancing at the lumpy body beneath the rug and the swollen ankles encased in tan, lightly wrinkled tights only confirmed it for Andrea.

She had to think straight. Stuck in this bloody traffic jam, she had little else to do—but thank God for it all the same. She couldn't take her eyes off the inert figure splayed on the back seat.

Suddenly, there was a slight movement beneath the tartan blanket, and an arm emerged. Bespectacled eyes stared right at her.

"Oh! How long have I been asleep? You should have woken me. What's wrong? Why aren't we moving?"

The voice sparked a vague awareness. The accent was nondescript—plain, or something equally unremarkable. But something was pinging in the mud that was Andrea's memory.

"I don't mean to be rude, but do I know you and what are you doing in my car?" I tried to keep this pleasant in case she was some sort of monster.

"Andrea what are you talking about it's me, Lynn." A look of genuine confusion on the woman's face, but also a smile. Do monsters smile like that?

Inside my head I'm screaming, just like that picture by Edvard Munch. Have I completely lost my mind and gone off the mental highboard? I must have as I have no clue where I am, where I'm going and who this crumpled-looking woman is in the back seat of my car, assuming this is my car, who knows? She is laid there like she owns the place. I can't take my eyes off her, is there anything about her that will make me remember?

"I don't mean to be rude." Manners cost nothing and might keep the potential monster discombobulated. "How do I know you? You might be some nutter for all I know, you know hiding in my car waiting for your moment to pounce. You hear about it all the time." Manners, Andrea, don't poke the beast.

"Are you serious? Hiding under a tartan blanket, come on, Andrea." Picking up the corner of the rug, to emphasise the point, and in case, Andrea did not know what a tartan rug was. Which to Andrea meant she had some knowledge of the confusion in Andrea's mind.

"I wouldn't know, would I? How would I know about them, only a serial killer would say that. So, come on, spill the beans." Which sounded aggressive, even as I said it. Perhaps it was me that was the monster. After all, I wouldn't remember, would I?

Lynn watched Andrea, she was beginning to feel a little frightened of her behaviour, maybe she wasn't taking her meds again? She had to think fast about how she was going to react and handle this all too common, yet historic, manic version of Andrea. The version they thought they had managed to put away and control the times when it showed itself.

"Andi, calm down. I think you may be starting to feel unwell again. Have you taken your pills? How's your pulse? I'm not here to scare you. Can't you remember who I am? I'm here to help you. You asked me to accompany you to visit Bill—you do remember Bill, don't you?" Lynn tried to keep the questions light. After all, she was in a car with a woman who was having one of her episodes, and while they were not moving, there was still a frisson of danger.

A sudden flashback of memory. Bill! Bill! Oh my God. I squeeze my eyes shut and try to wipe the thought of him from my mind. It's a mad world, all right. Bits and pieces come back, and my heart is definitely racing now. A moment of clarity in my mind—pills, yes, pills. Where were they? I knew they took me to a different place, a happier place. A functioning existence rather than this whirl of panic I was in. I searched for my handbag. Where was it?

Bugger! It was there next to this woman who claimed she was here to help. Perhaps she was trying to pinch my pills? I could watch her in my mirror. Thieving bitch! Clarity ensues—I can vaguely remember her. It's something about the way she said Bill's name.

A slow scream builds and builds, and then, as if making a mad dash for the light outside to escape the darkness within me, it rips from my lips as I hammer my head against the steering wheel. No! No! No! "I can't breathe! I need to get out of this car. Why are we stuck here?"

"Stay right there, Andrea. Take deep breaths to calm down. I'll get out and see what the hold-up is. Just try and get a grip. We've been planning this day for two weeks, so I can't understand why you're acting like this." A genuine concern now replaced the confusion on Lynn's wrinkled face, causing further creasing.

Lynn opened the back door and got out of the car. She was in a quandary, unsure how she was going to handle this. All the counselling with Andrea to get her to this place—for what? The training she had undertaken so she could help Andrea, ensuring she had stuck to the drug regimen, making sure she did her breathing exercises—none of it was any use now. Stuck here on a motorway, scanning all around her, she could see the snaking lines of cars, their red taillights gleaming and taunting her like beady-eyed devils or maleficent bats in a cave.

Two years had passed, but she could still vividly recall the scandalous headlines reporting the serious assault on the controversial author William Sullivan. He had been beaten severely, nearly to the point of no return. One of his volumes had been torn and poured over him like poisonous confetti. The several awards he had received in 2015 for his book *What is the Point of the Female?* had been put in a pile on his desk, his blood smeared over them.

The opposition and hate he had garnered from females the world over—even aligning some men behind the protest—had been overwhelming. It was rumoured he was planning a sequel, believed to be titled *Men Do Have a Point*. Andrea had been his editor and copyreader, and it was her discovery of the unfortunate William in his non-flattering repose that had sent her over the edge, as she had been a little in love with him. Even though she would deny this with her last breath.

Lynn got back in the car next to Andrea and placed a liver-spotted hand on her arm. She was so tense. Reaching across to Andrea's bag, she offered it to her.

"You need to take your pills, Andi," she said with warmth.

"You haven't stolen them?" I asked the woman who claimed to be Lynn while rootling around inside. There they were. With a bottle of water as well. Perhaps would-be Lynn wasn't a thief.

"No, love, I haven't. We are off to see Bill in the hospital. You remember. But you know you have to take your pills. Now, sip some water, and do your breathing. You know the way. That's it. Good girl."

Oh yes, Bill. Lovely Bill. The cocktail of chemicals quickly started to take effect, as I knew they would. How could I have been so daft as not to take them? Not taking them meant forgetting, blackouts, blind spots. I drew air in slowly and deeply—hold, four, five, six—and out, just as slowly. The quick action of the drugs had not yet been dulled by tolerance, like the last prescription I had. In, slowly, deeply—hold, four, five, six—and out, just as slowly. Yes. Bill. Lovely Bill. And Lynn was here with me now, so all would be well. Not such a mad world anymore.

*****

Ray thought some more about the possibility that the heads of the crime gang were indeed planning to blow something up as part of a diversion, and he offered a silent prayer that he was safely locked in his metallic cocoon. As boring as it was to be stuck in a jam, Ray and Tina had both been near a major bombing before. To be honest, "near" meant they had been diverted to help and had seen first-hand the devastation caused by a three-thousand-pound fertiliser and Semtex mix detonated in a high public transit area.

They both viewed themselves as more than fortunate not to get too close, mainly confined to traffic and public order on the periphery, but they knew by the number of response vehicles that it indicated a high casualty count. This was later confirmed—seventy-seven dead and over three hundred and fifty injured, some critically. The target at that time had been suspected to be religious, with all the connotations that would have for national security and community tensions.

York city centre on an Easter weekend was not only a soft target, but it was also a significant one due to the date in the Christian calendar, the school holidays, and the city being a World Heritage Site. The investigation was still ongoing, although in this case, all signs pointed to some sort of fundamentalist activity. This was the worst form of cowardice in Ray's opinion, but then—apart from Tina—very few people listened to Ray.

Especially now that Cheryl had packed her bags five months ago. But Ray didn't want to think about that either. This situation playing out outside seemed to be something a little different.

The question many people would ask—Ray included—was why a criminal gang, or OCG as they were collectively labelled, would revert to using bombs. The answer, he knew, was devastatingly simple—it was cause-and-effect logic. Even the dumbest criminal could have figured it out. And the tops of these organisations—well, they were many things, and most of those were not pleasant, but they were certainly not stupid.

The way it worked was simple. Feelings were running high against terrorist activities loosely linked to one religious faction or another, particularly after York and G-Mex.

This diverted resources from an already stretched security service and police force. So, by basic logic, if the OCG set off bombs occasionally in areas where the motive was unclear, they would gain more space to move and operate.

The last couple had been in unoccupied buildings, but with enough evidence to set the anti-terrorist branches twitching like a dog on heat. Casualties had been minimal—light scratches, compared to the York bombing, which had been far more than just a diversion. This tactic had a degree of intelligence that you could almost admire—if it wasn't a bomb. A standard diversionary tactic—a deadlier version of *Find the Lady*.

The trick was not to get caught, obviously—the stakes were too high for that. If Ray was guessing correctly, then maybe there had been a mistake, and fingers were now being pointed at the right person. Or it could be something else entirely. But the manpower deployed on this op suggested something more than trafficking or drugs. It was also not beyond logic, Ray thought, that this motorway delay was no accident. If it was an OCG intervention, they might be trying to scupper the NCA's plans—if those had been leaked.

Although that would be a new way of working and would take a lot of bollocks to complete, it didn't change the fact that he was already thinking about leaks. Also, the accidental and uncontrolled casualties would be anathema to them—or so Ray hoped. He hadn't voiced this concern to Tina yet. A late-night bomb in a comparatively soft target was easy; a coordinated accident big enough to snarl up the traffic and emergency services, perhaps not so much.

He turned his attention away from things going on in a world outside his control, stuck as he was, and for once, he was in a state similar to Tina's usual frustration at having nothing to do. As he watched, he caught sight of a slightly rumpled woman of later years exit a red car, look around, and then climb back in. Shaking his head at the things people did when they thought they were safe.

*****

5:42 pm

That old woman in the tweed I caught sight of had been a little odd, but she seemed to have started some sort of craze, as there was a bird from another car doing it now—getting out of the Mini right behind me. She had gone around the back of the van—what the fuck? She couldn't be robbing it; it was locked up tight. Probably one of those clowns who wrote shit in the dirt on the back. There were some comedians out there, occasioning a bit of humour that went beyond 'wash me'. My favourite had been, 'My wife can't wrestle, but you should see her box.'

You had to be there, I suppose. I'd have a look when I got where the van needed to be. If I got out now, it would freak the girl out, and there was every chance I wouldn't get back in once I took that first step—taking my chance with Chaz and the kids. Off down the road as if the devil himself had made an entrance.

A Hummer had now slid a few feet forward, but as it was about two hundred yards long, the driver wouldn't notice. It was pink and huge. Imagine those little people—what were they called? The ones that captured Gulliver. Imagine what they thought the first time he went for a piss and they saw his cock. That was this Hummer.

For a brief moment, a couple of over-made-up girls popped out of the massive sunroof, bottles and phones in hand. That explained it all—hen do. Fucking wasters. What had they photo'd? The flash had caught my attention. That other girl's graffiti must be good; I'd definitely have a look later. Although Chaz would go mental if the back of his van appeared on the net. I could easily deny that. What I couldn't deny was running late—but that was a problem for a little later.

Red Lights, Ignore Stop Signs

Tiff was very proud of her first car—a silver Mini and a present from her dad after she had passed her driving test. It was one of those presents that came with strings attached, but wasn't that always the way with parents? You don't get owt for nowt, or some such rubbish—that was the mantra her old man churned out regularly.

She only wished the car had Bluetooth that worked properly so synching music while driving would be seamless. Not that much of that thing laughingly called moving was happening right now. Instead, she had to use data on her phone, which would no doubt cause her some grief later when the bill came in. But what was a girl to do? She selected her favourite artist and began to sing along.

Muttering to herself, "God, I wish this traffic would move. This just sucks!" Surely, talking to herself was the last resort, she thought.

She had been late setting out for work, and now she was going to be even later arriving. She hadn't moved for at least fifteen minutes—probably even longer, if she was honest—mainly because time awareness was not one of Tiff's limited strong points. It was only a part-time job, which didn't pay much, but it helped cover the odd night at the cinema or those special iced caramel lattes she loved so much. The detour through the drive-thru Costa to pick one up for her journey to work had proved a good decision.

Now well past her boredom threshold, she decided to ring Willow. Oh, fucking hell! There was only ten per cent charge left. Rummaging through the glove compartment for her charger lead, she plugged it into the USB socket and was rewarded with the flashing icon in the top right of the screen, telling her everything was going to be okay again in her world. Well, in Tiff's rather self-centred world, anyway.

She glanced to her right and looked straight into the face of the driver of a red Ford Fiesta.

The face of an old woman stared right at her. She looked slightly deranged, thought Tiff, or on summat, and why was she staring at her like that? With a sneer she had perfected over many hours in her bedroom mirror, she gave her the middle finger.

"Mind your own fucking business, bitch."

She scrolled to Willow's number and tapped the screen. Not likely to get caught using her phone when she was sat like this, and anyway, she wasn't moving, so it was fine. But it just rang out, so it would have to be a DM.

Stuck in boring traffic. I'm gonna be waaay late. Can you make excuses? Tiffy. xxxxxx

As she was going nowhere fast, she decided to check her socials, knowing it would chew up another chunk of data. She prayed the wrinklies wouldn't kick off again when her monthly bill came in, although she knew that was as inevitable as it getting colder in winter.

They argued that if she wanted privacy, she should pay for it herself. Glancing at the iced latte, she thought, *Yeah, right—not that she would ever say it to them.*

Well, what else can I do while I'm stuck here, with nothing but an old woman staring at me and a stupid limo thing sucking in all the light behind? I mean, for God's sake, that thing is monstrous. At least she could offer her thanks for having the iced caramel latte to sustain her.

Casually flicking through screens, not caring if anyone saw her blatant disregard for the law, she couldn't help but snort when she came across a post from the group *Youandme2*. *How did I ever like this group?* When she was younger, she had worshipped them, but now she couldn't stand them. They were crap—she hated their wokeness, among other things.

Reading the latest post from one of the stupid bitches, she thought, *Who the hell cares what they think anymore?*

Tiff just couldn't help herself; her resistance was low due to the boredom. It would just have to be done—she would have to comment on their musings.

Switching to a fake account, *@tifftoffthebest...*

#Who the fuck cares anymore? Why don't you stupid bitches just disappear? Better still, do us all a favour and just drop dead! #dreamformeandyou2

There was a mild kick from doing that, and it made her feel slightly better. Washing down the anger with a mouthful of latte, topped with some spite, she was content.

What could go wrong now?

Tiff's phone lit up, and a groan escaped. It was her dad. She had better answer it; otherwise, he would only get all arsey with her later.

"Yo, pops." She knew he hated that, but he also loved her.

"Tiffany! Where are you? You didn't do your jobs. You know it's your turn to hoover and dust. You also left the dishwasher full after you said you would empty it. Your sister does it all the time—why can't you just lift a finger now and again? What excuse have you got this time?"

Tiff couldn't believe he had rung just to have a really boring dig. God, the old were a pain.

Cringing at the use of her full name—because she knew that always spelt proper trouble—she said, "Oh yeah, I forgot. I'll do it later. I'm on my way to work, but I'm stuck in a traffic jam and don't know what the hold-up is."

"Well, you had better have your jobs done by the time I get home from work tomorrow, otherwise you won't get another penny out of me!"

It always came back to money in some way.

"Okay, okay, I will. Don't stress about it." She cut the call. *God, he is so irritating.*

She took a large gulp of her coffee and turned back to the mad woman in the Fiesta, wondering why she looked so sheepish and kept glancing over her shoulder at the back of her car. Not only did she look bonkers, but she was also now acting it out. Tiff decided to ignore her for now—unless she got out, that is. That would be a different bag of bananas.

The only amusement was singing along with her playlist, watching the charge on her phone go up, and taking a few pics for her Insta account—iced caramel latte in hand, nutty woman in the background. She posed as she typed:

#Costa iced caramel latte and loony in a car—yaaay!

Taking another long glug of her coffee, she smiled into her phone camera, looking very pleased with herself.

After spending a few minutes flicking through her phone, she began to regret getting such a large coffee, as the need to pee was getting increasingly urgent. It was the story of her life—not really thinking things through. If she had thought about what went in having to come out, she wouldn't have swigged so much so quickly.

Now that she was thinking about it, the need only grew. Sod's law.

It was getting really bad, and the next song on her list didn't help. Bloody *Waterfalls* indeed.

OMG! I'll have to get out and see if there's a hedge or something I can dodge behind, she thought.

One glance was all she needed to rule a hedge out. There were some trees at the top of the grass bank, but they were miles away.

She was stuck behind a mucky white van and hemmed in by everyone else who was stuck with her.

As she watched, someone got out of the Fiesta. *No way!* she thought. *The doors are locked. I'm okay. Still need a pee, though.*

It was a different old woman. *Maybe she needs a wee as well?* Let's see what she does. It would take her mind off her bladder.

The woman was dressed like someone from one of those old black-and-white films she sometimes watched when lazing about at home.

The excitement ended when the woman got back in front of the Fiesta and started what looked like a row with the mad one.

Then the mad one pulled out a bottle of water.

Tiff thought, *Wee. Great. I'm going to have to do this…*

"Going to go for it," she said aloud.

Tiff got out and quickly scooted around to the space between the front of her car and the back of the white van. Looking around, she saw that nobody was really paying much attention to her. Nothing was moving, and she felt as invisible as she could be. The pink stretch limo still stood resplendent in the far lane, like a fat metallic worm. *Can I do this?*

This is torture! There was no other option—she had to relieve herself. As the situation was desperate, there was nothing for it; she would just have to crouch down and pee between the cars. Hoisting her skirt out of the way and pulling her knickers to the side, she let out a sigh of utter relief as she watched the steaming golden liquid stream in a slithering line towards the red car. Thankfully, the mad woman in the front was oblivious, preoccupied with the other tweedy woman.

As she crouched, she decided to write her name in the muck on the back of the van—*Tiff T 2021*. She had a quick chuckle as she finished, snapping a picture to upload later. *That was a relief! I don't know how I dared do that—I'd be disgusted if I saw anyone else doing it*, was running through her head. *Needs must*, thought Tiff as she straightened her attire and stood upright.

Her phone pinged in her hand. It felt good to be standing in the fresh air after being stuck in the car. *I might as well take advantage and stretch my legs a bit.*

It was a message from Willow. '*Tiffy T, is this you? Lol!* 😂 '

What?! She scrolled down the screen, and there it was. *Oh, my fucking God!* It was her—mid-flow, peeing in public. It was on the *YouandMe2* channel feed!

How was this possible? How the hell had those bitches done that? Someone else must have sent it to them. No—that was far too quick. *If I find out who did this, I will rip their bloody head off*, thundered through her brain like a panicking horse. She twisted her head around, scanning for anyone who might be looking at her, anyone who would get their kicks out of taking her photo while she peed.

Out of the corner of her eye, she noticed a couple of heads poking out of the top of the stupid-looking limo. She recognised one of them—it was one of those *YAM2* slags. *It was them!* They were there, and they had put the post out.

Her phone had begun pinging madly. A quick glance showed she was trending. Tiff only had the vague hope that nobody decided it would be funny to show it to her dad—that would give him something else to go on about.

She set off towards the limo. *Time to sort those cows out. I'll show them— they don't mess with Tiffany.* And for someone so conscious of the image she portrayed online, she seemed oblivious to the effect her actions were having on those around her.

*****

Tina went on alert as she saw a head appear briefly above a black saloon roof. Heading to do what was the question.

Immediately, she gave herself a bollocking. The head had been female, and unless something really weird was going on, she was no threat. Anyway, Tina thought, as she placed her hand on the stock of her Glock, it would break the boredom—and who knew, she might get to shoot something.

She looked in the mirror and saw that Ray had clocked it as well. He pursed his lips and shrugged at her, as if to say he had no idea either.

*****

5:43 pm

Now what the bloody hell was she doing? That young lass was holding her phone out and looking around. From this viewpoint, it appeared she was searching for something—or filming—or who the fuck knew?

After a few seconds, she seemed to lock onto something, and whatever it was had caused her to move quickly towards the stretch Hummer.

It was a couple of cars back and gave the impression it had a right to take over the whole outside lane. Fucking ridiculous thing—and fucking luminous pink.

What sort of mental arsehole would want to hire that, let alone buy it?

The driver of the dildo-wagon looked oblivious and only noticed the girl at the last minute, when she started shouting at the Hummer. And why the bloody hell was she taking off her shoe?

At least I had been pleasantly distracted by this little untitled drama unfolding behind me—but, as sure as eggs, my thoughts still slid quickly back to my own personal here and now.

Where Has His Luck Gone

The driver of the Hummer was as comfortable as anyone else in the jam, probably more so, and yet, despite this and the faux luxury surrounding him, he was trying his very hardest not to get annoyed by the four women in the back.

Women, he corrected himself—that was a bit of a push. They were nothing more than kids, albeit with more money than sense, all drawn from a seemingly bottomless well of imagined entitlement. Christ, he thought, he had underpants older than at least three of them. The music he had playing was designed to annoy them; after all, the stuff they normally requested and subjected him to was an insult to music.

"Tommy, can you, like, lower the volume? Me head's splitting, like. Ta very much," said one of the clones. He knew all their names but couldn't be arsed to put a face to them.

Working for them for six months had not encouraged him to change that stance. The older one he knew—that was a political act based on the fact that she was the one who paid his wages.

"Sim, I've got some painies. Here, take a couple, chicks." Clone Meghan handed the packet to clone Simone.

"No ta, Megs, I've already had some, like. It's just, like, not shifting. I hope it does soon, like, or I won't be able to go on, like."

Tommy almost ground his teeth. This sentence proved how manufactured this lot was—he could not imagine the lyrics they would write if they could, like.

"None of us will be going on if we don't get a move on. It's like those lyrics we've just heard—we are halfway there! Tommy, pet, do you know what's happening, like? What's the chuffing hold-up?" This came from the other one.

Tommy—the general dogsbody, chauffeur, gofer, and everything in-between and underneath—had, today as on most days, been given the tainted honour of driving the girl band Youandme2 to their gig. He wasn't a fan of their type of formulated pop music, but the one saving grace was that he loved driving their limo—a stretch Hummer. Sadly, it was in luminous pink, but he could largely ignore that from the inside. He would even put up with all their nonsense and poor taste in music just to be in this fantastic beast of a motor. He would drive it all day long if he was asked, so sitting still in this traffic was just as frustrating

"Can't you turn it over to the traffic updates, Tommy?" came a drawly whine from the back.

"I will in a minute. I like this track—you can't beat a bit of Bon Jovi to keep you awake at the wheel." He reached for the glass partition that separated the front from the back of the car. "That," he said as he slid it shut, "should cut the noise down."

Tommy lowered the volume on the radio slightly—he didn't want to turn it off completely. They had a bloody cheek expecting him to listen to their moronic conversations. He would rather listen to his favourite bands, so bollocks to that! He didn't hear the next comment as he cocooned himself in with the leather-clad ones.

"Urgh! It's not my cup of tea. Thank God for Spotti and pods, is all I can say."

Jade, who was the other one, sat with an obligatory phone attached, scrolling her social media, updating the fans on their every moment, trying to build the excitement leading up to the gig. This was the first leg of the new tour and the first since the restrictions of COVID-19 had been lifted.

The rehearsals had gone OK, but they were all nervous as kittens about getting back in front of fans after so long. Nervous and excited, to be honest. She didn't want to alarm fans that they might be late, so she started off a thread with a selfie of herself, glass of prosecco in hand, posing and pouting for all she was worth. She tagged it—#LovingThisLife! (But drinking sensibly lol!)♥

Trinny, their PR and a record company senior media assistant, sat quietly at the back of the limo, going through emails, calendars, and appointments, so she wasn't really listening to the exchange between the girls. This was something she had fine-tuned over the last few years, as it was very rare indeed for one of them to have anything interesting to say, but she needed to keep an ear partially dialled in, just in case.

She worked for Steve Carmichaels's company, the famous music mogul and slightly creepy Svengali. What she was, when all was said and done, was a company girl through and through, which was why she allowed herself to think that way. She dressed the part, with her sharp Ralph Lauren jacket, crisp white blouse, and high-heeled Louboutin shoes, trying to give the impression that she would not take flak from anyone.

Youandme2 were a manufactured pop group. Each of the girls had auditioned separately for *The Wow Factory* TV programme, which aimed to showcase new talent. They hadn't known each other until that fateful day when Steve appeared and pitched the three of them together after liking what he saw. A three-year recording contract, free promotion, and fifty grand each to boot was the reward! They couldn't believe their luck, and thankfully, they all got on—after a fashion.

Each had their own personality and a strong sense of independence, so it took a bit of work to suddenly be teamed up and have to consider the others' opinions, ideas and suggestions. But they rubbed along okay now. There was, however, no creative conflict, luckily, as they sang what they were told. Most of the fallouts were over fashion—usually over who had the most likes, followers and retweets.

The adage *two's company, three's a crowd* occasionally raised its ugly head. Trinny had her work cut out sporadically, but that was what she was paid for. If this thing worked out, she would make a sum that would put the money these three had received into the realms of pocket change—which was why she was a company girl.

"Jade, you know you said you would run everything by me first, remember? We have to protect your name and the company's ethics. Show me." She had to do occasional checks in case one of the young fools ever believed they were something they would never be. At least for five years.

"It's nothing much, Trin, just a harmless pic and caption. It's soooo boring being stuck here, and I'm nervous about tonight." Although Jade looked down as she said this.

Trinny's thoughts were preoccupied with concerns about whether the roadies had arrived, whether the stage was set up, and whether everything else was ready so they could just do the sound checks. She wasn't sure what time they would get there, but it wasn't looking too good. The updates on the news channel she was monitoring were forecasting long delays, which might even end in cancellation—but she would keep that to herself.

"I hope we've got a full house tonight. Like, since they eased the Covid restrictions, it'll be like old times. I've almost forgotten what it was like before. I can't wait for things to be normal again," said Simone, who, if things had been normal, would be back serving pints in a low-end public house.

"Me too, Sim. I'm getting a bit nervous 'n all. What if the fans have abandoned us? Fans can be so, you know—what's the word? Err, fickle. Who knows, they could easily have changed their taste in music since the lockdowns." This came from Meg, who had been on the dole before being plucked, primped, primed, and dumped into the limelight.

"Ah! We'll be alright, judging by the number of followers we have and the likes we get when we post stuff," Jade said, busy flicking through her phone, not looking up as she spoke.

Jade was the only one who had had a career prior to stardom—albeit as a clerk in a council housing office.

"OMG! Girls, we are being trolled. I can't believe it."

Disbelief loomed large on Jade's face as she frantically scrolled through the comments on Instagram, Twitter, and Facebook. Since the initial abusive comment, it seemed as if the world had woken up and suddenly everyone was hating on them. Darkness erupted on the six-inch HD screens—a darkness that had been waiting for an excuse to open a door and pour itself all over the lives of these three young girls.

"You should see this. The nasty comments on here have gone mental—wow. The comments are trending, not the gig, but the troll stuff. Trinny, stop it, for fuck's sake." Jade could not keep the panic out of her voice.

"Take no notice, Jade," said Meghan. "You know what these keyboard warriors are like. The thing is not to be hot-headed. If you answer, you'll regret it."

"B-b-b-but…it's just so awful. Someone on here has called you a really awful racist name and called Sim…well, see for yourself." She handed the phone to Simone.

This couldn't be happening. How could one stupid, inane comment result in a torrent of unsavoury, racist, and abusive messages?

Simone, you fat cunt, you've got thighs like beer barrels. Why don't you get yourself to a fat farm and sort yourself out? #youandme2shit @lippyjoyko…

Why does Meg straighten her hair? Is she trying to pass as white? We all know the bitch is a half-black bastard! #youandme2shit @loxylou124…

You're a bunch of talentless, toneless, pointless no-marks. You are so shit! #youandme2shit @pentelasue…

"What's wrong with, like, people? Have they got, like, nothing better to do?"

Simone was distraught. No one had openly called her out about her weight before. Okay, she wasn't the skinniest in the group, but c'mon—she wasn't *that* fat. She read some more of the comments, her mouth moving with the words, reading the occasional one out loud—only the really bad ones.

"Stop it. This is awful, Sim; I don't want to hear any more. What are we gonna do about it?" said Meghan.

"Jade, you're quiet—you haven't said anything."

"I'm trying to understand—why all this now? Just as we're about to have the first concert since the restrictions were lifted, you'd think people would be glad to be getting back to normal. There are some real sickos out there—and not just with Covid!" She was trying to be pragmatic—or would be if she understood the word.

"Well, it's alright for *you*, Jade," said Simone. "I don't notice any abuse about *you*, like—the perfect white, skinny girl!"

"C'mon, Sim," said Meg, trying to ease the situation. "You know you're just mad at the trolls. Like, there's no need to take it out on Jade."

"Well, I'm sorry, like, but you've got to admit it. Jade *does* consider herself a cut above us, like—she always has to do the talking during interviews and always pushes herself to the front during photoshoots. It's like she's saying, *I'm the lead, and don't you forget it.*"

It was enough to have Tommy grinding his teeth—or would have been if he had not been blissfully unaware in the front.

"Look," said Trinny, "just calm down, girls. There's no point in getting at each other's throats. If you implode now, those stupid trolls have won. You've got to rise above it. Why don't you open the sunroof and let some light and air in? See if you can spot what's going on while you're out there—and leave off posting stuff! I'll get someone onto it."

Trinny pushed the button, and the full-length glass roof started to slide out of the way. In a bizarre attempt to distract them, it was like rolling a ball in front of some puppies. It also lowered the temperature—figuratively and literally.

Taking a deep breath, Jade stood up, raised her head above the sunroof, and glanced around. Oh God—this traffic jam was worse than she had thought.

"This bloody traffic goes on for, like, miles. Aww, we're never gonna get there!" Simone had popped up beside her and was doing a full three-sixty. She nudged Jade and said, "Look over there, past the red car."

Jade sniggered and reached for her phone.

"Fucking hell, Sim, would ya dare?" The pair of them burst out laughing at the diminutive figure crouched down between a silver Mini and a scruffy white van, appearing to be having a wee.

"I've got to get a pic of this!" She clicked away. The two girls just creased. Jade plonked herself back down on the seat and frantically posted the shot of the public pisser, adding:

#*Do you know this person? Seems some people have no shame whatever! Come on, girl, where's your self-respect? #Crymeariverofpee.*

It was almost as if she had forgotten the previous few minutes and was determined to achieve a new level of stupidity.

Trinny sat with pursed lips, showing her displeasure. "What's going on with the pair of you? You were at each other's throats a minute ago."

"Oh, just a bit of harmless bants, Trin. Chill out."

Trinny saw the post, and it was as if her whole world had suddenly imploded. These stupid young fools thought this was all funny. They were supposed to be a family-friendly act—the teen girl sensation. A band your nan could listen to.

Something that could be shown on TV before the watershed. That silly little bitch had just posted a picture of a young girl urinating.

The comments were flowing in, and Trinny nearly laughed to herself at the pun. The personal attacks earlier were common and easier to manage, but this had opened a whole new can of worms. This was getting comments from mainstream media, even from promoters and sponsors. Steve would be going ballistic.

As Trinny glanced out of the tinted windows, she saw the object of the post heading their way. She had taken her shoe off and had started to beat the crap out of one of the windows, tears of humiliation streaming down her face. *I know how you feel, love,* thought Trinny.

Tommy saw the young lass, and when she started belting his beloved limo, he decided to intervene. Slowly getting out, he started to move towards her. The young girl spotted him, stopped mid-shoe strike, and looked at him directly.

"Do you work for these shits?"

"I do," he replied with slight trepidation.

"They have just destroyed my life. I hope they all die."

With that, she took her tear-stained face back towards her silver Mini, throwing occasional venomous glances over her shoulder. At one point, she turned and started to make her way back to them.

Bemused, Tommy got back in the Hummer, lowering the window, about to ask what that was all about, but before he could, all hell broke loose in the back. So much for his peace and quiet. He raised the glass partition again and turned up Planet Rock, secure in the isolation bubble of the armoured limo, knowing he wouldn't have to listen to the catfight in the back.

*****

5:44 pm

Christ, the bloke was a tank. He had got out of the Hummer and talked to the young girl with the shoe. I can't believe the looks the girl gave the slab, but it all ended in some sort of standoff. I would love to know what that was all about, but the big gadge had got back in the car.

The lack of movement and the deep feeling of inevitability about the next half an hour or so meant I spent a few minutes being a lot more chilled. I was taking more notice of my surroundings than I had when I'd been on autopilot, debating the problem.

After all, being realistic, Chaz and his meatheads would not hurt my kids—what would be the point? I would get there eventually, and as they say, no harm, no foul. If Chaz did harm them, then it would mean I'd be knocking on the five-oh's door quicker than you could say it.

If I squinted my eyes nearly closed, the red lights up ahead took on the form of red tracks. There was no need for autopilot with these tracks to follow. The tracks continued on their journey like an ironic, legless centipede, their final destination unknown for the moment. Was this my course, my route? Would this be the final culmination of this shit existence?

I had heard somewhere that this van was owned by Chaz's old man's freight company, but I strongly doubted that was true—it would be bloody stupid. Also, an insult to Chaz's old man. The van would be nicked, but the plates might belong to the company—a clone job—and therefore completely deniable. Easier to just clone some plates and nick a van.

I couldn't imagine Chaz having to explain to his dad why one of his vans was involved in a crime. I could have added *allegedly*, but there was no doubt the contents would be on the north side of dodgy. The panto I had played a part in, just to get the van from the lock-up in Leeds to this point, only emphasised the dodginess.

I tried to formulate my excuses and how I could explain to Chaz about the repercussions of the jam, as that was a conversation that *would* happen—albeit later rather than sooner. Being stuck as I was, the whole plan about taking my phone proved how stupid that was. Which was not something Chaz was renowned for—the actions he had taken to get it to this place relatively simply proved it and showed the amount of effort Chaz would expend to achieve whatever this *was*.

That was the track I was stuck on—a red one. One with a world of pain if I was caught and a bigger one, possibly, if I didn't complete the task.

Another one of those weird shuffles took place outside. Things moved about a bit—some of them familiar, some fresh faces to view. Another Beemer had pulled in-between the motorised phallus and the back of my van.

The sour-faced woman at the wheel caught my eye. I tried a smile, and she looked straight through me. *Bitch.*

Six Days and All Alone

I wasn't worried an hour ago, but now it appears I may miss my deadline. Miss Hotshot Reviewer, the influencer in the arts who spent all these years living a spectacularly secular life, is going to miss a deadline. Never happened before. Been close but never happened. As they say, not on my watch. Then I go and get stuck in this rubbish. The only option is that I may have to resort to the old-fashioned method of phoning it in.

Yes, girl, it may come to that. Girl, who am I kidding? Only myself. And what is the point of that? Anyway, Lisa, old friend, it's time to sharpen up your ideas! Who can I think of in the office that can take dictation over the phone these days? Tim? Liv? Mand? All of them, probably, but who can I trust to get all the inferences behind the words and not change something because they think I may be a little caustic or they want to exercise their wokeness? OK, where are my draft notes?

There, that solves one problem. I can get the words in my head straight and then phone it in—still a few minutes until the deadline. I know they all call me the witch, the ice queen, and a lot worse, no doubt, behind my back. When I started out, you had to be all of those things—a woman in a predominantly men's club. Nowadays, you can get away with a sunny personality and the ability to bounce around a screen like you were on springs. Or drugs.

Which, judging by the office dos I've been dragged into, was more than quite likely. They call themselves influencers, but influencing people by advertising for payment is not influence—it's blatant coercion in my mind. I offer an informed opinion. I can make or break anything—from a play, an artist, or a band through to a book or publication. Also, no payment, apart from my salary, passes to me. Just as well, really, as I can't see myself gaining many product placements or endorsements.

Those years as a food and restaurant critic served me well. Making and breaking reputations and eating well was a pretty rewarding existence. The arts stuff had sort of fallen into my lap and added a pleasant, if somewhat occasionally painful, diversion to food—and was considerably better for the waistline. Travelling the world is a thing of the past now, and I don't miss it. There is enough for me to do in my home environment. Keeps me busy enough to avoid cobwebs growing.

Reflecting on this was not getting me anywhere. Have I got the words I need? Obviously. Can I put them in the right order? Always the challenge and never the chore. OK, here goes.

"The Patron, main desk. Tim speaking. How can I help you?" chirped out the Gen Z drawl of one of the people I wanted. The BMW's speakers generated it in perfect clarity.

"Tim, it's Lisa. I just called…" I began.

"Hi, Lisa, we were just talking about you. We need your seven hundred for the theatre ASAP. We haven't got anything we can fill with."

And no hint of an apology for cutting across her.

"Tim, I know, that's why I am ringing. I'm stuck in really bad traffic. I've got the notes here. We will have to do this old-school," Lisa explained with all the patience of a mother.

"Old-school?" A pique of interest, his accent slipping slightly back to his roots. You can take the boy out of Sheffield, etcetera.

"Dictation over the phone." Lisa thought of the old music hall joke.

"Did they really do that?" The note of disbelief was not hidden at all.

Seriously? Oh, the naivety of youth. "Yes, Tim, it was how most of it was done. Before computers, you know."

"God, that is, like, really, really long ago." The disbelief still there.

Thanks, Tim, I needed to be reminded about my age about as much as I needed to have a Brazilian wax and labia piercings. "So, can we do it?"

"I suppose. I am just off out, but Mand is still here, and she is better on a keyboard than I am—quicker, anyway." The spirit of friendly competition had not been fully replaced in this century, it would seem.

"Can you ask her for me or put her on?" Just in case he had not thought he needed to do it.

There was an audible click before I was greeted with the unmistakably Mancunian and distinctly bouncy, "Yo, Lis, what's up?"

"Yo yourself, Mand. If I dictate, can you take my copy for the run? It's only about seven hundred, so should be fairly quick." Which may be repetition, but I was not actually sure what Tim had asked.

"Never done it before, but how hard can it be? How does it work?" Not much, it seems.

"I will just tell you what to type. I will tell you to stop at the end of each sentence. New para is as it sounds. Any odd words, I will spell out. Does that work for you?" See Spot Run. Cruel but accurate.

"Yep, let me get some headphones and sort my desk out. Will give you a call back in five," Mand responded, completely missing the patronisation.

The phone rang seven minutes later.

"Hi, Mand, you're late," attempting a weak joke, although my inflexion didn't sound as light to me as it should have done.

"Sorry, was just seeing if there were any other oldies about who knew about this way. There isn't, and oh, I got a drink," the bouncy one pronounced.

"Oldies, really? And you will need coffee for the next bit, so good idea." I realised that I needed her, so better keep it sweet.

"Nah, no coffee. Good old-fashioned health drink," Mand offered.

The picture of something green, gloopy, and vaguely sinister was my first thought, but then in our trade, it was just as likely to be something packed full of sugar and caffeine and called Geronimo or something equally inane. Parking that image, I suggested we start.

"Fire away. Ready when you are," came the chirpy reply.

"OK—title is A Soldier's View. No, scratch that. Trench Warfare? Question mark? That's better."

I wasn't used to editing on the hoof, so this was new.

I was rewarded with the click and tap of a keyboard.

"Sorry, before we go any further, Lis, what font and size do you want? Standard justi?" which followed the cessation of the clicking.

"Calibri, eleven, and yes, with double. The print guys will sort it from that." I had forgotten the technicalities, as I would normally have just submitted my own e-copy and that would be it.

"OK, let's go!" came the overenthusiastic instruction.

"A review of *Entrenched*, directed by James Gillespie at the Scorton Community Theatre."

"The centenary commemorating the end of the First World War has now passed, yet there are still events and offerings springing up as new material emerges—a butterfly with poppy red wings. The formats and venues will vary and might still inspire deeper thought and reflection."

"No, delete *inspiration*, Mand. Replace with *reflection*," I added.

"Got it," squeaked Mand.

She appeared to be keeping up and showing a level of skill that I had not anticipated, so I continued. "And in some cases, a more educated understanding of the conflict. Stop. I have seen many performances in the past five years, and the latest is titled 'Entrenched', by James Gillespie, a work based on the diaries of his great-grandfather stop."

"These diaries were revealed in an episode of open speech Antiques Roadshow close speech last year stop They depicted his grandfathers' actions comma thoughts comma and exploits in the trenches of Northern France from 1915 to 1917 comma from which he returned comma injured comma to his family stop."

"New para. I assume for maximum effect comma the director comma decided that the diaries would be best presented as a monologue comma the scenery comprising simply of three very large white screens set at slight angles to the performer stop My assumption was the performance would have some form of visual element supporting it stop."

"As the audience and I took our seats the screens were displaying a classic scene of poppies in a field comma presumably depicting Northern France comma which would be apt considering the subject matter stop My initial thought being that the visuals would change as the delivery unfolded giving a sensory support to the delivery from the narrator stop That assumption would be shattered as they were not changed once comma narrowing the focus therefore to the performer and the quality of the material stop. How are we doing Mand?"

"All fine." Still as lively as ten minutes ago.

"New para. The performance itself comma was well delivered by Alan Williams comma a young actor who I believe will have a promising future stop The intonation and nuances in the structure could be a tool for almost any subject matter or quality material stop That is the qualification comma the material in this instance whilst clearly of interest and value to the family is quite frankly dull stop

"This is not to denigrate the bravery of any of the characters referenced or to try and gloss over the horrors of the events stop This felt like the Edwardian version of Twitter stop All that was missing was open speech Today I ate a biscuit dash LOL close speech stop The stories depicted were naïve and shed only a little light on the daily activities of men in the trench comma but they had no depth or innovation of content stop

"There was nothing in this work that has not been produced before or that would be beyond even a limited imagination stop I could develop no empathy or emotional attachment to the narrator and began to doubt the veracity of the events themselves stop I wanted to see some of the famous humour comma a bit of Spike Milligan dash I know it was a different war but if you read his memoirs then you get a view of warfare that has that humour and a developed level of humanity stop"

"Two secs, Mand, just going to have to concentrate on the traffic a little, as it's moving and people are looking at me and gesturing." The traffic had moved in its sludge-like manner, doing one of those odd little shuffles that happen in jams, and there was a largish gap in front of me.

The blue Audi indicated and pulled in. Like you're going to get there any quicker, you idiot. I pulled up behind him, just as a Volvo, I think, and a small hatchback did the same behind me. I was pointedly trying to ignore the giant pink monstrosity to my right. Ah well, back to business.

"Hi Mand, back, sorry about that some clown wanted to get five yards nearer home. New para. The addition of some music could have helped comma if it supported the visuals that should have been part of the backdrop comma even the introduction of an interval would have helped stop Perhaps the reason for this last omission was the attrition rate could have been as high as the Somme judging by the amount of shuffling and fidgeting going on around me stop"

"After two hours of watching a poppy still-life comma listening to a professional and proficient delivery of some very dull adventures comma and I mean very dull comma the case of the missing socks being one in point stop I reached the conclusion that perhaps all this commemorative action has now run its course comma and perhaps at risk of sounding treasonous comma some of it should never have even seen the course comma let alone ride along it stop Nearly there Mand."

"It's okay, this—quite good fun, really." Followed by an energy drink-fuelled giggle.

Oh god, the simple pleasures of being so young.

"New para. My advice to James Gillespie would be comma whilst your relative was obviously a very brave and loved man comma his life is not necessarily one for sharing with an audience in this fashion stop There could be a good piece of work buried in the material comma if only it was repurposed possibly as a narrative poem stop If that is the case then despite my reservation's comma the delivery from Alan Williams could tempt me back stop Otherwise comma I would not recommend it stop That's it, does it sound ok?"

Not that I needed confirmation from a hyper Gen-Zer.

"Your usual style, Lis, no holds barred." Which didn't sound like an insult.

"It was very dull, Mand, but there was a glimmer of something. Can you read it back for me, please?" Not that I mistrusted her typing. Well, actually, yes, because I probably did.

Mand read back the words that I had pretty much blurted out based on some loose scribblings clutched in my left hand. I made one change. The line—"from which he returned, injured, to his family."—became—"Luckily, though injured, he managed to return to his loving family."

"OK, word count."

"Just about bang on. I'll get the setters to check, but it shouldn't be a problem. I don't know how you do it." And was that a little note of genuine admiration wrapped up in that statement?

"Long in the tooth. OK, send it—that'll keep the EIC off my back for a while." I didn't want to thank her, as that was not me, but I would in person should I ever get into the office.

"Will do. Take care, Lis. See you in the office sometime."

The call ended, and I was left back in the world of traffic, giving me time to contemplate a job well done, a job hinting at times past. Cocooned in my Beemer, comfort surrounding me, I was back to being alone. A brief foray into the world of the workplace would satisfy any cravings I had for interaction. I was back where I needed to be—self-sufficient, reliant on nothing but myself. I wondered about my fellow road users and what their level of human contact was.

They probably all had families or significant others—whatever the phrase is nowadays. I could see several on the phone, talking to them, I presumed, and they had probably assumed I was doing the same. The bloke in the grey Beemer, similar to mine, was on a call, giving him a look of happiness and amazement or something. One of his kids probably wrote his name in custard or something. I shouldn't mock—at least they had someone to care about.

What have I got? At least I wouldn't have to write my own epitaph, though I would like a review rather than some deep and meaningful parable. I wonder what would be on it?

Lisa proved the pen was just as mighty as the sword, but she had no trouble sticking both in if needed.

Ah well, we won't dwell on that. Tomorrow is another day. I have a production of *Carmen* to see—an alternative interpretation, apparently, with dance. Oh, joy.

I had drawn level with a tatty white van, and in my determination not to look at the pink thing, I could see the driver of the van. He caught my eye, and in what could only be described as a contortion attempt—was that a smile? I ignored him, as he was only a van driver, and who in the hell has the remotest interest in them?

*****

Tina was thinking of a conversation she had shared with Ray—what seemed like days ago but was, in fact, less than three hours. They had stopped at a service station at the top of the M6, as the Audi they were following had decided it wanted to. They had pulled in next to each other, positioned to see the Audi and its driver, who had gone off in search of whatever he needed from the services.

They weren't too worried about him running away—after all, they knew who he was and where he worked and lived, so picking him up wouldn't be the most taxing thing in the world. They couldn't leave the drugs, though, as that was guaranteed to get them new arseholes torn if they lost them while grabbing a coffee or a burger in Southwaite.

"How's Chris?" Ray said, breaking the silence as he opened his car window. Neither of them had taken their eyes off the target vehicle now parked up in front of them.

This meant that Tina had her passenger window down and would have to raise her voice to be heard, but it was a necessity in case it was a switch, and they needed to be ready to move quickly. The Armed Response Vehicle allocated to them was parked up behind some trees and not visible—they didn't want to spook any potential watchers.

"Gone, mate. Probably with Cheryl, ha." Tina could not hide her bitterness.

"Wouldn't wish that on Chris. She was alright." And neither could Ray.

"Yeah, well, doing this job tends to make you a bad choice for a lover. Which is pretty much what she said on the way out," Tina said with a tight smile.

"There must be a manual, as Cheryl said the same—or emailed the same, anyway."

Ray looked at Tina, trying to gauge how much she actually knew. He had never told her this, and yet there had been rumours around the office.

"I couldn't believe that twenty years of marriage ended by email. That is cruel, Ray."

So, she did know, thought Ray, and yet had not said anything. That was Tina all over—she would support you through anything if you asked, but otherwise, she did not want to get involved in anything too personal. Ray was usually grateful. As they were stuck here for a few minutes at least, perhaps they could talk about it now.

"It was the York bomb that was the camel thing, I think. The clampdown on comms meant she was trying to reach me and couldn't, and it broke her." This was true; it was also the culmination of twenty-five-plus years of perceived neglect.

"Still cruel, mate." Tina looked at Ray as she said this, trying to work out how hurt he really was—not that she would do much about it. She understood the concepts of empathy and sympathy, and the dictionary definitions. It was the practice of either that she struggled with.

"Yep. Anyway, that's one of the reasons I think this lot may be planning another explosion for a distraction," Ray said, moving the conversation away from his marriage. He knew now that he didn't want to talk to anyone about it.

Tina raised an eyebrow in what could only be called a quizzical manner. "Cheryl leaving you?" She added a smile to let Ray know she was taking the piss.

"Ha bloody ha. Just the size of the op and the secrecy. I have been known to be wrong, though." As he said this, he wondered how right he was, and it frightened him. After all, the Audi they were tailing might not have drugs in it at all—it could be something far nastier.

"No doubt we'll find out soon enough if your expanding gut has got it right—either we take down matey-boy there, or we get called out to help somewhere else." *This was the type of simple logic that Tina worked to,* Ray thought, *Tina did the other stuff, which is why they worked so well as a partnership.* "True, true, and it's not expanded that much. Still got the same waist trousers I had twenty-five years ago." He sucked his gut in as if he was trying to prove it to his partner, ignoring the fact that his action just made it look like he was farting.

"That's what elastic is for, Ray." She shot out with her trademark snorty laugh. "What do you know about him?" Tina flapped a hand generally in the direction of the blue Audi.

"Good job, no record, not even a traffic offence. The car is his dad's, as he doesn't even own one. Still lives with him, in fact. Long-term relationship with his girlfriend is what got him under our care, according to the gen." Again, had Tina been listening at the briefing, she would already know this.

"Do you know her?" Tina asked, with a hint that she knew something Ray didn't.

"Alice Riggs? No. Her record is clean as well, but intel points at a cocaine habit, and that's how she fell into problems with the OCG. Also, according to my mate, it's possible we have someone on the inside—which might explain the details we have about matey over there, and all the rest of it." He nodded in the direction of Matt Connors, who was now strolling back to the Audi with what looked like a Greggs bag and a can of pop in his hands.

"And him being a white knight—or in love or something—is now driving his dad's car, full of coke, to a meeting with a drug lord. He doesn't fit the normal county lines profile."

Which, as Tina said this, Ray knew was very true, and again, he felt he was missing something.

"No, but he'd fall under most radars—two-year-old car, late twenties, good job, lives in a nice area. So, not a normal profile, no, but then, if we're right, he has over one hundred kilos of pure coke in there."

This was a result in itself—but add the rest of the team they were following, and you had over a tonne of the stuff.

"Do you think he knows? Or knows that we know?" Tina was watching the car as it sat in the car park, doing very, very little. The only movement was one that indicated Connors was enjoying the fruits of his forage in the services.

"I don't think so. He's acting pretty normal and hasn't tried to evade us," Ray pointed out, though he had a nagging suspicion. Because Connors was such a normal target, he might have been set up to be far more than a coke runner.

But in fact, Tina and Ray could be following the means for the gang to cause their distraction.

This was something Ray was not going to share.

As Tina thought about this, she wondered if she was seeing it all. One of the things she allowed was for Ray to think she hadn't been listening. The truth was, she had been half-listening at the briefing and only needed Ray to repeat it so she could fill in any potential blanks.

The reason she was feeling a bit perturbed by this conversation was that she couldn't help but think Ray was holding something back—which was most unlike him. She amended that statement in her head. It was most unlike him when it came to work. Personal? Well, if she was honest, he could keep it all under his elasticated belt as far as she was concerned.

Tina went back to watching the Audi and the shifting scenery around her. Her headlights automatically came on as dusk continued to fall. She wondered why nobody had thought to disable this. If you were on a stakeout, there was no more obvious an announcement than your lights suddenly coming on.

It was too late now—Connors would have, or certainly should have, seen the momentary flick.

Although, going by the smoke coming out of the Audi window, she doubted he was paying much attention.

*****

5:45 pm

There was always that question of what had caused Chaz to slither out of the dark place he normally dwelt in, cohabiting with that other creep. What was his name? Sounded like a hat, but more Russian. People might look at a city at night and see all the lights, but what they don't see is the dark.

The dark makes up ninety-nine per cent of what fills your vision as you gaze out, thinking how pretty it looks. The dark is where things like Chaz hide until you aren't watching or the world sleeps. I wondered what had placed me back on his radar.

The thought of fight or flight kept popping up without a care, but that option was not open to me now, if it ever was, as I was stuck here. The only real option was to watch the clock tick down and make a show of compliance. After all, Chaz and his minions had grabbed my ex-wife and kids after telling me to drive a van to a car park that I knew would be shut in fifteen minutes.

Had I been on time, the kids would have been returned, and I could only hope that a similar fate would occur if I arrived late. Yet, that darkness had sucked me in again, and this time I was so far down its gullet that only a very big finger was going to get me vomited back into the light.

My thoughts were skittering around like one of those fish that lived and danced within the arms of an anemone. I was frightened to touch one and see what it was about, as every thought seemed to draw me further into the darkness of imminent doom.

Shaking my head, I noticed a large SUV that looked like a Lexus, but, to be fair, could have been one of many brands. The only real distinguishing fact was that it was being driven by a chauffeur—without a hat—but you could tell he was a pro driver, as why else would the other gadge be sat in the back looking like all the cares of the world had disappeared? He must be important, I thought, some business honcho who could afford a Parker.

A momentary distraction from the blackness that was enveloping me, threatening to pull my very world apart.

With The World Still Turning

There was a strong chance, judging by the traffic, that the first book signing I hadn't been able to finagle my way out of was going to be a no-go. That was ironic and, to be honest, a relief, as I hated the idea of these things. But being tied into my latest contract meant my pound of flesh was taken in the form of attendance.

Listening to all the platitudes and praise was so not my scene—it was bad enough by email and social media. A fellow author, who had been to many, told me that live fans were even worse, confronting you as if it was their right. They would have to get over the shock of meeting me first, which could have been a bigger smokescreen than it appeared on paper. If they managed that, I was sure they would then share their own insights into the story and characters.

It was as if these people thought I just made it up without putting any thought or effort into ensuring the series held together. I mean, if it was that easy, why the hell didn't they leave me alone and put their own scribblings down? Most of them would have to buy some new crayons first and upgrade their *My First Dictionary* if what I heard was true.

I knew I sounded unfair, but I had put fifteen years of my life and soul into these books, making sure there were no discrepancies, no blatant errors for critics to jump on—"I thought Pete died in the second book," or "How can the rulers pass that rule in book four when, in book six, they plainly break their own rules?"

It made me wish they would just send me some money to cover the royalties, leave my books in peace, and get a life. Look at what happened in the last series of *GoT*—absolutely panned, probably by those who thought it was a documentary. Or those who believed *Love Island* was a true reflection of how everyone else lived and wondered why they had missed out. Not that I had anything against them or the series, I just wished they would keep it to themselves—I didn't need to hear about it.

The sharing thing would be fine if it wasn't just pedantry or, in some cases, downright idiocy. Fandom—who the hell thought that was a good invention? I was sure Charles Dickens didn't have the problem of some Victorian lady telling him he had used the wrong ingredients in gruel for Dotheboys Hall or something similar. I supposed, if I was honest, I should be more than a little grateful—it had paid the bills and much, much more.

If I wasn't going to make it to the chain bookstore in time—and I was due there in an hour—the lack of forward movement and the array of red lights ahead, like Satan's pearl necklace, suggested a timely arrival was highly unlikely. My driver—oh yes, I had a driver—was either tutting or sighing frequently, a verbal counterpoint of annoyance to my secret happiness.

A happiness born of not having to reveal myself at last, plus not having to answer tomfool questions. One of the perks I most enjoyed was having a driver, though this guy wasn't my regular. His oral tics—sigh, sigh, tut, tut, sigh—were a new contrast to my thought process.

I could use my time more constructively. Opening my laptop, I stared at the Word document that was going to cause a shitstorm of hate mail. It would, however, set me free—even if it meant living in a fortified, guarded house for the rest of my days.

This was like wondering what would have happened to J.K. Rowling if Voldemort had won. That was the crux of my dilemma. I wanted to end it, didn't I? The series had gone as far as it could possibly go. The seventh and final book was complete apart from the last few chapters. The alternative endings were written, and in reality, I only had to make the decision. The publishers would bleat a bit, but they had taken their percentage—they could go hang.

The reason I had reached this parlous state was simple. If I was honest with myself, I was bored with the whole story. The creation of the words was fantastic, but the world I had fashioned now invoked tedium.

I had started it as a sort of laugh, a challenge to the writing fraternity. Could I, a middle-aged white northern male, construct a story from the perspective of a young girl? It had been done before and no doubt would be done again, but those who knew me would have bet their mortgages on me being unable to achieve any semblance of believability or even a smidge of credibility. I had picked up the tarnished gauntlet and created Clare and her alternate identity, H, as part of a dystopian world—a world that dealt with the suppression of women's rights by a minority in a brutal fashion. Morally and ethically questionable, it was *sort of* a *Handmaid's Tale* scenario, but not quite—it was my take on the mad world of dystopia.

Surprisingly, my peers had enjoyed it. Then the rest of the world appeared to accept it as well. Nobody was more gobsmacked than me when I was asked for the second and third books. Thus encouraged, I had taken my heroine on a journey through some dark adventures, raising, I hoped, some pertinent issues—all through the eyes of a teenage girl.

The feedback from the public was huge and strange in equal measure. I was getting fan mail from every flavour of reader. The most poignant came from teenage girls who related to Clare and the issues she raised.

I became complacent when they asked for another set of three. I had created the *Sanctuary* series—yes, *that* one—and nobody apart from a few select people knew.

It was a secret. It had been written under the pseudonym Paula Cassidy. Despite the best efforts of the press and fans, nobody had tracked me down. At one point, during the launch of the third book, the publishers had even hired a stand-in who seemed to satisfy all the chasers. When she—or rather, *I*, by proxy—requested privacy, it seemed to have worked. Or maybe something else had caught their eye out the window. Who knew?

The entire six-book set had just been released as a limited-edition box set—a none-too-subtle advertising ploy for the next one. The one I was sitting in the back of this… Jag? Lexus? Volvo? You know, I didn't have a clue. The driver was called Tim, though.

Back to the dilemma—I was bored with Clare. I could end on another adventure, but then a clamour would start for the next one. I wasn't sure I had that in me.

Not only was I toying with killing her off—the final act of rebellion by the heroine—but I had written the final chapters with that heretical act in mind. I knew this would cause pain to the readers. They all related to her as if she was real.

Therein lay the problem—she *wasn't* real. So, she couldn't really die. If someone wanted to create another scenario and bring her back, let them. I would offer no objections—just accept the royalties.

In an attempt to avoid flipping a coin, I decided to ask Tim for his thoughts.

"Tim, can I ask you a question?" I caught his eyes in the mirror.

"Course you can, Mr Castle. Not sure I can answer, but I've nothing else to do at the moment." A look of genuine amazement appeared in his eyes.

"It's Paul please, none of that mister nonsense, and that makes two of us. Ok you know what I do for a living?" Just in case he hadn't been told or indeed had ignored the brief.

"I was told you were an author, and that's why we are off to the bookshop signing in Sheffield," Tim answered meekly. Giving the impression that he knew how a hired driver should respond and would play that part to the full, although I noticed he didn't use the sir bit during the exchange, which was a relief.

"That's right. They didn't tell you anything more than that."

To be fair, how much more would he need to know? It was not like he was going to feed me and needed to know about any allergies or whether I had any peculiar riders for being a celeb. I don't, by the way.

"Nope." There was a tightening around the eyes, indicating Tim was worried about his professionalism being questioned or whether a test was forthcoming.

"Well, I'm going to tell you something that very few people know. Then I'm going to ask your advice. Have you heard of Paula Cassidy? The *Sanctuary* books?" Just in case he had been living under a rock—you never know.

"Have I! It's all my daughters go on about. They have them all and are already pestering for the new one. Do you know her?" That was the standard response if I ever brought up the books in company, polite or otherwise.

"Yes, Tim, very well, in fact. I'm Paula Cassidy." A thing that only five other people knew—six if you count me. The temptation here was to compare this to a *Spartacus* moment—after all, I was a slave to the publishers and Clare.

"You are fu...kidding!"

His eyes went wide in the mirror, nearly producing a turn-round-in-the-seat type of action, which, as we were still not moving, carried minimal risk—apart from him slipping a disc or giving himself a hernia. He managed to check himself, though.

"No, definitely me. You have now joined a club of around five or six people, and you didn't even have to sign anything. Anyway, it may not matter soon," I said with no pathos at all.

"If you don't mind me asking, how did you get away with that?" Tim asked. A question I often asked myself—not just about the anonymity but the whole kit and kaboodle.

"I don't mind. Mainly by luck and a bit of advertising skulduggery. Do you remember that interview a few years back? Well, the author was a fake—I was answering the questions for her via an earpiece." That had been fun in a bizarre and slightly fetishistic sort of way.

"Wow, well, it certainly fooled a lot of people." A note of admiration in his voice, which had not necessarily transferred to his eyes. He was probably wondering what I was going to ask him.

"It bought me some space and peace of mind. It all started as a drunken bet. You wouldn't have known that, would you, as the inspiration I gave—or rather, my doppelganger did—was to help young girls and all that entails. Now look at it—it has become a monster. Film rights, one already in production. I have a team of six who answer all the mails and letters. Not what I had in mind at all." That was as truthful a statement as I had ever been—either with anyone else or, indeed, myself.

"You've done all right, though. There won't be many on this road who have a driver," Tim offered, with a certain amount of pride, I think.

"Yep, it's done me well. But now for the advice." My mind was shouting at me not to do this, as I didn't know Tim from Tom or Adam, and he could go running to the press as soon as he had dropped me off.

"Go on, then. Still not sure what use I'll be." His eyes gave nothing away.

"As you say, your daughters are all over the books and will be with the films as well. So, you are my focus group. I'll value your opinion, as you don't know me and won't just be paying the lip service I normally get. I won't be offended by the answer—I am just curious and have a dilemma. You see, Tim, I am thinking of killing Clare off and ending the series with the seventh book." And there it was. From a club of a handful, my driver was now in a club of two.

"Woah. Wasn't expecting that. Can I think for a minute?" The shock was plain to see.

"Of course."

I watched his eyes in the mirror, showing a faint flaring of shock, etched in a red glow from all the brake lights around us. I could imagine he was doubting my sanity and wondering what he would tell his daughters—how he could console them. Then, being a cynic, I thought he might be calculating how much he could sell his story for. I wouldn't blame him. It could be a big payday for a bloke who was driving overinflated egos like mine around the country. I glanced out of the window, contemplating my fellow road users for a few moments.

I was sure they didn't realise the momentous decision being made a few yards away. Then again, it was the death of a fictional character—one that had rewarded its creator very well. It was hardly a decision to invade Europe or to assassinate Prince Charles. In reality, it was important to me—and several million young girls who identified with her. They'd get over it.

"OK, Mr Castle, I think I can answer you." No giveaway in tone or expression.

"Paul, please. And go on, then." I was genuinely interested to see if he came up with the usual flannel—the type I would expect from the sycophants that orbited Paula Cassidy.

"I think you are right. If you don't, then you risk it all becoming stale. At least nobody will see this coming. You may upset a lot of people, but as they don't know who you are, what does it matter?" Not the answer I expected—nor one that lacked insight. Maybe I wasn't such a bad judge of audiences.

"I may become more well-known if I do." A concern I had to admit to myself.

"That's true, Paul, but I am sure there will be something else along pretty quickly. It's like Pokémon when I was young—came, went, and then bizarrely came back again. So, if it was me, don't have her definitely killed—just possibly killed. Leave that door open, for, you know, a return at some point." This guy should be my editor.

"Tim, that is the best advice anyone has given me for ages. Thank you. I can just amend the last few lines. I would also appreciate it if you could keep this under your hat for a few weeks. I know it's a great story for the papers, but if you wait for the proper announcement, then you can sell a story yourself—how you were driving me when the decision was made and who I was, etcetera." Not that it mattered, but it would be nice.

"I wouldn't do that, Paul." And I believed him.

"No, I am telling you to. I have more brass than I know what to do with. Why shouldn't you make some off the possible death of Clare? She would appreciate the irony." If she were real.

The car lapsed back into silence. I amended the last few lines to a possible death. I couldn't take my eyes off the pages in front of me, reading and rereading the final passages of someone who, while not existing, had been with me for a third of my life. I could feel a godlike power over Clare, if I was so inclined.

It was more of a sadness, really—a necessary action to let her slip into a possible death and me to regain my life. I read the last few chapters of *The Awakening of Artemis* again. The capture and trial resulted in the ultimate sanction: to be erased from history, if not consciousness. I could almost feel the weight being lifted. It was like coming out to your parents and friends. *Yes, I am Paula Cassidy, and what can you do about it?*

The next day

The slam of wood hitting wood wakes Clare fully. She has glimpsed a face she will never see again. A face she doesn't know now, nor ever will. Then comes the rhythmic thud of a hammer, closely followed by an earthy thunk, repeated less rhythmically, like an out-of-time jazz drummer.

This is the musical backdrop as the casket is buried. There is still a tint of lemon in her nostrils—was she drugged? Her aching head is at least supported by a soft pillow. She can feel the diary tucked behind her in the plastic bag she had saved from her lunch earlier, preserving her thoughts and ideas for those yet to come. Tadum, tadum—her heart accompanying the sounds from above.

Tadum, tadum. Calming her breathing, she can feel her blood sliding around her body like sauce over pasta. Tadum, tadum. There is no sound other than her heart now. Tadum, tadum, tadum. Clare's right arm disappears into a hole and appears to be fastened at the wrist. Her vision is non-existent, so she would be guessing. Tadum, tadum, tadum, tadum.

A panic settles in her stomach like an undercooked dumpling—one you are aware of, hoping it subsides naturally. Tadum, tadum, tadum, tadum, tadum. The panic rises, a swirling sensation, like a child doing a random finger painting. A kid's painting—ironic considering why she was being punished. This is a Judgement Box, as proscribed by the Goodman, designed to remove all hope like a two-day-old mayfly without a mate.

Another warm hand slips into her trapped one. Tadum, tadum, tadum, tadum, tadum, tadum.

"Who's that?" Clare almost screamed.

A familiar voice replied, "Clare, it's me, Evie."

Tadum, tadum, tadum, tadum, tadum.

"Evie, you weren't part of the judgement?"

"This is the price of my failure."

"That is so wrong. This is my fault, Evie."

"The Goodmen don't need a reason to punish, just an opportunity."

There was silence for a moment, her heartbeat calming as Evie's own pulsed in Clare's fingers. Tadum. Tadum. A sadness descended on Clare and Evie, like a ten-day-old party decoration—the ones she had read about—as they reflected on the pain caused by that one simple crime, the lives that would now be lost to the law.

The liquid crept over her feet. Tadum, tadum, tadum, tadum, tadum. This was the final part of the sentence.

"They are really doing this. Why the drowning?"

"Because it is the Goodmen's way to show that they won't be defied. They are cleansing us of our sins in their eyes. Our deaths will be remembered, though, and we will become legends."

Came the calm voice attached to her wrist.

"Famous?"

"They have broken a rebel and think it won't be spread; we aren't the first, and not the last. Love you, Artemis."

Tadum. Tadum.

Clare's final thought as the water reached her head, and the warm hand slipped from her grasp, that second heartbeat taken away, was that she would like to take a few more breaths, to hear a few more heartbeats, to see the sun again take its first view of the day, and to hear the trees begin their dawn song.

"I don't want to be Artemis; I want to be me."

Tadum…

No more pondering—I wasn't going to make this blessed book signing. It was also highly unlikely I would be invited to many more once this was published. Putting on my metaphorical tin hat, crossing anything I could, I saved the file one more time, typed a quick mail to Ollie, my editor, explaining my literary-induced suicide, attached the full manuscript, and hit send.

Goodbye, Clare, and God bless.

*****

5:46 pm

The SUV had slipped out of my line of vision, the view now blocked by a van mirroring my own—in that it was a van. It was in better condition and had logos, indicating the corporate nature of its identity. It was being driven by a black or brown guy, or whatever the current woke name was, but this guy looked happy with his lot, so colour didn't matter.

The logo on the van informed me, and therefore the world, that it contained drug supplies. I do wonder at the sense of this, as surely it was like painting a target on it for all those in my fraternity to rob it. I can't help but smile, thinking that my van was probably crammed with drug supplies as well, but not the ones you could get on a prescription.

It was a feeling—but for one brief moment, it was like I had found a kindred spirit in this other van driver. I couldn't explain it, and I wondered if the other man had a family and was separated from them as well. Perhaps that was it. I doubted my new brown road pal was going through what was happening in my world, but you never knew, did you?

Anyway, the guy wouldn't look so damned happy if he was in my situation. I will stick to my own brand of misery, casually flicking my eyes and smiling at the guy in the other van.

They Let You Bleed

Since the first day he had arrived in this country, Haroon had been in awe of the traffic. There were busy times in Dhuusamareeb, his hometown—his old hometown, that was, he corrected himself. The traffic was usually caused by Habib's goats getting out or, in the worst case, if Al-Shabab were carrying out their poisonous road checks.

Here in the UK, there were only the devil's hours when the roads would be what would pass as quiet. Those hours between midnight and four were the ones when Haroon felt most comfortable driving his van, his job only allowing those sojourns sporadically. The odd thing was, he felt less lonely at these times, even though there were fewer people around. It was as if he felt more in touch with the world as he now knew it. "This traffic is a symbol of the infidel's arrogance" was no doubt what Al-Shabab would have said.

Haroon had lived above his little pharmacy shop, which would be considered a Somali success in most of his neighbours' eyes. It was a business he ran with his wife, Samiya—not that he advertised this fact, for reasons that included safety and keeping the eyes of the warlords firmly looking elsewhere. They had been comfortable—or as comfortable as they could be in Somalia.

Then the war came. It was no longer a fireside story; it was there in the town. And all of a sudden, he no longer had a pharmacy. His whole life was now a crater. Haroon and Samiya were left with their clothes and about a million Somali shillings in notes, which he later found out was worth about two thousand dollars.

Luckily, Haroon had also deposited about fifty thousand dollars with his uncle in Addis—money he had worked hard for over the last ten years, along with a small inheritance from a relative. They had no other option. Loaded with water and some loaves of bread, they set off on the long walk away from the only home they knew. They heard rumours on their journey that Al-Shabab had targeted their town because it was said to be harbouring Christians.

Haroon was Muslim, so he understood the vitriol pouring out of the warlords, but he didn't agree with them and paid only lip service to some of the more fevered and emotional pronouncements. After all, he was an educated man. He had a degree in pharmacology, and his wife, while not formally educated, was more than capable of holding her own in debates—the ones they had often had over tea in the evening. Haroon missed those lamplit, effusive discussions.

They walked steadily in the direction of the border with Ethiopia, aiming to get to Addis Ababa and his uncle Farooq. They would be able to plan from there. The walk wasn't that long, as they used some of their precious cash on a bus or two, keeping enough back for a bribe if they needed it at the border.

Haroon had an Ethiopian passport as well as a Somali one due to his studies in Addis, so he had been allowed to pass easily, and ten thousand shillings—around twenty dollars—secured Samiya's passage as well. Even so, this small delay caused them to miss the bus to Addis. The next one was scheduled a day or two later, so they had to wait nervously. The longer they stayed in one place, the higher the chance that someone would pay attention to them.

The trip to Addis took three days, and they formed a few new opinions on chickens as they travelled cheek-by-beak with them. They spent as little as they could, as the last contact with Farooq had been about six months earlier. Being profligate with their cash now would be suicidal if Farooq was not there. However, when they arrived at his house, Farooq greeted them openly and warmly. The news of the war spreading had already reached him, and his affection appeared genuine.

A day or two to recover—wandering the streets of Addis, trying to formulate a plan—was cut short when his uncle suddenly became a little evasive. The reason soon became clear when Haroon, over tea one evening, explained he would need his cash so they could set up in Addis, possibly buy into a small pharmacy. Farooq, to his credit, admitted he had only about a third of the cash. The rest, he said, he had sent to his wife's cousin, Ashraf, in the UK, as it would be safer there—less prone to cash flow problems in the Ethiopian banking system.

Being a calm man, Haroon had not overreacted. This made a kind of sense, and while disappointing, it meant a plan would have to be made to sort it out. Farooq explained that a transfer to Ethiopia was not possible at the moment. He suggested they might want to go to the UK to get it back, and who knew? They could live there and not have to worry again about Al-Shabab, civil war, and corrupt banking systems.

As plans went, this was maybe the best they had. Farooq gave Haroon around seventeen thousand dollars and generously paid for two tickets on the train to Cairo. Haroon considered this an attempt to ease his guilt over sending the rest of the money away but accepted the peace offering at face value. Saving face was very important to his uncle.

Samiya and Haroon left Addis on a train that was supposed to depart at five in the morning but, after a long and sweaty delay, finally left at ten seventeen. They bought a few clothes in a market and borrowed a suitcase from Farooq. A red rucksack that Samiya carried contained their passports, the sponsorship forms from Ashraf, and a few meagre supplies for the journey. Haroon had secreted their money about his body in small bundles of one-hundred-dollar notes.

The journey was comfortable this time, as they were in second class, which surprised Haroon—he hadn't expected his uncle's generosity to stretch that far. He offered a quick prayer to Allah in thanks for not having to share space with any feathered travellers. They were relatively untroubled, and another small bribe at the border with Egypt—paraded as an administration fee for the visa stamp in their passports—was the only notable event. There was little to see apart from the occasional glimpse of the stately, slow-moving Nile as it meandered northwards, mirroring their journey but without having to pay any bribes or squat over a hole in the carriage floor.

Their troubles really started when they got to Cairo. A phone call to Farooq informed Haroon that Ashraf was still in the UK. Even though he hadn't spoken to him, the news was good. Unfortunately, onward travel to Europe was impossible. Single fares were not for sale, even with a bribe, which was highly unusual. The return fares were more costly than they could afford.

Then, a surprisingly helpful member of the ticketing staff at the ferry in Alexandria told them that Samiya's passport would not get her out of Egypt. This was due to the breakdown of Somali government departments and the knock-on effect on the issue of travel documents. In fact, they were deemed fake. Haroon would be fine with his Ethiopian one.

They had no option but to go back and lose everything—or try to buy passage with people smugglers. The latter would take most of their remaining dollars, and Haroon had always poured scorn on the idea. He knew the lands of Europe were not paved with gold and that the citizens there would not be throwing euros at them in joyful celebration of their arrival.

He knew that qualified people from Somalia and Ethiopia—in fact, most of Africa—headed to Europe when they secured jobs. That was Haroon's only hope. He was a pharmacist, and even though his degree certificate was now a pile of ash, there must be a way to prove it.

Farooq's brother's nephew, Mushie, put them in touch with a contact who could help. Haroon had paid ten thousand dollars for the privilege of sitting in a smelly fishing boat with Samiya and around forty others, only to be dumped unceremoniously on a beach in Greece. They were among the desperate and endured some of the worst days of their previously relatively sheltered lives.

Samiya lost weight and was starting to look unwell, and Haroon thought he wouldn't have looked much better. He didn't want to dwell too much on the journey across the sea or the onward travel to the northern French coast. He would only ever tell his story once, and that would be to a border official in the UK. The rest of the nightmare he stayed silent about.

His passport was the key—he could travel to the UK as he had a sponsor, but Samiya couldn't. They could stay in France, but how would they survive without their money? They had long arguments about this. Despite her health, Samiya was insistent that he go ahead and then, once in the UK, find a way to get her across.

So, Haroon had left her in a refugee camp with some other women, a cheap mobile phone, and a thousand dollars stitched into her skirt. He had boarded a train as a legitimate traveller, buying a return ticket just in case. The letter of sponsorship from Ashraf was safely stored with his passport and the remainder of his cash.

The agents at the UK border were pleasant to Haroon—an attitude he hadn't expected, given the human tide breaking on the country's shores. He had lied, claiming he was a Copt who had been persecuted. There was no questioning of his religion, only acceptance. They grilled him and queried his sponsor; Ashraf spoke to them and confirmed the sponsorship. This gave him the right to stay for a while.

The fact that he had several thousand dollars seemed to work in his favour, as they could see he wouldn't be a drain or, hopefully, want anything. Once he was on UK soil, he met a charity worker who advised him on what he needed to do to get Samiya over. He was armed with forms and a list of numbers to call when he was ready to submit them. They were going to help him fill them in.

Haroon had headed to Leeds on a train—with no chickens this time—though it was very expensive and confusing when he had to change in London. He had spent several hours going round and round on the Underground, such a marvellous invention, until he arrived at Kings Cross.

Samiya was still okay, though her tension came through even in her SMS messages. This only spurred Haroon on to get settled and submit the paperwork. His determination drove him onwards. He could tackle anything in this strange new country if he had Samiya with him. Ashraf met him off the train.

Haroon struggled with the size of the city at first. The cultural differences were easy to spot, and it was freezing. Ashraf made good on the money, taking him into a bank and sorting it all out so that Haroon had an account in his name, with a card to withdraw cash from a machine. This, the charity worker said, would also reflect well with the Immigration Service.

Ashraf let Haroon stay with him for the first few weeks until he could find a job. Haroon constantly worried about Samiya, but she reassured him that she was feeling a lot better and that they would be together soon. Haroon offered up many prayers to this effect.

Despite an excellent grasp of English and a degree in pharmacology, he struggled to get a job as a pharmacist because he couldn't prove his qualifications, and Addis University's records were not reliable. None of this helped Haroon. The best he could do was take a job as a driver for a company supplying chemist shops with drugs. The irony wasn't lost on him. The charity said this was another positive and helped him with the forms. He had asked how long the process would take, and they said it could take up to six months.

Six months. Haroon did not have the words to express his devastation at this turn of events, but what could he do? He accepted Samiya's tears and wore them as his own when he told her. All he could do was get somewhere to live, work hard and offer up his prayers.

His faith, to a certain extent, was rewarded. His employer gave him more and more work, with longer and longer journeys, realising his trustworthiness. He found a small flat in Burley and, with Ashraf's help, furnished it. He had money in the bank, the right to reside, and, according to the charity, had done everything possible. The only thing missing now was Samiya.

Sitting in his van, day after day in the British traffic mess, gave Haroon time to reflect. His journey—and Samiya's—was still running its course. If he had been a dishonest man, he could have sold all the drugs in his van and funded a people smuggler to get Samiya over. But he was devout and honest; he would rather struggle than spend the rest of his life looking over his shoulder in the UK. This was a journey to safety.

The petition had finally been approved; he had heard the news from the charity that very morning.

It had taken nearly eighteen months, during which time Haroon sent money to Samiya so she could live in a house with some others just outside Boulogne. He knew she was safe and fed, and he had tried to keep his frustration wrapped up tightly. Finally, his patience and prayers were rewarded. Samiya had been given leave to travel to be with him as his wife. The call had rendered him speechless, as he had been nearly at the end of his hope. The prayers he offered had finally been answered, and his work for the mosque and charities around Leeds had borne fruit.

On Monday, he would take a day off to meet Samiya in Dover. She would be setting foot in the UK legally, and they could continue life's journey together again. He had tried to contact her earlier, but there had been no response. He would try again when he stopped. At the moment, the traffic was stationary, and he was surrounded by the melting pot of humanity that congregates on a motorway. He wouldn't use his phone while driving, not even to text, though his impatience to speak to Samiya nearly broke him.

But the looks from some of his fellow travellers—the guy in the old army truck, the white van—told him to wait. The big pink thing made him shake his head. It was not something you saw every day, not even in his present, and it would be another story to share with Samiya.

*****

5:47 pm

Once this horror film—starring me—was over, the one I would make sure had no sequel, I was going to take the kids away with Lizzie to try and repair some of the damage this darkness had caused. Or—and this was the more likely outcome—I was going to consume enough alcohol to make me flammable. Holding on to that thought almost made me smile. Either scenario was good, though the idea of Lizzie coming near me with a fag almost made me giggle—completely inappropriate, considering.

Was it Churchill—the man, not the insurance company—who blathered on about a black dog? Not a clue, really, but something was in my head about it. Lizzie would know, no doubt, and take great pleasure in pointing out my lack of learning.

But now, I could share some kinship with him. My own black dog was here, waiting to pounce—not a cuddly Lab or a designer hipster Cockapoo, but a Rottweiler with Chaz's face. Lurking, sneaking, circling my kids, ready to snap and devour, tearing them into only so many constituent parts and lumps of DNA.

My part in the creation of something good in this world was completely removed and scattered to rot without anyone to mourn. This dilemma was taking me to places that I hadn't thought about since getting with Lizzie. And I would be buggered if I was going to let Chaz or his avatar dog, tear anything up of mine.

There would be no dog, no devouring, there would only be a happy colourful place that if he could describe it would look like Disney or DreamWorks had vomited their entire palettes up at once. This was not going to be a black dog day. Unlike the guy who was wearing his knackered-looking Skoda as if he was surrounded by a pack of them.

As The Headache Fades

Glancing around him, Syd realises that even though he is stuck in this awful jam, rather ironically, it would seem that he has finally turned the last bend on his long journey to where he is now. It has been a journey six years in the making and has caused more pain than he wants to contemplate. He knows his right to continue on his way can be revoked easily, like a visa in an unstable country.

That's what he is—a volatile government that is lasting well but could be deposed at any point by one slip. A slip that should be in his control but may well fall foul of outside influences.

When he was at his worst, he was so bad he didn't realise how awful he was. His peripheral vision was not only misty but completely obscured by clouds—a myopia caused by the bottle, eyewear created by the bottom of a pint glass. The dependency had crept up on him gradually. He knew he was unhappy when it started and blamed it on everything: his job, his finances, his family, the dog, the bloke in the shop—anything but where the blame really lay.

Yes, he hated it. He had managed to hold onto a relationship, which, over the years, had never failed to amaze him. How his wife had, and still does, put up with him is beyond his ken. Even though he didn't like where they lived, they were stuck unless he did something about it, and that was unlikely to change.

Luckily, they had not wanted kids yet, so at least he had spared them his despondency and internal dislike. Thank everything that is sacred for small mercies, he had thought at the time. Perhaps now they could talk about that. First things first. He smiled as he imagined that conversation with the true hero in his life.

The woman in the black Beemer had caught his eye earlier. She was engrossed in a call by the looks of things, although whoever she was talking to didn't appear to be able to get a word in edgeways. Either that, or she was inflating her own importance by talking to herself, he thought. Takes all sorts. Probably wants to look busy so everyone marvels at her success. Silly bitch, he thought. Although he did wonder what she would think if she watched him. Wouldn't even notice him, Syd thought, and why would she?

He was an alcoholic who was now six years clean, and he was as proud of that as he had been of anything, he mused. He would never have thought it possible—an impossible attainment for someone who had made it his mission in life to try and keep Diageo's shares afloat.

The blue flashing lights of an ambulance caught his eye. It was stuck in the emergency lane behind a broken-down or abandoned car. The driver of the ambulance was trying to negotiate a way back in, but the motorway was packed, making it difficult for drivers to respond, even if they wanted to. Poor sod, Syd thought. That could have been me all those years ago. His reason for being, for such a long time, had been at the bottom of a bottle, and he had done his best to finish as many of them as possible.

The final hospital emergency admission had been the first step on this journey. Waking and seeing a glimmer of love and a whole bucket of worry in his wife's face had been the catalyst. Mentally, he doffed his cap to the occupant of the ambulance and wished him luck on his own journey.

This day for Syd had been more than a good one; it had been one of those that you write up as a truly momentous occasion—the type of day that people only experience a couple of times in their lives. The type of day you would have written home about when we still did such things. It had been that extraordinary.

A few weeks ago, Syd had applied for a job—one that was his dream role, and not a dream when he was in his cups. A Project Manager working with the NHS in the community. He had believed it would be an instant rejection; he didn't have most of the essentials and had padded out his CV. Not lied exactly, but he had become familiar with a definition of exaggeration.

A video interview had then taken place, as the current times dictated. First of the shocks—whatever he had said must have chimed with the guys interviewing him, as he had moved on to a face-to-face interview, which, until a few short hours ago, he had been in.

The experience he did have was sort of relevant but would not stand up to too much scrutiny. Luckily, they had focussed on him and his personality—something he had maintained even when he was at the worst of his addiction. He had also managed to keep a clean driving licence—another one of those things in the box marked *miracles*—and he would never be able to explain it. The number of times he would have been over the limit didn't bear thinking about.

Try every day for three years, and that would be about right—and very, very close to the truth. At the end of the interview, they had all but told him he had the job. They must have been keen, as within ninety minutes, they had called him and verbally offered him the role. He would double his salary, have better hours, and a whole lot more job satisfaction. Perhaps this was his reward for his sobriety. Perhaps they could now move, and he could talk to his wife about the kids thing?

The day was so joyous, despite the creeping darkness outside and the light drizzle that fell, that Syd was singing along with a rock radio station. He didn't even notice that the tracks were flicking between misogyny, drugs, depression and drinking—all things that would normally have caused a channel change. But hey, he was determined to enjoy the day.

He cast his mind back to the AA meetings he had attended and pondered how surprising it was that more of the attendees didn't turn back to the bottle, given some of the crap they spouted. He was particularly amused by the story of Judas—he was sure that wasn't his name—who had collared him at the tea table.

It had gone something along the lines of:

"The world could be flat, couldn't it? For instance, the rule that you can't fold a piece of paper more than eight times until it reaches its critical foldiness also applies to a map of the world, right? An astronaut takes a picture, and it just looks flat. Okay, it's round, but it is flat. Perhaps it is one big cosmic joke, and we are spinning like a coin, flicked by God so we look around yet are still flat. God is using the earth coin to answer the dilemma of how he managed to create a species so thick they think the earth is round."

Syd hadn't been able to answer or add much to Judas's thinking, but it did make him chuckle, and he had used it at one of the no-drink suppers his wife organised.

There were a lot of conspiracy theorists at the AA meetings. The most bizarre was Tom, who had also collared Syd at the tea table—a popular method, it would appear. He had told him that he knew he was really a dinosaur but had escaped extinction when the lizard kings saved him. Tom was waiting for the lizard kings to return and take over again.

Seriously, Syd had mused, this was why people drank. There should be a government harm warning on the meeting leaflets.

Now Syd could start planning for a better future—a much brighter future. One where he would have to wear shades, and not because he was hungover.

He remembered the night this journey to well-being had started. The memories were slightly unclear, but he recalled the dream he had been having. He had never told anyone, not even the denizens of the tea table at AA. He had been dreaming that the world had been invaded by tubs of margarine—lots of them, with little arms and legs and beady eyes on stalks coming out of the lids.

They were hunting him, and their little yellow mouths were shouting, "We will find you, Syd, and then we will be free."

That was the last he had recollected until he was brought back to reality in the A&E booth, where a tube was stuck down his throat and the contents of his stomach had moved so quickly, as if to distance themselves from him in embarrassment. Then his journey had commenced, and the final corner had been turned to a rosy, sunlit life.

"Hi, babe, sorry, not back yet—stuck in traffic."

His wife answered in a few seconds.

"That's okay. How did it go?" came an excited, gaspy question from the speakers.

"I thought it went okay, and it must have." He was not going to hang her out there—not only was it cruel, but she deserved the truth.

"What do you mean?" A cautious note of excitement was apparent.

"They sort of indicated at the end and then confirmed about an hour later on the phone. I got the job, babe." He could picture the smile that would now be building on Millie's face.

"Oh, Syd, that's bloody great. I am so proud of you for everything." And this was no lie—he could hear it in the statement.

"And I can only thank you again for sticking by me and believing in me." That was a bigger truth than he had ever really alluded to, and more than she would ever know.

"I love you, you clown. It hasn't been easy, but the last few years made it worth it. Now look at you—sober, a new job, and a drop-dead sexy wife to come home to." The pride came over the connection in waves.

Laughing, he said, "I love you too. I should be back in an hour if this starts moving, and then we can start planning. Going to call Mam now—she'll want to know." He didn't want to end the call.

"OK, darling, see you soon and take care. This is a really good day."

And she was gone—but not really, because this was their first faltering step towards a bright new life. There were days when he still felt the pull, when a bottle called to him, tempting him back to his old life. Those days usually came when he was stressed, depressed, or stuck in a traffic jam or a queue.

But here he was, in the worst of those situations, and stress was almost a given. Yet, he didn't feel it, because of the call with Millie and because he now truly believed. There would be days, no doubt, when that feeling might return, but this moment—this place, this precise time—would sustain him in the darkness should it come.

Disconnecting, Syd was about to call his mother and tell her his news when he glanced out of his window. The red light gave everything a slightly surreal and demonic effect. The pink stretch Hummer with the tinted windows caught his eye again. Earlier, he had watched one of those drinking visions of his past, as a young girl appeared to abandon her silver Mini and approach the monstrosity. At the time, he had wondered what could be going on here and whether he should offer any help.

The human instinct to avoid getting involved had kicked in, and Syd looked the other way. He would keep half an eye out in case he needed to play the Samaritan. A van nearby was clearly overloaded—it was sagging so low it almost wallowed against the tarmac. Not my problem either, he thought. He may have been sober, but he only had the energy and drive to focus on himself and Millie now. He turned his mind back to the wonderful woman he was married to and the future that was now theirs to take and run with—an opportunity that, six years ago, he would not have considered possible until that day he made the decision to be sober and to live.

*****

Tina didn't believe in existential crises—or existential anything. She believed in herself, and things were either right or wrong. Even if, on the odd occasion, something was wrong, then it was also right, because she put all her faith in believing it was right.

It was a simple theory, but it allowed her to do a job that required certainty of action to flourish. If you allowed doubt in, you would either lose the arrest or end up like her ex-partner—in a wheelchair. Or dead.

The fact that she now had doubts was something she was not prepared to deal with, and she was used to her innate certainty in her actions. They had crept up during various chats with Ray, all because she had detected something in what he was saying that wasn't right. There was something he wasn't saying.

This, in itself, was not unusual—Ray had a secretive side. But when it came to work, he would normally expound on anything and everything. He was not a keeper of secrets, was Ray. This was why Tina was glad he was taking his retirement, even though he had not yet plucked up the courage to talk to her about it. So, the fact that she felt he was holding something back was now playing on her mind.

What was it? That was the question. Their objective was fairly simple—see the car, follow the car, don't lose the car. When instructed, they would end it all by arresting the driver and seizing the contents of the Audi. It was simple, in no way complicated. It was what they did day in, day out. And yet something about it was troubling Ray.

He had mentioned the diversionary explosion a few times, hadn't he? And then, as if Ray had come up behind her and twonked her on the back of the head with a hammer, she thought she had it.

*****

5:48 pm

With a flick of my eyes to the left, I was drawn to the blue flashing lights still trying to move stubbornly down the inside emergency lane—one of many I had seen today. The reason for my interest in this one was unclear. Was it to do with the delay, or was it something else? At least it had broken the palette of red, white, and orange and hopefully signalled things moving along soon. Straining to glimpse through a gap between the two modern-day dinosaurs—the behemoths of the motorway that were hogging the road ahead—I could see that the ambulance had stopped a little way ahead.

"Bet something, or some arsehole, is blocking the lane, trying to be bloody clever because they think they're so important. Feel sorry for the poor bastard in the ambulance," escaped from my mouth. The glare from the lights added to the pain I was already feeling in my head, magnifying it and turning it into something entirely visceral.

I wondered what the risk would be if I tried to get over there and follow behind the ambulance, but getting all these others to move for a ropey old van would probably be too much. Add in the fact that I was an arsehole—but not that type of arsehole. My ex-wife would attest to that.

So Here We Are Just the Three of You

So here I am—yes, definitely here, and it's definitely me. Or I think it is. I suppose the question is valid, as I have no idea who else it could be. The only problem is that I'm not sure where I am, so how can I be me if I cannot nail down that specificity?

There are no clues to my location. It appears to be a small white room, complete with what looks like an oak desk and a black leather-looking chair tucked up under it.

A weird two-tone alarm sounds somewhere in the distance, but the Doppler effect makes it difficult to judge either direction or distance. This is punctuated by a beeping and wheezing noise that, on the face of it, seems to be coming from me. Since that is too strange, I will ignore it for now.

This space has no windows, filled only with a weird sense of unutterable silence—at least, I can hear nothing other than the distant alarm and the unidentified wheezy, beeping noise coming from somewhere close to or inside me. There also appear to be no discernible odours, unless my olfactory sense has gone into hiding along with my ability to work out where I am.

Lifting my hand to my face to conduct a simple experiment, I sniffed. It didn't smell of anything. Was that conclusive proof? I wasn't sure what odour my hand should exude in the first place, so scientifically, it was slightly flawed. I heard the sniff, so I was definitely not deaf.

"Hello," I said. No—I heard that as well. Unless it was in my head, which, as a thought, I quickly filed away in the drawer marked *not going there*. I needed to cling to the hope that all the other extraneous noises were outside and not go all *woo-woo* on myself. Based on the evidence I could present, I was possibly olfactorily challenged but not aurally. I was spatially unaware. And I was scared.

There was a feeling that I had only just noticed—nausea. Saliva was absent from my mouth, so vomit was not imminent, if I remembered the process of evacuation correctly. Then I corrected myself: I genuinely could not feel anything. Nothing at all.

I lifted the hand I had previously sniffed, put the side of it in my mouth, and bit down. There was no pain. The room spun—or did it? Since I now knew I could feel nothing, how would I know?

As I was contemplating this, trying to force myself to wake up, the wall opposite me shimmered briefly, causing me more consternation. I knew this did not happen in the real world—whatever that was.

There was a door, a regular industrial-looking door, designed to stop fire, with one of those little windows, complete with safety glass. There was no door handle. This in itself was not unusual—I'd seen thousands of them in my time. What threw me was the manner of its sudden arrival.

There was no reflection in the glass, which gave me no idea what I looked like. So I still wasn't sure if it was me. I had no explanation for my reflective absence other than *vampire*—which was nonsense—or *dreaming*, which might not be.

What was that wailing noise? And could you hear things in dreams? I couldn't remember.

The last thing I remembered before this was being fairly confident, for some reason, that it hadn't been long ago. Then it came flooding back. I was there—I could see myself. I was walking in a graveyard, along a gravel path, listening to music on some wireless earphones. Subconsciously, I checked for the earbuds. They weren't there.

I was listening to a song most wouldn't associate with my age group—*Gone Away* by Five Finger Death Punch. Why this memory was so clear, I couldn't comprehend.

When all my other memories seemed to flit around like the fantasy fairies in those faked Victorian photos, I knew one thing for certain: I was visiting my father's grave. Dead for five years. Probably communing with all the other clan members who were reposing and decomposing there. Although what was on my mind at that point, I had no idea. No matter how hard I tried, I couldn't pin it down.

I remembered rain and strong wind. I recalled seeing a flash of red out of the corner of my eye—a plastic bag, perhaps. A piece of human jetsam. I wasn't concerned with that. I was more worried about this piece of human flotsam.

That was my last memory—

That hillside graveyard.

The weather.

A song.

A plastic bag.

Children! I had children—two? No, three. But try as I might, I couldn't find their names in my brain. At least I knew they existed. Maybe if I tried to forget them, I would remember their names. That trick sometimes worked.

To distract myself, I turned to the small window in the door.

A corridor was all I could see, with a similar-looking door opposite—this one with no face at the window, which would have seriously freaked me out. Or, if I was honest, further freaked me out.

To the left, a short corridor painted a very pale blue—like the best quality duck egg—led to a small set of stairs rising at the far reaches of my view.

To the right, a similar passage, this one painted a very pale green—like the palest emerald—ended in a void. I wouldn't be wrong in assuming a downward set of steps. Applying logical rules that defied my current setting—because the human mind only lets you see what you *think* should be there—ergo, there must be steps.

Where the two passageways met, there was a seamless transition from one colour to the next. It was an effect an interior designer would approve of.

Where was that siren coming from?

Judgement time, Chris.

Hang on—that must be inside me.

A voice. Or two? A tangled, audible overlay.

But nobody was with me in the room.

Turning from the door, I saw a shimmering mass appearing beside the desk.

A sort of green, sort of grey, sort of blue—then a deep pink. A misfiring palette. A broken kaleidoscope performing a badly choreographed dance.

The voices again. But in my head.

This is your last day.

What the bloody hell?

We will want you to recount your life, Chris.

I mean—what the fuck?

Parents, came the voice/voices.

A pad and pen had appeared on the desk.

My brain kicked in and even though religion was not a part of my life, the stairs now made a kind of sense.

I was being judged.

Not by the angels of the Bible, but by something that might have come from a low-budget sci-fi CGI effort.

So, either I was having a breakdown of some sort, or this was really happening.

What harm could it do?

It was in my head.

Nobody needed to know about it.

I pulled out the chair. It should have made a noise against the industrial-looking floor, but for some reason, it smoothly glided in my hand—further confirming that this was a dream. Or, at worst, some sort of breakdown.

The pen felt real.

As I sat, the chair was the most comfortable I had ever experienced. If I got the chance, I might find out who made it. I wouldn't mind one of these in my own office.

There was what could only be called a *supernatural* throat-clearing.

The message was clear.

They, he, she, me, it—whatever the thing was—wanted me to get on with it.

Why that question first? Perhaps it was because they were here first, before me—my ultimate point of creation—and therefore, they took precedence. Maybe it was because it was the hardest part of most people's relationships and was at the core of who you were or what you would become.

So also, the hardest. To be honest, my father was a bully, and my mother didn't notice. I had the unhappy experience of being bullied at school and then going home for it to continue. Not the psychological stuff that kids get all worked up about today, but the full-on physical abuse that scarred not only your body but your mind. Not sure why my dad did it—perhaps growing up without a father made him act that way.

It was just me, completely bypassing my sisters, even though I would admit that I wasn't the most well-behaved kid. But I don't think I deserved being beaten black and blue. So much so that I used to skive off games if it was bad or blame it on rugby training if I could get away with it. I was ten years old, for fuck's sake. To be honest, it took me until my late thirties to stand up to him. I could have battered him at any point after I turned fourteen but wanted to save my mum the embarrassment.

In hindsight, I blame her as much as him, and I'm quite glad he's dead now, as the physical stopped, but the mental carried on until he died. So, good riddance, Dad. I looked down at the paper and, without realising it, I had written this all down in my own scratty script. So that was my first question answered for the amorphous mass, wasn't it? I put the pen down, wondering if it was strictly necessary—if this was inside my head, then surely I could will my thoughts onto the paper. The pen, in one of those poof moments, disappeared in front of my eyes. So that was how it worked.

'Family is next', said the voices.

I have never liked my family. I got on with one or two of them, but to be frank, if I never saw them again, it would be too soon. Not my kids, though—I know they are okay as far as people go. Gem, Matt, and Coral. I remember their names now, though only Gem and Matt ever lived with me. Two diverse sets of genes—the diametric of my family branches—could not be more different and never more apparent. The Scouse ones just seemed intent on breeding. There are more first and second cousins than I could count, or would ever bother to remember. It was like having a replicator. Most of them will be dead by the time they hit sixty, though, as they all smoked like chimneys. The Scottish ones—fewer of them, but more insidious.

My cousin Euan tried to fondle my younger sister. I lamped him, told my parents, wasn't believed, and got a beating from my dad. Is it any wonder I hated the whole mess of them? I exacted my prosaic revenge on Euan fifty years later—got him drunk at my dad's funeral and then reported him for drink-driving. Bang goes his marriage and his hard-earned respectability. Well done, me.

Another cousin tried to rip my dad off when he was dying, and I gave her short shrift. Even though I hated him, she wasn't taking advantage of my mum—no fucking way. As I said, they were far more insidious. So, does that answer the question? Yes, I have a family, but I fail to see their influence beyond a mild one. Yes, a negative one—my anger, which probably came out elsewhere, but no doubt we will get to that.

I noticed that the first sheet had disappeared. Concentrating on the last one, it started to fade and then, with a slight pop, it went, taking my projected thoughts with it. A new one appeared in front of me, blank and ready for my thoughts, confirming that this was in my head—what had just happened was impossible. And still no explanation for that siren or alarm call. I paused for a moment and tried to will the gyrating colour mass out of existence, but for reasons I can't explain, it didn't work.

'Do you believe in law?' the colourful echo pronounced.

Doesn't everyone? To some degree or other. Forgotten to pay for something and not gone back, had a drink too many and driven? Maybe a bit of weed, or taking revenge on someone by putting their car windows out with a golf club? I mean, I have never done anything really bad—just the type of thing the majority might have done.

'Children', my subconscious was having a field day.

Oh, great! Two lived with me until I split up from the mercenary that masqueraded as their mother. The other I didn't meet until I was thirty-seven. I knew I had got her mother pregnant but assumed she had gone back to Wales to have it—or not. Never crossed my mind until that phone call. Not sure we have a relationship, but it is what it is. I have tried to support them when I can but have left them to get on with it.

'Tell me about your marriage'.

There were two. The first time, she ran off with someone else after six months while I was working away. I had a sincere hope that she had a happy life. The second—I just said she was mercenary, though we stayed together for fifteen years, for the kids mainly. In my case, anyway. She just stayed for my wallet. We get on well enough now, though, which is odd—still wouldn't leave my wallet lying about.

Other than that, I don't trust women and am happy in my own little world, where I can pick and choose who I talk to and am master of my own destiny. Might sometimes be lonely, but that was a small price to pay.

'Likes and loves—have you had any?'

I like wine. I like my kids most of the time. I am not sure I love them, though. I think I loved my first wife, which could explain the pain I felt when she ran off. Have I loved anything since then? No, I don't think I have. I may have loved my parents when I was really young, but that's unconditional—what they did later burst that bubble. That's a sad little list.

"Where is that siren coming from, and what is beyond that door?" I said out loud, I think. *Why are you angry all the time?*

So, they ignored me—which was an impressive trick if they were in my head, like ignoring your wife as she sits in front of you, stark naked, with a glass of wine poured for you. People ignoring questions was one of those things that angered me. However, as it was me asking, I knew this would come up, and I'd better answer. Not that it sounds weird at all.

Why am I angry? I just am. I am angry at the state of the world but can do nothing about it. I am angry because my life hasn't really amounted to much. I am angry because I am bored. I am angry because—well, just because. I don't really know why, and if I could tell my younger self something, it would be to try and turn from the anger, as it has given me no real benefit.

'Revelations to you as a child'.

Okay, this was getting very weird now. But I was stuck in this. So here goes. Only to trust a little more, stand up to your dad, and—no matter the hurt—report him. Learn to like people, try to contribute more, and try to find meaning in your life. Really help your kids if you have any. Even keep your family close—you may need them. That's it, really.

You are in my head, so to deny you is to deny myself. I don't believe in any form of God, so you can't be anything like that. Therefore, I must have had some sort of breakdown, and this is my brain having an overload. Anything I say will stay right here—it's hardly a court of law. The one thing I can't rationalise is that bloody siren.

'Can you change?'

What difference would it make? I don't believe in anything beyond. I think I have been happy. Even if I tried to drown my demons, they would have learnt to swim. As for you and this—well, it's all in my head, isn't it? So, I can sleep peacefully, knowing it makes no odds. I will declare myself content and unrepentant for my actions. So, come on, figments—do your worst.

The door swung open of its own accord. From the right came a pale green light. Cautiously, I entered the corridor. To the left, the view was only of a pale blue wall, strangely flashing and pulsating—a curious counterpoint to the background siren.

So, I had been proscribed to go down. Did that mean I was going back to my old life, returning rather than venturing upwards? Hell would never be described as pale green, so I must be going back. A small laugh—one of relief or victory—escaped me. I descended half a dozen of the previously imagined steps and felt a slight vertiginous moment, like air-pocket turbulence when flying, quickly passing.

I opened my eyes—or thought I did—and what was that annoying noise? Beep, beep, beep, beep.

Then a voice cut over the beeping. "Is he okay?"

I recognised the voice as Gem, my eldest. I tried to speak, but nothing happened. I also couldn't move—or so it seemed. I could hear my chest moving up and down, but it seemed to be in time with the beeping or the whooshing that was its counterpoint.

"It's okay, Mrs Waite. We nearly lost him there. Your father is in a coma. We'll get him to the specialist unit as we agreed, but with this traffic, there's very little we can do. He is comfortable and can feel no pain, although he may still be able to hear you, so please talk to him."

I heard another voice that I didn't recognise, but this one, I didn't think, was in my head.

"Sorry about this, doc. Some idiot has blocked the shoulder. We'll have to try and get back in and out of the main traffic. Good—that wagon's letting us out. We'll get going again soon. This blockage isn't great."

Then Gem came back in. "Hang in there, Dad. We'll get you more comfortable soon. I hope you can hear me." Then she started to cry.

What the absolute fuck? I was conversing with angels two minutes ago. The metaphorical coin dropped—I had been judged, and rather than rewarded, I had been punished. Found wanting, I had been returned to my own private hell. So who's fucking laughing now?

*****

The driver of the Ford had seen the ambulance manoeuvre to get in and back out in her mirror and had offered a silent thank you to the driver of the wagon who had let it through. There was a tricky moment when she lost sight of the car she was following—although "following" wasn't technically true, as she was in front of it, which meant she was leading it.

However, as the driver of the other car didn't know she was there, he couldn't know he was being led. Alice Riggs sighed. It was her fault that Matt Connors was driving the car for the gang she ostensibly worked for, so she felt a certain responsibility for him. Tasked with finding a driver, she had used Matt. That was what it was—nothing fancier or more convoluted than that. And now, here he was, with the contents in the boot of his dad's car, stuck on a motorway.

This would not sit well with the crime bosses, as they would brook no delay, but Alice had already tried to explain and had been cut short. Her real bosses, though, would be apoplectic if they knew she was here, as she was supposed to be as far from it as possible. "Plausible deniability" had been a phrase bandied about a great deal in the last few weeks.

Alice also knew that Matt was being followed—the two Volvos stuck out like clowns in a nunnery. But that wasn't the problem. All Alice was concerned with was ensuring no real harm came to Matt. If he was arrested, that would be the best thing; dead was something she did not want on her conscience.

That was why she was here. She knew where he was heading and what might happen when he got there, and she was damned if she wasn't going to try to extract him to the relative safety of arrest by the two who were following him. She sighed again, wishing this scenario would play out soon—her nerves were shot.

*****

5:49 pm

Chalk and cheese—on the surface, anyway.

He had now dropped back level with the second wagon from the fast-food outlet. This driver looked like a right miserable twat; the other had a jolly vibe going on. This second one reflected himself, more than likely, as he was fairly sure he wasn't portraying a cheery countenance.

Well, he would leave him to his musings, as he must consider that, despite his most positive thoughts, he could not possibly complete this journey as instructed. He had seen the ambulance that had struggled to get moving, even with its lights and sirens doing their thing. So what chance did he have, as nobody got out of the way for vans?

The instructions were to get to the underground car park by six at the latest, as the barriers would deny any unknown vehicles after that time. A special key was needed to raise them once this deadline had passed, and, incredibly, given the connections, nobody had got one of these. Chaz himself had delivered these instructions personally, along with the van keys.

Limping up the path, dragging a leg like it was trying to reject the idea of being attached to him. He wouldn't come in, as he knew that I might get a tad volatile when he told me the reasons I would do this. Seeing his limp and him being out in daylight and all made my desire to inflict pain no less—just more so.

My kids. My bloody kids and my ex-wife. I had wanted to turn him inside out, but he held the nap hand.

Promises Are Broken

I am getting bored of looking at the back of Ian's wagon. It is not the most edifying of views, especially as it probably looks very much like mine does. I hope the passenger in the taxi, which I can see in my rear camera, enjoys my arse-end—after all, he has been sat there for the duration. God, he must be on the meter. How much will that be running to?

Unless he got a flat fare, in which case, more fool the driver. I would want to top myself if I were sat there watching the meter click off every minute. It would be like watching your life being dripped out at one penny per second. At least, I suppose, he has something to look at other than Ian's backend. I could call him, I suppose, as I really could do with talking to someone. But was it worth the slap on the wrist from the company for using a mobile while driving, even though we have come to a halt?

I know there is no difference in law; I just feel a bit pedantic today. I mean, I was there for Ian when Michela left him for that teacher, wasn't I? I listened to his ranting and raving, poured him out of pubs, and told him what was important. He managed to turn the corner and has done a damn good job, despite his daughter being a borderline ecoterrorist.

That wasn't his fault. He may have been a little indulgent with her, but considering her mother had fucked off to Spain, it was quite understandable. I look at my kids and know they would step over me in the hall and only raise slight concern if I started to fester and smell.

I can't even blame them, really. I feel like a doormat most of the time, and I do nothing to break that description. Jan gets away with everything and anything, and the kids just follow her lead. Once, when Katherine—who was fourteen at the time—came home with a haircut I would describe as a techno version of a new realist Dali on her head, rather than her normal brown bob, I questioned her. I think any parent would.

The phrase "Dad, you just don't understand" was used, and therein lies the problem—I just don't. I don't fit in with my own family. It's like they have accepted my presence but are not quite sure what I am for, apart from carrying a wallet. As long as they don't poke me too hard, then perhaps I will just sit quietly in the corner with my open wallet in my outstretched, cold, grey hand.

The similarities with the guy in the taxi became clearer. I was coasting along sedately, watching my life drip out a tenner at a time. My sympathies, pal.

Ian would offer me some advice, or had it gone too far now, and I was stuck in a circle of reality that had now also become a circle of probability? In other words, my acceptance of my fate was now, in fact, more than likely what I was due. It would have happened anyway, as I had just laid back and thought of England. I had taken the easy option—and still do.

The only reason I am still driving this bloody wagon is that I can escape from my family. I know that I should front it out and tackle this head-on, but I can't deal with being told I don't understand, because, again, I don't. Ian's voice in my head was now telling me the same thing, and I didn't need him to repeat what I already knew deep down.

So, no, Ian. No moan. I will talk to him face-to-face if we ever get the chance again. It has not been so easy since he became a single parent. He once jokingly said he sometimes worried that when he went out, Caz—his daughter—would move some squatters in or some protestors trying to save hedgehogs. But he understood her, and I think he admired her and her passions. There's a difference.

When we were younger, I am sure Jan loved me. She must have—otherwise, why would you tie yourself to someone? Unless my doormatiness was apparent even then. The damn circles again. The fact that she seems to have accepted that I will never really be anything but a provider, and will largely let her get on with whatever she wants to do, appears to be her strategy. She even managed to fit in a couple of kids, and I am sure I was there for their creation.

Though, as they grow up, they are even less like me than they were as infants. I am sure that Jan wouldn't do the cuckoo thing with me, would she? I don't even want to open that box. I have fed, watered, and sheltered them all their lives. That makes me a dad, even if I am now doubting whether I had managed to get up off the hall floor long enough to make them personally. These thoughts were doing no good to my mind or my health.

I shouldn't even be driving. The doctor told me so, and for once in my life, I had made a snap decision. There was no way I was going to let a juvenile doctor take away my one last piece of perceived freedom. It had only been a bit of indigestion. Or so I thought. I had finally dragged myself to the local surgery, due mainly to an overreliance on Gaviscon. This had not had the effect I had hoped for and had prompted the call to the surgery and the battle of wills with the receptionist—the ones who insist they are medically qualified enough to diagnose your needs over the phone and not just there to answer the bloody thing.

When I finally managed to get in front of someone with a medical qualification, I sat there while the kindergarten medic told me I had an irregular heart rhythm, that I needed more tests, and all that stuff. The tests had shown that I had a condition that was a precursor to real heart problems unless I took it easy and swallowed a multicoloured cornucopia of tablets every day. Most people would have shared. Most men, in particular, would have run home and told their families what had happened and what could be done about it. I say men mostly because, for once, they would be justified in their illness and not up for derision.

"Look, darling, it's not just man flu! I am ill."

I had the chance once. Jan asked me if I was okay, as I was looking tired. I was about to tell her, but she was distracted by something shinier, like a hennaed magpie. The chance was gone, and, as I was stuck in my circles, I just shrugged and went to work.

I am slightly jealous of Ian. Even Michela running off was something to be jealous of. The only time Jan would run would be if I had won the lottery. "You have got to be in it to win it, Jan"—isn't that what they say? Looks like you have lost, love.

I will need to sit down with her and the kids and explain that I am ill. I know I will be greeted with looks of mild disappointment, as if I had done something so out of character.

Something that didn't revolve around their needs. How could I be so selfish and only think of myself? I should feel guilty for not putting them first. The health service does not understand that my needs are not paramount—there are people far more important than some silly little heart condition.

If the other road users knew I was driving this beast with the possibility of heart failure, they would be rightly angry. Although, with the way the traffic is now, if I did cark it here and now, it would be a minor bump up Ian's back end and some mild disapproval from those behind when I didn't move forward a few yards. I would not even make a ripple in life's pond. The circle of reality was being drawn again by the circumstances around me—a life filled with mild disappointment and disapproval.

My heart went out to the bloke in the taxi. I was stuck somewhere I didn't want to be—and stuck for the foreseeable. We had something in common: the steady drip, drip, drip of our lives disappearing before us. I wondered if he had anyone who cared where he was or what he was up to. I sincerely hope so, but the old guy looked slightly lost and alone.

I know the feeling, mate; I know the feeling. If I could, I would get out and talk to you—then at least you'd know I cared, even though I don't know you at all. Perhaps you might even care for me a little, listen to my woes, and help me get through today—and hopefully the next.

In the meantime, you get to stare at the back of your driver's head and the arse-end of my wagon, advertising something you've heard of but probably never experienced. Perhaps your circles should align more so you could experience them. Or perhaps not—your circle already looks like mine: closed and predictable.

*****

5:50 pm

This whole situation was a slow-moving—or rather, not-moving—nightmare. I knew this was some sort of karmic payback, and I was paying a price for my past. The relationships I had fostered once school was done had led me here. In fact, they had led to this very moment—sitting in this van with a predicament I hadn't envisioned when I'd shit, showered, and shaved that morning before leaving the house to collect this van from Burley.

Chaz was always bloody Chaz. I had steered clear of him at school, mainly because of some perceived juvenile rivalry—postcodes or street nonsense, something like that, though I couldn't remember. He had been on the school football team and was even scouted at one point. Then he came off a stolen motorbike and screwed his leg forever. That was the end of any pretensions about sport for him. That explained one of the many chips Chaz seemed to carry on his shoulder, all wrapped up in newspaper.

Only after I left school did Chaz come back into my orbit—only more unbalanced than ever, both physically and mentally. The offer of occasional work had been too tempting, with real jobs being thin on the ground and my qualifications for anything normal somewhat lacking. The path I had taken was entirely of my own making, though I had been prodded down it by creatures who cared very little for me or mine.

I glanced at the clock. With only a time jump as a solution to reaching my salvation on time, the reality of the situation had been apparent for a while. And yet, I still hoped the monsters who had cornered me would show some level of understanding—either allowing me to complete the task when I could or offering an alternative. I would know soon enough. Or would I?

The old guy in the taxi—would he have a better story than his own? Very probably. I had always enjoyed sitting in the pub, listening to all the old buggers in their suits with jumpers underneath, telling war stories. Some of them might even have been true. They sure as hell all acted like they had fought in a war.

A Coin That Won't Get Tossed

The journey back today was nearly done—an expensive way of completing the last leg, but he had missed the connecting train. Rather than wait around the station in the gathering dark, he had jumped in a taxi. The driver seemed pleased to have such a long trip, a welcome alternative to the usual city rounds. He didn't even mind that they were now stuck on the motorway, waving away the driver's apology as if it didn't matter anymore.

This was the last long journey he would take apart from the final one. The taxi driver—Piotr, it said on the badge (Polish for Peter, he guessed)—had tried to engage him in conversation, only stopping when Stanley indicated he wanted to nap, while secretly all he wanted was to reflect on the last few hours and his trip to his memories in Whitby.

He had started the day with a clear picture of where he was going and what he wanted to achieve. He had set out on his journey with determination, even if his body could no longer impart any sense of urgency. The first part of the train ride had been pleasant, and he had even managed a brief conversation with the passenger next to him.

Although he had skirted around the reason for his day out—unsure how sane he would sound if he revealed everything—the transfer to the express coach to York had been hitch-free. The next part of the journey had ended with him looking at the sea, the sand, and some hardy souls walking out.

Stepping off the bus onto the grey pavement of Whitby bus station, his powdery white hair unrestrained by a cap, he had screwed up his eyes against the wind as they watered. Glancing up at the scudding pale grey clouds high in the northern sky, he was pleased to be wearing his warm tweed jacket. The autumnal weather was notoriously cool, and there was a promise of rain later. It was colder than he had hoped—or perhaps he was simply older than he once was—as he rubbed his hands together to get the circulation going.

A cap, pulled from an inside pocket, soon had his hair back under control. In the old days, he would have set it with Brylcreem, and no wind would have shifted that. He had no wish to tempt fate with the cold—he didn't want another chill like the one that had lingered a few weeks ago.

Clusters of people sat in the bus shelters and on the plentiful public benches, protecting their fish and chips from the seagulls, which flapped and danced around, waiting for scraps. They reminded him of the monochrome punk rockers of the seventies—all noise and attitude.

It always amused him how the scavengers paraded around the rubbish bins, waiting for discarded crumbs, before swooping away with the spoils clamped tight in their yellow beaks. He had seen this spectacle many times over the years—the discordant chorus and squawk of the gulls as intrinsic to the seaside as day to night, or the tide to time.

He had not been in a rush, so he had taken a gentle meander past the ice-cream parlours, fish and chip shops, and the ones selling what Kathy would have called *tat*—all done far more slowly and stiffly than in days gone by. These things made Whitby what it was now, stepping reluctantly away from what it once had been. Perhaps that explained his latest journey—or at least part of it—as he too slipped into an older version of himself.

There were small queues—relics of the COVID years—snaking along the narrow pavements, people eager for a ninety-nine cornet, an ice-cream with monkey's blood drizzled on top, or a bag of chips. Usually, he would have joined them, but not today. He had come for something far more important. He had no time to spare, nor any appetite for food.

He had tottered on, thinking, when did I start doing this old man's shuffle? He reached the zebra crossing, waiting until it was safe to cross, recalling the little sweet shop that had once stood next to the penny arcade. 'Pastimes', it had been called. He had always thought it was a strange place for a confectionery shop, but it had been successful—especially after the council built the new bus station overlooking the town centre.

The station had stood directly opposite the little shop. It had become the go-to place for families straight off the bus, grateful for anything to pacify the kids while they organised their day out. A Chinese restaurant called the Golden River now stood on the spot. He had thought of the shop many times on his visits, wondering what had become of Susie—and whether she had made a journey to Whitby, just as he had.

The view in the other direction was enough to have him shaking his head at the eyesore that confronted him. A steel wire security fence skirted the ruined remains of a long-forgotten building. It had stood abandoned and derelict for years, and at some point, a fire had ripped through it, reducing it to a pile of scorched bricks and ash. A metaphor for life—and for the one he now missed.

They had been married fifty years ago. Their honeymoon had been their first of many visits to Whitby—three whole days. How different everything had looked then, as they had stepped off the old bus outside their B&B. Oh, what a day that had been. The sun shining, the cloudless sky a deep blue.

The tears came to him then, and he felt no shame as he took out a crisp white handkerchief to wipe his eyes. The memories came flooding back—the ones of his beautiful Kathy. An image of her, head thrown back, eyes crinkling in the corners, shoulders shaking with laughter, as he had bumbled around the dance floor at their wedding do, to Elton John's *Saturday Night's Alright for Fighting*. *Stiff Hips*, she had called him, and it had remained her affectionate nickname for him until she had passed on.

He had moved slowly forward along the harbourside, reflecting on the task ahead. While there was no rush to reach his destination, there was a strange impatience to get it over with. He was unsure how he would feel afterwards, but he knew it was for the best.

Using another crossing, he had continued along the promenade, pausing a while to breathe in the cool, salt-tinged air and to give his stiff hips a rest. Leaning on the speckled sea wall—mindful of the splatters of bird droppings—he had spotted small yachts with their sails unfurled, bounding over the wave crests like marine antelopes.

To the north stood white wind turbines, like giant anaemic sunflowers, turning as they harnessed the power of the northerly winds. Further north, the Cleveland Hills were cloaked in a purple haze that shimmered beneath the autumn sky. It was a view he had always loved—it signified where he had started out, tying him to this land.

A short walk past the War Memorial, standing at the start of the short pier—a statuesque column resting on a cobbled plinth. Wilted flowers of red, white, and blue, wrapped in flimsy plastic, flapped in the breeze, commemorating those lost in two world wars. They would all be replaced with fresh ones in the coming weeks. He regretted not bringing a bunch of flowers to pay his respects.

The weathered old bench sat silently, watching over the sea opposite the Memorial. Once, long ago, it had worn a glossy green overcoat, but now the paint was cracked and peeling after years of exposure to the salty air. He had sat on the bench many times over the years, relieved to finally be resting his aching hips.

Sighing deeply, he took in the view before him. The sands were just visible as the tide turned.

There were remnants of sea coal on the sand, and black shadows scraped across the beach—a legacy of the industrial heritage further up the coast. The scene reminded him of when he was a lad, and his pa would take him to the beach at home in the early hours of the morning when it was deserted. They would fill sacks with the gritty black stuff, then trudge home, taking turns to wheel Pa's bike and being mindful not to let the sacks fall off.

He smiled then, still able to visualise his dad scooping the sea coal out of the sacks into cones made from newspaper, which he would then sell door to door to the neighbours. His mam was always grateful for any extra income when times were tight. The jet-black remnants of the mines from further up the coast perpetually washed up on the beach, and he supposed it would always be that way—though now, no one collected it, as everyone had gas.

A glance southward, and there stood Whitby Abbey on the promontory above the old part of town. It looked closer to the sea than he remembered, but perhaps his mind was playing tricks on him. His one regret was that he had not gone to visit it one last time. He made himself comfortable on their bench and said aloud:

"Well, bench, I've shared some memories with you over the years. There was a time when there were three of us—do you remember? You, me, and my beloved Kathy, God rest her soul."

He lowered his head as the welcome memories came flooding back, like the tide in front of him had just turned and was sweeping up the beach in its inexorable journey.

"You were our favourite bench, and we would sit here for as long as we wished, every time we came back, telling you what had happened in our lives. There was a time when we sat here eating fish and chips. Kathy had been to the hairdresser's and was looking all lovely and radiant. I loved the sprinkles of silver in her hair, but she hated them and had them removed. Either way, she always looked beautiful to me."

Another sigh escaped his lips, this one followed by a chuckle.

"I'll never forget that day—can you remember? The skies turned metal grey and blotted out the sun, then huge raindrops poured out of the sky into our fish and chips, turning them into a soggy, vinegary mush. It was so awful we couldn't do anything but laugh! Kathy laughed the loudest as her lovely hairdo dissolved into straggly wet strands framing her face. By then, we were so soaked it was pointless trying to get out of the deluge."

He creased his brow, a distant look appearing in his eyes as he stared into the distance.

"Oh! Yes! I remember. She said, 'Look at our lovely bench—the droplets of water on the top look like little diamonds.' And I told her she should be covered in diamonds, but not the wet kind, and we laughed even harder. We sat until it stopped raining, and when we stood up, there were two perfect dry patches in the shape of our backsides. Talk about leaving a lasting impression, eh? We always felt more at peace after talking to you. We could rant and rave, curse, laugh, and swear, and you never criticised. You know our life story better than we do."

The corners of his mouth turned up in amusement, but then his brow contracted in a scowl.

"Even after I had that fall and broke my hip, it didn't stop us from coming here. Kathy said I needed to exercise and keep walking."

'Move them stiff hips!'

"She would shout, and we walked more every day until I was able to walk the full length of the promenade. Only then would she let me sit down for a rest. Boy, was I relieved the first time I managed that walk, though I don't know what I would have done if you weren't here for me."

"Do you remember the day Kathy told me she wasn't well? We cried and held onto each other, and your presence was comforting. We stayed for what seemed like a lifetime, holding hands and making plans."

The tears came again.

"But things have never been the same since my Kathy went, and I'm not coping so well. I find myself thinking about the good old days more and more. I know I will never forget the times we spent here, looking out at sea and reminiscing. I came today to say farewell, old friend, as I've moved to Mansfield into a home so I can be near the kids, and I won't be back here again."

"By all accounts, you won't be here yourself for much longer, as I heard the council is going to take out all the old benches along the pier and promenade and replace them with fancy modern ones. Things will never be the same again. But there's one thing I'd like to do, if you don't mind—leave you with a reminder of our friendship. It's something I should have done long ago when Kathy was still here to appreciate it."

He took a small penknife out of his pocket and carefully carved a small heart on the back of the bench, scraping the initials K & W inside. Satisfied, he returned the knife to his pocket. His eyes twinkled, knowing he had done something he never would have dared to do as a young man, but he was happy knowing Kathy would have laughed out loud at his audacity.

Contentment filled his soul as he bid farewell to his old friend.

"Thanks for the memories. I'll always remember them with great fondness."

Standing slowly, he cast a final lingering glance over the pier wall and beyond, capturing the scene forever in his heart. He saluted his old ally and stiffly shuffled away to catch the express bus for the last time.

The poor old bench was once again alone, overlooking the sea—the only one remaining that would remember the loving couple who had visited it all those times. But who would remember it now that the old man was gone?

Rudely awakened from his memories by a sharp braking, and thoughts of a lonely bench, Stanley smiled at a day well spent. He was going to be near the family now, and that was what was important. He would always have this day and the memory.

A job well done, as his mam would have said.

There would be others in this traffic jam who, no doubt, had suffered loss or were getting as old as he was, and he wondered about their stories.

*****

The radio chatter had become repetitive now. Tina only heard updates on where the other targets were, and everything seemed to be going as the planners had no doubt expected—except, of course, for Tina and Ray, who were effectively the fly in the ointment. She allowed herself a little smile as she thought of the girls and boys who sat at desks all day having some sort of hissy fit and ripping up their Post-It notes—all because Ray and Tina had become embroiled in real life.

What was interesting was that, apart from Ray updating their leader a few minutes ago, there had been very little traffic directed at them. Tina changed that from interesting, in her head, to somewhat worrying. Her previous thoughts on what exactly was in the boot of that car were now firmly entrenched, allowing nothing else to infiltrate. She was fixated on it now, even if she might be wrong.

Her internal argument went along the lines of—the powers that liked to think they were on top of things were, in fact, aware that the contents of the Audi were something other than what had been advertised at the briefing. Therefore, they were trying to find a way out of it that would make it appear they didn't know—thus avoiding having a very angry Tina pointing her weaponry at them.

Her reputation as a kickass lesbian copper—which was largely in her own head—did have a kernel of truth about it. She was not a bear you wanted to poke with anything. This whole thing was beginning to smell more than a little fishy. Tina wondered if she should ask Ray, but then he was a natural worrier, and projecting her own madness onto him felt a tad unfair.

She puffed out her cheeks. There was nothing she could do, and until otherwise instructed, she would sit tight.

5:51 pm

I could only assume that the underground car park was where whatever nefarious activity Chaz and his troupe of performing apes had planned would go down. Am I one of those monkeys? Yes, I suppose that was true, no matter how hard I denied it. There must be a backup plan—I had now convinced myself of this—and I could cling to the notion that they were tracking me, this shitty van, and its load. So, they would know I was stuck. Let's attach some logic to a non-logical situation.

The thing is, I hadn't ranted or raved—my default setting in situations I neither understood nor, more crucially, wanted to understand. Instead, I had applied logic. I was angry. I wanted to hurt something, or rather, one Chaz-shaped something, if I was honest. Yet I hadn't let these feelings explode out as I normally would. Perhaps this was a new me. Perhaps it had taken someone threatening my kids to make me realise what was important, and this was quite a shock. This new, calmer me was accepting the situation and looking for a way out of it.

The pink thing was still intimidating everything around it, and the small-space shuffle kept changing around me. I caught sight of the minibus—the guys in there were still giving it large with beer and song. As much as I would hate it, I would swap into that bus, somewhere with no trouble. A new Peugeot had arrived on the scene, an old bloke shuffling some papers, by the looks of things. It all came to a halt rather suddenly.

The flaring of the brake lights, apart from adding to the pressure behind my eyes, was starting to look like fireworks. Really crap ones, but still. I remember the fireworks of my youth and when the kids were little. Only this country would celebrate an act of treason and spectacular failure by letting off slightly ironic detonations to mark it.

In the old days, it was a couple of beers or a can of pop, a bonfire, and some low-grade explosives. Now, they have become major productions. There's something to learn there—perhaps all the terrorists in the world would have achieved less notoriety and a more sympathetic ear if they had detonated their bombs to *Ode to Joy* or *O-fucking-Fortuna*.

No, things were certainly simpler back then in my younger days. No sociopaths taking your kids and holding you over a flame.

Now There's Revolution

I am not quite sure how any of this happened—not being stuck in this blooming traffic, but how, at my age, I had become an internet sensation. Apparently, I was seriously trending and had about two hundred thousand followers who read my blog uploads or followed my musings on Twitter and something else that I can never remember the name of. The very strange thing about all of it is that I am seventy-one years old, for crying out loud.

Now, most people would assume that I was followed because I was a silly old man who got stuck in his bin, fell over his dog, or some such nonsense. No, it had all started as a joke—well, not exactly a joke, but certainly a relatively simple request. I had asked my grandson to show me how to dictate into my PC and all that entailed, as I wanted to be able to get my thoughts down and recount all the stories from my past.

Mainly because I was mildly interested in the family tree and realised only too late that all my parents' and relatives' stuff had gone with them to the unknown. All the knowledge and anecdotes that had been dragged up at every reunion were now no more than wisps in a breeze. Then the surprise had been laid at my feet.

My grandkids viewed me, I think, as a source of reasonable Christmas presents or birthday money—no more, no less. They came to see me under sufferance, I am sure, but they were still relatively passive and accepted the trips to see the grumpy old man. In an effort to entertain one of the clutch and appear vaguely interesting, I had asked the question about the PC. The next time they turned up, Simeon—the one who had shown me—asked how I had got on, with what appeared, on the surface, to be genuine interest. What I did not expect was a genuine teen endorsement.

"This is really cool, sort of funny and sad, and I would read it. You should post it."

At which point, I envisioned envelopes, etc.

"Who to?" was my response.

"The web, Grandpa. We could set you up a blog, and you could just do this regularly. The oldies like you would love it, and some others too. People always like to remember back."

"Reminisce is what you mean."

"'Spose."

That was that. Simeon gave me a comprehensive old-people instruction over the next few weeks. In other words, talk very loudly and slowly until I got it. I must have got it because a call from Sam, my daughter, informed me I had two thousand followers and that I should get on Twitter. My first thought was, yes, love—because really, I had no idea what on earth she was talking about.

I was half tempted to look out of the front window and see if they were in my garden. I suggested she come over with Simeon as I was obviously missing something here. I knew how to post—yep, down with the kids—but not what to do from there or, indeed, what would come out of it down the line.

The following Saturday, I think it was, Sam arrived with a very eager Simeon in tow. This was an unexpected side to Simeon, as his mother was always extolling his complete lack of enthusiasm for anything.

"Gramps, you are like the most famous person I know," was his opener. "I only have thirty on Twitter, and two of them are Mum and Dad, though they don't think I know."

Sam, at this point, did look a little sheepish. He then showed me the comments on my first couple of blogs, and I was genuinely amazed. Mainly because I had not seen them before—as all I did was ramble and post, the fact that this was a two-way thing had failed to register.

However, if I was being critical, then the grandkids could have pointed this out when they were old-mansplaining. People were commenting on what they remembered and adding their take on certain things I had raised. There were followers who seemed to want more—well, they would get that—and old people who wanted to thank me for taking them back to a time before the internet.

Which was kind of ironic, but we will skip over that. Simeon was good enough to tell me to ignore the bad ones, as they were called trolls and just got pleasure from being nasty. I did wonder how I was going to prove I was in my seventies to *oldpeoplesmell*. Thankfully, Simeon's advice was pertinent, and the good far outweighed the bad.

The next hour was taken up with explaining how to post bigger and better and how to add Twitter feeds into it. This was all fascinating, and my brain was engaged in a way that I only managed on a Monday night when trying to fathom *Only Connect* on the telly. I was now set up to be more than a silver surfer looking at pictures of cats in hats or the football scores. I was now a surf master, and I had a two-thousand-strong—and growing—army following my every word.

That's what it felt like, though what it was in reality was just what I blurted out every week. I am sure most of my devotees would not care about the trauma I suffered when I lost a slipper or the shouting match I had at the news. But we can all dream.

That was nearly two years ago. The army has grown to two hundred thousand, and the hashtags #grumpyrememberings and #anunremarkablebriefhistory were trending. Simeon did explain this to me, but to be honest, if I stick a couple of lines out there—which had grown to short story length, if I was honest—and someone still reads it and sends it on, then they really need to get out more. However, the new kudos I had in the eyes of my kids and grandkids was worth it.

The real bonus was that I was now attracting small sponsorships. Some companies paid me hard cash to endorse their products. How messed up was that? I asked Simeon what that was called, and he said I was now what was called, in the new world, an influencer.

Though why anyone would be influenced by a slightly confused, out-of-place, and lonely old man was beyond me. Cash helped, though, and the family got better presents than they were used to.

There was a wish that Lou was still around to hear and see all this. She would have greeted it with a slight grunt and surprise as to why anyone would listen to me—as she rarely did. Although forty-five years had fine-tuned this ability in her, I think. So, I have a few years yet before everyone stops listening.

Now this internet star—or geriatric fool—was stuck in traffic. All because I had gone out to get some inspiration for my next blog, and I thought some country air would help. Rather than staring at four walls—as nice as they were—getting out was the new luxury following the COVID thing. It appears that everyone had the same idea, and they had all got out. At least we couldn't spread the disease, entombed as we were in our metal coffins.

Anyway, I had spent the day sitting in a café on Ilkley Moor, idling away time, occasionally laying claim to my space by buying something. I think the novelty of seeing an old man with a flat cap, sitting pecking away into a

MacBook Air, must have had something to do with their tolerance. Two years ago, I would probably have tutted at me and made some uncharitable remark about acting my age. How things change.

I had achieved my mojo and my zen.

At first, I had just rambled aimlessly with no real structure until my daughter pointed out, near the start, that I should do it as a timeline type of thing—and for once, she was right. Previously covering the fifties and sixties, I had now reached the heady milestone of 1971.

This was now becoming interesting. Even though the Swinging Sixties had been dealt with, these years were probably the most formative for me personally.

The Swinging Sixties didn't really reach the part of Yorkshire I lived in. It was more the slightly off-kilter sixties, to be honest. My day—apart from being filled with coffee, a bacon sandwich, more coffee, and a rather delicious scone—had delivered a piece for this year. I was now in a rush to get home to my workstation—yes, I know—and get this out there. My army was hungry and needed my wisdom. It would appear that these thoughts were coming from a new persona.

Perhaps I should wear my flat cap backwards and loosen my braces so my trousers hang down. There's a thought to put out on Twitter later. I was addicted to this now and felt a slight regret that I was missing my self-imposed deadline.

Not to worry, I could use the time constructively. Flip on the inside light and read the rough draft—see if I could make any improvements or alterations. There would be some between now and the post, but hopefully, if I sorted them now, it would mean less work when I finally got home.

Picking up the sheets I had printed out in Ilkley library—discount for seniors today, don't you know—I commenced a scan. A pen was stuck in my mouth like one of those non-smoking aids, though the pen may have tasted better. What I must look like to the others surrounding me in the jam was of no consequence. One glance and they would no doubt be thinking, *Have you seen him with his hat on the car? Does he know that it doesn't rain inside?* Anyway, who cares?

A brief history unremembered and unremarkable—edition 22

#grumpyrememberings #anunremarkablebriefhistory

Whoa! I am an adult—1971

I believe a certain awareness came over me during this year. I had achieved a level of physical, but certainly not mental, maturity. As for sexual maturity—

according to a magazine I once scanned in the dentist's—I was already past it. *Cosmopolitan*, I believe. I also think I blushed when I read this.

The counterargument to this would be: should we ever really get mature about sex? I will leave that one to you.

As I write these memories down for you, one of the comments I constantly hear and read is the refrain: *It was always so much better/cheaper/cleaner/less crowded/more polite/easier to understand* in 1XXX** (*delete as needed and add the year of your choice*). I think some people are reminiscing about a time they clearly could not remember—unless they were hallucinating (which is entirely possible in the era we have just finished reliving) or lived in an augmented reality.

I have challenged some to elucidate and put some substance behind their statements. Those who responded mostly invented some random relative or uncheckable piece of history to add weight to their pronouncement. As you all know, I try to avoid the rose-tinted sort of memory. Certain things may indeed have been better back then, but I am not dead, so I think that is one improvement those of us of a certain age can all live with.

Now we have entered the 1970s, there is a huge elephant in the room that would only come to light thirty years later: the celebrity paedophile, the not-so-celebrity paedophile, and the fat sweaty bloke who worked for the council. Not making any excuse for any of it, but life was more trusting then. We had all been given lectures about strangers, cars, puppies, etc.

The problem was that kids were less supervised, and the chance of some free sweets or playing with a puppy would knock all that out of their heads. Years of having nothing, and a country that was finally recovering, were the open-door catalysts that enabled this scum to get away with it. If he was on the telly, then that was a cast-iron guarantee he was okay. Wasn't it?

I don't suppose the habit of calling any family friend "Uncle" helped, nor did the well-documented fondness for sweets. Luckily, Operation Yewtree and others sorted all that out—but just too late for many.

Heading back to my ramble of 1971, this geriatric rumination through time. I had my first set of wheels, a red 1964 VW Beetle, called Arthur (no idea about that – blame my then girlfriend – a relatively new if not quite understood development). A pint cost fifteen whole pennies, the new ones, remember the pain of decimalisation, the panic of getting all your saved up threepenny bits changed into the new stuff. So, a pint in old money was three shillings. I believe the majority of readers think there was a con here. Were things cheaper before and then after the change more expensive? As all our concentration was on working out what was what, we didn't really pay too much attention. I am just confident that we would never be able to prove if they had taken the opportunity or not.

I don't suppose the habit of calling any family friend *Uncle* helped, nor did the well-documented fondness for sweets. Luckily, Operation Yewtree and others sorted all that out—but just too late for many.

Although this does add weight to the *everything was cheaper* jibe, I would say. I only took home fifteen pounds a week from my job (and that included tips but no devil tax as yet).

We can shoot a hole in the argument about life being cheaper, as we had less to spread about. I am sure some whizz has done a calculation and a graph to show it all. I just know I felt richer in 1971 than I do in 2021, and you can't put that on a graph.

I put down my notes for a minute as the traffic was moving slightly, and it wouldn't do to have to explain to some young police officer that I was reading my blog so I could update my two hundred thousand followers. The next step would be a council-run home, and my driving licence suspended.

There was a very happy-looking man in a small French car, chatting away on the phone. The phone thing in the car was not something I subscribed to—mainly because I viewed it as an escape. Turning it off because you were in the car—just try it. It brings a certain sense of calm once you've finished panicking because nobody can ring or message you.

The traffic stops again. The final light is fading now from the sky, only highlighting the redness ahead, giving everything that infernal glow. This is a good time to go back to my notes, as I believe I moved on to technology next.

Technology sort of existed. Admittedly, we had allegedly put a man on the moon two years ago, but in most cases, tech was large, expensive, and basically limited in functionality. For instance, I had just acquired a state-of-the-art (or so I was told) record player, which had the added integration of a tape recorder (the ones you had to wind with a pen) and a radio that operated on two whole bandwidths. The definition of integration wildly differed between me and electronics giant Bush.

A radio and tape recorder had essentially been welded onto the record player and encased in faux teak, which had the desired effect of making a music centre.

It was stereo, though, which was a step up from the portable thing I had been using up to this point. It also needed a very strong shelf to hold it and at least two power stations to fuel it. I still had this thing until a few years back, when my grandson admitted he was collecting vinyl—which is apparently the new hip thing. The machine came out of the loft, and my son laughed—not quite the desired effect, but understandable in hindsight.

I had really started to get into music by this year, hence the record player. Basically, music was still being invented back then, so we can excuse a lot of the trash that was produced in the '70s. However, as we progressed into the '80s, there is honestly no excuse to be offered for any of that decade's output—no doubt I will touch on that if I ever get there.

I had seen my first proper band at the beginning of this year. The City Hall in Sheffield, on January the fourteenth, I think. They are still a part of my life today; they have never left me. That band was Black Sabbath, who were still going until 2017 and inspired me to have a tattoo done in tribute when I was in my fifties. Who says you don't carry your influences a long way?

One other thing that has stuck is that mobile phones were only things you saw on the back of a Post Office lorry when they were installing new glass-walled urinals—otherwise known as call boxes. There were rumours that somewhere in that there London, something was happening that would allow mobile phone calls. Wow.

Twenty-five years later, and we would be on the verge of everyone having some form of the wretched things. Considering that the majority of you will be reading this on one, that's probably a bit harsh. And even I will admit they do make life a little less stressful. In the old days, the advice from your parents was always to carry a two-pence or ten-pence piece for the phone, along with a hankie (for the smell, I presume).

A parental mantra so ingrained in all of us to ensure that emergencies could be phoned home—a message reinforced well into the next decade (thanks to ET or BT—one of them). Nowadays, in my case, it is a ten-pound note. Not sure I can explain it, other than inflation and a desire to hold onto the past and all that was good and innocent. Still can't go out without a hankie either.

Food—I'm not sure it really existed unless something mushy or offal-based, accompanied by potatoes, vegetables, and gravy, counted. Fish and chips were exotic, and a trip to a Wimpy bar was a birthday treat. I will cover curries in a later ramble, but they hadn't reached this far north yet in any great amount. As for Michelin stars and celebrity chefs—tyres and Fanny Craddock would have been my answer to that particular pronouncement.

There wasn't a lot to be said about it. It was a means to an end, wasn't it? Sunday lunch allowed your dad to spend an hour and a half in the bog with the paper, making smells that no human should be able to produce. The north hadn't quite caught on to the garlic mushrooms and Black Forest gateau revolution. Worcestershire sauce with your pickled egg would be as exotic as it got.

There was, however, a predilection in my family for weird and wonderful puddings. These had arrived from the post-war years and rationing, which we talked about earlier in the series. Most of these things had the look and texture of roadkill. The taste was something you would never forget—and never repeat if lucky.

Though you will all recall the statement: eat it all up, then you can leave the table. The young ones reading this today probably wouldn't even know where the table was. This was a remnant of the war and its side effects. Oh! And there was a fondness for Black Bullets (which a) still exist, b) are still called this, and c) can't be sold in a list of places that include, but are not exclusive to, Compton, Brixton, Soweto, etc.).

I will end this edition on a slightly gloomy thought: this was the beginning of a decade where, by the end of it, we thought electing Margaret Thatcher was a jolly jape. Some things may well have been better in the past.

Tara for now.

Joshua, the old man with several chips and no gravy.

Next week: Yorkshire Born and why I would follow Newcastle United!

#grumpyrememberings #anunremarkablebriefhistory'

That would do it, I think. There may be a couple of last-minute changes, but overall, I'm quite happy.

There was an admission I had made to myself shortly after this had all started—that I may have been suffering from some sort of depression when I lost Lou. God, I hate that phrase—I hadn't lost her. I knew exactly where she was, but she had left me in the most permanent manner.

This allowed me to stop thinking about her and wanting to put an end to it all so I could go and see if there was an afterlife. She will always be there, but only in a good way. I have a new life now, and I will enjoy it as long as I can.

I put down the pages, turned off the internal light, and caught the eye of the dodgy-looking bloke in the white van. There was no way of communicating anything to him, so I returned to watching the traffic move in slow motion—just like me on a winter morning.

*****

5:52 pm

This period of inactivity had been eye-opening as I viewed some of the people I was trapped with. But this takes the biscuit. I mean, look at this tosser—does he not know I and everyone else around him can see him? He is not fucking invisible.

Yeah, okay, we aren't moving, but still. It was like that lorry driver earlier, who had clearly got up and gone into the back of his cab. One minute, no tea. Next time, a mug of something. It was madness.

What I was looking at was a whole new level of—I don't even have a name for what it is. I could try to ignore the fucking balloon, but if I did, my head would return to the not-ticking clock. Only eight minutes to go, and the mystery of what would follow.

I had a van full of who knows what—an inherent and overt threat to my family, which I had to hope was not a promise to me if I failed. The urge to run away and take my chances had long since faded, but the sadness in this was that there was no way out unless I got out and ran.

Even my time inside had not been as bad as this. I may have been locked up, but I felt more like a prisoner sitting in relative comfort in this shitty van. There was no irony in that statement—this was worse than when my release date had been approaching. My parole was due in seven minutes. I would either be a free man—or locked into something even worse. But I had to hold onto the optimism that the worst would be that I was in hock to Chaz—or further in hock.

Less than One Million Years from Today

This is no good, no good at all. I should be at home now, sitting with a cup of tea, pen in hand, and my stopwatch engaged, getting ready to test myself—testing my mind, testing myself against those who claim to have a superior intellect. Those who think they can bamboozle, twist, and hide. Little do they know, I am their master. My record is there. I cannot share it, as I am not one for singing my own praises or going anywhere near the mouthpiece of a trumpet. You just never know where or who it may have been with, even in a metaphorical sense.

The lights will have come on by now. I can't, and don't want to, think about the timer working without me or that my electricity is being used with no known benefit. At least it will be thirty minutes till the heating comes on. I should be back home then. I can hang on that long without dwelling on it. Really, I can.

There is no point in getting worked up about it; this is neither the time nor the situation to have one of my things. Thank God for the moist tissues. I can occupy myself with wiping. Wiping is good. It takes my mind off the elephant in the room—well, sitting in the front seat in my briefcase, to be completely exact. Sitting under that report on water levels and the imminent issue of flooding in Wharfedale.

The one I have meticulously prepared for the perusal of the other engineers. It is as meticulous as they knew it would be. They may think I am a tad anal about the detail, but this report is really important, and not just because I say so. There can be no further incidents of inundation of dwellings. There can be no further talk of the introduction of beavers to sort it out.

This is more along the lines of cold-hearted, old-fashioned engineering. Not that I am getting as obsessive about it as the beaver lovers—well, yeah, perhaps I am. Modulation by building something to interrupt the flows is one of my things.

It is still sitting there, stationary like the traffic. Perhaps I could have a look. If I use the stopwatch, I could stop and start it as I move. I have nothing else to occupy me apart from the wiping that people worry about. The wipes will only last so long, and there are only so many wipeable areas that I can reach.

Perhaps it would distract me somewhat. Sneaking a glance to my left and right, I see no interest in my activities; even the wiping appears to have escaped detection. Right, that's it. The stopwatch function on my phone engaged. Undo the locks. That's it—there it is. Today's cryptic, taken from the paper I only buy for appearances, as the news is of no interest unless it has floods as its centrepiece.

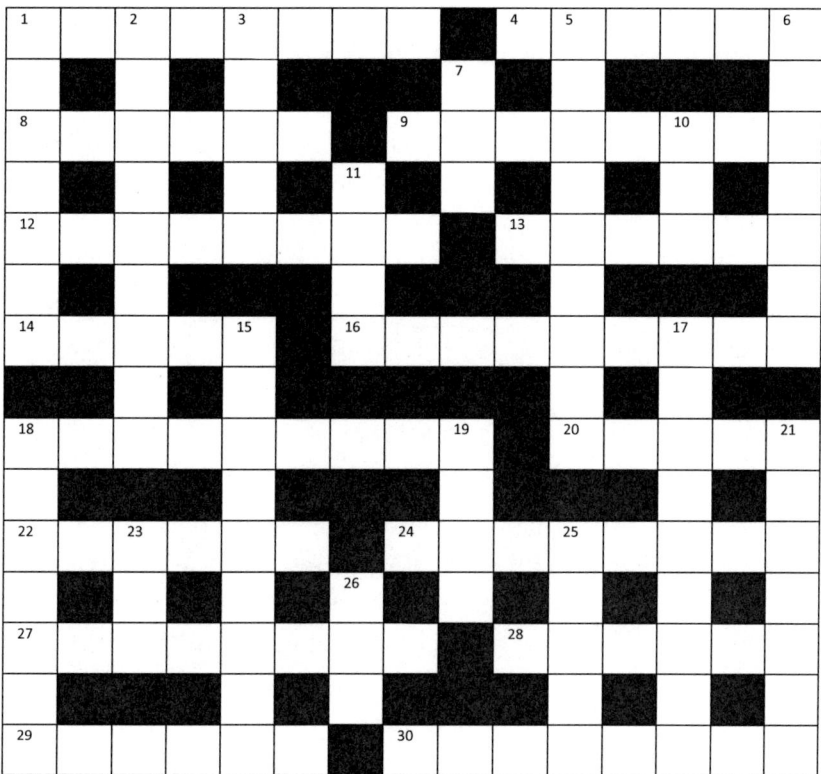

Click. One across. University leader, indeed, is suppressed (8). Really, that's it? My record should be on if that is the best they can come up with for me. So that means one down begins with D. Let's have a look. Samuel Pepys, for instance, could have easily written about some milk farms (7). Oh, for crying out loud. These people are morons.

This is six-year-old kindergarten rubbish. Click—watch off, as there is a need to move the car forward. Still, nobody is paying me any attention. Even if they were, they would probably be glad I had stopped wiping and was doing something more prosaic, even if it was a crossword.

My mind flips back to the report I had moved to get to the crossword. The flooding would only be an issue to all the propertied classes who had kicked up a stink, despite knowingly buying their identical houses in an area that flooded every ten years before houses were built on it. Money talks, despite the higher insurance costs. They could obviously afford it—arrogant enough to think that dirty floodwater would not dare enter their conservatory.

I know better. I could tell them stories. I store these stories, mainly to tell myself, as nobody will ever really listen. Then again, I am a pawn to be moved in the battle of the middle classes. I am one of the ones supposed to fix their problems. I most certainly should not tell them the truth. Who am I to say the builder, who has now gone bust, was wrong to build there? Who am I to obsess over the fact that, if the land had been good for housing, then perhaps—just perhaps—someone would have built housing there sometime in the last millennium?

They called the area the Golden Triangle. Croesus himself would be proud. All the monied types escaping to the country—yet only twenty minutes from the office in Leeds or two hours on the train to London. So, Yorkshire Water, sort it out, as we cannot afford the time to have Tamsin's pony airlifted again, and it is really inconvenient for me to have to get the 4x4 dirty in all this water. I find it incredible that this has been allowed to happen. Was York not enough?

Years and years that has been going on. I have submitted so much in my reports that I have to wonder whether anyone reads them. I have lived in York, and I have first-hand experience of how and why it floods, but what can I say anymore? Money talks, so just fix it. Not that I could or had put much of this in my report. Lights have been on for five minutes now—only twenty-five till the heating.

Click. Two down begins with A. One of the main themes for Stephen Hawking is perhaps (5,4). Move on in one second. Three down—E starts. The Spanish and German are senior (5). A little tougher, or it would be without the E. Next. Eight across—A something, O something, D something. Conflicted at the bookies (2,4). Yes, got it. OK, twelve across—I something, T something, R something, three spaces. Part of a performance to bury little Valerie (8). Very good. Looks like they are warming up after a poor start. Click. Moving again slightly. The record may not be challenged, but the time so far isn't bad. Circumstances may play a part. I could start a new book of records.

At home, at the kitchen table, in the car, in a restaurant—etcetera. I could keep this book with the other ones. The main one being my mileage, petrol amount, and cost—going back to nineteen eighty-one and my first car. The pricing of all my food, if I am honest, is quite comprehensive too. I don't believe the figures they bandy about inflation, and keeping these helps me prove they are lying.

Or it will when they make a false pronouncement. I will be ready with the ammunition. They make very interesting reading, honestly, they do. Like the copy of all the water flows I have measured, the official ones, and the ones I go back to when I can as a sort of hobby.

The red lights are all flaring, and nothing has moved for a few minutes. Time for some more clues.

Fourteen across, S-I--, hides family aboard Brunel's flagship (5). Move on, too easy. Four across. Starts for example may be full of rubbish (6). Yep, good, but quite easy. Five down, that's apt. Real idiot rewrote opinion column (9). Six down, S at the start. Contraction of psychiatrists? (7). Back to Janet and John! In fact, I am being unfair more Spot the Dog. Seven down. Men leave maiden to get help (3). For crying out loud. Nine across, -I-I---R. Inwardly, sibling is terribly frightening (8). Next. Thirteen across -O---N. Carry out principal sphere of influence (6).

Come on guys, or girls, this is terrible. I am glad now I am not at home, as this would have been annoying. My cup of tea wouldn't even be cool enough to sip yet. Ten down, I can guess without looking. Something about a drink with jam and bread, or a snack in Plumstead? What a shock I am right. Eleven down, -A--, curse sacred vow (4), oh goody a Sun crossword clue.

One more clue, and that's half of it done. I will have moved about thirty yards. So much for the distraction. Click. Ten gone, twenty to go. Sweat is starting to form; I am beginning to worry about it. Use one of the remaining wipes—that will work. That mark on the window is outside; I can't get to it. Now it will stare at me in defiance. It will be more of a challenge than this bloody crossword.

The water game has been my living for thirty-five years since I completed my master's. I am proud, I am. Being a leading—or one of many—experts on flooding, water management, and everything associated with the natural movement of it was gratifying. Largely being ignored and asked to put a certain gloss on reports wasn't. Over the last ten to fifteen years, the amount of redaction and language change I have completed was borderline criminal. The excuse was that reports had to be lawyer-proof. That was the logical next step post-consultation, apparently.

Even though they could be watertight—pun intended—they were always picked apart in the tribunal or planning meeting. It stank almost as much as having several thousand gallons of sewage rampaging through your living room. I know the report sitting in my briefcase will go through several iterations before emerging like an albino butterfly that has been in its pupal case far too long and has missed its moment in the sun—devoid of anything contentious or of content that would act as a scent for the hyenas in suits.

Click. Sixteen across. H---I---S. Where trips to the theatre send you to sleep (9). This is getting very dull; I may have to write and complain—or email, anyway. I have been doing their damn puzzles for twenty-five years. Perhaps that's it. Perhaps I have now done every clue; I have seen everything they can produce. What should I do if that's true? I can't go to another paper, can I? No. Same paper every day—that's the mantra. Keep the puzzle till evening. What can I do?

Eighteen across. E is the third letter. 'Surgical birth!' says Aryan aloud (9). Okay, so a little more thought in that one. Mentally pencil in that thought and see if anything backs it up. Fifteen down starts with S, nine letters. Reinstate the mentor with hidden records of transactions. Okay, so that fits what I thought. Praise too early, I think. Never mind. Click. The rain is getting slightly heavier, as I knew it would. There is a storm on the way—physically and symbolically.

If the predicted fall happens over the next few days, then the occupants of lower Wharfedale will need very big buckets. The ground is already saturated, and even the beavers would struggle with this one. The flak for us will be huge, despite the warnings. Despite the saying that people in glass houses shouldn't throw stones, you will find that they are usually the ones throwing the most. We will counter with another report, and the compulsive cycle will roll along yet again.

Fifteen gone, fifteen left. The house could be blown apart if I am not there, and I am not going to be. Should I ring a neighbour and ask them to check for me? No. They already think I'm odd for measuring the distance of their wheelie bin from the road. Don't they know the regulations? This would just add fuel to the fire. No—wrong statement. There will be no fire. The house has never blown up when I was there, obviously. So why would it now, just because I am not? Obviously. I can still see that mark on the outside. Should I get out and get rid of it?

The red lights are so bright now that they appear angry, mimicking the red faces of the soon-to-be flooded. The warnings will have already been put out by the Environment Agency, but I would lay a pound to a pinch of salt that the Golden Trianglers have largely ignored them. Such is their mindset, fuelled by the arrogance of their bank balance.

Click. Eighteen down. Should begin with C, if I am correct—and now that I suspect I have seen every clue, then I am. Where you hope for better luck when the chips are down (7). I am correct, then. What a surprise. Seventeen down—I will look at this and hope for more of a challenge. Beginning with A, nine letters. Publicise the drive east, for a change. Not even a sniff of a challenge.

Is that gas I can smell? Stop it! Twenty across. L-V--. Led Zeppelin broke this, perhaps. Back to the sun again. I am going to persevere with this insult to my brain, as I know it will have to be completed before the heating comes on. House blows up. No!

Twenty-two across. S---E-. City road follows walls or fleet. I mean, seriously? Twenty-one down. An E at the start. Sends goods abroad from former ports (7). Nineteen down. Even Anna will fasten with a hammer (4). Twenty-four across. -I---R-P. Runway provided heir's trip, we hear (8).

I think I can hear my brain slowly giving up the ghost. Click. Twenty past. Ten for an unknown future. Only seven clues left, and I am no further forward on the road than I was. The rain is still light. The other travellers will have different views of it, I hope. I am sure they won't care for it as much as I do.

Rainfall has been my life. I have travelled all over the world to study it. My flow records can attest to the locations and changes that have occurred. I get mails from my contacts in India, South America, and the US, telling me what changes in flow they have seen. I record all this as if I were there. It makes for worrying reading.

I think I can hear my brain slowly giving up the ghost. Click. Twenty past. Ten for an unknown future. Only seven clues left, and I am no further forward on the road than I was. The rain is still light. The other travellers will have different views of it, I hope. I am sure they won't care for it as much as I do.

Rainfall has been my life. I have travelled all over the world to study it. My flow records can attest to the locations and changes that have occurred. I get mails from my contacts in India, South America, and the US, telling me what changes in flow they have seen. I record all this as if I were there. It makes for worrying reading.

As for Europe, my little camper van and I have drawn a very grim picture of the ups and downs across most of the mainland. But if I don't do it, who else will, and I am used to being ignored, but I will persevere. The end of the world may not be coming, but a bloody big change is, my records tell us so.

Click. Big push. Twenty-three down. Makes fun of inferior paper (3), R--. Bit of a nerve there, I can make fun, but surely don't highlight it. Twenty-seven across, N-G-E---. Disregards strange leg scent. I have definitely seen them all, I am not even thinking about them. Five to go, and then release from puzzle purgatory. Twenty-five down. Stylish trams have returned. I mean seriously? Twenty-six, devoured eight apparently (3). Three to go, thank God.

Twenty-eight. -A-I-R. After middle age, a glazier is less active. I hope my pen runs out—at least I would be saved.

Talent agents find them at jamborees (6), beginning with S. Oh, I wonder what that could be?

Last one, and then I can concentrate on what is really important. ---T-E-S. Oh, for the love of puzzles. He stands in front of the Greek capital to see pagans.

Finished. Completed.

Click. Not a record—for a time, anyway. Can there be a record for simplicity, or is it, as I suspect, that I am complete?

It has now been twenty-four minutes since the lights—and only six until the heating does or doesn't blow my house up. That mark is still not shifting, even with the light rain. The guy in the white van is looking at me oddly.

I wonder what he would do if I got out. The girl over there has left her Mini, and there is no real commotion over that. Perhaps, then, nobody would mind. After all, I would be increasing everyone's safety if I removed a mark from the screen.

Put the crossword away under the report, ready to be filed with the last twenty-five years' worth. Get a wipe and get out. Nobody will notice.

Then you can relax.

Your house will still be there—just warm.

Relax, Peter. Just relax.

*****

Tina had done a double take—surely, she had not seen that? It had really taken the Jammy Dodger.

The bloke who had just edged past in the far lane had been doing a crossword. A fucking crossword. Had he had some sort of episode and thought he was at home? Tina was becoming more and more aware of the characters and fuckwittery going on around her. It was almost as if some strange occurrence had created a microcosm of the world and shoved it onto the motorway for her entertainment.

Except she wasn't entertained. She was so gobsmacked that she hunted for a pen and took note of the clown's registration number. She would pass this on and ask the starchy-suited ones to have a word. At least it distracted her from the boot of the Audi, she thought.

*****

5:53 pm

My spell at Her Majesty's pleasure had been many things. Salvation, if I told the truth—after all, I was fed three times a day, I was warm, and I had somewhere relatively safe to sleep. The whole being homeless thing had, at the time, been the cause of my latest set of criminal activities. Or so I believed. Most would probably say I was just a bad 'un.

It had also been a deterrent—I was never going back. Not that I would stop my activities; I just would never get caught again.

Bizarrely, it had also stopped my possible decline into the drug scene—a route that had been as inevitable as the dawn when I was on the streets. Inside, despite all the drugs floating about, I had stayed clean through sheer bloody-mindedness and a will to grasp this cure for my bad luck. It was ironic that I viewed prison as good luck. But I had never been back.

Despite my three years inside, I had definitely come out changed. I had developed a streak of self-preservation that, before prison, had been smothered in recklessness. That was the thought now as I again reviewed my options. The selfishness was being beaten over the head by the vision of my kids. I hoped they were sat in front of a TV and had not been tied up in a cupboard. My ex-wife—I couldn't give a toss about her, only in so much as how it might affect the kids.

There was not much point in watching the traffic anymore. My attention was now firmly fixed on the clock on the dashboard and its inexorable climb towards the top of the hour—a time when I would find out my fate and that of those I love.

A Silver Spoon on A Chain

I am so glad that I won't have this commute anymore. This traffic is abysmal—although this is worse than normal—but still, it will soon be a thing of the past. Buying the new flat made so much sense, even allowing for the increased costs. Despite the official moving date not being until next week, I had asked if I could mooch around, as it would be fun to see the flat without its trimmings.

In other words, completely devoid of human detritus or the stuff we carry around with us all our lives. All the stuff that we must have—yet if we lived off the back of a donkey and cart, we just wouldn't, would we? No, we damn well wouldn't. I now have the keys—picked them up earlier. I just couldn't resist. Well, no normal person could, surely. The place was empty, a blank canvas, and I could see it before all my stuff was dumped there in seven days.

The whole thing, my mini adventure, had made me approach it with a degree of juvenile excitement—something I had not felt in quite a few years, not since the incident with the slippers and the music teacher. I had approached my black, newly painted front door—my new door—singing a little ditty and strutting like Mick.

I stood on my new mat—one with ponies on it for some unknown reason—and inserted my new key. I am sure I would stop thinking about things as new once I had either reached the age of three score and ten or become bored with myself. Hopefully, the latter.

The two vehicles up ahead looked like they were moving house as well—how exciting. I knew pondering over the vehicle types was pointless. I was crap at that. I basically put them in simple categories: very small one, small one, large one, lorry, and bike—the last two being all-encompassing for anything not in the first three.

Oh, of course, there were the stupid twat ones—or "twit" if telling my mother. Those defined anyone who insisted on racing around the car parks opposite my old house at two a.m., doing what I believe is affectionately called doughnuts. The fact that they are round with a gap in the middle would be more suggestive of arseholes—a more fitting description considering the occupants' behaviour. Not that the little darlings would be a problem for much longer. In a matter of a week, they would be nothing more than a smudge of burning tyre smoke in my rear-view mirror.

House or flat buying is certainly interesting and usually comes with an unexpected twist—not just those created by the creatures of the night around completion dates. Unless you have only ever bought and moved into a new house, arriving at it armed only with a piece of paper to write your snagging list for the builder who took your house out of its box, then you should always expect something left by the previous occupant—other than carpets and electrical fittings, that is.

Although I have a friend, Katerina, who can tell you about all the light fittings and carpets being taken—and the battle she had to get anything done about it. You should expect something, even something nice, like a bottle of wine welcoming you to your new home.

In most instances, I hear tell it is more likely to be a squashed toothpaste tube by the sink in the bathroom, a slightly brown and crusty cloth on the taps in the kitchen, or even a bag of spuds in the cupboard in the hall. I had none of those little gifts, which poked holes in my generalised statistics. But what I did have waiting for me as I entered the flat completely blew them out of the water.

What was there, basking like a cat in a patch of prenoon light cast across the lounge in all its scruffy and slightly abused glory, was a piano! I don't remember a piano when I viewed the flat—and that had been twice. I cannot and refuse to believe that the previous owner had purposefully got one for me as a housewarming gift, so I can only assume that I need to hone my observation skills. Surely, there was no way I could have missed this.

Admittedly, the previous owner was old, and the house had been stuffed full of—well, old-person stuff. A testament to a life spent diligently collecting and arranging it. Surely, though, as a fairly intelligent woman with highly satisfactory eyesight and a job where I had to spot issues and problems and offer solutions, I would have noticed one—even if it was hiding behind the jardinière with a macassar for a hat, like a faux walnut-encrusted ninja.

The guys in the two small cars, with all their possessions in tow, didn't look like they would leave a piano lying about. They would have a mate with a van, and if they were really stuck, they would probably just bounce it down the stairs. I would ask the previous owner, but this was impossible due to her suffering from dementia and now being ensconced in a home. The daughter who dealt with everything said she was no longer in the same postcode as everyone else. The only nod to reality was that her mum knew all the words to "Hello" and some other song about evergreens.

What an odd world we live in. There had been nothing in the contract about a piano, and I had a sudden urge to keep it to myself—along with the words to a Pink Floyd song running through my already cluttered brain. Something about a grand piano and a silver spoon—none of which was really relevant in this instance—but stuck in traffic pondering a piano squatter seemed to have slightly pushed my synapses.

I had looked at my new flatmate with an eye more used to spotting typos in contracts, and my new flatmate looked at me like a piano sitting on an orange and brown carpet in the sun would. Not wanting to get too morbid, but I was moving into a new house and was on the wrong side of half of three score and ten, and the previous owner, Mrs Dalgleish, had left the building—figuratively and metaphorically. Was the piano the cause—like in that film with the amputated hand that commits all kinds of badness before being thrown on the fire? Was that how the piano was looking at me—daring me to light the gas fire in its presence? Upon closer inspection, my new flatmate did have a certain elegance and did not appear to exude any malice—only a slightly forlorn sadness.

Casting my mind back to when I was younger—oh, so much younger than before—piano lessons had been on the parental agenda. So yes, I could play a bit. Might be a bit rusty, but at least I wouldn't have a dried-up old witch hitting me with a stick on the knuckles when I erred. This old bitch had been the catalyst for everything that followed—all the pain I had to go through.

The abuse had only happened twice, but my new teacher—the one I had moved to after the incident with the old bag—had been at it with all his pupils. I might have recovered quicker if it had not been for the forces of law and order and the protracted court case. Which is why I am single, why I spend my time with pieces of paper, and why I find rogue pianos a challenge to my senses.

To distract myself from the darkness that could creep up occasionally, I wondered what to do about the piano—how we could have a bit of "us" time, enjoy a getting-to-know-each-other period. Like having a man about, but without the toilet seat problem. In fact, the rest of the problems that come with having a male weigh anchor in your life would not have to be negotiated—one of the other reasons I stay on my own.

So, what to do? Mrs Dalgleish—not an option. The daughter—her name will come back to me—might lay a claim and want it back. If I move in properly next week, then it will be stuck and hiding behind my Barker and Stonehouse sofa with a fluffy pillow on its head. I could go down the solicitor route and check, but scenario two would still be an issue. Or I could keep it.

With this in mind, and having lost far too much of my life trying to work out what to do with it by watching daytime telly, I used the said accrued knowledge, taking off the back to see if I could identify the maker, model, or any other useful fact. Who knows? It could be worth something—enough to retire to more daytime telly—and wouldn't that be ironic?

The label read *JD Williams, Newcastle, England* and was dated—5th December 1934. Surely not? This had me envisioning a life of absolute idleness and sofa-moulding with a remote in hand. When I Googled it, my world instantly deflated. Two hundred quid if I was lucky—unless it was a concert grand, then forget it.

What had me wondering, and was vaguely interesting—well, to me anyway—was that the keys were made of ebony and ivory. The real stuff. A Google search also revealed that, as the piano was from at least nineteen-thirty-four, it predated the 1947 CITES agreement. The one I kept hearing about on daytime telly and *Antiques Roadshow* and always thought would never affect me—well, there you go. At least it meant I wasn't going to get raided by trading standards or other council-invested warriors.

Because of this Google-inspired revelation, I wandered around my lounge, trying to get rid of the worst earworm I had ever experienced. My life is often punctuated with snippets of songs or the application of lyrics to situations. Thanks to the deities of the internet, I now had that really annoying eighties refrain from Wonder and McCartney threaded through my head.

The slightly cruel streak in me then thought of regaling any or all of my friends, family, and acquaintances with this integral part of the story. If I had to suffer, then they bloody well would as well. Even now, sitting here in a frigging traffic jam with all these people around me, I wanted to get out and inflict this worm on everyone. Just thinking about those lost minutes earlier today made it resurface. Bloody hell!

This metaphor for world peace—and an affront to music—took me to a slightly different place, however, one that wasn't as prevalent or publicised when it was written. The keyboard itself didn't just represent a weird marketing version of harmony; it was an eighty-five-year-old tangible example of man's destruction of the planet. Ebony, one of the rare timbers, was being illegally forested in the rainforests, commanding an obscenely high black-market price.

The travesty of the ivory market is well reported and, despite the nineteen-forty-seven agreement, is still happening. Yet should my guilt be assuaged by this agreement? My thought process—sitting in my Toyota hybrid (yes, I was being as green as I could be)—was now being driven by a darkness that the two songsters had not even considered. A metaphor for destruction was sitting in my lounge. My new lounge was a haven for a lament—an epitaph to the world as it is.

Before I had locked up and left my new flat, I did a quick calculation on the ivory. Nothing scientific, you understand, as Emily doesn't do science. Scribbling on the back of an imaginary fag packet produced the possibility that, sitting in the sun, was not a piano cat or a walnut-robed ninja but about a tenth of the tusk of an average-sized elephant.

I had entered my new home with a spring in my step—not quite joy in my heart, but mildly stimulated. Within a few minutes, once the surprise had worn off, there, sitting on my new carpet, I could see the destruction of our planet played out without sound on an old piano that had escaped my notice. All valued at less than two hundred quid.

I felt my newfound elation evaporate. My happiness was now as extinct as the elephant nearly was. I now feel conflicted—destroying Pontus (yes, I have given it a name) would remove it from my sight but not my conscience. If I keep him, then a long-dead animal and tree will at least have a purpose, even if it is just to sharpen the awareness of our human stupidity.

If this piano was not a metaphor for our blinkered view of the natural world, then I don't know what was. I could weep. I hadn't done so throughout the earlier trauma, but something in this had really touched a nerve.

Yes, I could weep, but the fellow dwellers on the motorway, all burning up the residue of dead marine creatures, would wonder at me. And would they be right? After all, it was just a surprise piano.

*****

Ray resumed watching the red lights and the car that was his and Tina's baby, a brief silence falling as he further considered the repercussions. The radio chattered away, updating the veritable army of field officers working at various points in the country, the whole thing like background noise—something akin to chickens in a coop. Unintelligible to any other than the listening chickens.

The traffic was still moving sporadically, doing its shuffle thing, yet Matt Connors had made no effort to move any quicker. It was strange. The whole thing was now playing on his mind, and for some reason, he wanted to call Tina and suggest they let the Audi move a bit further away—just to be on the safe side, of course. The clock now read *17:53*.

*****

5:54 pm

My vision was momentarily diverted from the non-ticking clock and my troubles by a heap of shite belching all sorts of crap into the atmosphere. Most of it seemed to be going through the slots on the front of the knackered old Land Rover I had seen earlier. I considered waving at the Landy driver and telling him to shut his slots, but if the guy hadn't worked it out yet—well, fuck him.

How the driver of that rusty old Vauxhall Corsa got away with being on the road was beyond me. I know my van was no oil painting, but at least it was a good runner and probably nearly street-legal—even if the plates weren't its real ones. I mean, for fuck's sake, love, spend your pennies on getting it fixed or buying a better one. Even in the bad old days, I hadn't driven anything that crappy.

It had been a while since I had thought of her, but for some reason, she popped up, and I wished I could call Lizzie and let her know what was happening. She would be worried, and if she rang his ex-wife, then I wasn't sure what would happen there. They talked to each other—nearly on a civil level—but would Lizzie go around if she got no reply?

I hoped to God she wouldn't take that course of action, because as far as I knew, the bastards were at my old house. Only because that's what I would do—it was better than trying to move unwilling hostages. I would offer up a prayer if I believed in there being anything out there. The sadness that descended was due to my complete impotence. I may as well have had my hands tied as well.

The despair was shifting upwards now that the appointed hour was only six minutes or so away. Soon, I would know my fate, and as much as I was hanging onto the hope that the threat might be empty, that hope could well be hollow.

And God I Know I'm One

This car really was a heap of crap, and I would be the first to admit it. However, what all those others out there didn't know was that it only had to get me home. That was a comforting thought—this was its last hurrah. It was almost as if it knew and was quite happy to be sitting here, belching out all sorts of crap. The grinding noise from the front wheel—which can't be good either—was its way of telling me its woes or saying goodbye.

What must all the others think? Most of them are insulated inside air-conditioned cocoons, probably just tutting at the muck. The smell will be kept from their rich little noses. Apart from that bloke in the old Land Rover—last time we moved, he got a double-barrelled belch right across those slits in the front. You would have thought he'd have closed them by now. Well, they are his lungs.

If I could tell you people, I would—this car will be hitting the scrapheap or banger circuit shortly. The dents, rust, and general disordered state of it were synonymous with the state of my life—until last night, that is. There would be no more cold mornings where a start was as rare as a politician answering the question they were asked. No lower back pain from a seat that may have been designed by Torquemada.

I will no longer have to endure being stuck on Radio 3 or listening to the Christmas CD that's jammed in the player. Life is certainly going to be a lot different—all because of that one little thing, or that run of little things, that has effectively made me something I haven't been for so long. Not just solvent, but a happy human being with more money than I have ever had.

Yes, the endorphins help—boy, the rush over the last few days had practically burnt me out. A new dawn will rise on my relationship with my husband—the one I have been wilfully destroying over the years, denting it and causing the rust to form. There is one more obstacle to overcome, and I can see the arguments unfolding in front of me. Sadly, the traffic cannot be said to be doing the same.

My problem had been under control—whether everyone else would agree with that statement is open to question, but I would defend it. I liked to gamble a little, mainly on scratchcards—that sort of thing—never spending more than I had. I mean, someone has to win, right? I did okay, won a little, lost a bit more, but it can't have been a problem, as no one was giving me any shit over it.

My husband was usually silent. There might be an occasional raise of the eyebrow if he found the carcasses of dead scratchcards in the bin—much as he would if they had been chocolate wrappers or wine bottles in the recycling. I usually managed to get rid of those a little better, ha-ha.

It had been a slow spiral, and I had been in a little trouble financially, with only a limited exit strategy. Then the pandemic hit, and bloody COVID was to blame for the escalation—not only of my gambling but of my husband's disapprobation. Living in his orbit for nearly every hour of the day had raised the stakes considerably, and it sure as hell wasn't one of my wedding vows. I could almost feel the disapproval through the wall if I opened my laptop in another room.

Once, I even tried the garden shed, having realised that the Wi-Fi worked out there—a solution that, on the surface, looked golden. I even got over my stupid fear of insects and arachnids. What I couldn't get over was being stalked by my own life partner, who snuck up to the shed and entered with a violence more appropriate for a cartoon. I had half expected a speech bubble to appear above his head with "Aha!" in it. Mine would have been more along the lines of "#@t!c%*."

The violence was directed at the door rather than me, as I don't think he would fancy himself in a scrap with me—or so I kidded myself.

That was the price of COVID. I was now gambling online—on anything, but mainly slot machines. I had tried poker once, but that just made my head hurt. This was my escalation from some poxy scratchcards and the occasional tenner in a fruit machine. Enforced boredom and closer-than-normal proximity to my husband were the driving forces behind my new hobby.

I loved my husband, but I liked to put that love into about thirty per cent of my existence. Once that existence starts creeping up to ninety and above, the pot is stretched thin. I am sure he was having the same problem, but the main difference was that he had more control and wasn't pissing everything up the wall on gambling websites.

My mind wandered back to my life, to this exact moment, sitting in this car. I had a day-old smell. I would have loved to have freshened up before I breached my front door, but that was just not going to happen. There would be some wet wipes in my bag, and a squirt of perfume or deodorant would have to suffice. Let's have a look now—better to be sure I have the makings of some sort of freshening up.

The first thing on top of my bag was the envelope with the casino logo on it—the reason for my happiness, the reason for my optimism, and the reason I will only have to endure this car for a little while longer. The reason my husband may have me back and may even find a way to start down the path to forgiveness. I know he still loves me—or a bit of me, anyway.

The bit of me that doesn't want to shout 'heads' at the flip of a coin or who can give you the payout ratios on a roulette wheel. That envelope will be the equivalent of surgery on the bit he doesn't love. If there were a cure for the cancer of gambling, that envelope could be it.

Never had more hope ridden on such an innocuous object. In the dark ages, they would have built a shrine to it and worshipped it as part of the True Cross. It was my True Cross. I had carried my problem for so long and had seen many who believed in me—or believed me—fall by the wayside. I had endured the ridicule and resentment from those I would have called close. Yet, I had made it to my personal Gethsemane, even if it was an upmarket members-only gambling establishment. There, I had received my salvation and, hopefully, my redemption.

I had time on my hands, and I recalled a dream I had had a couple of times. It was odd, even by my standards. I was in my garden, and the echo of two shotgun retorts was rebounding off the shed wall. Yes, that shed. What was more unusual—apart from the shotgun—was the large pile of seagull corpses near the Leylandii.

It appeared that I had blown the fuckers away—the rats with wings that had been a personal nemesis of mine ever since I was little and one of the greasy, smelly, noisy bastards had pinched my chips at the seaside. As far as I was concerned, I would be performing a public service if I could blow their fish-and-chip-smelling brains to kingdom come.

However, I knew it was a dream because I was fairly sure nobody would let me have a gun. All this was because of the trauma of losing a few chips of the potato kind—the others were in the future.

The significance of this dream now came to me. I had spent the last few years losing more than a few chips. The seagulls were my inner voices—demanding to be fed and making more and more noise the hungrier they got. I had finally found my figurative shotgun and blasted the little bastards out of existence. I now had more chips than I had ever had, and that was the way back from the nightmare I had endured. Freud, eat your weird, blackened heart out.

Putting aside the envelope physically, because I couldn't escape this one mentally. I rummaged a little more and found the required wet wipes. Time for a little underarm and neck maintenance. That felt better—under my tits as well. I felt nearly human. A quick squirt of body spray advertising forty-eight-hour freshness. The world could be wearing roses twined through its auburn locks or artificially created freesias anyway.

The human fug had dispersed, though the car not so much. I was still belting out all sorts of poisonous-looking fog. Just ignore it—busy yourself with putting all your crap back in your bag. Have a little dream of the next car you will have—something sporty, something girly for you, and something for the husband that would make him feel like he had the biggest dick in the world.

A little lie wouldn't hurt. It would, though, wouldn't it? That was where all this started. One little lie, a slightly bigger one to cover the first, and soon, you needed a spreadsheet to keep track of all your deceits, deceptions, and downright untruths. The money was the hardest thing to hide—or rather, the way I had siphoned off any I could to feed my seagulls.

The money was killing him indoors. We both had reasonably well-paid jobs—a modicum of success, if you like. The kid thing was not an issue for either of us, as we had both said virtually from day one that we didn't want them. That was still true today, on my side anyway. If he decided he wanted to have them now, then he would have to find another greenhouse to plant his cuttings. Not going to happen here. Fairly confident he still feels the same.

Up until last week when I disappeared, anyway. But not much would have changed in seven days in his world. Working from home had been a nightmare. Neither of us was deemed sufficiently important to justify travelling in. Slight kick to the old ego there. So, we laboured through, each in our 'office'—his in the spare room, mine at the dining table. I did what I needed to, but the constant pressure of work being absent let me into a world where the seagull voices were louder and more convincing.

At the start of lockdown, we still had some savings. Our credit cards were almost balance-free. The mortgage was small and had only a few years left. We were comfortable—more comfortable than a lot of our friends and most of our families. You could have said we had it all. The key word, in hindsight, was had. So why did I fuck it all up?

Everything. I had fucked up everything in six months. Although, to be fair, the first three months were okay, so the fucked-up-ness only happened in the second half. After that, I spent all my energy constantly reinventing lies and deceptions, keeping him at arm's length from anything vaguely financial. I told him that since I was the one with the most free time, I might as well use it to keep everything up to date. The circle I found myself in was so vicious it would need the RSPCA and a taser to take it down if it ever got out.

By the end of lockdown, I had managed to spend all our savings and max out my cards—even after doubling the limit. There were loans in my name on the bank account, and the seagulls were demanding more. Their voices cried out for another session on the slots or the virtual roulette.

My world came crashing down three days after I returned to my company's office. He had been unwell and stayed at home. I am sure at that moment, fate, with its taste for cheap melodrama, came out of the darkness and created its mischief. The bank was now concerned and sent an envoy—not under a white flag, but under an umbrella and carrying a metal briefcase.

Unsurprisingly, my triumphant return home that evening was not accompanied by flags and trumpets. It was more of a Pinteresque production, where the main character—me—really had no clue, and everything was very gloomy. Gloomy, in this case, was sitting at the breakfast bar, surrounded by lies and deceptions, all of them bearing the logos of the various financial institutions I was indebted to. Technically, it was we, but I didn't want to point that out at the time.

The opening scenes of *Saving Private Ryan* had less drama than the next twenty minutes. It culminated in my dismissal from the field of play. He had even packed my bag. The instruction? To go, reflect, think of the future, get my head straight—all the other clichés you could imagine. I was still sick of the sight of him from lockdown, so I took the opportunity. I had a couple of hundred in my purse and a membership at an international chain of casinos that had promised me some credit, so who was going to argue? Not me, for one.

The seagulls squawked me to the casino and the promise of happier times. My entry into this establishment was slightly ignoble. They required seventy-two hours to validate the credit—or some other administrative stalling technique. The seagulls went berserk. Checking into a conveniently adjacent budget hotel, I managed to eke out a shotgun shell by playing low-stakes games and enjoying the general ambience. Avoiding alcohol was key, as drinking, as is common knowledge, lessens inhibitions. My purse couldn't stand lessening anything. Booze was off the cards—at least until the promised credit came in.

Three very long days later, the credit arrived—like a ship of the line returning from plundering some foreign field in the name of empire. The casino, based on my up-to-then impeccable deceit and the supply of out-of-date financial information, gave me an account with ten grand credit. Ten grand. I mean, ten thousand shotgun shells. Time to shut those seagulls up—for a while, at least. The roulette table was calling, and with that simple decision made, my life changed forever. That's how I feel about it.

The sequence of events was quite quick, but pressing the button for a nuclear attack is quick and simple compared with the consequences. The results here were just as cataclysmic. I placed a one-hundred-pound chip on a corner—that's four numbers and pays eight to one. It came in. Not a bad start. I split the winnings in half and let it ride three times on the third dozen, and they all came in. Yes, they all came in. Only a two-to-one payout, but I now had three thousand nine hundred in winnings. It took less than five minutes.

I then lost a couple of spreads and was down to two and a half of my winnings. The seagulls were watching rather than flapping about. I took a massive chance and went back to my original corner, putting all my winnings on. When the ball dropped, I was up to over ten-k.

You would have thought that this would be the point when I realised the seagulls had gone and my luck had to change. Everyone knows this—if you have a big win, don't chase another one. It won't happen. Ignoring all this was simple—I still had my credit in the account. If I used all my winnings and lost, then I hadn't really lost, as I was back to where I started. Impeccable logic.

All sense left me at this point. My tactic had worked quite well up to now—better than it ever had in the virtual world. Why would I put ten-k on a single number? Why? Because the payout was thirty-five to one. I would be clear. I could go back home, reflect, and be contrite, a promise on my lips to cease and desist and get some help. That's why I did it.

In the movies, a crowd would have gathered round the table as my run went on. In reality, I was accompanied by two sweaty members of the middle-management fraternity and the croupier. He had made the call to accept the bet on number six. They let it go. It dropped in—almost in slow motion, or so it appeared. The looks of sheer jealousy on my gambling cronies' faces were priceless, as I am sure the look on mine was. I had just won about three hundred and forty thousand pounds. Life-changing? It most certainly could be.

Now, sitting in this traffic with a cashier's draft for three hundred and sixty thousand pounds in a manila envelope. Slightly smelly I may be, but who cares? He would have to take me back, wouldn't he? Everyone would take me back. Everyone would believe in me again. I had walked away. The cure was in my bag.

Will this keep us happy? Will it keep the seagulls away? Or will they return, and I find out I have run out of cartridges?

*****

Which was true—not that the driver of the blue Audi, Matt Connors, knew about the tail. He thought he knew what the something in the boot was, but not conclusively. His mind was on other things as he sat in the queue with thousands of others, looking at the not-so-pretty lights.

Ray and Tina could only guess what he was doing or thinking and react if needed, being the professionals they were trained and programmed to be. They knew they would probably not have to fire their weapons, although they would no doubt draw them if the intel was right—that is. They might have to shout a lot if the takedown came while they were in traffic. Ray had his fingers crossed that they could do it away from prying eyes and, more importantly, smartphones.

Realistically, they both knew the days of being camera-free had gone, which only put more reliance on their professional training. The problem was that even in the most competent and rule-abiding takedown, it could look brutal and violent, and the current public view would use this as a stick to beat the security services with some more. Even after the disaster in York, the public was more interested in posting on the internet than helping. The distress for the victims' families could only be multiplied by this, but the caring had been taken out of the majority of our civilised society.

A sadness descended on Ray, mixing with the guilt for his inaction during the ongoing incident, meaning he was not in a good way. If action was needed, he could only hope his head was right—not only for him but for Tina, who would expect him to have her back, and for the driver of the Audi. The clock had done its clock thing and was announcing that it was now 17:55.

*****

5:55 pm

Not having any music or even talk radio in the cab had just allowed the silence to foster—or perhaps fester—my thoughts, all ending up in tighter and tighter circles. The outcome stretched into the distance like this jam. Perversely, time appeared to be slowing now as the hour of my fate approached. All I was doing was going over and over the same ground. I had to face the fact that my life of petty and occasionally more serious crime had led me here to this point.

My kids, by virtue of being my kids, were detained somewhere, and I had no idea—apart from running away—how to extricate myself and them. The van slightly in front of me looked even worse than this one, but at least it was carrying a kosher cargo—or so I assumed. Then again, why would I assume that? My last assumption had not worked out so well. I had been confident this would be a simple in and out when Chaz approached me—the call with the incentive only coming when I was on the road. Chaz obviously didn't trust me, and why would he—or indeed, should he?

Watching the other van, now just inside me, there was nothing to do but allow the despondency to settle, wait for whatever might happen to happen, and then pick up whatever pieces of my life were left. I was definitely not staying around to be used again by Chaz. I could go all *Die Hard* and wreak my revenge on him, but I was fairly sure that getting anywhere near him would be a struggle and ultimately futile.

The likely outcome would be my probable disappearance, and that would be no good for the kids. Better to have the occasional visit wherever I ended up than to become the subject of teenage angst and speculation through absence.

This was a fucking mess.

You Can't Take a Joke

Serves me right, I suppose—last in the depot, crappiest van to take out. Although not quite as bad as the one next to me, this one really takes the prize biscuit. It should be condemned. Perhaps it is an ironic judgement for all my past sins—or perceived ones, anyway. If they knew them all, well, that would be a different story.

Do I, deep down, really deserve this? I had taken the day off yesterday for a damned good reason—not a pleasant or facile one, but a real one. I had filled in all the forms and gone through the process, and yes, it may have put someone out, giving me an emergency day off, but it couldn't be avoided. To be perfectly honest, I wish I could have swerved it, retaining my dignity and some self-esteem. That seemed particularly important at the moment, and that was what the day was for—but there was no space on the e-form for that excuse.

This van is really stalling my thought process. I was hoping to have some time while I drove about to consider the repercussions of yesterday's little tête-à-tête. What is that smell? It's not the cargo, as that is all in cardboard and plastic, and I am fairly sure I am not carrying repackaged body odour with a hint of dog shit. Although sometimes, some of my cargo does seem to border on the bizarre. This one seems to be located more front and centre. A quick sniff of myself confirms it is definitely not me.

Concentrate. This is the ideal time to think while we are stationary. Luckily, this is a there-and-back drop, so only one call if needed to advise of a delay. The destination is twenty-four hours, though, so only a minor inconvenience for them, even if it messes up my day. Night, to be precise—but who cares? Indeed, who does care? My wife—sorry, soon-to-be ex-wife—sure as hell wouldn't. The only one who would miss me is the cat, and only when his dry food ran out.

Perhaps I should show more drive—ironic, considering—and I might even agree with anyone who told me that. Perhaps I should stand up for myself more, and I might even agree with that too. This van is the evidence before the jury. I should have said no on the grounds that it smelt funny and that the seat had been set for a three-foot-six, four-hundred-pound primate with very short legs, and I couldn't fix it. So, not only do I have to put up with the smell, I am uncomfortable while doing so.

For the last ten minutes, I had been jiggling around, trying to move the bloody seat in a vain attempt to remove the pain in my arse—unlike my wife, who had hired a very good solicitor to remove hers. I am sure the other drivers around me are amusing themselves as they watch the skinny bloke in the van do some sort of dance, culminating in him sniffing himself. The sad fact in all this is that yes, I could push myself more—but I was happy with my lot.

Put aside the smell and the seat, the job allowed me a lot of thinking time. I got to go to places I hadn't been before, even though most involved a warehouse. Occasionally, I got to stay away. So, what was not to like? The pay, if I am honest—but I was happy. Ish.

Pulling the lever very hard finally made my seat shoot back like I was in the cockpit of a fighter jet. Luckily, I was stopped from joining the cargo of crap that nobody wanted in the back by the cabin wall. That and the fact that the back of my head wouldn't perform some weird osmosis through steel. At least I could stretch my legs now, even though I couldn't quite reach the cup holder. If there were a magic button to jettison the smell, I would find it.

Now free and clear, I checked the bottom of my boots just in case and confirmed it was definitely not me. Looking at the manifest on the board beside me, I checked that it wasn't something I should worry about. No, it was cartoon character Christmas decorations. As I thought—crap that nobody wanted, but I could bet they would sell out. I had four hundred boxes of two hundred. That is a shitload of crap. Mine is not to wonder why and all that. Just drive the stinky van, Dan.

Yesterday had been one of those days—when you are there, you don't want to be, and you feel a quiet disconnect from reality. The day off had been spent—well, three hours of it anyway—being torn to pieces by my own solicitor. To be fair, she was just recounting a whole load of stuff that her—the wife's—solicitor had passed on. A particularly vicious game of Chinese whispers, in my opinion.

My brief didn't seem to get any visible pleasure out of it, though she looked like she would affirm to my wife that she agreed with all the points, given half a chance. That's what you get when you are neither too picky nor too pushy. You get whatever it says on the tin—and in this case, it said divorce lawyer. And all in the spirit of bad frigging karma, I got my particular version.

A hunger had crept in, and as I could just about reach my bag with the pre-packaged dinner in it, the choice was simple. There was a need for sugar, so I ignored the sandwich for a minute and went for the sweet hit. Chocolate, washed down with something packed with enough chemicals to be a by-product of Union Carbide.

Once that was all sorted, I could safely say my mouth tasted sweet enough to make a bee gag or attract a herd of wasps. I felt better for it, though—so I could reflect, slightly more comfortably and suitably chemically enhanced, on what my member of the legal sisterhood had recounted the day before.

The list, when narrated, was slightly sad, in no way spectacular, and probably familiar to the millions who had gone before me. It was like an anti-shopping list—all the things you would avoid as you walked around your supermarket of choice. Only, you were looking for a life partner. Sex didn't matter. In that sex did matter, but the actual derivative didn't.

It was similar to a mental tick list of all the things a quick-witted or shrewd parent should have told you before you left home—the things you should look out for. If any of those things were present, then you should run a mile, even if they had a discount sticker or were part of some other hard-to-ignore deal.

I had managed to use delaying tactics as I didn't want 'divorced' written on my CV. The easiest excuse was hiding behind COVID. Meetings weren't possible, post went missing, and my internet connection was up and down. I had managed to delay yesterday for a good few months. Not that this impressed anybody. It did make me feel better, though.

The cat had understood when I told him and had given his approval by yawning—which, as we all know, is cat for 'yep, got that, now move on.' I had sat in front of my personal legal Amazon—the one costing me a fortune I was fairly sure I didn't have—and listened to a long list of grievances. Was that the right word? No, because 'grievance' points a grubby little finger at injustice. I don't think at any point I had not been justified in the way I existed, so by that logic, I think Shona was being a bit harsh.

On the flip side, once you saw the list, you could almost write it down as a betting accumulator—one that led to the jackpot payout of irreconcilable differences. In normal person talk, I think that means I had fallen well short on the tick list of must-haves. Shame Shona hadn't done this before we got married. Perhaps I should add that to my list!

My advocate read the list with so little emotion I expected her to add 'amen' at the end—it was so much like a sermon, it took me back to being eight years old. That was the last time I had been in a church, apart from funerals and weddings—not that there's fundamentally any difference in my jaded world.

Both ceremonies were attended by people who, if they thought about it, didn't want to be there. I had been distracted during this diatribe by Ms Jenkin's earrings. They were so bright and sharply pointed as to be almost aggressive. I could imagine her going into the jeweller's and asking for some angry earrings. Made me smile as I listened to the droll list.

The broad highlights of Shona's gripes were as follows: I apparently went out of my way to be unpleasant and rude to her family. She was right about that, as her sacred family were not—they were basically irritants who wouldn't know privacy and personal space if it bit them. So, yep, score one for Shona.

I am told that I talk to people in a way that can offend. This apparently embarrasses her, and she is not prepared to continue living in constant fear of a stranger's umbrage.

Next on the gospel of vindictiveness was my inability to admit that I am ever wrong. In fact, I am apparently steadfast in my belief that I am always right— that I also inform people they are wrong and I am right in a manner likely to cause upset. You can see a picture forming here.

The next one is even harder to believe (and the pun is intended, I think)—I don't uphold her belief in God. This is great, considering her conversion was only a few years ago due to some perceived trauma one of her friends experienced. I failed to see the connection and held steadfastly to my absolute atheism, a point I am quite proud of.

I had no drive or ambition and consistently poured scorn on anyone with these attributes, including her good self. The list had gone on further, and to me, each point was more and more trivial. It was like a cumulative score—family, one point; God, five points; stubborn, two points; offence to strangers, etc., until you reach twenty points, and then you have irreconcilable differences—the lawyer jackpot.

The sad thing about this was that at no point was I asked my opinion on any of it; it was a fait accompli. If I had been asked, I would have pointed out that I didn't want to reconcile them, as the differences were all on her part. I was always right, right?

If I had time—and as I actually did, sitting here in this bloody traffic—I would write an alternative list. I grabbed the clipboard and, on a spare manifest from the back of it, started to scribble my thoughts on what I perceived as Shona's irreconcilable differences—or, more to the point, the things she should have accepted as normal behaviour.

Firstly, just because the people on the TV can't hear me doesn't mean it isn't perfectly acceptable for me to argue with them. Next, I am entitled to my opinions and therefore have the right to express them, even if they shouldn't be aired in public.

This is great—I should have done this ages ago. I will hold any belief that reflects the way I want to run my life; stick ambition and drive where the sun doesn't shine—or even where it comes from. Just because I don't like highbrow literature doesn't mean I can't read what entertains me. It doesn't make me a philistine. I will only wear a tie when you do.

On the fashion note, there is nothing wrong with telling you that only a man can iron a shirt correctly—because it is true.

I was starting to really enjoy myself and could imagine Miss Angry Earrings reading this back to Shona's hired advocate. At least it was helping me ignore the traffic, and to be honest, there was no great clamour or world shortage for the crap in the back of my van. If I were so inclined, I could get out and take a straw poll of my fellow travellers on their need for Homer Simpson fairy lights.

But, as I am always right, there would be no point—apart from stretching my previously compacted legs. I will add that to the list about being right—at least we can agree on that one. Also, taking instructions is not a priority for me, so be forearmed, Miss Jenkins—I am more likely to completely go off on a tangent.

Anybody who doesn't like sport of some kind is genetically flawed and should be shot. I think my list is starting to get a little trivial, but as it is not legally admissible, I think I will continue.

I feel no obligation or guilt about being a carnivore—I will be vegetarian only if I feel like it. Puppies and kittens are never cute. Tables are at elbow height for a reason. Sitting in my pants watching TV and eating crisps is perfectly acceptable behaviour in my culture.

There is nothing humorous about sitcoms, particularly reruns of *Friends*.

As long as there is alcohol, there will always be a way.

So, there you are Shona my darling you may have found me wanting, you may think that I didn't love you, but as you know I am always right. In this instance however it looks like there may be a shred of truth. Who knew. This is what feels like to admit I was fallible. Perhaps this is the dawning of a new age. Nah. Let's just drive this van with its cargo of crap to wherever. That's enough drive and ambition for me for now. Roll on the divorce. At least I wasn't driving the other van, the one that looked worse than mine, only it had knackered suspension as well, judging by the wallow as it slipped behind me in my mirrors.

*****

The tension was too much for Tina. She wanted to go and point her gun in Connors' face and get him to open the boot of the Audi. At least then she would know.

She had even considered pulling over and letting the Audi move away a bit, as sitting this close to something she was beginning to think was a lot more than a boot full of Class-A drugs was not in her job description.

She knew she was winding herself up about it, and it could be exactly what it said on the tin—but this waiting for something to happen was playing on her mind too much. And, as most of her acquaintances knew, an overstimulated Tina was not someone you wanted to be near.

5:56 pm

The traffic was still trying to slither around, like slugs that have been doused with salt. Although the emissions from this lot would be a lot more damaging than a bit of slime from a dying slug. One of those funny little SUVs appeared in my peripheral vision. The one made by the company where the guy was telling us to do the math. I think they were from Poland or somewhere like that, and supposed they might be practical for those that needed something to carry a large load in. A dark thought popped in about being a body to carry, perhaps. The driver didn't look like the type though. I tried to attract their attention as her front plate was hanging a little loose, and the old bill would pull her for it if they could. She had studiously ignored me, so much for the good citizen bit. Well, fuck her. I hoped she got pulled and did have a body in the boot, would serve her right.

The satnav appeared to have gone to sleep, as it hadn't uttered a word for at least fifteen minutes—probably given up, just like I nearly had.

Well, fuck the satnav as well.

Fuck Chaz and his bully-boy tactics.

Fuck the motorway.

As I ranted, I realised—fucking hell—I am surrounded by complete barm pots and loons.

What was it all about? Who the fuck knew?

I sure as hell didn't.

I just hoped I would find out eventually.

I Think We All Could Use Some Sleep

The thing is, I shouldn't have got myself involved. I should have let Aleesha sort it out herself, but it was hard when you lived next door to someone—practically in their pocket. So, I had stupidly stuck my head above the parapet, or whatever the phrase is. From a war, I think, and so apt when I think about it. Hindsight is a killer—no shock there. It just couldn't go on: Aleesha and Darren shouting at each other, one or both of them throwing things about.

The violence was there, but I just couldn't make out the reason for it. It was like listening to a horror film set piece without any visual clues and with your ears stuffed with your fingers. Their voices were distinctively muddled—it couldn't be anyone else. The level and intensity had deepened over the months. Trying to talk to Aleesha about it was difficult, bordering on impossible. She couldn't hide the marks, but she effectively told me to piss off and mind my own business.

A cultural difference—her pride and upbringing not allowing her to admit anything to strangers. This was despite the family schism that had developed when she moved in with Darren.

A couple of weeks ago, I had even grabbed her sister in a car park in town, trying to get her take on it. She was cagey and admitted she was worried but, like me, had not been able to get through to Aleesha. Perhaps it was time I grew a conscience. Perhaps—and this thought was one I couldn't shake—I should take a stand and do something about it myself. This had been sitting with me for a few weeks now, the little voice saying, "Go on, Trace, do something."

The normal attitude would be to ignore it, but how could I? Aleesha was a victim here. Darren was a bully. Admittedly, not a particularly impressive one—physically, anyway—but do you need physical size to achieve any level of domestic violence? My campaign had started with a leaflet and a phone number, given to Aleesha as if we were doing a drug deal. Hidden inside a magazine like a bookmark, easily explained if asked.

The next day, I picked up the leaflet from my floor under the letterbox, covered in the unmistakable smell and evidence of human shit. A shock ran through me, nearly striking my newfound conscience down. What thought process could possibly have led someone—and I assumed Darren—to do this? It was a real eye-opener.

This new level bothered me greatly. Darren had, up until now, largely ignored me. On the occasions we did cross paths, he was more interested in the contents of my jumper or t-shirt than anything I might have said. I could live with that, as pervy as it was. I didn't feel dirty, like some would say—I just felt sad for this little man who got his kicks looking at women's chests.

This, however, was different. I just found it hard to compute—how he, and again I was assuming, could have done it. What imagined course of thought had led him to believe this was a good idea? I would definitely have preferred direct confrontation. If that happened, I would know it was him. This, however, could have been Aleesha—unlikely, but still, there was a small element of doubt. She could have been pressured into it, couldn't she?

I thought about this for a couple of days. I didn't want to force the matter, so I studiously ignored and avoided both of my neighbours. This was mainly because of the shock but also because I wanted to formulate a plan. How would I approach either of them? It was not something you casually brought up in conversation. "The weather is rubbish, isn't it? And thanks for the shit." The passive approach suited me better at this point.

My best friend, Aoife, told me to go to the police. I had considered this, but I saw only a difficult conversation, and the evidence was already flushed away. There would be no opportunity to go all CSI on it. The likelihood of one of them admitting it was on a par with the police's interest in doing anything about it. Parking was the chosen course for all these reasons.

It was two in the morning, and I had been listening to them going at it for about an hour. The muffling was as effective as usual. Coming only a couple of days after the letterbox event, it pushed me into calling the police. I even gave my details. When they asked if anyone was in imminent danger, how could I answer that?

The dampening of sound gave me no point of reference, so I answered that I didn't know. What that meant, in reality, was that they woke me up three hours later, asking if it was still going on. It wasn't. They said they would send someone round later in the day to talk to them. Emergency response, my arse. They didn't attend at all the next day, and when I rang to query this, they did their diplomatic best to tell me that they couldn't, really, because of manpower etcetera, but could I ring them if it happened again? Before I hung up, I asked them if my tin star was in the post. They didn't answer that one.

Seeing Aleesha a few days later had been tough. I tried to pretend nothing was wrong and blathered on about work and any mundanity that came into my head. She didn't seem any different than normal—a little more subdued, perhaps—but there were no marks visible to me. Could the other night just have been a rather high-volume row?

One thing she didn't do was look guilty, so I got rid of the tiny bit of doubt that had put her in the frame for the post-incident. I made up my mind at that point—I was going to do something about it. I might just confront him and shame him in front of others and see where we went from there. He was a bully, so he might back down, and all would be well with the world. I didn't rule out further repercussions or an escalation.

In my mind, putting human waste through someone else's door was fairly intense, but my experience of anti-social behaviour was quite narrow. The last thing I said to Aleesha as we parted on the stairs was that I was there for her if she needed to talk or a place to seek refuge. She had smiled at me—slightly forced, I thought—and walked away, leaving me to puzzle over my decision to interfere.

Things had been relatively quiet for a few days—the occasional shout, but not the full-on screaming match that had occurred before. I had largely bypassed or been ignored by them both—a couple of encounters on the stairs that were polite but strained. I even considered forgetting about staging an intervention, if that's what it would be, as things were in a state of truce. That all changed a few days ago.

It was Sunday, the middle of the afternoon. Both of them had come home together—I knew this because it was one of those strained encounters. There had been a tension behind Aleesha's eyes, or had I imagined it? Darren, I couldn't judge—he was too busy trying to look down my top as we sashayed around each other. Me going down, them going up. I said hi and continued on my way to get some bits for dinner.

Thirty minutes later, I was on my way back up the stairs with my M&S ready meal and a bottle of Pinot when I noticed—or rather, heard—the cacophony from just ahead. This was on par with previous episodes but heightened by the lack of brick walls between me and the source. I hurried up the rest of the stairs and was just about to ring their bell when it all descended into absolute silence.

The only sound was my own breathing and possibly the tattoo of my heartbeat as it attempted to come out of my chest. This had proved a quandary—I could stand here like an idiot with my finger poised over the bell, or I could retreat and observe. There was literally no sound coming through their door, so I took a cautious approach and retreated behind my front door.

Just settling down thirty minutes later with a glass of Pinot in my hand and my vegetable curry doing its thing in the oven, I was surprised by my front doorbell. Wary of excrement-based activity, I took a view through the spyhole.

It was a uniform of some sort, all high-vis and reflective flashes. The distortive effect of the viewer didn't allow for service determination, but I assumed I was safe, as this would be an elaborate subterfuge for a man whose known level was posting shit through your door.

The police officer, PC Watson, explained that there had been an incident next door and asked if I had heard anything. At this point, they took Aleesha downstairs on a stretcher, her face uncovered, so she was still with us. I asked the officer in, as I could give him some information.

Once my door was closed and I had my wine in my hand—a point the officer seemed to notice and not approve of—I started to fill him in on what I knew, interrupted only by the oven timer telling me my curry was ready. I apologised and went to the kitchen to tend to the warning. I was slightly surprised when I turned around to find PC Watson right behind me, noting, I think, the empty bottles by the recycling and the lack of any duality.

I continued my story for him in detail, adding that I wasn't surprised it had come to this and that he could check the reports, as I had rung in previously. I offered him tea or coffee. He declined, saying that CID would probably want to talk to me and that he was aware of my previous report.

The impression he gave me was that he wasn't quite engaged with my account. When I asked what had happened, he blithely told me he couldn't give me the details, but there had been some sort of incident resulting in injury, and as such, they were duty-bound to investigate. Such blandness—my neighbour and friend had been carted off in an ambulance, and they were talking about duty and 'some sort of incident'. He said that as I hadn't witnessed any violence, he wasn't sure what else I could add, but that he would leave that to CID.

With that, he thanked me for my time and let himself out. I was fairly sure my testimony would be tarnished by the perception of the bottles and my singularity. But you never knew, did you?

I knew then it was time to roll my plan out. Despite the mushy information from the police, I knew Darren had hurt Aleesha and that the 'accident' wasn't one at all. My femininity was against me—even though Darren was not, as my grandad would have said, 'built like a brick shithouse', he still had certain male strengths I couldn't counter. My plan was far more subtle, far more devious—one of the benefits of reading way too much crime fiction.

Aleesha did not return, and everything quietened down once the emergency services had stopped tromping up and down the stairs—closing the door quietly seemed a feat too far for them. I was spared any domestic drama from next door due to the hospitalisation of one of the cast. This played nicely into my plan.

On Tuesday, I returned from work, and before I could get stuck into the bottle of merlot that was a prop for later, I made my first move. This involved the primary wile of our sex—namely, sex. I dressed in my tightest jeans and the most figure-hugging, low-cut t-shirt I possessed. Fortification by downing a glass of merlot also served the purpose of possible inebriation.

Ringing the bell next door, I heard a shuffling noise, and as the door opened, I was greeted by a male of our genus. Sleeveless t-shirt, jogging bottoms, and flip-flops. A picture of absolute hot manhood. The stale smell coming from his direction could surely not have been created in two days, but I smiled and took breaths through my mouth.

There was a furtiveness and edginess to my neighbour's demeanour—one indicating that he spent half his life being surprised by everything that happened and the other half scared, deciding to live in a small, dark space to get away from it all. He only came back out when there was no threat to his manliness. Impressed, I wasn't. His eyes had been drawn to where I wanted—namely, my tits—so he couldn't see the disgust on my face.

My first foray was to get on his good side, using the term only loosely, so I suggested he might help with the wine I was waving about in front of him, as he must be lonely with Aleesha away. The male psyche is so easy to manipulate, and we girls know it. He was already thinking: wine plus lonely plus sexy clothing must equal a shag. It was almost possible to see the computation running across his brow, like the world's worst calculator. It may have been in his eyes as well, but they were fixed elsewhere.

The next hour was the worst I had spent in my life; his telling of the 'accident' took up all of twenty seconds—Aleesha had fallen off a stool and smacked her head on the kitchen unit. I couldn't wait to get back to my flat and bathe in bleach.

I made my excuses, telling him I was going away for a few days with work and that if Aleesha wasn't back by Thursday, I would pop round again. Leaving it hanging, letting his mind fill in whatever gaps he wanted. I was flirty enough to let him know that he might get to touch rather than just look if he played his cards right.

The rest of my plan then came into action. The conference was genuine—about the only real thing in the whole piece. I had set off on Wednesday morning, at stupid o'clock, to get to the venue—a country house turned conference centre. Checking in with the venue reception and the conference had been done in full sight. I wasn't sure about the cameras, but visibility at this point was key.

Myself and a hundred or so other witnesses—or attendees, to be precise—went through a very thought-provoking yet torturous death by PowerPoint. Nothing exciting or untoward occurred. That was all for later. I was nervous, I admit, but this was revenge—not just for the shit, but for all other women who had suffered like Aleesha. I was staking out the moral high ground—a justification for the actions of the next few hours.

I had dropped enough hints during the day that my early evening involved a long walk to clear my head and then a video call with a new provider from the US, but I would join everyone for a drink later. I had left my car away from the two cameras in the car park, hoping there were no others.

To counter this, I had borrowed a set of number plates from my ex-brother-in-law a week ago. 'Borrowed' being a loose description of *stolen* in this issue. New cars today can just have the plates popped off with a screwdriver. Who knew? The internet, for one. I stopped around the corner and used double-sided tape over my own. Hopefully now anonymous.

I made my way back to the flat. Parking two streets away and dashing home in the rain was a pain, but necessary to cover my tracks.

The bin door was my way in; the camera on the front would have caught me, but I had disabled the lock on the back door—where there was no camera—last week. Internet to the rescue again.

So, I could arrive undetected—that being the plan. Grabbing a quick shower and freshening up in my flat, I waited for the sound of Darren next door, knowing Aleesha was not home, as I had rung the hospital to check on her. Catching the beat of some bass-heavy tune coming from next door was my cue. Armed with two bottles of wine—one red, one white—two glasses, and a plastered-on, ferocious lipstick smile, I pushed his buzzer. A killer smile, if I thought about it.

The surprise on his face was a picture, quickly fading to lecherous as his eyes dropped below the horizon of my neck and settled on the girls. Like a pervert sunset. He was dressed as if he had been created in the dark by someone listening to radio instructions without the benefit of a pause or rewind button. Shabby and derelict wouldn't even cover it.

The smell was still there and had amplified to a level of sourness only found in wheelie bins. I felt a moment of pity for Aleesha if she had to come home to this, but I quickly dispensed with the idea, as it wouldn't matter much longer. He accepted my offer of a drink, not even questioning my early arrival. His hormones had dulled what little sense he had, and the girls were doing a sterling job of keeping him docile. He didn't taste the first glass, more concerned about getting to the main event—something I encouraged by telling him about a trick my girls could do with an empty wine bottle.

Once his eyes started to glaze, I knew the diamorphine I had put in the red was taking its sinister effect. An invitee to the party he had not anticipated—a dastardly ménage à trois. His breathing had slowed, and I knew that, with what he had ingested, he would slip into a coma, and that would be it. I had dosed him with enough to floor a rhino—a leftover from my knee surgery two years ago. I picked up my untouched glass of white, both bottles, and retrieved Darren's glass.

Locating his phone, I made a call to my number, lasting several minutes, which was still in my room at the conference. CSI taught me about triangulation and cell sites. While the call was happening, I quickly wiped anything I may have touched, although I wasn't too worried—as I was Aleesha's friend, my presence could be expected.

A quick check of his pulse revealed it was slowing to a barely detectable state. His death would come within the next hour. I then poured the rest of the doctored wine into one of their glasses, wrapped Darren's hand around the stem, and placed the empty packet of diazepam next to him. I reset the CD to the beginning and selected repeat. Checking the hall, I put all the paraphernalia from my flat back in there. Locked up and left via the back door, retrieved my car, and headed back to the conference. The poisoning had taken less than an hour.

The traffic was light heading back, and I only stopped briefly to remove and replace the plates, parking roughly in the same spot as earlier. Joining my colleagues in the bar, I consumed several glasses of wine—not such a good idea on an empty stomach but an excuse to retire early and get some kip.

This morning, I rejoined the conference on Social Care and Cost Benefit Reductions, leaving just after lunch. I had not been summoned by the police; nobody had called me to ask where I was. I began to think I may possibly have got away with it. I had my explanation off pat: if asked, I would say that Darren had asked me for something to help him sleep as he was struggling while Aleesha was away.

Being a good neighbour, I told him to use the spare key and help himself. How was I to know, Officer, that he would pick the diazepam that I had legally and take it with wine? I had no idea of his state of mind, Officer—he sounded fine. Perhaps there was more to the accident with Aleesha, and he was feeling guilty?

When I got back to the flat, I had a look of surprise already in place on my face when a police officer told me I couldn't park in the car park as it was sealed for now. The music on repeat and at volume would have attracted someone—that had been the plan. It was all blue tape and flashing lights. I told him I lived there, and he allowed me to park illegally on a double yellow line near the entrance to the car park.

As I watched, I saw a stretcher being carried out of the front door—this was a full body bag, so I knew he was gone. Aleesha had an alibi, I had created a solid one, I thought, and Darren was gone. Darren could rot in his stale-smelling hell.

The police asked some basic questions and then let me into my flat. PC Watson knocked on my door again—luckily after I had finished cleaning up the glasses and bottles—to tell me they weren't treating it as suspicious, for reasons they didn't divulge, but they had to investigate as a formality.

Breathing a huge sigh of relief, I asked if I was needed for anything, as I had some recycling to do. He laughed at the number of bottles I had in bags. I told him I was taking them to the tip as our bin was full. He laughed again and said it was fine. Setting off for the tip became an aimless drive to nowhere—or anywhere.

I am now stuck on this motorway, watching my fellow users and wondering if any have just committed a murder. A completely vindicated one. I felt no guilt. Or was it a mercy killing?

I knew of the controversy and appalled outrage around honour killings in her culture, but I knew me—indeed, our honour was now intact, as was that of our sex. I will call it an honour killing. I am sure I would get my reward someday, even enduring this slight hiccup in my karma.

I sure as hell wasn't going to lose any sleep over it.

5:57 pm

I wished the clock had an audible tick—not just the silent flip over every, what I assumed was, a minute. But it may well have been two, ten, fifteen, given how slowly the change seemed to occur.

There were only three minutes left until I was unofficially late. One hundred and eighty seconds—fuck all when you say it like that.

What happens then is one of those imponderables now. They will know I am late; they will have a man outside, and he will be telling them they haven't seen the van. This is the least I would expect if they weren't tracking me.

Will they think I have gone on the run with the cargo? Taking my chances because I didn't care for my kids or ex-wife? Only one bit of which was true.

How will they let me know I have failed? Apart from the clock clicking past six, I had no way to find out. Was there going to be a party popper exploding out of the dash with a fanfare announcing my time was up?

The thought that they couldn't lose the cargo reaffirmed the little hope I had that this may end well—may end okay at best. I would hold onto that glimmer as the light faded further into dusk and the lights on Satan's Christmas tree grew brighter, reflecting hard off the windscreen of the Subaru that had its system up so loud I could almost taste the bass.

Someone should have a word, but nobody would.

People Call Us Renegade

Stuck here now for what feels like days, yet only forty-five minutes have passed, the music not even acting as a distraction. I'll ring her back in a minute—she can't expect me to take in news like that and talk about it while staring at taillights. If I were brave enough to say it, I'd think she had done it on purpose.

The ringing me, that is, as there was no doubt she had done the other thing on purpose.

That's the way she ticks, a beat of her own, a chiming only she can hear. Hooking up with her at the start had seemed like a great idea. She was different, exciting. Unconventional and possibly dangerous. What was it they said about some poet—mad, bad, and dangerous to know? Who was that dude? Shakespeare? Nah, someone else. Was a smackhead, but they didn't call them that then—they were arty.

Byron, that's it—fucked off to Greece and got off his tits. Not that Kelsey is a smackhead, she just acts like she's on something all the time. The excitement wore off months ago when I realised she wasn't right. It was the way she looked at people sometimes—or most of the time, if I'm truthful—as if she was thinking about how to get rid of their body once she had topped them. I never caught her looking at me like that, thank fuck.

When Johnnie-boy pointed it out to me, I was like fuck me mate, what are you on? He said, look at her face bud when she can't see you, and you'll see.

Which was a bit rich coming from a mate. Fucking scary Frankie was his last. So, I'd watched, and JB was right—she had this look, dark scary eyes, and a little smile. Not a laughing smile, not a cute smile, not even a camera-forced smile—more of an I am going to fuck you up sort of smile.

Never at me though, but she had now fucked me up in another way. Rings me when I am out on a drop and tells me Francis, I am late. I say late, babe, where are you off to? She says no late as in 245 late as in no decorators this month. I go, oh for fucks sake Kelsey, how did that happen? Stupid bloody question as she went all sort of sniffly and said you know and don't swear. I went, for fuc…God's sake what are you gonna do? She said, me do? and hung up. I'll ring JB. It was his fault, sort of—he should have pushed me more and told me to run for the hills after hiding the knives. It connected.

"Johnnie-boy." Let's see what he comes up with.

"Frankie, dude, how's it gannin'?" Was that a hint of a smirk in his voice?

"JB, I'm fucked, mate, Kelsey is up the stick." I could almost hear the old lady tutting in my head—fuck knows what I was going to tell her.

"You tool, you really want Chucky Three running about?" Definitely a hint of something.

"Not funny, mate, she just rung, got all teary, and hung up after telling me." I regretted this call now—I needed him to focus on me.

"What you gonna do?" Which was not what I wanted from the fucker—help, not stupid questions. How was that helping?

"That's what I said."

"I thought you were going to bin her off." There was a trace of I told you so in that.

"I was, man, but never found the right time, and you know…" I started to say.

"Yeah—fucking psycho look you would get." Definitely told you so, as JB completed.

"Right, and now she's got one in, what can I do?" Another tut from me invisible mam.

"Will she not get rid?" JB asked reasonably—for me, anyway.

"No idea, but I doubt it." Which was true—after all the trouble she had gone to in getting this way, I doubted she would take that course.

"Fucked then. I'll buy you some nappies." Back to taking the piss.

"Fuck off." And I hung up—he was no help at all.

Absolutely no sodding use—so much for being the best mate. Can I ask her to get shot, or do I want her to make me a dad—or more of one? I'd be a better one than mine, wherever or whoever the fuck he is. Me mam will go off one—never liked Kelsey. And Kelsey, well, was just Kelsey.

No amount of moaning by me mam was going to change that fact. She has to get rid—the grief isn't worth it. Also, how the fuck can I pay for a kid when I'm doing this crappy job for minimum wage? Only just keeps me straight.

If there was owt to blame, it was that bloody COVID thing—too much time on my hands, not as much work, and sitting at home with her. Man has his needs and all. She was supposed to sort out the protection—fuck all else to do. What was I supposed to do, wank myself raw? Now I know—keep it away from her was what.

Now look—a frigging kid. Nah, it has to go. I'm not ready for all that shite, and Kelsey, well, she's just slightly mental. I know women lose the plot when they're carrying, eating coal, and all that bollocks. What Kelsey would do when she got fat—she'd be pickling kittens or summat. The type of bird to chop my dick off for getting her that way.

Kelsey had been a nurse when I met her—she'd looked after me when I was in with a smashed-up shoulder. Smashed up because, pissed up, I had tried to catch a sheep—the bloody thing was a rock. Trying to impress another bird—

what was her name? Oh yeah—Roz, that was her. Fantastic jugs, if I remember. JB had nearly shit himself laughing from the field to A&E, back to mine.

Kelsey gave me her number, and I rang her, thinking she was a class above the normal bird I would have a run at. A couple of weeks in, she had gone on sick leave—mental stress from COVID, she said. After six months of being in the same space nearly all the time, I could see her mental bit was just her normal self. She never went back to work—just sat in the flat with me, doing nothing but pecking my head and letting me shag her too much.

As I ain't going anywhere fast, I may as well speak to her.

"Hey, babe." When she picked up.

"Francis." Said like she had a rod up her arse.

Bloody hate that—only my gran used Francis. "Sorry about before—was a shock and all." It wouldn't hurt to play nice.

"It was for me too." With the uptight voice thing going on.

"You really pregnant?" One of those things—what were they—where you ask a question you already know the answer to. I could always hope she had been pulling my knob earlier and it was a wind-up.

"Yep, did a test." With an inflexion of duh in it.

"Where did you get that so fast?" She couldn't drive because of the meds she was on.

"Maisie brought it around," Kelsey announced.

"Fuc… Maisie? So she knows." Last thing I needed—Maisie was a gob on legs, so it would be all around town by bedtime.

"It's not hard to work out," came the almost-hissed response.

"How late are you?" Clearly it was as I hadn't.

"About three months." Which was a massive mic drop.

"What the fuck? Why tell me now, or were you gonna just pop it out with the toast in the morning?" Playing nice was no longer an option.

"Francis, you mean you haven't noticed? There hasn't been a week when we haven't had loads of sex, but the last few, well…"

She had turned to whiney now.

"Now you say it…" If I hadn't been getting it somewhere else after escaping COVID, then I might have noticed. She clearly had.

"Typical. Anyway, I am, and I have put it on Facebook." Now that was the real mic drop.

"Oh, for Chris' sake! My mam reads that—she will go postal. I need to ring her before she—oh fuck, Kelsey, why couldn't you wait until we had talked about it?" This was even worse now. I didn't need Maisie and her big fat blabbermouth, not when it was on the net.

I realised I was talking to space—she had hung up again.

Message from JB: "Mate, you are so screwed, it's all over everything."

Message from Mam: "Ring me, Frank, now!" She had seen it then.

There was nothing I could do—stuck here with a psycho girlfriend at home, a mother on the warpath, and my best mate who just couldn't stop taking the piss. Glad it wasn't him, at a guess. I was going to sit here, enjoy the peace, ignore everyone, and hope a solution jumped out and hit me in the gob.

Other than that, a wish for a fucking big hole to appear and swallow me up would have to do.

*****

5:58 pm

From my new point of view, I could now see a dark grey Skoda sitting patiently—one in front and two in the back. One of the ones in the back was extraordinarily pretty, yet appeared to be male—so was it handsome? Who the fuck knew what I could say anymore? The other two looked official—the dark fleeces over white shirts were the giveaway and indicated old Bill.

However, on closer inspection, they looked too worn around the edges to be police, so I went for prison service based on my time there. The guy or girl must be shackled in there if that was the case. Poor bastard. I mean, poor bastard as well—as if I had been that good-looking when I ended up in prison, my life would have been a nightmare. The lad would be meat of the worst kind. If he thought he was a victim now, then he was about to join a really nasty club—one where every weakness and vulnerability would be exploited by those who knew they were stronger.

Welcome to the club, my friend.

The clock now told me that my time was nearly up. I could still do the *Falling Down* thing—get out and just fuck off into the gloom. If I could trust Chaz and his mates not to hurt my kids. Although they could hurt my ex-wife for all I really cared.

But would Chaz really hurt kids? Did he even have kids himself?

If I went and took my chances, then a life on the run from Chaz would be my sentence. Could I do that? The answer was no, I couldn't. It was a chance not worth taking.

So, I resigned myself to sitting here, trusting that someone other than me knew what the fuck was going on, and waiting for a decision telling me what to do next.

Don't Go Hiding

Picking up Stephen earlier had been relatively straightforward—moving him into the dark grey Skoda and securing the prisoner's wrist to the reinforced pillion in the centre of the back seat. Jim, the driver, was already in position and waited until Pete was set before getting ready to move off.

"Ready, pal."

"Aye, Jim, let's get our young friend to his new home," said Pete, the second officer sitting next to Stephen in the rear.

The remand hearing had been shorter than the board meeting that followed by some considerable margin. The pair of POs sat around, knowing the inevitability of the hearing, mainly drinking tea and spending what little cash they had on vending machine chocolate.

There was a considerable delay in dotting i's and crossing t's in the judicial system. They both had enough experience to know this and were therefore not particularly put out by the ordeal. They were just glad that the court had reacted quickly—an extremely unusual action—in getting the Transgender Case Board convened.

Perhaps it was in response to the unusual set of circumstances being played out in the name of the young man sitting in their car. The normal post-remand three-day window had been bypassed. The general chatter among all the visiting prison officers was that it was a new protocol to move quicker because of the repercussions of COVID. Stopping unnecessary movement around the country seemed like a sensible option. Seven hours of hanging about and getting numb backsides was a small price to pay in this instance.

The reason for the board was simple—Stephen, who was born female and named Josie, now identified as male. While not fully transitioned, he had started his treatment. The complication was that his remand for burglary with violence, assault occasioning grievous bodily harm, and vehicle theft, along with all the associated traffic violations, had to be at an establishment of his legally recognised gender. The board could supplant that regulation by decreeing that Stephen could be remanded to a male prison.

This meant their destination would have to make some allowances and put him in a secure unit, as the risk to his safety and well-being would be more than threatened in the general population. While inconvenient, it would avoid the scenario of the Prison Service being criticised for the alternative. The outcry would be deafening if a self-proclaimed male were installed in a female prison. Stephen would just have to put up with segregation and the harsh lockdown—although it was not quite as severe as the one that had happened due to COVID.

Pete Morley was known by many nicknames, but most of them were not used to his face. Pastor, pious, pompous, preacher, saint, and apostle were among the many. Imagination among his colleagues was not a job requisite, and all of the names made a sometimes sly but usually unsubtle rejoinder to his beliefs. He was a Christian—one of a dying breed.

Dying in public, possibly. Perhaps more people privately admitted to a similar set of values. He was what might be classed as a retrograde Christian—some might even label him a fundamentalist, as some of his views were extreme. The name-calling—well, that was between them and what they viewed as their God. Pete was outwardly and yet covertly religious, wearing a small crucifix pin badge on his lapel and having a special dispensation not to work on a Sunday.

This dispensation came at a cost, though, as his shift pattern was never constant nor particularly pleasant. He had not raised this as an issue, understanding the resentment and conflict his stance caused. His faith dictated that he shouldn't take offence but instead turn the other cheek.

This he did—enduring split shifts, frequent changes from late to early shifts, or from nights to late shifts—all with stoic acceptance. His colleagues were not overly aggressive about his lack of Sunday work, as Pete, to his credit, would pick up all the rubbish shifts, like Boxing Day or New Year's Eve—unless it was a Sunday, of course.

Secretly, Pete enjoyed one of his nicknames. *Prophet* was one he had overheard, and even though pride was somewhat anathema to his faith, he had typed up a card and stuck it in his locker. *Prophet Pete* was now official and even appeared on some other documents. All the old stagers—officers, that is—called him Prophet, and the younger ones were quickly corrected if they did not.

Pete viewed his role as one of teaching, which was why he liked the name. He knew he was there for more than that, but if he could improve the lot of even a small number of the thousands of inmates he had come into contact with over the years, then he would feel vindicated, just as he was sure even the prophets in the Bible had felt a certain pride in their achievements.

Perhaps that was one of the contradictions that his more friendly colleagues would point out. That revelation would imply they demonstrated more knowledge and insight than he had previously experienced. Dinosaurs and their absence in the Bible were more on their level. Something Pete didn't respond to—he usually just laughed it off.

One of the benefits he had found of his public-facing stance was that, once inmates understood his strict beliefs, they generally behaved more acceptably. This was a result of Pete's determination to write up and report any prisoner who transgressed his personal moral code. It wasn't an overly strict code—just one that he hoped would encourage those locked up to act as normal human beings—or as normal as possible, considering the situation.

COVID had put a strain on this course of action, but Pete was determined that normality should be an objective. The effect for Pete was that he was rarely assaulted and had very little cause for concern when on duty. Some of his more macho colleagues suffered an entirely different fate. This was a small victory for Pete, yet not one he chose to rub in the face of his colleagues. They chose their own path and therefore bore the consequences.

Some assumed he was naïve in his overt acceptance of inmates' behaviour. This was a misguided view—he was more than aware of the violence, the drugs, the petty rivalries, the racist hatred, the homophobic bile poured out, and the religious invective that was always bubbling away like a forgotten pot on a stove. Prison had more than its fair share of problems—it mirrored the society these prisoners came from.

The fact that it was condensed into a male-dominated and bottled-up environment was like God looking through a microscope to see what sort of society He had created. Pete was sure He wouldn't be impressed. But Pete was determined to do his small bit, even if his teachings and faith were tested daily by all that went on around him.

This was the reason for Pete's feeling of disquiet about the current situation. Morally, he was one hundred per cent certain of his feelings on homosexuality. In Pete's mind, transgender issues, body dysmorphia, and anything else not outlined in the Bible belonged in the same tarnished, rusty, and dented pot. He was firm in this stance, but Stephen, sitting next to him—albeit involuntarily—was causing a glitch in his thoughts.

Here was a woman who wanted to be a man, now going to a man's prison. In Pete's estimation, that was either the most foolish or the bravest thing he had ever seen.

It would require some re-evaluation on his part. He wondered if he could ask, and if he did, what would he ask? He would need to have a conversation with a prisoner that wasn't dictated by his uniform. The only way to dig deeper was to drop the shield of his status. He hoped Stephen would respond to a friendlier side—one more amicable than he had experienced so far.

Stephen was twenty-three, but in Pete's mind, he could assume a juvenile frame of mind, as the decision on the whole looked immature and ill-informed. Then again, was that right? Pete pondered as they sat in traffic. To change, in effect, everything you had outwardly known based on an urge might be more mature than he was giving Stephen credit for.

Pete was still the adult here, in the back of the car. Jim, the driver, was concentrating on his driving—or staying still, to be precise, which could be Jim's descriptor for life, in all honesty.

Pete was sure Jim wouldn't interfere if he started a conversation with the prisoner. Having had his natural beliefs challenged, Pete felt it was his duty to question—perhaps even to offer guidance to Stephen, based on his teachings. Maybe that was the opening—using the family gambit and seeing where it got him.

"It's a bit rubbish, this, Stephen. Looks like we might be stuck for a while."

No response came from the slight form slumped in the left-hand rear seat. He was secured, and if viewed casually from outside, he might have been thought asleep. Only the occasional blink reflected in the side window, giving Pete any hint of life.

"I thought you might want to talk about what to expect back in the unit?"

Nothing. Only another slow blink. Even the prisoner's breathing was so minimal that it barely ruffled the prison-issue sweatshirt.

"Look, Whitehead, we have more time than we would on a normal transport job. So, we may as well make use of it. Do you have any questions—about the unit? About the routines? What about anything mentioned at your board this afternoon?"

There were a couple of quick mirrored blinks and a slight hitch of breath. At least he might be listening, thought Pete, which was a step forward in his mind.

"I'm not the enemy, you know, Whitehead, despite what you might think about POs. What do you think, Jim?" He directed the question to the hulking driver in the front and received a grunt in return, indicating some sort of implied assent. "We've been around this job a long time—sometimes it feels like a lifetime—and we can help you, answer some questions, try and make it easier for you, considering your situation."

"My situation?" was the response, although there was no movement from the prisoner. Even a small shift in his position would indicate engagement. Pete was used to the constant movement inside the prison; staying still acted like a magnet for trouble, so most prisoners were constantly on the move when they weren't locked up. Although, it may have been the locking up that instigated the need for movement.

"You know, the whole transition thing—or the fact that we are taking you to a male prison, at your request and with the instruction of the board. You must have questions. I know I would if I were in your shoes." He tried to sound empathetic and not give away his ingrained disgust.

Stephen turned to Pete without a pause. "Well, you ain't, are you, boss? You haven't been fucked over all your life, have you, boss? I knew I was someone else even when I was really little, just didn't fit in. I wanted to, like, be a lad, if you can understand that."

"As I grew up, it got worse. I cut me own hair like a lad, all that sort of shite. The stuff that doesn't really matter. The stuff in my fucking head was chewing me up. And then I made the mistake of telling me mam and dad. Mam just blanked me, probably off her tits as usual, and me dad decided to take me pain to a whole new level."

"You haven't been told you're as shitty as a basketful of arseholes, have you, boss? You haven't had your dad telling you that you'll be nothing without a dick, which is why you want one? That you'd only be fit for one thing? Made to feel completely and utterly worthless? Boss, I was living the worst life. I wanted to be something that I wasn't. I was fucked up, boss. Only when the twat left did I do something about it, and going into care helped."

He had stared at Pete all through this speech.

"Stephen, please, don't swear. That's one thing I won't tolerate, as you will learn. You get a free pass this once, as you are upset, but that's it." Pete tried to process what he had just heard.

"Yes, boss." He turned back to gazing at a white van they had drawn level with.

"Stephen, I'm not messing here or even trying to scare you. This is going to be hard for you, and we could do with understanding a bit more. That way, we can advise you and offer a little more help. It would also be good for you to know you have officers you can confide in if it gets too much." Although Pete wasn't sure he would be the best one to be a mentor.

"OK." Still with a fascination for the van.

"You will have counselling as well, and I'm sure the medical side will involve some well-being and mental health assistance. We, though, are there every day and night, so if you need someone to turn to, it would be better if we knew more."

Pete realised he may mean this more than he would have thought possible. There was something about this young woman—man, he corrected himself—that was pulling him in.

Stephen turned back towards him then, leaving the van to its own devices, with what could only be described as a look of sadness written all over his face. He looked Pete over, and then a small snort escaped. A smile appeared, like the sun at dawn just popping over the horizon. Pete thought it made him look pretty—sorry, handsome—but he also feared what would happen if Gen Pop got him in their clutches.

"I see your little cross. Some sort of god-botherer, boss?" He nodded at Pete's crucifix.

"We call him P…" From Jim, who, for some reason, was paying far more attention than Pete thought—probably through boredom, as they were still hardly moving.

"I have a strong faith, yes. Why? Does that bother you?" Pete interrupted this overshare.

"No, boss, but me being like I am must bother you." The perception could only be the result of perpetual persecution.

"It's caused me to question, I must admit. That's why I wanted to talk—so perhaps I could understand more. I can't work out whether it's very, very messed up or very, very brave." Pete thought this sounded more honest than he had intended.

"That's your mob for you. Unless it's black and white, no room for any in-between, is there? It's simple, boss—I was born a lass, but I never wanted to be. My father, before he fu…left…made sure I knew what he thought. It was so in my face—he was—from eight years old. The insults and the hurt. But I knew, deep down and in my head, that I was born wrong." There was a tear in his eye.

"If he left, though, you should have found it easier to cope?"

"I were twelve when he left, and by then, I knew what I wanted, like. His was just a bully action. It felt right—I felt right—acting like a boy. At least the punching stopped when he left, which were summat." A strange look came across Whitehead's face, almost as if he were admitting something to himself or acknowledging a truth.

"Why didn't your mother stop him?" Although Pete had a suspicion he knew the answer.

"She loved him, boss. She didn't want me. And most of the time, she was off her head with smack. She had no idea what I wanted and couldn't even understand why I was so unhappy as I was."

"Stephen, sorry. It's a story we hear a lot." A sad reflection on society.

"Then, boss, I find out he wasn't even my real dad. Apparently, my real one was some no-mark my mum shagged—sorry, boss—on a night out." There was anger there too—so many emotions that Pete knew needed to be reined in before he was in the unit.

"I still can't understand why you carried on wanting to be a man, though." His religious preconceptions would not leave him alone.

"You think I can, boss? It had been with me since I was small. It was something that didn't leave my head at all. It was always there, a reminder I was wrong, like. Then the bullying just added to it—made it easier. When I was taken into care, I carried on with it, and you know what, boss? People actually listened to me. Me. They wanted to help me. And so I ended up, after some doctors talked to me a lot, in the programme."

"The drugs first, to start with, and now planning the surgery. The law means I can still have it, even stuck in prison, so it will go ahead. I know what will happen in Gen Pop, but it's what I believe in, boss. It's the way I want to live my life. So if I have to spend a bit of time with the paedos in seg, then I will. Anything else you want to know, boss?" He turned away and resumed looking out of the window. *Was he trying to hide something*? thought Pete.

This monologue had temporarily deprived Pete of words. The sadness was in there, but also, he could see the courage of Stephen's convictions. It wasn't some scam. It wasn't to try and pull the wool over anyone's eyes. He was committed, and Pete could understand that.

Pete had been on a slippery path, one that would not have led to where he was today. He had been messing with the counterculture around drugs and squats. Then came an epiphany—one night that was a complete blank—and that was it. Clean living and faith in a higher power had seen him grow and develop, leaving him content and secure.

"No, Stephen, I may think of something, but I see you believe in your choice, and that I can relate to. My own choices need that level of conviction. One thing I noticed—you don't have any visitors listed on your paperwork. Do you want any added?"

He was trying to drag this back to something that would not necessarily upset his sensibilities.

"I should add me mam, I suppose, boss. Thanks," Stephen said without turning back.

"What's her name? I'll add her to this form." He poised his pen, ready.

"Monica. Monica Whitehead."

As Pete wrote this on the form, he felt his faith rattled to the core. Surely that couldn't be right. There must be more than one, surely? He would have to raise this with his senior officer, as this confused yet brave young man sitting beside him could be his son—or would have been his daughter. Well, it was certainly a possibility, wasn't it? Those wild days with Mon.

Twenty-four years ago, wasn't it? It was time for prayer, as it fitted, even though Mon had not been monogamous with her affections. What a fitting testimony to his life before God had arrived—a mockery of his faith and beliefs, if you like. The result of his earlier days. His last fling had been Mon. Surely not. If it was true, it would challenge him—and his God.

Stephen looked back out of the window, watching the traffic milling around outside his mobile prison—one he would soon exchange for a more stable one. He was unaware of the conflict his name drop had caused, nor the repercussions for two of the three car occupants if it was true. He would eventually be rid of the prison of the female form, emerging like a butterfly into the dawn.

*****

Tina had clocked the two in the Skoda. They were wearing the ubiquitous dark fleeces of people more used to uniforms, which, in her considered opinion, meant either police or prison officers. As far as she knew, the police had very little use for Skodas—some hang-up from the old Cold War or something—so her still-flat yet definitely empty gut told her they were prison guys. Which meant that the bloke was, in fact, a bloke? And with them was a prisoner being shuffled off somewhere.

A sudden flurry of movement in front of her brought her back to the here and now as she narrowly avoided running into the back of Connor's Audi. That would have taken some explaining. It would have taken close surveillance to a whole new level—not to mention the paperwork and a personal hatred for Tina that would have ensued for scratching an NCA Volvo.

*****

5:59 pm

At a time when I had a lot on my mind, it was odd that one of the things I thought about was why I was noticing some cars around me but not others. It wasn't that they were invisible or had some weird superpower. It was more that they had formed a strange pastiche of colour, shape, and definition that constantly slid around me—a technological herd jostling for position at a tarmac waterhole, or the sway of a crowd in a mosh pit at a gig, constantly changing and evolving.

Some of the occupants, I would probably say, were somebody, doing something, and going somewhere. Most of them, though, were likely superfluous to my consciousness—nobodies, doing nothing, going nowhere. How did they all fit into the picture I was conjuring up, sat here in traffic, while a life-and-death situation played out somewhere else—one over which I now had no control?

All the pieces seemed to fall haphazardly, but was that really true? Was there a bigger picture? Was this the hand of God, or a god, or a bunch of gods? Or was it something else from the other side, directing this very personal drama? Cruelly dictating the situation according to some spurious or frivolous whim. Decreeing the fall of the puzzle pieces and their apparent randomness. If I glanced at the pieces from one angle, the picture would be clear—but then a thought occurred, and like a blink, that image disappeared.

If this was a jigsaw, and all the pieces were scattered, then there must be a starting point, like getting all the edge pieces. But this situation had no edge—it was a kaleidoscope of shifting patterns, directed by something that may or may not be a superior being, or may or may not be fate. Only these things could see the picture and move the parts around to form what was needed at that exact moment.

I was kidding myself if I thought I understood any of this. I knew of karma—was this it? My punishment for the life I had led and the path I had followed? The mystery was beyond me; the mastery of the puzzle, beyond my grasp. All that was left was for me to silently acknowledge that when I did eventually see a picture in the puzzle, it would probably be a picture of nothing.

My Life Was Empty

There was a fundamental truth at play here: my life had really come to something when all I thought about was my next hit. I wondered if anyone would actually notice if I sparked up again in the car now. After all, there was nothing much else to do but look at the not-so-pretty lights or the arse-end of another car. I still felt quite mellow from the toke earlier, but another little one wouldn't hurt. Would it? And from what I could see, nobody was taking a blind bit of notice of me.

It was all there—my gear—sitting on the other seat. It might as well have had a label saying *Smoke Me*, which would make *Alice Through the Looking Glass* far more plausible.

Go on, just a little toot, I could hear its voice. *You know you want to. Relax and take yourself back to that better place. If you need to, you can pretend you're invisible or that the glass is one-way if it makes you feel better.* The sad truth was, I knew what would make me feel better. Better than what? Just better. It didn't need clarification; it was simply the way I always felt after that Moroccan-spiced hit.

There was another voice, though—one of reason—and it told me that I should just look at it for now, as I was still chilled from earlier. I could use my sense and let myself come back down more, as driving like this and getting stopped wouldn't be a great idea.

The fact that Dad would go ballistic—mainly because it was his car—said a lot. Although, the drug use wouldn't be far behind in his spirit of approbation and paternal bullshit. As if I had summoned him into my presence in his work's Audi, I could almost imagine the conversation.

"I don't care if you want to waste your education and your life, sticking whatever into your arm or up your nose. I can't tell you what to do anymore!" He would say it in that whiny *I know better than you do and always will* voice.

I would respond with something like, "It's only a bit of a blow, Dad," and that would set him off further.

"For now. But it's a slippery slope, and before long you'll slide. But as long as you can pay for it yourself and don't hurt anyone else, then, to be honest, I know I can't do anything—except point out the waste of your health and wealth."

Or any combination of the fatherly pearls of wisdom and guilt-laying. I would then point out a simplistic view. "Dad, I've got a good job. I enjoy a joint or three occasionally, so no harm, no foul."

He would then huff off, leaving me to think over the way I was leading my life. "That's what you say. You live in my house, but you refuse to listen to me. My views, my feelings don't even count in your selfish little world, do they?"

The truth was, I would then let him storm off and continue in my self-centred little way.

Therein lay the main crux of the problem. Life had been relatively simple—until three weeks ago, that was all I had to contend with. Settling my mind on a different plane, a little relaxed during or, more than likely, after a hard week's graft. The money I earned from a reasonable job had been great. My girlfriend, Alice, was great. I would even admit that the work had been sort of great.

I suppose, as I was having this enforced static session of honesty, Alice was only really sort of great too—possibly verging on I wasn't sure where it was going, really. I mean, don't get me wrong—I enjoyed being with her, even though neither of us owned our own place. Alice had a flat she shared with two others who appeared to hate me—or so Alice said. I had only been there when they were out, which was rare, so I wasn't sure where this Matt Connors hatred emanated from.

Unless we splashed out on a weekend away, sex tended to be snatched in the afternoon or on the odd occasion when we could grab some time at my folk's house. Even in our late twenties, we still felt like teenagers—but not in a good way—grabbing a quick fumble when we could.

We had been doing this and living this way for two years, for God's sake! We couldn't get on the ladder without a massive deposit, and we wouldn't get a deposit if we rented together. So perhaps that was the problem I was feeling with the relationship. It was only half of one—if that.

Don't get me wrong—I think I loved Alice. I certainly tolerated her more than anyone else in my life, and I knew that wasn't exactly a glowing endorsement, but there you go. Was it love? One little voice said it could be. The other, fuelled by the smoke, would say, Don't be daft. Just chill and enjoy and forget all the bobbins about love.

This was why I shouldn't be left in an enclosed space like this—like a prisoner in a covered shopping cart, unable to really move quickly and with too much time on my hands. Whether the pot helped me think, calmed me down, or just added a perspective that I wouldn't normally consider, I wasn't sure. Like, you don't really think about clouds or rabbits unless you look up in the sky or run one over.Rabbits, that is—I'm not that stoned.

Are you sure? Oh, here we go—the little voice was back, so I must still have been a little out of it. *Are you sure you're okay to drive?*

Oh, shut up! Yes, I had got this far without killing anyone, hadn't I?

I'm hungry—feed me some smoke.

Haven't we been through this? I can't spark up again in the middle of a traffic jam. Someone will notice this time if they didn't with the last one.

Paranoia now?

No, just common sense. Why poke the wasp's nest?

So where—and why—had it all gone to shite? This was pragmatism, not paranoia. Life had been good. Not great, if I was honest. And now I was reduced to this—sitting in a poxy car, in a poxy traffic jam, with no hope of getting out of the mess I was in. Even considering what I was now doing to try and solve the mess that Alice had dropped on me.

Did I love her? God, the pull of my gear was really strong—like a visual itch that would only go if I rolled up and inhaled the smoke as my inner voice wanted.

When Alice first broached the subject, it had been during one of those rare 'alone' moments that we had to try and somehow manufacture. I had to admit—I was a little stunned. Alice was no sink estate chancer—not trying to denigrate anybody who had escaped them—but to try and draw you a picture: Alice was from a middle-class—and I will use the word—respectable family.

She was well educated. Better than me, in fact. If I was honest, I *think* she had a good job. She was on par with me in the monetary stakes anyway, though on the kudos level, she probably trumped me. Mainly due to the altruism associated with working for a charity that she mentioned regularly—telling me it had to do with offender rehabilitation and their families. I did wonder how a charity could afford to pay all of these people when that really went against the word *charity*—but what did I know?

Anyway, I hope you get the picture—she was not someone you would put in the stirring pot of this mess. Yes, like me, she enjoyed a joint at the weekend as a reward; we weren't hurting anyone, were we? Unlike me, she said she had also occasionally dipped into the Ecstasy waters, mainly when she went to festivals like Download or Glastonbury. To be honest, as far as I knew, that was her way of chilling—I went for the music, she went a little further. Hardly a major crime. But don't ask my old man his opinion, as I already knew it would not be quite as chilled.

In that quiet moment under my duvet, relaxing as only two comfortable adults could, with nothing to do for the rest of the afternoon except some more of what we had been doing and possibly a cup of tea, Alice dropped her not-quite-atomic-sized bomb.

"Matt, I have to tell you something," she said into my shoulder where she was snuggled.

"Dumping me when we are naked and in bed is not good form, Al." I sent a ring of smoke towards the ceiling—I always impressed myself with this skill.

"No, this is serious…" And indeed, she sounded a little uptight.

"I refer the dishonourable lady to my previous answer," I said, because I can be a pain in the arse.

"For fuck's sake! Stop it and shut up a minute." Which was the same as pointing out that I was actually conforming to type and being a pain in the arse.

Therefore, and however, I shut up, as the look on Alice's face, which had reappeared from my shoulder, was not one I wanted to test my humour on any further. In fact, she looked slightly worried—not quite frightened, but getting there. We weren't splitting up, so what could be so bad?

I could carry on tolerating Alice and having sex occasionally, so life was okay. Again, what did I know? The joint that I had relit after we had spent ten minutes pretending to be conjoined twins was still smouldering away, so I took another hit, sent off another ring, wrapped my arm around Alice, and waited for her to spill the something that wasn't a breakup.

"Listen, I have got into a bit of a mess. Oddly, you sitting there with a joint is both a symbol of and part of the problem. I have been stupid, really, really stupid. I thought I could handle it; it was only going to be the once, and then it wasn't. Then it was every weekend, every night out, and then pretty much every day. Matt, I lost control, and now it's going to cost me everything—and it could hurt you, which was not the plan," she said in a strange, squeaky-sounding voice.

"Al, what have you done that's so bad? You are worrying me." Sort of.

"I'm in big-time shit—coke has got me, and I owe a dealer a lot of money. I know you don't check my savings or bank account, but if you did, you would see I haven't stuck anything in it for about six months. I'm blowing, literally, everything I earn up my nose. I'm so ashamed and don't know what I can do. Or, well, I do—apart from giving up, that is. But I need your help."

"To give up? You don't have to ask."

I was slightly irritated that I hadn't spotted the problem, but then I had no experience of cokeheads. If indeed Alice was one. Sounded like it, didn't it? Yep. Then again, it was like spotting someone with HIV—unless you knew how to look, then how would you know? Pretty rubbish defence to indifference, but there you go.

"No, not just that—to get out of the hole, the debt, the fucking circle that is more than vicious—it is closing fast." And she sounded genuinely scared.

The whole story came out then, surrounded by the semi-ironic fug of Mary Jane. No, I hadn't put it out, nor considered Alice's feelings on this. I needed the calm, as the stuff Alice was telling me and what she was asking me to help with would have sent me off on a spiral.

One that wouldn't end—like the world's longest helter-skelter, only this one couldn't decide whether it was going up or down. So I continued pulling in and holding in the sweet smoke while the woman I had tolerated—or loved—for two years unfolded a tale so bleak, I still couldn't fathom why I hadn't spotted it.

The reason for this new honesty, she said, was that she had been suspended from work in the last week. If I was cynical—and I am—that seemed to be a big coincidence, but I suppose I should give Alice the benefit of the doubt. There had been a management change or policy shift at the charity where she worked—or had worked. One of those things that blow into the workplace like a fart in a crowded room—someone knew where it came from, but no one would admit it, and you could never quite pin down the source.

Anyway, because the charity worked indirectly with kids—although re-offenders were deemed more important (another tick in Alice's previously unblemished altruism box, I can hear you say)—they brought in a random testing regime. Not one that checked that you weren't doing dodgy stuff on your work PC or that you could add up or spell. The type of testing that was becoming more common in the corporate world—possibly explaining the fart emitter—testing your hair for illegal substances.

Alice said she was caught out. Suspension followed, and a dismissal would probably follow too, if the current occupants of that particular ivory tower had their way. Please don't give her any sympathy—I didn't. If she was stupid enough to do marching powder, then she had to be a big enough person to accept the consequences. I think she understood this; it was the knock-on repercussions she was more worried about. As was I, and the little voice in my head wasn't helping.

Alice was into her dealer for about thirty K. How much stuff she had stuck up her nose was incredible. The dealer had been quite accommodating—until he found out that she had probably lost her job. The narrative then shifted to a slightly more intimidating one, as the option to pay was being removed by that test.

I asked her to explain how she got so far into it, and she offered nothing, only that the need outweighed the common sense, and before she knew it, she was in a very deep hole. The spiral was in complete control of her, and because of my tolerance, it would appear, in my life too.

The deal that Alice had given us—to be honest, she had taken it and was now including me—was simple, if you liked cut-rate crime drama. Make some deliveries for the gang, and the debt will be forgotten. Alice didn't count naivety among her list of qualities, but in this instance, she had a flush of it, like a cold sore in summer. Sounds simple. Nothing is that simple, piped up my little voice. Perhaps it had a point.

Here I was—yes, me, not Alice—sitting in a traffic jam on a motorway, in my dad's car, with a boot full of God knows what. You are a trusting idiot, squeaked my voice. Yes. Yes. Of course I am, but the logical side of my id was telling me that if I didn't know what was in there, then it would be better in the long run. Alice's naivety was obviously contagious.

I edged across from the outside lane and then the inside lane. Thankfully, everyone was fairly courteous, and I only received a couple of beeps and middle fingers. If I could get off at the next junction, I thought, then I could make the drop—a little late, but hey, what's an hour between friends? I could see an ambulance up ahead, blue light strobing.

It made a pleasant change from the red glare, but it appeared to be stuck on the hard shoulder. I would let it out if nobody else did—one good turn and all that. As I watched, the ambulance extricated itself from the hard shoulder and, after negotiating the blockage, disappeared off into the distance, blue strobe fading into the descending darkness. At least someone was having a better day now.

My phone chirped into action, and the hands-free picked up the call—Alice. I pondered briefly whether I should ignore it, mainly hoping that the agent of my predicament would go away. But then again, we were in it together. *Yes, you are.*

I caught a glimpse of my reflection in the window as I pressed the answer button on the steering column. I looked like I had been painted by Bruegel—if he had managed to colour in eyes with a red drawn from the outside illuminations. I looked bloody, slightly deranged, and dishevelled—a bit like that guy in *The Shining*, although without an axe, thankfully.

"Matt, where are you?" came through the speakers.

"Stuck in traffic on the motorway." Which was entirely true and had no trace of smartassery.

"Oh God, I am getting calls from you-know-who, wanting to know why you are late."

My palms had started to sweat, which was a new one. *It's the smoke,* piped up my voice, *only the smoke. Go on, light up—the sweating will stop.* Wiping my hands on my battered old Levi's eased the voice slightly but didn't stop the sweat, which was back as soon as it was gone. Perhaps I should, shouldn't I? I would rather be frowned at by other road users than have sweaty palms. Wiping again made no odds.

"Matt?" came a frantic enquiry.

"Sorry. Tell him to ring me, and I can tell him. Or I'll send you a picture of the crap I'm stuck in, and you can show him," I managed to get out while I moved my gear closer.

"Do that, 'cause I can't hold him off, and we don't want to cross him."

Well, duh. And perhaps you should have thought about that earlier. She was testing my tolerance, was my love Alice.

"Yes, love," I said, without managing to point out the problem with her statement.

Then I killed the call and snapped a shot of the red lights stretching into the distance—like something out of *Star Trek*, or a demonic necklace, which would be evidence that I was indeed stuck. Hopefully, that would keep Alice's dealer from a rage.

I stole a wistful glance at the pouch on the passenger seat, the irony not even occurring to me. *Go on, roll up the smoke.*

No, I won't. Look at the trouble we're in because of it, piped up something I rarely listened to—my conscience.

Not true. It's only weed.

Yes, I know, but that's how Alice got there.

You are stronger than that. You enjoy my smoke, my feed.

I won't, so you can shut your yap. I need a clear head. I need to help Alice. I love her.

Love, is it now? I thought it was tolerance.

Same thing, same thing.

Another thirty minutes had gone by. My phone had rung more times than I could be bothered to count—all either Alice, an unknown mobile, or my dad. All with the same question but different reasons for the request, or variations on a theme, if you like.

Where was I? Well, I was still here.

The spark from the lighter briefly caused me to lose sight but was a welcome change from the unending redness outside.

One deep breath, and I was back where I wanted to be, sucking in the smoke like a newborn foal takes its first feed.

That makes it all so much better.

It does, doesn't it?

*****

Alice knew the game was up now and that Matt was never going to make the drop on time. The implications of this would be too horrible to contemplate, and suddenly, his arrest was by far the best option.

There was nothing much for her to do but try and get to the drop first—which would take some explaining to more than just those at the drop.

Her only hope was that they would accept a rearrangement.

*****

6:00 pm

There were a lot of things I had seen over the years. Most of them would probably edge on the side of pleasant—or, more accurately, not fall into the *offensive to the eye* category.

The situation I was caught up in now was definitely on the side of the unpleasant, even if nothing could be seen.

I had lost count of the times I had looked at the clock, which had a certain irony, as it was blinking away my moments and clearly hadn't lost track of time.

The punishment I was envisioning was getting worse by the minute. There would be a beating, certainly. But would they get rid of *him*? Surely, Chaz would have some form of loyalty to an old mate—if that was not too strong a use of the word.

There were massive odds stacked against that—sort of *roulette table, house always wins* type of odds.

My thoughts turned back to the possibility of death and what would happen.

My old man had once said to me, "What you have to remember, son, is that everyone wants to go to heaven, but hardly anyone wants to die to get there."

This was a philosophical aberration from a man who smoked sixty a day in a bid to get there a bit quicker.

The afterlife was of no interest. Dead was dead.

I just didn't want to join that particular throng in the next few hours.

Not that I was brave. Not particularly. I could hold my own—but only when told to.

History, though, told you that if you scratched the surface of many a battlefield, you would find the bones of the brave.

Those who advocated and acted with a tad more caution would come home and get to cut the grass on a sunny Sunday afternoon.

Not that caution could help me here.

I was effectively trapped by fate.

A fate put into motion by my actions and my lifestyle for the last thirty years or so.

Scaring the Nation

The gang in question they were after was a two-headed beast: Ilya Fedorov, who was the international arm, if you like, even though he lived in luxury in London—a modern-day criminal with a past that was murky at best and completely obscured at worst. He had come from nowhere with a bag full of cash and a hard man at his side, who controlled his army of assorted lowlife. That hard man was also the UK branch of the team of crooks—Chaz Dumfries.

Ray thought about Chaz, a rogue operator if ever there was one. After showing his predilection for extreme violence, he had gone on the run and reappeared under a new name several years later, but Ray knew it was Chaz. Just because the box said Jack Kennelly didn't mean it didn't contain the body of Chaz Dumfries. Both men were violent, Jack/Chaz particularly so. It was thought he was behind the shootout that shuffled Tina's old partner off into the sunset.

There was no exit due for a while, so Tina relaxed a little, happy that she could react if needed. The only issue was the lights from the brakes going on and off—they were starting to give her a headache, and she hoped it wouldn't affect her vision if she was called to action, either with the Audi or anywhere else. Apart from putting on her sunglasses and drawing derision from Ray and worried glances from other drivers, there was not a lot she could do. So, she told herself to suck it up, or grow a pair, man up, or any other offensive masculinised epithet.

"Lima 46, Lima 47, please acknowledge. Lima 2, over," crackled their radios rather loudly. They were amazed that, out of all the background chatter, they could pick out their call sign. It was like how you always pick out the English language in a gathering of foreigners and vice versa.

"Go ahead, 2. 46, over," said Ray, thumbing his mic.

"Do you still have the target on visual?" came the disembodied query from their control.

"Affirmative. Approx. ten—one zero—metres to the front," Ray responded, now in full professional mode. He knew what was coming—someone had made a decision.

"Hold, please, but prepare for the go," which all but confirmed Ray's thoughts.

"Confirmed, 2. Over."

Ray and Tina shared a look in the mirror, both automatically releasing their seatbelts and settling their Kevlar vests. They couldn't risk pulling out their Glocks and checking them until they went full approach, as if the public saw them, it could cause as much panic as if they suddenly got out of the car and ran down the road shouting "fire".

Trained as they were, they both slowed their breathing and looked to the carpet to minimise any glare. Adrenaline was doing its dance in both, and controlling it took more energy than either of them wanted to expend. The technique of slow, deep breaths lessened it.

A slow minute passed—though Ray would have sworn it was longer by about thirty—but that was the adrenal system for you. The clock had now flipped over to 18:00.

"Lima 46, Lima 47, the signal is green. Confirm, Lima 2," burst out of the radio, raising the adrenaline a further notch. So much so that Tina thought she could smell it.

"Confirm signal is green, Lima 2. Lima 46, out," Ray snapped.

Ray and Tina shared another quick glance, took a large gulp of fetid car air, and opened their doors. Both crouched low and automatically placed their gun hand on the stock of their sidearm. Moving quickly past the first few cars beside them, they were accompanied by the sound of horns being pressed as other drivers assumed they were abandoning their car—because that would be normal, wouldn't it?

As Ray ran, he glimpsed the white van from earlier about fifty yards ahead. Taking either side of the Audi, Ray and Tina pulled level with the front doors. Ray was at the driver's side, surrounded by a cloud of smoke. Tina caught a sniff of it and nearly laughed—this balloon who was about to be nicked was smoking a joint.

Tina needed to get into the car, so she smashed the passenger window with the butt of her Glock and shouted, both of them now pointing their unholstered weapons into the space.

"Armed Police! Armed Police! Put your hands where we can see them!" they called in stereo.

The driver looked nothing other than panicked and complied almost immediately, dropping a fat roach onto the carpet and then panicking even more. Tina had the door open now and was getting ready to swiftly cuff Connors and drag him out of the vehicle.

"Matt Connors, you are under arrest for the intention to supply Class-A drugs. You do not have to say anything, but it may harm your defence if you do not mention when questioned something which you later rely on in court. Anything you do say may be given in evidence," Tina churned out the well-known phrase.

Ray was just conscious of all the little lights on the smartphones pointing at them and wondered if Cheryl would see him on the news or the internet.

*****

6:01 pm

The truth is, I had a brief moment of panic from the sudden appearance of an armed bloke in my mirror—one who had completely ignored me before running further up the motorway to a blue Audi a bit behind me. Panic? Who am I kidding—I had nearly shit myself. Then the bizarre thing was that I had sort of hoped they were for me, as that would take away the dilemma and offer me an answer to what would happen now that I was finally and officially late.

When they started pulling the guy in the Audi out, looking to cuff him over by the hard shoulder, I had just thought—poor fucker. The lights from the numerous camera phones had given the scene a slightly surreal look. I hoped I would be able to hear or watch the news later to find out what it was all about. Armed coppers usually meant serious shit, so probably drugs. Though it was a bit of a stupid place to do it.

But who was I to criticise? Given the situation I was currently stuck in, this was not exactly the most sensible place to be, yet I had no choice. I wondered if the young gadge they had gone all *Sweeney* on was there of his own free will. I had no time to waste on another who lived on my side of the line. Although the guy did look as though he had been turned inside out unexpectedly by the arrival of the filth. Perhaps he was one of those who spent more time in the daylight, and this was only a new experience—being dragged across the line to darkness.

6:02 pm

Even as I knew it would, the clock had slipped past the agreed delivery time. The van was supposed to be in the car park right now. I felt no new despair washing over me—I was resigned to whatever came next and relying on my employers' ability to know I had been effectively stationary for thirty-three minutes. Nothing around me had moved much in that time—the odd shuffle and the stop-start crawl that had been the pattern breaking the boredom.

The guy from the Audi had been cuffed inside the car and would soon be marched back beyond his viewpoint in the back. One of the coppers would move the Audi into the emergency lane, no doubt, and then follow his colleague. It would sit there, as there was nothing else to be done. The shoulder was blocked by the broken-down car that had stopped the ambulance earlier, which must be halfway to wherever it was going by now. I hoped there was a way out of this now. Surely, they would know.

What good would it do to harm my wife and kids? I fervently hoped they would believe in me and that my family and girlfriend would forgive me. I would offer a prayer up to whatever was up there. The fact that this had happened at all was just further confirmation that there was nothing there to help me. I was on my own.

I further considered again that getting out and walking away was the thing to do. If it hadn't been for the kids, I would have been long gone. The punishment I would have received would have been survivable—probably. Ultimately, though, I had to stick with it. I had to put misplaced faith in a cast of criminal characters that wouldn't normally stimulate any. I had to believe they would know I was stuck and do something less severe than the threat they had made.

Hear the Black Death Rising

"It's nearly time," said the passenger.

"It is," the driver grunted in response.

The two companions in the grey Mercedes were also stuck in traffic. The radio and their contact confirmed they would have several miles of this to battle through, making their escape—if needed—very awkward. They were at least two miles behind the white van they had been shadowing via an app on a stolen phone. They knew where it was supposed to be at this time but were also acutely aware that the van wasn't going to make it to the final destination in time.

The decision had to be made. They knew that Mr Kennelly and Mr Fedorov would not accept failure. They also knew they would be removed if the operation failed. Additionally, they were very aware that the action was only supposed to be diversionary, and if they acted now, there would be deeper consequences than planned.

The dilemma was solved when a text arrived on the phone: *We know where it is, confirm it is to be actioned now. Then return when you can.*

This meant that if they were clever enough, they could climb up the bank to the industrial-looking units just visible over the hill and call in a lift back from there—or hide out, whichever worked.

"Well, that's it then," said the passenger.

The driver looked at him, perhaps not understanding the next phase.

With a glance at the driver, Lev pulled out another nondescript simple phone. The number he wanted was pre-programmed. He pressed firmly on number five, activating the speed dial, and the world in that area of the north changed for a while.

*****

6:02 pm

If You Could Get Out of Life Alive

Had he been able, he would have sworn he heard the first *dee* of the Nokia ringtone from the back of his van. His consciousness was vaporised along with his physical form, scattered in the blast that erupted outwards from his van, as if a door had been slammed shut in the story of those lives going on around it. The explosion destroyed and dismantled everything within thirty yards in either direction—wrecking some, thumping others with debris, ripping some inside out, and bending road furniture and gantries. The surface at the epicentre appeared to have melted.

An overhead bridge suffered deep gouges as it was hit. The peripheral edge of the explosion's diameter may have escaped obliteration, but it would bear the scars for many years to come. The edge of the motorway was heavily banked, and this saved further catastrophe, containing the force and preventing it from reaching houses on the other side of the bank.

A small mercy—one none of those caught up in it would ever truly appreciate. The fury may have been contained, but later reports would attest that the sound and vibrations were heard and felt many miles away. The devastation dug a crater several feet deep where once a little-noticed and nondescript white van had stood.

That sound and fury obliterated and scattered anything that had shared the unremarkable space that was no more, like a child's game of jacks. As if the devil had arrived, raised his foot, and stamped on it in a fit of irritation. The darkness that had been lurking and developing in the countryside on this autumn evening had been displaced by a more insidious one—a darkness of humanity, a darkness of the soul. One that would leave far more of a mark on those it touched.

The echoes died away, leaving a brief silence, punctuated by the pop of an overheated tyre or the *woof* of a tortured fuel tank. Only then did the screams, shouts, and recriminations begin.

*****

Playlist

The tracks that I have listed below all played some part in the creation of the characters. They may not be lyrically sound or follow the actual stories that I have told. What they manage to be, are bloody good tunes.

Ian	Polar Bear, (2004), Therapy?, Spitfire Records.
Greg	Happy Hour, (1986), The Housemartins, Sony Records.
Kelly	Family Affair, (1971), Sly and the Family Stone, WB Music.
Julie	It must be love, (1981) Madness, Two Tone.
Eric	The first time ever I saw your face, (1972), Roberta Flack, Atlantic.
Phil	Another Brick in the wall, (1979), Pink Floyd, Harvest.
Edie	Dream On, (1973), Aerosmith, Columbia.
Kal and Dina	Love can build a bridge, (1990), The Judds, RCA.
Ty	Whole Lotta Rosie, (1977), AC/DC, Sony.
Ronnie	I can see clearly now, (1990), Hothouse Flowers, London.
Rick	Circumstances, (1978), Rush, Anthem.
Tag	Gone Away, (1996), The Offspring, Columbia.
Andrea	Mad World, (1983), Tears for Fears, Mercury.
Tiff	Drivers Licence, (2021), Olivia Rodrigo, Geffen.
Tommy	Livin' on a prayer, (1986), Bon Jovi, Mercury.
Lisa	Me Myself I, (1980), Joan Armatrading, A&M.
Paul	(She sells) Sanctuary, (1985), The Cult, Beggars Banquet.
Syd	Because I want you, (2006), Placebo, Virgin.
Haroon	Medication, (1997), Primal Scream, Reprise.
Chris	God Take 1, (1978), Ian Hunter, Sony.
Ed	Heavy, (1999), Collective Soul, Atlantic.
Stanley	Old Man, (1972), Neil Young, Reprise.
Joshua	Living in the past, (1969), Jethro Tull, Island.

Peter	Waterfront, (1984), Simple Minds, Virgin.
Emily	Nobody Home, (1979), Pink Floyd, Harvest.
Bethany	House of the Rising Sun, (1964), The Animals, Columbia.
Daniel	Don't have to like you, (2008), Pack A.D., Mint.
Tracy	Behind the wall, (1988), Tracy Chapman, Elektra.
Frankie	Knocked up, (2007), Kings of Leon, RCA.
Stephen	Shade, (1994), Silverchair, Murmur.
Matt	Sweet Leaf, (1971), Black Sabbath, Warner.
Tina and Ray	Police and thieves, (1977), The Clash, CBS.
Lev	Bomber, (1979), Motorhead, Bronze.
The Driver	Knockin' on Heavens Door, (1991), Guns 'n' Roses, Geffen.

Read the first chapter of the next part of Tina's story

Once In a Lifetime

Alder Markson

Just after

The violent and unexpected reverberations of the explosion were fading slowly, like recalcitrant waves on a turning tide. The final ones retreated with only the vaguest hint of any vibration left in the air, soundless yet strangely almost tangible. A silence then began to fall—one that was beyond profound, an absolute, immutable existence in this brief snapshot of time. It would be seen as momentous and yet measured in less than a few seconds.

The last echo faded into the gloomy October dusk, and then a far more tortured and pervasive aural percussion began. A percussive pop from an overheated tyre as it blew itself apart, a soft flump as the fuel ignited in patches around the scene of devastation that had once been only an irritating yet normal jam on a busy motorway.

This modern mechanical sonata was joined by a much more primally animalistic one, as the screams and yells of the injured and the dying were accompanied by the shouts and wails of those who, by some quirk of the Gods, had been completely spared. The latter could be a symphony to good fortune, an opus to surprise, but at this moment, it was the anthemic aria of all those who were arriving in a new hell.

Time had not remained still, even though the scene would be frozen in many memories. Seventy seconds had elapsed since the explosion ripped its path outwards. The man-made construct of order had crept across the land, showing the world that things must and would move on. But this time, the creeping inevitability of order would not disturb the scene before it—it would only heap more distress on those that remained. Time may not have stopped, but to those present, it showed that they were involved in what was a particularly malicious game of statues, in no way resembling those innocent days of a remembered childhood.

What had been a mixed yet ordinary collection of vehicles on a busy motorway—some prized, some not so much—was now a burning, twisted landscape. Deformed hunks of metal competed for space with the ones that bore only an unbelievably random slight scarring. Dents, missing panels, and smashed glass accompanied by flames stood in sharp contrast to the destruction of the misshapen lumps that would not appear in any catalogue or slick showroom again.

There was either a twisted hand or a miracle at play in those that seemed to have escaped completely—a slight scorch or a burst tyre, a cracked headlight or a dented panel, were the only distinctions of their place in this chaotic endgame of their journey, one leading towards the infernal path of nihilism.

The fury at the centre had removed most of the plain white van from existence. The remains of its contents—the cause of such a drama—were now only so much detritus.

Several unlucky vehicles in its immediate vicinity had suffered catastrophic damage. These were the ones that burned most fiercely, a ready supply of fuel ensuring a ferocity that Dante would have recognised and no doubt envisaged. The unfortunate occupants of these vehicles were frozen in place, held in the firm embrace of the inferno raging around them. If they could have shown shock, they would have done so.

They, however, wore the rictus grins similar to a mummified Iron Age corpse pulled from its boggy resting place by an archaeologist in Norfolk. The steady rain that had formed from the light drizzle added to the misery but made no impact upon the flames—almost as if it was fuelling them, making them more intense, such was the ferocity at the centre.

The encroaching darkness of the October evening valiantly attempted to punch back this new source of light, finally settling for a state of passive neutrality. Its animosity towards this surprise interloper into its shadowed domain was held at bay by the ferocity of the new artificial light.

The darkness held itself, as if recognising the kindred spirit of the death-wielding fire. Its time would come again, once more joining its brother in the darkness that was the orchestrator of this. A new kind of being was created out of this darkness, triumphantly proclaiming its mastery for now. The night was driven back and would wait with a patience born of age.

As the first shoots of life appeared, as if they had been warmed by the flames, they were the survivors—wandering like automatons, heedless of any further dangers. One or two shapes on the ground may once have been human, identifiable only by the presence, in most cases, of shoes. The rest of their features were largely indistinguishable from the tarmac.

A surface that had given up its recent semblance of smoothness was now humped and moulded into bizarre and tortured patterns. The heat and force at the centre had reordered this stretch of road—this little part of Yorkshire. A landscape used to the ravages of industry and the natural erosion of its famed weather had now been riven, its very fabric scarred in a few short, violent seconds.

Nobody at the scene—those who came to their aid or those who helped clear it all away—could imagine that this piece of the county would not bear its scars forever. But as with the scars of another part of this same motorway and its aeroplane-shaped tragedy, where the scars were no longer visible, drivers nowadays may pass comment as they drive past Kegworth, if they remember—but most don't.

*****

6:05 pm

SEO (Senior Executive Officer) Tina Rawson had been very lucky, although she was unaware of just how much luck she had been given yet. When the van had blown, she had been shielded from the larger part of the blast as she was in the act of cuffing Matt Connors and was therefore mostly tucked into the passenger side of the Audi. There would be some bruising on her side where she had reacted in shock, colliding with the doorpost. She was also aware of what felt like tiny shards of glass in her hair. That would mean brushing and washing with more than her customary lack of care, as well as having to listen to a lengthy moan from Lesley, her stylist.

Tina quickly recovered her sense of surroundings. With a sharp glance around, she noted that Ray Pickard—her work partner and fellow SEO in the NCA—had disappeared from the other side of the car. It would seem the luck he may have had was the kind that nobody wanted, on a par with some of the others in the traffic jam, or what was left of it. Tina couldn't see him anymore and certainly couldn't hear him, though that didn't mean much, as she could hear very little other than a high-pitched ringing at the moment.

The blast had given her tinnitus, rendering that sense largely useless—temporarily, she hoped. Grimly, she had to ignore the dilemma of the missing Ray conundrum. So, she refocussed on the here and now, which was the man still cuffed in front of her.

Ray and Tina had been shadowing Matt Connors as part of a nationwide—or the northern bit of it—operation to take down two senior members of an OCG. They had been given the green light to arrest Connors and were in the process of doing just that, even though the location was not ideal, being at the side of a motorway, when the world had shifted significantly.

Connors, who had been driving his dad's car, had a boot full of cocaine—believed to be up to a hundred kilos, according to the intel. While he was only a mule, it needed to be taken off the street. This was a coordinated effort involving multiple takedowns, which was why the go signal had been given while they were still on the motorway.

Tina had voiced her concerns, but as usual, they were largely ignored, and it became a question of just getting on with it.

Connors, still cuffed and appearing superficially undamaged and relatively unbloodied, was also giving the impression of being only semi-conscious. His body position, caused by Tina having half-dragged him across the front seats, had shielded him from the effects of the window blowing in. He was covered in fine powdered glass, resembling a large, grotesque Christmas decoration—although who was she to talk?

It was best to put that particular festivity far from her mind—she was never a fan anyway. More pressing matters took precedence. She wondered if the prisoner was still doped up, as the smell of cannabis in the car was noticeable, despite the inferno raging around them.

The smell of smoke outside the car, however, was growing even more pungent—understandably pervasive, but also rising in intensity. It was this that brought Tina's head round hurriedly. Flames were flickering at the back of the Audi, posing a whole new set of dilemmas.

As she couldn't see Ray, she had to assume the worst for now. Dealing with what was in front of her had to be the way forward. Connors was still alive, and one of the mantras that was churned out was the preservation of life—so preserve it she would try to do.

Based on this snap decision, she reached across and uncuffed him, not even contemplating the miracle that she still had the key and, even more so, had managed to locate it. Pointing her Glock at Connors, she told him to quickly slide across the front seat—she was going to save him, not free him. This was a hard-earned prisoner, very hard-earned indeed, it would seem in Ray's case, and she would be fucked if she was going to lose him now.

Looking around while Matt made many sounds as he started to slide across the front of the car, she caught a glimpse of her face in a miraculously undamaged wing mirror. What this revealed was that she was ruffled around the edges and a little second-hand. There was an argument that some rouge wouldn't have gone amiss. However, in the grand scheme of things, she was largely intact, and only now did it start to dawn on her how frigging lucky she was.

"Come on, move, you arsehole," she shouted at him. With her ears still ringing, it was louder than she intended. Matt flinched slightly but slid across the seat a little quicker.

"Your dad's pride and joy is starting to smoulder, and unless you want to go up with it, you'd better get a fucking shuffle on!" she continued at a panic-inducing decibel level.

This warning had the desired effect. Whether it was the glance behind at the flames creeping around the back window that was enough incentive or the fact that he had a Glock pointed at him didn't really matter. Connors shot across the passenger seat and landed on the damp tarmac, wrinkling his nose as he realised the dampness was, in fact, fuel.

It was not petrol, but his mind seemed to be showing him the image of another imminent fireball. A sudden roll of smoke, carrying with it a weird barbecue smell that had wafted across them from the burning fast-food wagon behind them, only seemed to spur him on further.

"Not so fast, matey," said Tina, grabbing Connors as he started to make a slow, unsteady bolt for the scarred but comparatively safe grass banking in front of him. She noticed a phone sitting in the console, and without thinking, she palmed it and stuffed it in her pocket. Her reasoning was that there might be something of evidential value in it, as the main incriminating stuff looked in danger of imminent combustion.

One of the things Tina managed to be was predominantly a good copper. The instinct never left her, and as much as she wanted to tend to Ray, this was winning out for now. Tina grasped Connors' cuffed arm and half-frog-marched him up the bank. The rain was falling steadily now, adding to the general level of misery she was feeling. She may have lost a friend. She was temporarily hearing impaired. There was carnage all around her. There was a possibility she might yet lose a collar. And to cap it all, she was getting wet.

Giving herself a mental shake to disperse the self-centrism she had dragged up, and really seeing for the first time the devastation in front of her, she felt a new wave of emotion. But those tears would be for later. There were jobs to do—most of which she wasn't remotely trained for or had ever expected to be anywhere near in her lifetime.

Tina dragged Connors in a quick shuffle about thirty yards. It was Yorkshire, after all, and she had no idea how many metres that was or thereabouts from the burning Audi. As they moved, the heat from the larger conflagration faded back to more of a campfire comfort, although you wouldn't want to be toasting anything on this one.

Tina shoved Connors down, recuffing his arm to a conveniently located electricity company marker. That would secure him for a while. He was a prize hard-won, and one she would have to leave for a while, as she scooted back to check on the magnificent disappearing Raymondo. As she turned, the Audi burst into what would soon be an all-consuming inferno, adding its flickering to the general Bruegelesque scene playing out beyond and around it.

The diesel from the wagon her prisoner had worried about would not ignite yet, as it might not get hot enough to combust. Tina crossed her fingers that her Hazchem training was correct in this, but watching as the flames rose, she wasn't sure how long that unqualified equilibrium would last.

"Fuck, shit, bastard, fucking bollocks."

Tina, it would seem, had lost her ability for coherence as she saw the evidence—still in the boot of the Audi—literally disappearing up in smoke. This hard-won arrest might now be completely scuppered by something beyond the explicable or predictable. One minute she had been sprinting down the road, Ray in tandem, guns out and ready to bring a bit of fresh-out-of-the-box pond life down. They had been accompanied in their travails by the nowadays de rigueur audience of lights twinkling from the ubiquitous camera phones.

All of which meant they would be famous by teatime, Tina remembered thinking. Now she was reduced to wondering where the fuck Ray was. Her prisoner was safe, but the route to conviction had taken a very abrupt turn for the defence counsel. The evidence of the existence of a boot-load of Class-A drugs would be circumstantial at best and laughed out by the CPS at worst. There was nothing she could do about it, which was a bugger.

Having never been in a war zone—unless you counted Leeds city centre at nightclub throwing-out time—she envisioned this was a damn fine impression of one. God knows what people did when their war went on any longer than the few minutes that had just played out here. How do people cope with this day after day?

On one side, she was incredulous at what her fellow bipeds were capable of doing to each other—if, in fact, that was the case here. On the other, what shite people actually put up with while the violent classes were swinging their dicks about was amazing.

Tina's heart was now pounding like a Taiko drummer, and she could feel a dampness at the base of her spine—the only place that sweated when she was stressed. It had been five minutes tops, so the adrenaline rush was well underway. What had gone missing in this case was her common sense—or even her flight instinct.

She had nothing to fight, so why had the sense she was born with disappeared, replaced by what, in the olden days, would be called derring-do? Arriving back at the here and now—flames tend to focus you on exactly that— she reholstered her Glock. Running around the set of a very real disaster movie with a gun in her hand was, at best, not quite the calming image she would want to portray.

At worst, she would get taken out by a trigger-happy first responder reacting to the scene, whose initial reaction would be to taser or shoot. Time to call it in. She clicked the officer-in-need-of-assistance button. That would summon the cavalry and every other bugger in the neighbourhood who could respond. The tinny voice in her ear asked her to update the request for assistance.

"This is Senior Executive Officer Tina Rawson, badge number four, four, eight, two, one. There has been some sort of explosion on the M1. Multiple vehicles, so assume there are multiple casualties. I'm only slightly hurt, my colleague is missing, but we need everything. Out."

"Roger, we are aware. We were alerted by the camera team, and responders are on the way. Can you identify yourself when they arrive? Should be no more than two minutes. Out."

"Will do."

So, the cavalry was on the way. Now to do her bit—or do something, anyway, as she wasn't quite sure what her bit was in this new set of scenarios. The training team at HQ hadn't put together a set of PowerPoint slides for this one.

Quickly pondering what had happened, she recalled the conversation in the car with Ray.

Was it only a few minutes ago?

He had thought Jack Kennelly and Ilya Fedorov, the heads of the OCG they were trying to decapitate, were, in his considered and singular opinion, planning another bomb. Surely this wasn't it?

They had discussed it over the radio as they sat watching Matt, knowing that the pair's style was material damage to create a diversion.

This wasn't a deflection; it was utter devastation. As she looked around, she saw bodies and burning vehicles everywhere—this was more a terrorist modus, surely? The more she thought about it, the more certain she became that this wasn't them, so she dismissed the idea. It couldn't be that pair, she tried to convince herself. Perhaps it was just an unlucky accident—a fucking catastrophic one, admittedly, but still just one of those things.

Right place, wrong time for her, Ray, and all those others caught up in it. She discounted Kennelly and Fedorov because they would know the hurt and pain that would be brought to bear on them if it was proven to be their doing.

Enough of this conjecture, she told herself—Ray had to be her immediate focus.

D	E	A	D	E	N	E	D		B	E	G	I	N	S
I		B		L			A		D					H
A	T	O	D	D	S		S	I	N	I	S	T	E	R
R		U		E		O		D		T		E		I
I	N	T	E	R	V	A	L		D	O	M	A	I	N
E		T			T		R							K
S	K	I	N	S		H	O	S	P	I	T	A	L	S
		M		T				A		D				
C	A	E	S	A	R	E	A	N		L	E	V	E	E
A				T		A				E		X		
S	T	R	E	E	T		A	I	R	S	T	R	I	P
I		A		M		A		L		M		T		O
N	E	G	L	E	C	T	S		L	A	Z	I	E	R
O				N		E				R		S		T
S	C	O	U	T	S		H	E	A	T	H	E	N	S